They emerged in chaos.

The fold collapsed behind them, but the sound was swallowed in the cacophony of battle that raged before them.

"By the gods!" ChuKang roared. "Where are we now?"

KriChan turned on Braun, grabbing the edges of his breastplate with both fists. "Where have you taken us? Where are Jerakh and the rest of the Centurai?"

"I . . . I don't . . ."

KriChan shoved Braun to the ground, his lips curling up around his fangs in disgust.

"Wait!" Drakis shouted above the noise. "I know where we are! This is it . . . the Ninth Throne of the Dwarves!"

The throne room was enormous, the hollowed out core of the Stoneheart nearly a hundred yards in diameter. All the Impress Warriors could see the Last Dwarven King sitting on his throne, his crown shining in the explosive light of the invading army. Scattered about the room was the last of the wealth gathered from all of the Nine Kingdoms, but it was the crown that riveted the eyes of every Impress Warrior smashing against the dwarven circle of defense.

"Is that it?" KriChan shouted, pointing toward the throne even as he began charging toward the writhing slaughter around the base of the steps.

"Yes!" ChuKang snarled through his clenched, bared teeth, running alongside him. "We take it and we go home!"

The Annals of Drakis
by
Tracy Hickman:

**SONG OF THE DRAGON
CITADELS OF THE LOST**

Tracy HICKMAN

Song of the DRAGON

THE ANNALS OF DRAKIS: Book One

DAW BOOKS, INC.

DONALD A. WOLLHEIM, FOUNDER

375 Hudson Street, New York, NY 10014

**ELIZABETH R. WOLLHEIM
SHEILA E. GILBERT
PUBLISHERS**

www.dawbooks.com

First Paperback Printing, July 2011
1 2 3 4 5 6 7 8 9

DAW TRADEMARK REGISTERED
U.S. PAT. AND TM. OFF. AND FOREIGN COUNTRIES
—MARCA REGISTRADA
HECHO EN U.S.A.

PRINTED IN THE U.S.A.

For Gerry . . . my hero.

ACKNOWLEDGMENTS

We all stand on the shoulders of giants and all are worthy of thanks but to two women especially I owe public acknowledgment: Laura, my wife and partner without whose muse I would have no tale to tell nor song to sing; and the brilliant Sheila Gilbert, who showed us where to find the fire beyond the smoke.

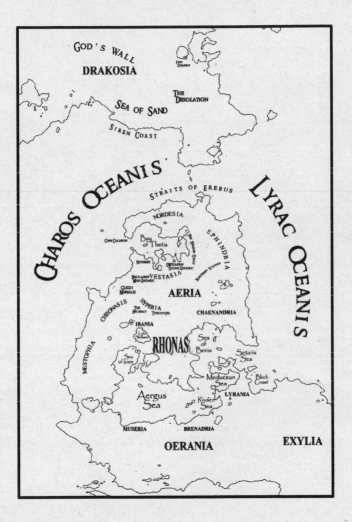

TABLE OF CONTENTS

Contents

BOOK 3: THE FORGOTTEN   285

BOOK 4: THE SIRENS   405

Book 1:

THE JESTER

CHAPTER 1

The Song

T HE SONG would not leave him.
    *Nine notes . . . Seven notes . . . Nine notes . . . Seven
notes . . . Five notes . . . Five notes . . .*

*Circles in circles, endlessly spinning through his mind,
filling its space with an endless melodic wheel. It pulls at
him, calls to him, drawing him into a whirling vortex of
music that engulfs his thoughts, his actions . . .*

"Drakis! Wake up!"

Drakis, Impress Warrior of the House of Timuran and
Leader of the First Octian, shook his head and tried frantically to focus his eyes in the stark light.

The enormous, broad face of ChuKang, Captain of the
Timuran Warriors, swam in front of him. ChuKang was a
manticore—a lion-man from the Chaenandrian Steppes—
and was therefore forced to bend his towering, eight-foot
tall form down to face the human. ChuKang's lips curled
back on his flat, fur-covered face as he spoke, exposing his
sharp fangs. "Drakis! Do you have the count or not?"

Nine notes . . . Seven notes . . .

Drakis found it hard to catch his breath in the stifling
heat of the narrow corridor. The stone hall was barely
twenty feet wide and packed shoulder to shoulder and
wall to wall with his brother warriors as far as he could

see in both directions. Their faces stared back at him, cast in the stark and unnaturally cold light of a number of globe-torches distributed among them. They were mostly made up of towering manticores mixed with nearly an equal number of four-armed chimera and the occasionally emerging face of an impatient Mestophian goblin. Each of their heads—shaved from the top of their foreheads running back to the base of their necks—was marked with the *sinque* tattoo branding every one of them as the property of House Timuran.

Each warrior-slave knew his place—just as Drakis well knew his own. He was the third of eight warriors that made up the First Octian, first of the ten Octia that made up House Timuran's eighty-warrior Centurai. Timuran's Centurai had been attached to five more from neighboring Houses on the Imperial Frontier to form the Second Cohort of the Western Provinces—just short of five hundred warriors—which in turn was united with seven other Impress Cohorts, an additional War-mage Cohort, plus a Warlord Cohort creating the four thousand and eight hundred strong Legion of the West. Three such Legions made up the army grandly named "Blade of the West," which was then joined with two other such armies—"Emperor's Blade" and "Blade of the Marches"—to fill out the enormous Imperial Army of Conquest.

Over forty-three thousand Impress Warriors bringing their bright-edged steel against the last bastion of Dwarven Mighty—and Drakis was but one among them.

Nine notes spun through his mind, sounding hollow as they fell into a vast, surging sea of blood . . . Five notes singing of his insignificance drowned out by the nine notes that dragged him downward into an abyss of sound. His dying breath made no impression on anyone else at all . . .

"Drakis!" ChuKang roared.

"Captain! I have the count!" Drakis blurted out, his eyes focusing on the captain. "First Octian through Fourth Octian are at full strength with eight warriors each. Seventh Octian has combined with the Sixth and are now reporting seven warriors strong. Eighth and Ninth Octia are also at full strength of eight warriors each. Archers of Octian Dista are answering with four."

"What about Fifth Octian?" KriChan growled. He was a fierce-looking manticore with a long scar running from just above his right eye across his face—and also second-in-command of the House Timuran Centurai after ChuKang.

"Fifth Octian does not report," Drakis answered. He was sweating profusely now. "I think we lost them just before the last fold."

"Lord Timuran will not be pleased," KriChan said quietly. "Committing the entire Centurai in this campaign was more of a gamble than an investment . . . and we've yet to garner a single prize."

ChuKang gave a warning glance at his Second. "Without a prize of honor it might be better if we *all* came back on our shields. We need to get into the fight. Braun! What's taking so long?"

They all turned to the only other human present, the sole Proxi for the remaining warriors of House Timuran's Centurai. He was a short man with a stocky build, easily distinguishable by his large, hooked nose and piercing, dark eyes. Like most of the Timuran warriors, he wore a hodgepodge of protective armor, but instead of a weapon he carried the Proxi staff of the Timuran Centurai—a tall wooden shaft with an onyx claw headpiece gripping an Aether crystal at its top. As the Proxi, he was the connection between the elven Tribunes who ran the battle from their hilltop thousands of feet above and many leagues distant from the combat underground. The Tribunes experienced the war from a command tent filled with the breezes of an open sky, their bodies far removed from the blades of the enemy. Bound by the power of Aether magic, the Proxi was the projected presence of the War-mage Tribunes at the battlefront. What Braun saw, his Tribune saw. What Braun heard; his Tribune heard as well. More important still, Braun and all other Proxi were an extension of the Tribunes' magical powers wrought from the Aether, the conduit for the Tribunes' spells. Thus their elven masters leagues away could experience and contribute to the battle through the Proxi in nearly every aspect except one: In agony and death a Proxi was always alone.

Braun cocked his head to one side, as though he were listening to the rocks overhead. He flashed a crooked smile, but his eyes were fixed on a scene far beyond the close walls around them. "Can't you hear it? Don't you see? The dancers and the puppets are all moving across the stage, each one playing his little part, just as we are—our own little part! And now we're coming to the great finale— the headlong rush into death itself. It's all going exactly as the masters have promised it would be. Death, blood, and glory all threshed like fall wheat with our deaths and our blood as dross and the glory all neatly gleaned for House Timuran. Smell the applause!"

"What in the name of all the gods . . ." KriChan began.

Five notes . . . Five notes . . .

Drakis drew in a deep breath. "Captain ChuKang, Braun is not—Captain, it's been three days since his last Field Devotion."

It's been three days since my own devotions, Drakis thought. *Three days of this song rolling through my head . . .*

"Three days for any of us," ChuKang snapped. "What of it? Is that a *problem, hoo-mani*?"

KriChan's eyes narrowed as he stared first at Braun and then back at Drakis.

"He'll do fine, Captain," Drakis said, his own eyes focusing on the scowling face of ChuKang. "I'll see to him."

"You had better see that he doesn't break, Drakis," the Centurai commander grumbled while shooting a glance at KriChan. "His folds got us into this and, by the gods, his folds had better get us out! Proxi's minds always break first in battle. We're too deep under this mountain to have our Proxi snap like some dry twig."

"Deep?" Braun said, crouching on the fitted stones that formed the floor of the corridor. He reached down to the paving stones at his feet, his fingers brushing against a pattern of interlocking rings etched into the stone. The symbol glowed faintly at his touch. "Yes, we are deep and far from home. See the gate symbol here? They have been growing weaker with every fold farther from the Aether Well of House Timuran. What shall save us if the way is shut? The cords that bind us to the House of our master unravel, and does not our future unravel along with our past?"

KriChan opened his mouth to speak, anger flashing in his eyes.

"Yes, Captain," Drakis inserted quickly before the manticore could speak or, worse, act. "I'll take care of him."

Nine notes of the dwarven kings laughing in the darkness . . . Seven notes in his screaming as his world falls in glittering shards five notes at a time to the ground . . .

I'll take care of him, Drakis thought, *if I don't unravel first.*

Drakis drew in a deep, shuddering breath and tried to breathe slower. The armor he wore was mismatched and pinched him. He fought the panicked urge to tear at the straps and cast off the torturous steel tomb—and tomb it was, his mind screamed at him—and run blindly away to anywhere but here in the darkest heart buried far beneath the Aeria peaks. He considered praying to the gods of the House but then stopped.

There was nothing special in him that the gods might want to save, he thought. He was a human—a defeated and moderately rare race—talented with a sword, perhaps, but otherwise unremarkable. He was of only average height for his kind. Broad shoulders and a strong body, perhaps, but the skin of his face was pocked, and a small scar at the corner of his lips gave him the affectation of a crooked frown; not handsome in the way of the gods but of average looks for a warrior of his race. The campaign had done nothing to improve his appearance either, as the tattoo brands on his scalp—usually shaved cleanly bald before the daily Devotions of House Timuran—were now slightly obscured by a fuzz of dark brown hair that had pushed its way through his scalp over the last three days. No, he realized, there was nothing remarkable enough about him to command the attention of the gods. All he had was himself and his brother warriors from his Octian to keep him alive for one more day.

Drakis squeezed his wide-bladed short sword tighter, desperately willing the strength of his hand to overcome the sweat and dark dwarven blood that coated the grip. He did not dare close his eyes, tempting as it was to banish the walls closing in around him.

He had won victory in many battles, slain many enemies in the service of the Rhonas Empire—may his allegiance and loyalty to his elven masters ever be on his lips—and the glorious House of which he longed to be a part.

He was only a warrior-slave of House Timuran—as he had always been, as the gods had made him.

Nine notes rolled around Drakis on shattered shields, a chorus of screaming slaves all singing in madness . . . Seven notes drew him back, running from the flames burning down his life . . .

"It's here! The last judgment of the gods!" Braun shouted. The Proxi suddenly knelt down in the corridor, planting the steel-spiked base of his staff against the glowing symbols in the paving stones and leaning forward. A blue glow grew within the crystal fixed in the staff's headpiece.

"This is it!" ChuKang shouted. "Drakis! First Octian stand to the sides of the fold! Jerakh! Murthas! Second Octian leads those on the right! Third Octian leads the rest on the left"

Drakis tried to ignore the notes turning through his mind in an unending circle as he stepped back, pushing his back against the corridor wall. *Nine notes . . . Seven notes . . . Five . . . Five . . . It was his sanity that rotated on a melodic wheel careening across an endless plain toward a dark tower atop a pillar of stone . . .*

The Proxi staff's crystal flared with brilliant light. The air in the corridor before the Proxi twisted, flattening into a vertical disk that cut across the width of the corridor. Space itself contorted, collapsed, and compressed. Dark hallway, rock, stone, passages, walls, lit rooms, dark halls—all rushed forward inside the magical oval whose edges writhed with arcing light. Just as quickly the rushing motion stopped. The sounds of battle rang out through the magical fold, and Drakis could see clearly a huge underground plaza lit by hundreds of burning torches. An enormous statue filled a rotunda just beyond the plaza around which a line of screaming, enraged dwarven warriors were charging toward them.

"For the glory of House Timuran!" ChuKang roared as he and the rest of the First Octian stood aside, pressing their backs against the walls. They would be the last to enter the battle.

"For the glory of the Emperor!" Drakis shouted in chorus with the rest of the Centurai around him.

Second and Third Octia rushed forward as though charging to collide where the glowing oval from Braun's staff bisected the wall between them. Drakis felt the brush of armor and whiffed the stench of drying blood as the Second Octian rushed past him, followed immediately by the Fourth and Sixth.

"Keep moving, you slave bastards!" ChuKang shouted. "Win me enough room to kill some dwarves!"

KriChan continued to roar. "For the Emperor and his Imperial Will!"

The ranks of warriors surged forward like a confluence of rivers, leaping into the vertical glowing disk on both sides as though in collision . . . but the folded space of the elven war-mages and their Proxi obeyed a reality that was uniquely dictated by the power of Aether magic. Drakis watched as the converging warriors dashed headlong into the magically wrenched space, and, from where he stood, he could see that those entering from his side were rushing into the distant illuminated plaza and engaging the charging dwarves. He knew from experience that those warriors charging in the opposite direction were rushing from the opposite side of the fold into that same plaza.

The screaming Impress Warriors of Timuran continued their charge through the blazing mystic portal until the four remaining members of the Octian Dista—all of them goblin archers—leaped through to the other side.

All that remained were the warriors of the First Octian—Drakis' brothers in combat for as long as he could remember. ChuKang, the Captain of the entire Timuran Centurai, was at the heels of the goblin archers, roaring in battle rage, a massive sword in each hand as he turned and pushed through the portal. Ethis—a four-armed chimerian with the wonderfully durable physical structure of his kind—leaped through. He was followed by TsuRag and GriChag, both manticores from the Southern Steppes of Chaenandria as were ChuKang and KriChan. Behind them came Megri, the goblin with quick eyes and quicker fingers. He flashed a bright, sharp-toothed smile at Drakis before hopping through the fold.

KriChan hung back a moment, turning his narrowed eyes on Drakis. "Is the Proxi still good?"

Nine notes singing of the Dwarven Thrones . . . Seven notes ringing of the Octia losing one . . .

Drakis' head hurt, and he was not sure he heard the manticore correctly. "Master?"

KriChan wrapped his massive paw around the back of Drakis' neck. The human could feel the sting of the great warrior's claws pushing against his skin, and KriChan drew him closer. "I have no time or patience to waste on you, Drakis! You are *hoo-mani* . . . Braun is *hoo-mani*. Tell me now! Is the Proxi broken?"

Braun knelt next to them, watching them both with bemused interest even as he still held the fold open with sweat pouring down his face from the effort. "Tell him, Drakis! Tell the big, pet cat that he need not get his fur up. I've never felt better in my life, Drakis! I've never seen the world so clearly! Layers of cloth have been unwinding from my eyes, and for the first time, I'm beginning to see just what a lie we're all living."

KriChan growled as he suddenly turned on the Proxi, baring his teeth menacingly.

Braun's blissful smile fell only slightly, his eyes suddenly focusing and his words tinted with menace. "Of course, if you *kill* your Proxi, who will extract your hide from this farce of a battle then, eh?"

KriChan shook violently but knew better than to harm the Proxi. He turned his wrath on Drakis instead. "He is *your* Proxi, Drakis! You keep him doing right by his brothers or I'll see that *you* pay for *his* insolence!"

The manticore leaped through the fold, his weapon raised to strike.

The sounds of terrible battle flowed out of the fold, filling the now empty corridor. Devoid of the globe-torches, pitch darkness had once again reclaimed the cold, stone emptiness, except for the bright light coming from the fold that illuminated the two humans that remained.

"I don't think he likes me," Braun said through a smile to Drakis.

Drakis grabbed the Proxi by the elbow and dragged Braun's shaking form to his feet. "I'm beginning to wonder if I do either."

"Oh, I think you'll *know* soon enough," Braun said, giving Drakis a shove through the fold portal. Then Braun's smile took on a darker, more vicious aspect. "I think we may all *know* soon enough."

With that, the Proxi stepped through the fold portal with his staff. The fold collapsed at once . . . choking off the light from the distant plaza and plunging the abandoned hall into utter darkness.

CHAPTER 2

The Folds

DRAKIS STEPPED into a killing field.

The fold behind him collapsed into a thunderclap, the sound joining the rolling chorus of other booms that shook the enormous subterranean plaza as four more folds delivered their own warriors into the battle. More than three hundred Impress Warriors erupted into the square, pouring from their own folds at the base of an enormous, bas-relief covered wall and onto the plaza floor.

The enraged dwarves were already upon them. The Warriors of the Ninth Throne ran with incredible speed from the towering rotunda at the far end of the plaza, their bright-edged axes and swords swinging in their hands as they rushed headlong toward the Impress Warriors.

"They're engaging us before we've formed up!" KriChan shouted.

"Timuran Centurai!" shouted ChuKang above the battle cries of the charging dwarves. "Battle line! Now!"

The manticores and chimera scrambled to find their places as they had practiced so often in the sunlit fields south of the shining towers of their home...but the dwarves broke upon them in a mad fury, shattering the lines of the four Centurai in the hall before any of them were prepared. Mad dwarven warriors bowled heedlessly past enemies at hand, their eyes fixed on the First *Octia*n of the Centurai.

Drakis glanced at ChuKang.

They're after the captains, he thought.

ChuKang's face broke into a vicious grin.

A hand fell on Drakis' shoulder. Drakis spun about, his sword swinging up instinctively.

"Drakis . . ."

It was Braun.

"I don't feel . . . well . . ." Braun's eyes were blinking furiously. "I'm seeing too much . . . hearing too much . . ."

No, not the captains, Drakis realized. *It's the Proxis the dwarves want. No Proxi, no fold . . . no fold, no escape.*

Drakis gripped Braun's shoulder too hard, shouting words into his face in the hope that they might somehow be heard. "Braun! Stay near me! Understand?"

Braun grinned back in reply, his eyes unfocused.

Drakis turned back to face the onslaught, his voice breaking as he screamed the command. "*Octian! Octian!*"

Time slowed in his mind. The formation of the Centurai had dissolved completely into a sea of vicious, desperate combats.

He saw the face of GriChag glance in his direction, then turn to face a dwarf whose ax was trying to find the manticore's knees.

Ethis took several steps backward, trying to join Drakis, but a berserk dwarf launched himself against the chimerian, dagger in hand.

The song overwhelmed the sound of death and steel.

Mountains of stone and of dead fell dreams . . .

Seeds that are planted in dark . . .

Long for the sunlight . . .

Wait for the sunlight . . .

"DRAKIS! WAKE UP OR DIE!"

Drakis heard the warning from the chimerian barely in time. He flattened his back against the cold stone of the plaza wall, thrashing about with his sword as he desperately tried to parry the dervish flailing of the enraged dwarf pressing his attack. The ornate granite wall immedi-

ately chilled the back plate of his armor, pulling the heat
out of his body with painful swiftness. He was grateful for
the pain; the shock of it focused his mind. Drakis thrust
fiercely, kicking hard away from the stone behind him with
his right leg, rolling into his opponent before the dwarf
could counter the blow. Drakis trapped the creature's
weapon arm in his own and forcefully bent it outward.
He felt the thick bones crack as the dwarf howled, but he
kept on, pulling the dwarf forward by his broken arm and
throwing him to the ground. Desperate, Drakis reversed
his grip on his sword, plunging it downward toward the
dwarf's chest—but another dwarf suddenly sprang onto
his back, his thick arms wrapped around Drakis' throat.
Drakis panicked, trying to strike at the beast now throt-
tling him, but his sword only flailed ineffectively at his
back. What little vision remained to him was rapidly going
blurry.

"He's an insect, idiot!" Ethis yelled at him. The chimerian reached back with his fourth arm and shoved Drakis
toward the cold wall behind him.

Drakis lurched back, smashing the dwarf between himself and the stones of the plaza wall. The impact rattled the
dwarf enough to loosen his grip—but not enough to make
him let go. Drakis staggered forward, hoping to smash his
unwanted rider once more when he saw—incredibly—the
dwarf with the broken arm running toward him. Blood
streamed down his face as he screamed, his ax in his good
hand. Flashes of light danced around the edges of Drakis'
vision as he watched the berserk dwarf charge at him. At
the last moment, Drakis spun away from the horrible spec-
ter just as the gleaming edge of the ax blade swung toward
him. He felt the impact of the blow behind him. Hot air
suddenly rushed into his lungs as the second dwarf, still
clinging to his back, took the thrust and released his grip.

Drakis swung around again, drawing his blade up swiftly
behind his head. Too late. The berserk dwarf had already
shoved his dead confederate aside and leaped toward the
human, his ax blade descending toward Drakis' face.

The flight of the dwarf was suddenly arrested in midair

by the blur of a massive club swinging out of the darkness and connecting with the body. Drakis heard the dwarf's armor crumple under the blow and the collapse of its rib cage just before the dwarf flew backward, vanishing under the feet of the raging combatants.

"Nice hit, GriChag," Ethis commented, slightly out of breath himself. Drakis could barely make out three still shapes lying at the chimerian's feet. "That one was worthy of the Imperial Games."

"Not good," GriChag replied with disappointment, his deep voice rumbling. The manticore's massive dark head shook with disapproval a full two feet above Drakis. "I was aiming for his head."

Drakis, still choking, stepped quickly back to the relative safety of the plaza wall and tried frantically to catch his breath. His Octian was forming a defensive circle around him, pulling ChuKang and KriChan both within their perimeter.

"When all else fails, depend on your Octian, eh, Drakis?" ChuKang yelled over his shoulder as he drew his twin swords across the throat of a dwarf before him.

"That is what you taught us," Drakis shouted hoarsely as he rubbed his throat. Panic suddenly gripped him and he turned quickly. "Braun!"

"I'm here, old friend," Braun replied. The Proxi stood next to Drakis, his sandals and feet covered in blood from the bodies about them, but he took little notice of either. Instead, he gazed at the bas-relief covering the wall towering behind them. "There are cracks in the wall, you know. I've been looking at them for some time now, and I think I can see light coming through them. They're getting wider all the time."

Drakis squinted at the Proxi. "What are you talking about? We're leagues underground!"

Before Braun could answer, ChuKang and KriChan stepped back, standing on either side of the Proxi. "Braun! This is a disaster! What does the Tribune want us to do?"

"Well, he hasn't . . ." Suddenly Braun's demeanor changed; anger and disdain showed on his face, and his voice was suddenly nasal and condescending in tone. They were used to it, for they had seen it every day of their lives: The Tribune was once again pulling the strings of his puppet Proxi. "Gather the individual *Octia* cells together and re-form the Centurai. Flank the dwarves in the plaza on the left and make for the rotunda. The dwarves are fanatical, but they have gambled on this charge and lost—they have extended themselves too far, and their reserves will not arrive in time. Flank them and get to the rotunda."

"Master, should we plant a gate symbol there?" KriChan asked.

Braun turned to the second manticore, his features contemptuous. "No! There are grand halls leading away from the rotunda. Take the Centurai to the end of the right-hand hall . . . then have the Proxi plant the gate symbol there and propagate it as many times as possible along the promenade you find there before the dwarven reserves arrive."

ChuKang asked, "But how long before the dwarven reserves . . ."

Braun turned back toward the captain, his face nearly purple with rage. "Just do it! We need as many gate symbols as possible established on the promenade at the end of that hall. Do *that* and you may yet salvage some honor from this debacle, Captain ChuKang."

In an instant, Braun's face changed again to a gently smiling countenance. "Did I miss something?"

"Captain!"

It was Jerakh, the manticorian warrior in charge of the Second *Octia*n. "Second, Fourth, and what's left of the Eighth and Ninth *Octia* have formed with you here. Third and Sixth are fighting off to the right. I haven't seen the Octian Dista."

"Let's move!" ChuKang shouted. "Let's push to join with the Third and Sixth—then swing the formation to the left. We're to make for that rotunda."

"But our casualties . . ."

"We'll count the dead later, Jerakh," ChuKang said. "Drakis! You have the Proxi. Let's go bleed some dwarf!"

The battle was still raging in the plaza when the Centurai from House Timuran broke around the left flank, trampling underfoot the dwarves who had not already succumbed to the Impress Warriors' weapons. The broken dwarven line contracted, and with shocking suddenness, Drakis found himself running at full-gait through the rotunda with Braun's shoulder armor gripped firmly in his left hand. What remained of the Timuran Centurai ran with them as well, their ordered battle lines once again dissolved by the necessity of the moment. Everyone was having trouble keeping up with Captain ChuKang, who dashed headlong from the rotunda and bolted down the grand hallway to the right.

Nine notes of stones polished, statuesque dwarf glowers . . .

Seven notes of watchful guarding doom and loss . . .

Five note halls of gleaming onyx . . .

Five note halls of black entombing . . .

The stones were polished under their feet, and they passed the thirty-foot-tall statue of a dwarven hero. The hall they entered to their right was filled with warm light from lit torches set in iron wall sconces. Ornate carved pillars of polished stone rose nearly fifty feet overhead to support the intricately carved arched ceiling.

Drakis barely noticed it. His eyes were fixed on ChuKang as he ran down the hall toward blackness darker than any night beyond the arch at the end of the five-hundred-foot-long hall.

"Keep running, Warriors!" KriChan shouted. "Don't stop! The end is in sight."

Come answer the call of lamenting . . .

Drakis gritted his teeth as he ran.

Come answer the sky that fell . . .

His feet fell into the cadence of the song.

Forgive the lament . . . Forgive promise torn . . .

"Shut up! Shut up! Shut up!" Drakis muttered under his

breath, but the song kept revolving in his mind with every measured footfall on the stones passing beneath his feet. The great black void filling the open end of the colossal hall slid toward him, and still he ran, following ChuKang and holding fast to Braun because that was what he was told to do and the music in his mind overwhelmed all other thought.

ChuKang passed the arch at the end of the long hallway and abruptly stopped. The rest of the Centurai followed his lead, raising their weapons in caution as they approached the darkness.

"By the gods," ChuKang said in awe as he stood looking out into the void. He called over his shoulder. "Timuran Centurai, set up a defense. Octia Two, Three, and Four protect the hall. Octian Eight to my right and Octian Nine to my left. Octian One to me! Drakis! Bring me that Proxi!"

Drakis glanced over at Braun.

"It's going to be all right now," Braun said to him quietly. "Sometimes it has to be truly dark before we can make out the stars in the sky."

Drakis took in a breath to speak but then let it out again as a sigh. He stepped between the Impress Warriors even as their masters were organizing them into defensive lines. He was blind as he stepped quickly toward their manticorian captain, the darkness seeming a complete void beyond.

"Captain?" Drakis spoke as he came near.

ChuKang turned to the Proxi, pointing to the stones beneath his feet. "Gate symbols! The first one right here, and then start propagating them along both sides of this landing as long as possible! Do it now . . . we may not have much time."

Braun bowed slightly and then shrugged his shoulder out of Drakis' grasp.

Drakis looked at him with slight embarrassment. He had simply forgotten to let go.

"As the Emperor wills," Braun said with a crooked smile. The Proxi immediately swung the Standard around smartly, its steel point jabbing into the stone as Braun knelt next to it. The stones beneath it were cut by the strange purple glow at the staff's tip—an unnatural color that Drakis found difficult to look at. Meticulously, Braun moved the tip across the stones, inscribing their surface with the familiar interlocking ovals of the gate symbol. Once completed, any Tribune could use them to transport their own Centurai to this same spot—the last location of their most forward progress. Many a valiant warrior had died for the honor of moving these symbols a few yards forward on the battlefield.

"KriChan," ChuKang said quietly to his lieutenant at his side. "Have you ever seen the like?"

Drakis watched the two manticores stare into the darkness together.

Then Drakis realized that the darkness was not entirely dark. As his eyes slowly adjusted from the brilliance of the halls they had just left, he could make out fires burning in the distance, their vague reflection on still waters and in the distance ...

"The Yungskord!" Drakis breathed.

ChuKang turned at the sound. "Yes, Drakis. The Yungskord ... the last cavern of the dwarves. It's said to be over a third of a league long."

Drakis stepped up next to where ChuKang stood. He could see now that they were standing on a wide, stone landing that ran across the face of the dwarven city from which they had just emerged. Below the landing, the natural cavern sloped downward to the edge of the fabled underground Lake Kigga. The fires appeared to dot a rugged island in the center of the lake that rose upward toward an impossibly regular and enormous oval of stone. Drakis pointed toward it. "Is that ... ?"

"The Stoneheart?" KriChan said through his fanged grin. "The last throne of the dwarves? Yes, Drakis, I believe we have found it."

The Stoneheart, Drakis thought. Every Impress Warrior had been thoroughly instructed in it from before the battle began. It was a single, massive granite disk, polished by the dwarves to a glassy smoothness, though Drakis had wondered why dwarves would want to go to so much trouble to put a brilliant finish on something that would never be touched by light. It was nearly a hundred yards in diameter and perhaps twenty yards thick in the center. Most remarkable of all, the entire stone sat atop an enormous geyser whose channeled energies pushed upward with such force that the stone seemed to float atop it. It was the flow from this geyser that fed the torrents raging across the floor of the cavern.

"We may have found it, but how do we get to it?" Chu-Kang mused. "These gate symbols we're laying down will make this the entry point for the entire army once they are engraved, but charging that island with an army isn't going to get them any closer to the throne. Look—to the left—that small dwarven city on that side of the cavern. There's a causeway that runs up from those buildings to that gate . . ."

"The Thorgreld," Drakis said aloud.

The Stoneheart was accessible only via a single bridge carved from the stone that extended from the doors to the Heart outward toward the Last Gate of Thorgreld. It was the final defense of the Last Dwarven Throne, for on the order of their king the entire Stoneheart could be rotated atop the geyser by the dwarves within, moving both bridge and entrance door away from the Last Gate and making it unreachable. The Tribune had told them a great deal about it as they prepared, for battle within the Stoneheart was the prize coveted by all the Houses of the Rhonas Imperium, but hearing it described did not convey to Drakis the enormity of the experience of seeing it himself.

"We've got to get to that causeway," ChuKang said, his voice rumbling as he considered the problem.

"Were any of our warriors over there before?" Drakis asked.

Both ChuKang and KriChan turned toward him. "The Tribune would know . . . but if they were that close to the causeway, wouldn't they have pressed the attack?"

"Maybe they didn't know it *was* over there," Drakis replied. "They might have been fighting in the corridors as we have ... perhaps they didn't know how close they were to the prize. We can only see it now because we're over here."

"If that's true, then they *might* have abandoned some gate symbols there," KriChan said quickly. "We could fold there and make for the throne ourselves!"

"Captain!"

ChuKang turned abruptly toward the sound. "Here!"

"They're coming!" Jerakh said. "We can see them moving toward the rotunda."

"How long?"

"Not long."

"Braun!" ChuKang called.

The Proxi was still kneeling next to the gate symbol glowing faintly from the stone next to him. Braun moved his Standard over the symbol, and a spark arced upward and over the heads of the arrayed warriors until it landed nearly five hundred feet farther down the landing. There it burned briefly into the stones, carving out a duplicate of the gate symbol. "That's ten, Captain!"

ChuKang reached down and picked up the Proxi with his massive hand, lifting him bodily from the ground and pulling him to stand next to him. "Do you see that city to the left?"

Braun squinted slightly. "Yes ... the one built into the face of the cavern."

"They're coming, Captain!" Jerakh called.

The sound of the slow march of dwarven boots became a growing thunder in their direction.

"That's the way to the throne," ChuKang said. "There's a causeway next to it—a road that leads straight to the gate. Do you *see* it?"

Braun smiled. "Yes ... and so does the Tribune."

Braun turned at once and knelt again next to the gate symbol in the floor. He planted the Standard, and its great crystal flared into brilliant light at once.

The fold opened.

Drakis shuddered. He could see nothing at all through the ink-black fold.

"Timuran Centurai!" ChuKang called out. "Fall back! Into the fold by the numbers! Octian Nine!"

The group leaped from their positions on the landing, dashing at once through the crackling oval into the darkness on the other side.

"Octian Eight!"

Warriors from the other side of the landing jumped up, scrambling toward the fold and vanishing into the blackness.

"Ethis! Megri!" Drakis called out.

The chimerian and the goblin both called out in ragged response, "Yes, Octis!"

"Each of you stand guard on opposite sides of the fold. TsuRag! GriChag!"

"Yes, Octis!"

"Keep your eyes on the dwarves coming up the hall! We're leaving!"

ChuKang continued to call out the *Octia*. In quick succession each pulled back, running quickly through the black opening of the fold.

Drakis stared down the hall. The dwarves were running now, seeing that their enemy was trying to elude them. Their battle cries filled the hall, their blades flashing in the torchlight.

"Octian Two!" ChuKang shouted.

Jerakh and his warriors leaped up, dashed between the members of Drakis' Octian and, without hesitation, jumped through the fold.

The dwarves shouted their rage in terrible chorus.

"That's it!" ChuKang roared. "Fold out!"

Drakis turned toward the fold. Ethis and Megri had already jumped through. TsuRag and GriChag were following the captain, and KriChan as he watched. That only left . . .

"Braun!" Drakis shouted.

The Proxi stood up. The Standard still emitted the magical Aether, holding the fold open, but Braun now held it casually in his hand.

"Let's go!" Drakis barked.

Braun's form was silhouetted against the bright hall.

Beyond him, Drakis could clearly see the dwarven warriors less than a hundred feet away and getting closer with every thundering step.

Braun made no move.

"Braun!" Drakis shouted.

"It's all right," Braun replied, standing perfectly still. "You don't *see* it, do you? The walls have all crumbled, and here—here in the darkness—the light comes at last!"

The dwarves cheered. Fifty more feet and their enemy's blood would flow.

Braun smiled but made no move. "Do you *see* the picture? Do you *hear* the music?"

Nine notes . . . Seven notes . . .

"What did you say?" Drakis asked, his eyes going wide.

Twenty feet. Eight more steps.

Drakis lunged forward, pushing his shoulder into Braun's stomach. The Proxi doubled over the warrior's shoulder in surprise.

Axes and sword blades alike were raised. Two steps more to strike.

Drakis wheeled with the Proxi over his shoulder and leaped headlong into the fold.

Chapter 3

Empty Rooms

DRAKIS FELL SHOULDER FIRST against the stone floor. The impact shook the Proxi from his grip. Drakis felt Braun tumble away from him just as the thunderclap of the closing fold shook the air next to him and plunged him into absolute darkness.

Something fell with a dull thud and a resounding clang next to him. Drakis started, rolling quickly away from the sound. Instinctively, he reached to his side, drawing his sword from its leather scabbard, but though his eyes shifted back and forth in anxious anticipation, sight was useless in the total absence of light.

Black is the sightless light smothering . . .
Dead to the waking world sighs . . .
Dead is the hero . . . Dead to all lament . . .
Buried past memory here below . . .

He was alone with the song.

Drakis' hand began to shake uncontrollably in the darkness.

"Octian!" Drakis called out, his words swallowed into the black void around him, echoing small and hollow. His fellow warriors had passed through this same fold just a few moments before him. They should have been arrayed all about him with their globe-torches shining.

Yet he crouched in the darkness, and there was no reply to his call.

The wheeling melody surged forward in his mind once more. Drakis quickly muttered a prayer to Rhon—god of war—and drew enough courage to shout again.

"Octian!"

The gentle, answering voice coming from so near in the darkness unnerved him with its quiet calm.

"I am here, Drakis."

The warrior spun around in the dark. "Braun? Is that you?"

Dim blue light grew stronger as he watched, pushing back the smothering black as it brightened. Drakis fixed his eyes and his sanity on the glowing, expanding circle. Drakis' world settled with each revelation of the brightening sphere. The headpiece, then the shaft of the Timuran Proxi staff that he had followed to victory in every battle of his life emerged from the darkness. Then the bald head now obscured with three days' growth of gray-flecked hair, the hooked nose and the piercing eyes . . .

. . . The figures of Impress Warrior dead.

The bodies of an Imperial Octian lay about their feet. Drakis frantically started examining the mutilated corpses but then stopped.

"These aren't ours," Drakis said.

"No, they've been waiting for us here for a day or so now, as you might have guessed by the stench," Braun nodded. He pointed over to the decapitated body of a human nearby with a broken Standard staff still gripped in his cold, discolored hand. "He's how we got here. That fool managed to do his duty to the last; and carve the gate symbol before they got him. I guess we arrived a bit late to be of much use to him."

Drakis looked down at his feet. The freshly severed arm of a dwarf with an ax in its hand lay bleeding onto the ground.

"And if we had been a little later, we wouldn't have arrived at all. Braun," Drakis struggled to make his voice calm as he spoke. "Where is the rest of *our Octian?*"

Braun looked up, considering the question, then smiled knowingly. "Not far, I should think. No doubt they have been called away by some glorious and pressing cause on behalf of our masters. Still, I should think that they will need us more than we will need them in the end, wherever they have gone."

"Are you hurt?"

"Hurt?" The Proxi asked in amused surprise. "No, Octis Drakis . . . I am remarkably at peace."

Drakis stared at his companion for a moment. "Braun, stop that talk. You're pushing KriChan's fur the wrong way. I think he's about ready to tear your limbs off as it is."

"And how would the big cat get home then?" Braun answered simply. "How would he be able to lie on his master's feet and be petted? Who would feed him his table scraps then? And who would remember him, buried here under the mountain? Not a one, Drakis, not a one."

Braun peered into the darkness. "His memory would be buried with him here—and with it he would have ceased to exist at all."

Drakis shook with a sudden chill. "Now those are *exactly* the kind of words that get you into such trouble with . . ."

"Look!" Braun said, pointing with his free, right hand. The glow from the top of the staff was now shining with a brilliant white, revealing a great underground avenue running between facing sets of narrow structures. All featured an arched opening next to large, ornately framed windows fitted with thin plates of polished crystal through which Drakis could see with almost perfect clarity. Yet, in spite of their common features, each was uniquely appointed with different carvings and strange dwarven symbols.

"What are they? Drakis asked.

"Shops, I should think," Braun replied.

"Shops?" Drakis asked. "What are shops?"

"You don't know what a shop is?" Braun gave a sad little laugh.

"I am a warrior of House Timuran," Drakis said, setting his jaw. "I have had no need to know of such things before, nor do I see any point in it now."

"Let's find out anyway," Braun replied, stepping toward the open archway of one of the buildings. The light from his staff shifted the shadows across the buildings as he moved.

Drakis realized he was being left to the darkness. He quickly sheathed his sword and fell into step behind the Proxi. "Braun! We've got to find the *Octian!*"

But the Proxi was already inside the archway of the structure, his light shining out through the gentle ripples in the polished crystal window. Drakis ducked quickly through the low arch. He was stopped almost at once by a vertical wall beautifully carved with dwarf figures, some carrying baskets over their shoulders filled with vegetables and grains while others were enjoying eating loaves of bread and drinking from tall mugs. He easily stepped around the wall and into a large room. The fitted stones of the floor shone like a white marble mirror under the light from the Proxi's staff.

Drakis shook his head. He knew they had to move, to rejoin the Octian and press the battle forward. ChuKang had told them time and again that to stand still on a field of battle was to invite death to find you. Drakis had to join the battle, had to find some honor in this debacle. More importantly to him, he secretly dreaded the silence and the stillness around him; it gave the music in his mind space to grow.

"What do you think, Drakis?" Braun said as he stood in the center of the room.

"I think we need to find our Octian and . . ."

"No," Braun snapped, an angry edge to his voice. "Do you *see* the picture? There's a large flat platform inside the window. There . . . back there . . . is a carved stone counter and behind it . . . can you see it? . . . there are three ovens."

Awaken the ghosts long forgotten . . .

Recall the loved dead . . .

Drakis began to sweat in the chill room. "It's a . . . a kitchen . . . a kind of dwarf mess hall . . . a place to eat . . ."

"You *look*, but you don't *see!*" Braun urged, stepping closer to Drakis. "The spirits still breathe whispers of their passing in this place. Their voices shout to us from the silence, and you! You hear *nothing*!"

They eat here. They love here. They laugh here.

Better if left and forgotten . . .

Nine notes. Seven notes.

"I *hear* enough." Drakis swallowed hard. "Leave me alone, Braun!"

"It isn't what is *here*, Drakis; it's what *isn't* here that you need to see!" Braun swept past Drakis to the window. "Here on this shelf were the wares of this shop: baked goods, breads, meats—can you smell them still in the air? There . . . there in the archway that we came through, there is *no door*. There have been no doors in *any* of the openings or halls through which we have come in the three days we have been wandering down here in our graves. By all accounts, the dwarves love their gems and their precious metals and their stonework—we are told they are all even more covetous of such things than our righteous elven masters. Why, then, are there *no doors* between the dwarves?"

We kill without cause. We kill without thought.

Five notes . . . Five notes . . .

"What difference does it . . ."

"And this room," the Proxi continued. "The floor is cleaner than any plate I've ever eaten from in the Centurai barracks of our great Lord Timuran. No dust. No dirt. But where are the chairs? Where are the tables? There are images of them carved into the wall facing the archway, but there's not a stick of either to be found inside. Look, Drakis! *See!* There are hooks in the ceiling above the counter, but where are the pots, the pans, the kettles, or the spoons? Where are the *tools*? Where are the kegs and the stores of grain or tubers or roots or whatever the dwarves fed upon?"

"Stop it, Braun! I don't care . . ."

The Proxi turned again to face Drakis. "Where are the children who squealed through the streets with joy, Drakis? Where are the women who breathed life into this place? Where are the gray-bearded elder dwarves with their frail bodies and their wisdom aged like fine wine?"

"I don't . . . I don't know!" Drakis answered.

"No, you *don't*," Braun said, stepping toward him with a strange twisted smile on his face. "*You* don't know . . . *I* don't know . . . but at least I'm beginning to understand just how *much* I don't know!"

Drakis reached behind him, feeling for the archway as he carefully backed away from the wild-eyed Proxi.

"It's all unraveling, Drakis," Braun said softly. His tongue flicked to the corner of his mouth, drawing in the spittle that had formed there. "Here in the darkness I can *see* . . . here in these rooms that are so like you and me. Perhaps it is the distance from the Aether Well of House Timuran, perhaps it is the three days we have gone without renewing our Devotions. Maybe it has something to do with being so deep beneath the mountain of the dwarves. I don't know, but whatever it is, the cords, soft and silken as they have been, are unraveling from my mind, and I am beginning to *see* the picture of truth at last."

Drakis felt the edge of the archway with his left hand and carefully stepped back into it, His right hand slowly reached across his body almost without conscious thought, his palm resting on the hilt of his sword. "Braun, we're warriors . . . Impress Warriors of House Timuran . . ."

"No, Drakis, you're wrong," Braun breathed through clenched teeth. He would not stop advancing. "Who are you, Drakis? Why do you fight so well? What makes you so determined to live?"

"I fight . . ." Drakis swallowed, taking another step back through the archway. "I fight for the glory of Rhonas, for her Emperor, and for the glory of House Timuran!"

"Pretty speech, hollow words," Braun spoke, his words dripping disdain. "You dance like a marionette and vomit out the words spoken by others behind the curtain. I've *seen* what's back there. You take a peek at the truth and tell me. It's just us here . . . you and me buried in our crypt, and there should be no lies between the dead. You know the answer! Tell me!"

Drakis' breath was coming hard.

Five notes . . .

For the love of her ... For the loss of her ...

"Tell me!"

He suddenly thought of Mala—his beautiful Mala working in the foundations of the magnificent palace of Sha-Timuran. Her image floated before him in his mind; she reached up with her hand to wipe the sweat from her clean-shaven head before she returned to scrubbing the path stones beneath the graceful towers of their master's citadel that floated above the garden. He could almost catch the glint of her emerald eyes, feel the curve of her cheek in his hand. He had to return to her—for her and with the honor that they both so desperately needed. She was unaware of the danger he was in—that his life could end at any moment—and the thought of her not knowing comforted him.

He could almost hear her humming to herself as she worked in the garden ...

Nine notes ... Seven notes ...

The dwarves have no doors ... The dwarves are no more ...

Braun was smiling at him. "So you *do* know something honest after all! Tell me!"

Drakis gripped his sword, pulling it from the scabbard.

Braun anticipated the move. The Proxi's staff lashed out suddenly, gripped with both his hands. The shaft caught Drakis just behind the knees, cleanly sweeping both his feet out from under him. The warrior landed heavily on his back, the breath knocked from his chest. As he sucked in a painful gasp, the light from the headpiece carved a brilliant, blurred arc over him, and he felt the cold steel point of the staff against his throat. He fought for air, trying to speak, but the sound would not come.

Braun leaned down, his head and shoulders silhouetted against the light from the Aether crystal on his staff.

"We're empty rooms, Drakis, all of us," Braun said in short breaths. "Nothing but the form of what our masters have molded us to be. But I've *seen* the reality of who and what we are. The walls have cracks, and the light shines through. The cords that bind us unravel, and we see at last that our rooms are *not* empty but filled with ghosts, Drakis—ghosts and demons more terrible and wonderful than we know."

Drakis reached up with both hands, gripping the staff at his throat. "Braun! Stop!"

"I can't stop now," Braun answered, shaking his head with an unnatural smile. "You've got to see the ghosts! They're waiting for us both—calling to us—longing to take us to a better destiny."

Braun looked up. The roof of the avenue was a great arched ceiling barely visible beyond the light from the staff.

"The ghosts come in the darkness," Braun giggled. "Some things are seen better in the dark . . . some things are *easier* in the dark . . ."

The glow from the staff began to fade. The impenetrable darkness slowly closed in on them again as the light shrank.

"Soon your soul will be open at last," Braun nodded, the features of his face vanishing into a vague shape as the light receded. "The ghosts will spill from you and you will *see* the vision."

Darkness enveloped them.

"You will *hear the song!*"

Stars appeared.

Impossibly, above him in the pitch blackness two-thirds of a league below the mountain, the night sky filled his vision.

Nine notes . . .

Come to us and bring our redemption . . .

The stars shifted as he watched in slack-jawed wonder.

Seven notes . . .

Weep for the pain and the loss . . .

He felt as though he were falling up toward them.

Five notes . . .

The past is our sorrow . . . The past is our shame . . .

Faces started forming among the stars. Faces he had forgotten. Faces he once knew.

Ghosts.

Drakis screamed.

"Drakis! Are you injured?"

Drakis opened his eyes to see the faces of his Octian, lit by a single globe-torch, staring down at him.

The human warrior sat up on the stones of the avenue and drew in a painful breath. "No, Captain ChuKang. I can fight."

The manticore stood up, pulling Drakis to his feet as he did. "We thought we had lost you, *hoo-mani*. There was a reserve of dwarven warriors waiting here when we came through the fold. I think they were more surprised to see us than we were to see them."

KriChan chuckled darkly. "They ran, but not fast enough."

"It was a blessing from the gods," ChuKang continued. "Chasing them down showed us the way to the causeway."

"At least we thought it was a blessing," Megri chimed in. The goblin was grinning as he picked at his fingernails with the point of his dagger, "until we realized the Proxi had gone missing."

Drakis turned. Braun stood nearby, still smiling at him with the same strange grin.

"The Centurai is assembled up ahead," KriChan said. "Are you ready to go?"

Drakis shuddered.

"More than ready."

CHAPTER 4

Firefall

THE TIMURAN CENTURAI had lost nearly a third of their number by the time they emerged from the dwarven avenue. Regrouped and organized, their well-ordered phalanx emerged shoulder to shoulder onto a courtyard that was completely engulfed in hot, steaming mists.

Their carefully ordered and classic formation suited the plans of the Ninth Throne Death-dealer Dwarves well—who waited for the Centurai to emerge from the avenue and then set upon them from both sides simultaneously. Hot, wet mists swirled in utter blackness around them, illuminated by the frequent, diffused flashes of blue and red in the distance, each flash painting silhouettes of slaughter in the mists. In the confusion of the vapor, the carefully ordered Centurai collapsed again into frantic and desperate fights with an enemy who kept appearing out of nowhere and vanishing just as quickly as they came.

Drakis adjusted his grip and pushed his way into the battle once again. He needed to bring order to his Octian. If he could rally them, then he might use them to bring order to other Octia in the Centurai, but that couldn't happen until he could *find* his own brother warriors. He was blind in the thick vapors around him.

He waded into the milky conflict, killing before being killed and struggling to keep his footing on the blood-slick stones.

"There is a place that calls my soul home." Unbidden, Drakis' lips began to move with each blow of his sword, and through his chattering teeth he began hesitantly to sing. "North far beyond horizons . . ."

He cut his sword deep across the gut of the dwarf before him.

"To my place of resting . . . of testing . . ."

He drew the blade out just in time to parry an ax blade from his right.

"Centurai! Centurai Timuran!" The call to rally was shouted unmistakably by ChuKang—yet his words sounded strangely muffled, their direction and distance diffused through the steaming fog. One after the other, the leaders of each Octian were being summoned to rally to their leader. "Centurai!"

Drakis thrust his sword into an ax-wielding dwarf, then, looking up, caught a glimpse of several large figures running past him, their dark outlines illuminated by flashing pulses of light against the steaming mists. The first two were manticores—judging by their size and the enormously broad shoulders—followed closely by a lithe shadow with four arms.

"Hey, GriChag! TsuRag! Ethis!" Drakis called out as he dragged his blade quickly from the quivering body of his last opponent. His own Octian at last. So long as he had his Octian brothers with him, he was invincible. His eyes remained locked on the shadows as they quickly stopped and turned in the sticky fog.

"Yes, Warlord?" Ethis said flatly as he came closer.

Warlord was the title reserved for the master of the combined Legions and ludicrously beyond what any human could dream to attain. Drakis frowned. "Knock it off, Ethis. GriChag, where's Megri?"

"With ChuKang and KriChan," the manticore said quickly.

"And Braun?" Drakis urged.

"Yes, he's with them, too." GriChag turned his massive head away in disgust.

Drakis gave a sudden, violent shake. The steaming fog was unnerving him. "Then let's form the Octian on Chu-Kang. *You* show us the way, GriChag."

The manticore curled his lip, barring his fangs, but he turned and obeyed, followed by TsuRag and Ethis. Drakis' own feet stumbled on the uneven ground, but he knew that both the manticores and the chimerian could see far better than he could in these conditions. Better to keep his gaze fixed on them and risk a few missteps than to risk falling down some bottomless shaft.

With a startling abruptness, the mists twisted, writhing in the cavern wind, shredding apart. He could see the Yungskord again, but this time Drakis was looking back to the distant promenade that the Timuran Centurai had folded away from not that long before. He had stood there and seen this place in the distance; now, thanks to the folds, he was standing here and looking back on where they had so recently been and where Braun had propagated so many copies of the gate symbol along that wide promenade. The young warrior took in a breath, for the sudden vista filled him with awe and pride; those quickly set gate symbols had borne fruit.

Drakis stood atop a cliff face looking down onto a battle the likes of which he had never before witnessed. It raged all across the floor of the enormous Yungskord cavern. A tide of Imperial Warriors—three full Impress Legions, he was sure, over sixteen thousand strong—charged from a line of folds all along the promenade and down toward the carefully prepared positions. Imperial catapults, hastily arrayed on the promenade, launched supporting balls of flame over their heads. The dwarves waited for them, dug into a series of trenches crossing the craggy ground between the raging cascades of water that were still flooding into the enormous grotto. Long torrents of magma streamed down from the ceiling of the cavern; their brilliant yellow-orange ribbons fell crashing into the flooded cavern floor and flashing into scalding steam, boiling both the water and the Impress Warriors around it. Still, the slave-army of the elves pressed their attack, led by ranks of enraged manticores, their fangs bared in their feral faces, their roars sounding before them as they charged across the field of battle. Following on their heels were chimeras and an entire Cohort of Proxi—nearly five hundred strong—in support. They were casting sheets of electrical fire over the heads of the charging manticores and into the trenches of the dwarves. Their effectiveness was lessened, however, as the Proxi, too, had to run forward or risk death literally pouring down on them from above. Their flashes of lightning and the magma cascades illuminated ghastly scene as the manticores were suffering under the withering assault of catapult fire raining death across their ranks. The great lion-men never took their eyes off their prey, however, and in a wave leaped over the battlements and into the first line of dwarven trench works.

"Drakis!" ChuKang snarled through the flat muzzle of his face.

Drakis turned at once, unquestioningly obeying his leader's command. "Captain! I do not yet have the count . . ."

"Forget that! There's no time," ChuKang said, pointing up along the cliff face. "Get this Octian organized and moving . . . now!"

It was the causeway; the same causeway he had seen from the far end of the Yungskord, but now it lay open before them, rising along the side of the cavern, winding between the spires of impossibly large stalagmites straight to the gates of the Thorgreld—and Stoneheart just beyond.

"You heard the voice! TsuRag and GriChag—you're the leads with swords bright!—Megri, you follow ChuKang and KriChan. Braun, you're with me. Ethis—you watch our backs. Stay tight. Let's go!"

ChuKang was already charging up the inclined ledge, and Drakis was finding it hard to catch up. Now in the clear, Drakis could see what remained of their Centurai emerging from the steam. They were far fewer than he had hoped, perhaps not quite forty—less than half their original strength. With the song still sounding in the back of his head, Drakis yelled, and his entire Octian yelled with him as they led in the charge.

They ran up the fitted cobblestones of the causeway as it wound its way upward following the side wall of the cavern. Their path was illuminated by their globe-torches and the increasingly frequent brilliant flashes from the battle on the cavern floor behind them. Every step up the inclined road brought them closer to the Last Gate of Thorgreld—a bastion carved into an enormous stalactite hanging from the cavern ceiling nearly a thousand feet above the cavern floor. Beyond that, in the dim light of the battle raging below them, Drakis could see the Stoneheart—last stronghold of the dwarven kings.

The blessings of the Emperor may yet be with us today, Drakis thought. He could see the Last Gate ahead of them as they charged up the causeway, and the way still looked open. There were no dwarven warriors on the road between them and the gatehouse. Out of over forty thousand warriors, the fates had conspired to place what remained of Centurai Timuran within reach of the greatest prize of the war.

"Hey, *hoo-mani*," huffed the goblin as he sprinted alongside Drakis. "What is this treasure we've come to liberate?"

"It's the most important treasure of this entire war, Megri, but you're going to have a hard time finding it if you don't know what it is," Drakis grinned. "Weren't you paying attention?"

"Yeah, dwarf barter—I forgot."

"Can someone please tell Megri why we're here?" Drakis called back, not slackening his pace.

Ethis spoke up at once. "Destroy the last of the dwarven thrones . . . capture the Crown of the Ninth Throne . . . and return with it and any other bounty we liberate in triumph to Lord Timuran."

"That's right," Drakis called back, his voice starting to get hoarse from long use during the day. "We get to return with great honor and glory added to the House of Lord Timuran."

"Maybe even a reward, eh?" Ethis chuckled. Drakis had long ago learned to listen carefully to chimera. Looking at them was useless in trying to gauge their intentions since chimera barely had a face, let alone facial expressions.

"Sure, Ethis," KriChan, the captain's manticorian second, responded. "Se'Shei Timuran himself will give you a big kiss, pat you on the head, and elevate you to Sixth Estate just so you can join him for breakfast."

"More likely *eat* him for breakfast!" Braun laughed. "But you shouldn't worry, friends, because we'll never have to worry about another breakfast ever again!"

Drakis eyed Braun as they ran side by side. He had known Braun all his life, but he had never acted so strangely before.

"Thick-bones—thick-head," Ethis, snorted as he laughed. "You know the saying? *Hoo-mani* are poor at everything—great at nothing."

Both the chimerian and the goblin laughed heartily.

"Quiet, both of you!" ChuKang growled.

Drakis grimaced. Chimera approached battle with a lot more finesse than the manticores. They weren't particularly strong, but they were fast and difficult to damage; their skeletons were telescoping plates and cartilage instead of the more rigid and brittle bones of the manticores or humans. They could change their skin color to blend into their surroundings and alter their skeletal frame at will so that they might be nearly as compact as a dwarf to nearly twice as tall as Drakis. Chimera made fine warriors but tended to be clannish and exclude others. He didn't have anything against the chimera and always remembered them as maybe a little playful but never cruel to him. But now Ethis was making racial jokes?

"We're coming to the end and the beginning all at once," Braun huffed next to Drakis. "The whole pointless bloodletting and death dealing—all for the amusement of the elven children! We should stop . . . savor the moment . . ."

"We're almost there," Drakis snapped. "We can't stop now."

"You cannot run from yourself, Drakis," Braun shook

while he ran. His craggy face was sweating profusely. "The ghosts are lurking, waiting to pounce on you given any opportunity. They'll leap from their little box and bite old Timuran right in his skinny ass!"

"Shut up, Braun! The Tribune will get the wrong idea . . ."

"Do you think so? I thought I was speaking very clearly!"

"Just keep your mouth shut and we may salvage a way out of this yet. If we get hold of that last Dwarven Crown, the glory to House Timuran will be . . ."

"I don't give a damn about the House glory!" Braun spat back. "It's not *my* glory—it's not *your* glory--so why should we care . . . let alone die?"

"You know why as well as anyone!" Drakis shook his head. They had fought their way so far, lost more than forty brothers from their own Centurai in the last hour, and now their Proxi wanted to just walk away from the reward? What in the name of the gods was wrong with everyone today?

Nine notes . . . Seven notes . . .
The last dwarven king . . . My death-knell did bring . . .
Five notes . . . Five notes . . .

"Well, it looks like none of us are going to have to worry about the spoils today," Ethis grumbled. "Look up ahead."

They were rounding a towering stalagmite when they saw it. More than a hundred yards beyond TsuRag and GriChag, three full Cohorts had erupted from folds appearing on the causeway in front of them. More than a thousand Impress Warriors were now dashing madly toward the Last Gate ahead of them.

"Where did they come from?" Drakis asked sourly.

"What difference does it make," Braun sighed, "so long as they're the ones doing the bleeding?"

"Damn you, Braun!" KriChan's golden eyes flashed in the darkness. "If you weren't our Proxi, I'd tear out your heart right here and now!"

Drakis turned toward ChuKang. "Come on! We've come this far—we can still beat them to the throne!"

"Wait! Something's not right," ChuKang snarled.

The human stepped in front of their manticorian captain and angrily turned. "ChuKang! The lead Cohorts will break against the gate tower. Let them do the dying and then we ..."

ChuKang was not looking at Drakis; the manticore's gold-hued eyes were fixed on something at the top of the causeway.

Drakis could feel the heat growing on his neck. He turned and drew in a sharp breath.

The front Cohorts had engaged the Thorgreld Gate; an upside-down tower suspended from the cavern ceiling down to meet the rising causeway, but the dwarves once more were anticipating them. A cascade of molten lava, held in check for uncounted centuries against this day, was loosed by the dwarven defenders from above the gate. Its brilliant, blinding stream arced out from the inverted tower's spouts and poured down on the ledge below. Flashes of blue could be seen near its base—evidence of the desperate attempts of the Tribunes to hold back the incinerating river of liquid rock through their Proxis while keeping the lead Centurai still battling for the gate and the throne beyond.

The lava, however, continued to pour from above, rolling in a devastating torrent over the remaining warriors and into the entire Cohort behind it. The warriors of the Second Cohort broke ranks, running back down the causeway directly toward Drakis and his comrades, but the river of lava was rapidly overtaking them.

Drakis glanced at his feet. The fitted cobblestones of the causeway had been formed with a slight trough in the middle—the perfect channel for a river of molten rock.

"Back!" ChuKang shouted. "Back down! Now!" His commands were pointless as those behind him were already trying to move. But the causeway was packed now with other Centurai from the Imperial Army who had appeared behind them. Those closest to the front started shouting and pushing at those behind. Panic rose like a tide among the warriors. Drakis plunged into the fray, trying desperately to get away from the onrushing death. He heard the screams of several warriors as they were pushed over the edge by their terrified companions.

The deadly tide hissed menacingly behind him as the mass of warriors compressed around him. The air was being pressed out of his lungs.

A massive hand grabbed the back of his breastplate and pulled him back. He felt himself swinging wildly, his head banging against his own shoulder plate, and then suddenly he was spinning through the air. His scream was cut short as his back slammed against stone and he tumbled down a rock face.

His fall was only a few feet down from where he impacted, but it felt as though he had fallen much farther. Still panicked, he scrambled backward, clawing at the ground until he reached the wall. Only then did he take in his surroundings.

He was sitting on a rock outcropping above the causeway. The other members of his Octian were there as well, a few of them a little bruised but otherwise intact. ChuKang was pulling himself up the cavern wall to join them.

"You toss well for a *hoo-mani*," Ethis chuckled.

Braun was shivering, curled up in a stone niche at the back of the outcropping. Ethis was looking intently over the edge. KriChan was helping pull ChuKang up to the ledge.

There were two younger manticores on the ledge who were almost identical, as well as another chimerian.

"Belag! Karag! What are you doing here?" Drakis asked. "I thought you were in the Sixth Octian with S'Kagh."

"We were, Drakis," Belag answered at once. "But we're both just as glad to be with you, considering the alternative."

"And you, warrior!" Drakis tried to stop his hands from shaking as he turned toward the chimerian. There was something familiar about him, but the memory would not push past the music. "What's your name?"

"Thuri," the chimerian said evenly. "Fourth Octian under Ophas."

"Well, you're all First Octian now," Drakis said and turned toward the captain.

"Should have foreseen this," ChuKang said with a rumble in his voice as he gazed toward the gate. "A waste of warrior-flesh."

The ledge shook. A great slab of stone sheered away from the rock face under the ledge, crashing down into the magma with a shower of molten rock. The heat rolling up the face toward them was blistering. "We can't stay here," KriChan roared.

"Captain!"

Drakis turned toward the sound, faint over the roaring of the magma flowing below their ledge.

"Look!" Karag shouted as he pointed across the glowing flow below. "On that rock pillar!"

Drakis saw them.

It was Jerakh, the manticorian leader of Timuran's Second Octian. Half a dozen other warriors from their Centurai had joined Jerakh in climbing to their own cramped haven atop a broken stalactite on the far side of the causeway.

"They're trapped like we are," Ethis yelled over the din. "If the molten river on the causeway does not kill them, then it must be at least three hundred feet to the floor of the cavern."

Drakis was finding it hard to breathe.

"Well, Drakis, trapped at last," Braun said with a sick smile. "I guess no one is going to know why you fought after all."

Five notes . . . Five notes . . .

Mala will forgive . . . Mala will forget . . .

"We're not trapped!" Drakis shouted as he picked up Braun with both hands, dragging the Proxi to his feet. "Can you propagate a symbol far enough to reach that pillar?"

Braun shook violently in his hands, his eyes refusing to focus.

"*CAN YOU?*"

"Of course," Braun drooled slightly, his words slurred. "I'll have to draw a gate symbol here first."

"Do it!" Drakis spat, releasing the Proxi with a slight but emphatic shove.

The ledge shook again. KriChan leaped back just as a section of ledge gave way under his foot.

ChuKang grabbed the human warrior's shoulder. "What are you doing, Drakis?"

Drakis turned. "Those warriors don't have a Proxi. They cannot fold off that stone pillar without one."

"Then they're lost . . ."

"No!" Drakis shouted perhaps too emphatically. "We have our Proxi make a gate symbol here on our ledge then propagate it across to *that* ledge where Jerakh is sheltered. We get the Tribune to fold us all over to that other rock and then *all* of us fold out from there."

"There isn't much room over there," KriChan added, his heavy brow furrowed.

"They'll *make* room . . . or cook."

ChuKang nodded and turned to the Proxi. "Make it happen, Braun."

But the Proxi was already finishing the inscription of three interlinking rings in the stone of the ledge. Sweat was pouring from his brow and he looked up with unfocused eyes, but the arc of bright light flew from his staff and fell with precision exactly in the center of the stone pillar on the far side of the molten causeway.

"Now, Braun! Call on the Tribune!" Drakis shouted in his face.

Braun's eyes suddenly focused. He shoved Drakis away, knelt down, and jammed the end of his staff into the stone of the ledge, sweat pouring down his face. The terrible cries of the dying on the ledge below him receded farther from his mind as he connected with other thoughts . . . other powers.

"So we rescue our brother warriors . . . then where do we go?" Thuri gripped his four blades in his hands once more.

"Does it matter?" Drakis shouted, drawing his own short sword. "We've come this far . . . how can the day get any worse?"

The air twisted in on itself, then suddenly tore apart. ChuKang did not wait to see what was on the other side. He shouted, and everyone jumped through the opening just as the outcropping crumbled beneath their feet, eaten from under them by the continuing stream of lava.

Chapter 5

The Last Throne

THEY EMERGED IN CHAOS.

The fold collapsed behind them, but the sound was swallowed in the cacophony of battle that raged before them.

"By the gods!" ChuKang roared. "Where are we now?"

KriChan turned on Braun, grabbing the edges of his breastplate with both fists. "Where have you taken us? Where are Jerakh and the rest of the Centurai?"

"I . . . I don't . . ."

"Why did you bring us here?" KriChan shouted in the Proxi's face.

"Not me!" Braun yelled back at the manticore. "*I* didn't bring us anywhere! It's the Tribune . . . he's the one who determines where the folds connect, not me! *He* sent us here!"

KriChan shoved Braun to the ground, his lips curling up around his fangs in disgust.

"Wait!" Drakis shouted above the noise. "I know where we are! This is it . . . the Ninth Throne of the Dwarves!"

Every available Cohort from almost two full Legions—perhaps six thousand warriors in all—had folded into the room just ahead of them, a charging army of warriors who could smell impending victory in the air and taste the final

fall of the dwarven kingdoms. Their influx gushed into
the vast space as though they were a torrent from a swollen river, flooding into the rotunda and the last stand of
dwarven might.

The elite Warriors of the Ninth Throne were there to
meet them, their axes already wet with the blood of their
enemies. This was the last throne, where all of the dwarven
kings came to council with one another. It was the most
honored place in all the Nine Kingdoms under the mountain and home of the greatest of the dwarven kings—
whose name was not known.

"What about Jerakh and the rest of our Centurai?"
KriChan swore. "Damn the Tribune!"

"Or may the gods bless him," ChuKang replied.
"Braun?"

"Yes, Captain."

"You say the Tribune knew about Jerakh and the rest
of our warriors?"

"Yes, Captain."

"Then he'll bargain for another Proxi to get to them and
bring them here," ChuKang said. "The Tribune wants us
in on the end—wants a prize that will bring honor to our
House. *That's* why we came!"

Five notes . . . Five notes . . .

I fight for a life . . . I fight for my wife . . .

The throne room was enormous, the hollowed out core
of the Stoneheart nearly a hundred yards in diameter.
The domed roof was supported by nine enormous statues
of dwarven kings, each carved out of the native stone as
though they supported the weight of the mountain on
their shoulders. In the center of the room was the elevated
platform at the top of a truncated cone of stairs where the
dwarven kings once met in council. Now all the Impress
Warriors could see the Last Dwarven King sitting on his
throne, his crown shining in the explosive light of the invading army. Scattered about the room was the last of the
wealth gathered from all of the Nine Kingdoms, but it was
the crown that riveted the eyes of every Impress Warrior
smashing against the dwarven circle of defense.

Drakis realized that they had arrived late—by moments only, but that was enough. The converging Impress Warriors of the Rhonas Empire had already swarmed down on the dwarven defenders, shattering their forward lines in what must have been a horrific collision. Now all lines between the defending dwarves and the Rhonas warriors were blurred into a confused, seething mass of blood and blind rage.

"Is that it?" KriChan shouted, pointing toward the throne even as he began charging toward the writhing slaughter around the base of the steps.

"Yes!" ChuKang snarled through his clenched, bared teeth, running alongside him. "We take it and we go home!"

"Home? How?" KriChan exclaimed.

"All the other Centurai are trying to hold their formations together," ChuKang smiled with relish as he spoke. "There's no one left to hold us back! Just don't stop!"

The crown was the prize above all others coveted by the elven Houses that had engaged in this war. Any House that returned with the crown would be lifted beyond its previous status, possibly even elevated in its caste among the Estates. Every Tribune directing the battle from the distant command tent on the plain knew it—and made doubly sure that every Impress Warrior knew it, too.

Drakis was running as fast as he could just to keep up with the manticores. "We'll never make it! Someone else is going to fold right to the top, and it will all be over!"

"No! We have a chance. Look!" Ethis ran next to him, pointing with his third arm. "Look!"

All around the throne folds erupted, but even as each sprang into existence, another fold would appear too close by. The tearing of space collapsed, and the folds shredded each other.

"Greedy bastards, our Tribunes," Thuri shouted through a wide grin splitting his otherwise featureless face. "Pushing each other out of the way now that the end is in sight."

"All we need is to get our Proxi up there to etch a gate symbol. That will anchor our fold, and it's all over,"

KriChan shouted from behind them. "Drakis! Take Braun and follow ChuKang! Don't stop!"

"This is it, Braun!" Drakis shouted. "Let's go! Follow me!"

"Of course, Drakis," Braun answered cheerfully as he picked up the Standard staff in his hand, "as far as the ghosts will allow."

ChuKang charged into the battle with a wide-bladed sword in each of his massive hands, but he did not stop to engage any of the enemy. He continued his run, weaving between the warriors engaged in battle, his great blades occasionally striking out at any dwarf that moved to engage him, then dashing past.

Drakis followed, keeping his eyes fixed on the Sinque—the Devotion tattoo on the broad back of his manticorian commander's shaved head. He was only dimly aware of the other warriors of his Octian weaving their desperate way near him in pursuit of their leader. Flashes of battle caught his eye as he ran: a manticorian warrior from another Centurai being dragged to the ground screaming under a rush of dwarven axmen; a human, his face covered in blood plunging his sword downward into a dwarf prone at his feet; a chimerian, shifting in size to nearly nine feet, swinging a pair of curved-bladed swords against three dwarven dart-men while trying to stanch the bloody stump of a severed arm with his remaining free hand. Their cries receded in his ears, echoing in his mind as from a distance, replaced by the torturous melody that ran through his mind to the rhythm of every running step that he took.

"Keep going!" KriChan's shout sounded far away, behind the wall of music in his head. "Up! Go up!"

Drakis tripped over the body of a fallen dwarf, breaking his stride and threatening to bring him crashing down to the bloody floor beneath him. He lurched forward, desperate to get his feet back under him.

ChuKang's blades flashed again through the thicket of combat as Drakis lunged after him.

They were through. The curving stairs rose before them to the dwarven thrones above.

ChuKang roared, rushing up the stairs with KriChan and Belag already behind him. Drakis followed without hesitation, his own battle cry in his throat. He glimpsed Thuri to one side as he rushed up the stairs ducking past the still erupting and collapsing folds.

The dwarven defenders, distracted by a threat on the far side of the throne, were too late to regroup for ChuKang's sudden assault. They tried to release the cauldron vents beneath the topmost step so they could pour a molten cascade down on their enemies, but they were too late. ChuKang's blades cut into them as the remaining dwarves of the King's Guard, all in ancient dwarven armor, tried desperately to push the manticore off the platform of the Nine Thrones. KriChan entered the battle next to Chu-Kang as did Belag, and in moments they had engaged the last stand of dwarves in mortal combat.

Drakis then saw the Dwarven King, the crown fixed to his battle helmet.

Drakis, sword drawn, rushed forward.

The Dwarven King's long beard hung down over a shining breastplate of ancient design. He held a shield on his right arm fixed to his bracer, and his left hand gripped a sword. The jewels on the crown flashed in the light of the magical bolts still being cast through the hall. The helmet itself was fabulously ornate–sharp dragonlike wings extending backward on both sides and a faceplate molded into a fearsome countenance.

Drakis grinned. He always preferred it when the faceplate was down; somehow it made the killing easier.

Drakis made a few probing thrusts, studying the Dwarven King's reactions. Time seemed to be slowing around him, and the world contracted until all that existed for him was the armor-encased dwarf in front of him. Parry. Parry. Thrust. Slash and parry.

Drakis bared his teeth in a savage smile.

The king was skilled . . . but not skilled enough.

Drakis lunged forward, his blade flashing in a series of blows. The dwarf quickly parried, backing from the onslaught. Their swords locked, Drakis pressing downward until both their blades smashed against the dwarf's shield.

Drakis reached down, pulling his dagger from his belt.

The human pushed away from the dwarf but not quite far enough. The king lashed out quickly, cutting just under Drakis' breastplate, his blood welling into his tunic beneath. Drakis cursed but knew it was a risk he had to take. He needed to remain close.

Drakis parried the next blow and then again pressed a savage set of blows against the dwarf, pressing him against one of the thrones. He was tiring quickly and the pain shooting across his chest was distracting, but the thought flashed through his mind that at least the song was leaving him to his work. He swung high and downward, again crashing both their swords down on the shield arm, then suddenly spun, the dagger in his free hand cutting through the air.

It found its mark between the helmet and the breastplate. Drakis turned the blade and felt the warm, sticky wetness gush over his hand.

The Ninth—and last—of the Dwarven Kings released his grip on his sword.

Drakis let go of his dagger. The dwarf slumped back onto the throne.

Drakis reached over and pulled the Crown of the Ninth Throne from the helmet of the Dwarven King, his voice shouting with unparalleled joy, "We've done it! We've won!"

ChuKang straightened to stand with his stained blades in both his hands. The last of the King's Guards had fallen before them. "Well done, Drakis! A triumph!"

"Lord Timuran will honor us all!" Thuri nodded.

"Perhaps even a Sixth Estate?" Belag purred. "Surely, ChuKang, you are due to be so honored."

"We'll brag ourselves into glory later," ChuKang said, shaking his head with pride. "Let's get out of here before anyone realizes . . . where's Braun?"

"He was behind me," Drakis said as he turned. "He should be . . ."

Drakis' eyes fixed on the Standard of the Timuran Centurai. The staff lay abandoned on the ground at the foot of the dwarven throne.

"He's gone!" Thuri yelled as he picked up the staff.

"Gone?" ChuKang shouted. "Where could he *go*?"

Drakis frantically scanned the battle around the foot of the stairs but could not see the Proxi anywhere among them.

"Here!" Thuri shouted, thrusting the Standard into Drakis' free hand. "*You* do it! *You* get us out of here!"

"I *can't* . . ."

"You're *hoo-mani* . . . just like Braun!"

"It doesn't work that way," Drakis spat his words in anger and frustration. "You have to be trained for it . . . linked to the Tribune through the House Altar . . ."

"How long before the Tribune can get another Proxi to us?" ChuKang asked quickly.

"He'll know the link was broken," Drakis answered. "He'd have to negotiate use from another Tribune . . ."

ChuKang turned to look down from the platform. "We don't have that long."

The battle was quickly winding down, the Centurai of other Houses were breaking free of the failing dwarves, moving up the stairs toward them.

Toward the crown.

The Imperial Army of Conquest was made up of units donated to the campaign by various Houses of the Empire. Some of the larger Houses had been known in the past to donate an entire Legion—an extravagance of maintaining over four thousand slave warriors. That was not true of the current campaign. The largest single House commitment— from House Plincian of the Paktan Guild Order—was five Cohorts of two thousand, eight hundred warriors. Several other Houses contributed full Cohorts of their own, but the majority of the Imperial Army of Conquest was made up of Legions and Cohorts that were cobbled together from donations of between one and three Centurai from many individual Houses.

Cohorts from the larger Houses were regrouping, strug-

gling to reestablish order in their commands for their own
organized assault on the crown. But the Centurai from the
smaller Houses knew that their only chance at the prize
was to seize it now. For the majority of the warriors in the
vast throne room, the military order of Legions and Cohorts evaporated at the sight of the prized crown.

The warriors from the different smaller Houses, battle
fever still raging in their blood, started up the stairs toward
ChuKang and the remnants of his Octian. As one Octian
pushed forward, the others grabbed at them, dragging
them backward. A blade strike. A scream. Then suddenly
all of the Impress Warriors of the Rhonas Empire—each
vying for the glory and recognition of their own House—
turned on each other. Combat erupted among the warriors
of the competing Houses, each of them desperate to reach
the top of the steps and claim the crown for their own.

"What do we do?" Thuri said, his large, blank eyes
blinking furiously. "How do we get out of here?"

"Without the Proxi?" KriChan barked. "We have no
way out!"

"But what about Jerakh? Tribune Se'Djinka . . ."

"Look around us! The Tribune can't open a fold here
any better than the rest of the Tribunes!" Ethis snapped.
"*We* were supposed to rescue *Jerakh*, remember! If he gets
here, it would only be through a fold opening on the *outside* of this mob . . . then there'll be our own army between
us and him. What good would that do?"

Karag drew in a sharp breath. "We're on our own?"

"Unfortunately," Ethis replied, raising his four swords
once more as he gazed down the stairs. "Not for long. We
are about to have far too much company."

The scrambling warriors from the other Houses were
coming closer. As the cone of stairs got narrower in cir-
cumference with each step, the fighting among the manticores, chimera, gnomes, and a few humans became more
constricted. They stepped over the bodies of their former
comrades, slew anyone who got in their way, only to be
felled by those behind them intent on one thing.

They each wanted the crown for the glory of their own

House. They had killed the dwarves for this prize. All that was left for them was to kill each other.

An ancient manticore, scarred and missing one eye, was the first to reach them. ChuKang met him with both blades, but the seasoned warrior traded him blow for blow. Two more manticores swiftly moved to join the combat. KriChan and Karag rushed forward to help. Ethis stepped backward toward Drakis, his narrow head swiveling about, looking for approaching enemies on all sides. Belag rose up against a chimerian from House Sutharan, cutting him down just as a human lunged toward him.

Drakis held the crown in his hand.

The dwarves have no doors . . . the dwarves are no more . . .

A goblin lunged at ChuKang from behind. The Centurai commander howled in pain, falling forward into the blades of the Tajeran manticores. KriChan sliced downward, nearly cutting the goblin in two just as one of the Tajeran manticores thrust from the side, running his blade upward. KriChan took a single gasp before collapsing. Karag stepped forward, impaling the Tajeran manticore on his own blade, but the blow left him open to the third manticore on his right.

Belag roared at his brother, rushing toward him. Karag did not see the danger. The blade cut into his leg behind the knee. The manticore howled, turning just as the blade swung again, this time downward into his chest.

"What do we do?" Thuri yelled at Drakis.

For the love of her . . . for the loss of her . . .

The song was raging once more in his head. The melody sounding over and over.

"Drakis! By the House gods!" Thuri yelled again. "What do we do?"

For the love of her . . . for the loss of her . . .

Drakis' eyes suddenly focused.

He looked at the crown. He could have bought a life of his own with it—but if he kept it, he would never live to claim it; none of them would.

Drakis leaped up to stand on the arms of the throne,

holding the crown high over his head. He felt more than saw more than a thousand pairs of eyes fixed on him.

He searched at the far edge of the army. He could see the larger Cohorts, now organized, making a determined run toward the thrones.

He caught a glimpse of the glowing headpiece of a Proxi staff beyond the edge of the pressing mob. There was the face of a manticore next to it. Was it Jerakh? Had Tribune Se'Djinka sent them help at last?

For the love of her . . . for the loss of her . . .

With all his remaining strength, he hurled the crown toward the distant manticore next to the familiar looking staff at the far edge of the mob.

It sailed out high over the heads of the Impress Warriors, tumbling in the air above hundreds of greedy, outstretched hands. The warriors who were on the stairs groaned but turned almost as one, charging back toward where the crown was falling.

"Madness," Ethis said, shaking his head as he watched Rhonas Warriors converge on where the crown had landed in its flight, killing their brothers-in-arms to claim it for their own.

Drakis just looked down into his empty hands.

CHAPTER 6

Spoils

FOUR FIGURES WANDERED LISTLESSLY among the dead.
Drakis reached down, turned over a broken shield
and peered beneath it under the hard radiating light of
a globe-torch in his hand. The pale, glazed eyes of a dead
dwarven warrior stared back up at him. The warrior was
stripped of all of its armor and weapons. Even its tunic had
been torn open, leaving its bare, unmoving chest exposed.

"There's nothing left," Drakis muttered to himself.
"They've taken it all."

Drakis stood upright and, stretching his stooped back,
surveyed the results of their victory. The battle had raged
briefly below the throne as the various House factions
fought one another for possession of the crown. Drakis'
aim had been true; he was certain now that the crown had
landed among the warriors from his own Cohort. In his
recollection it was Jerakh himself who had caught it. A
Proxi bearing the standard of the Cohort of the Western
Provinces—no doubt where Tribune Se'Djinka had secured a replacement for Braun—managed to open a fold,
and the crown was gone. The outraged other Octia from
the various Centurai remaining in the great throne room
immediately fell to pillaging anything of any worth that
they could put their hands on. These were set upon quickly

by the larger and now regrouped Cohorts, who took what they wanted from the hall by virtue of their size and unity. Once they were sated, the Centurai of the smaller Houses fell to their own pecking order. They cleaned the hall of its treasures, and when there were none left to be taken from the ground, they began to strip the dead. When there was nothing left of value among the dead, they began once more to fight and kill each other over those treasures they had already looted.

Drakis and his three remaining warriors from House Timuran had tried at first to secure their own portion of the fortune to be sacked from the last dwarven stronghold, but without a Proxi to fold their gains safely away, their choice was either to fight interminable battles with those who *did* have access to a fold or give up their spoils.

Now, all was silent. The Impress Warriors from the other Houses had all folded out of the hall with their prizes. Drakis and the few living members of his Octian were all that now moved under the enormous dome of the rotunda.

Drakis surveyed the scene with revulsion. He had seen many battles in his life, but none had struck him as being so senseless, vicious, and pointless. All these dwarves were dead, and for what? So that Timuran or Tajeran or any of a dozen other Houses could have bragging rights about their Cohorts? So that they could carry away some metal crown?

I fight for a life . . . I fight for my wife . . .

Drakis shook his head. The words weren't right.

He looked up into the glaring face of an enormous dwarven king hanging above him. It was one of the nine statues supporting the domed ceiling, illuminated by several fires now burning in the rotunda. Books, Drakis supposed, dwarven histories or journals or other such nonsense that had no value at all. The flickering light cast strangely moving shadows across the face of the statue, and the smoke gathering in the dome left a hazy distance between him and the face looking down on him with such disapproval.

"Anyone find Braun?" Belag shouted, his voice echoing in the vast hall.

"A couple of charred humans over here—one of them looks like it was Braun," Ethis called back. "Why?"

"I want to kill him!"

"He's already dead."

"Not dead enough!" Belag roared.

"Keep looking!" Drakis urged.

"Nothing!" Ethis said with disgust as he kicked over another dwarven body nearly sixty feet away. "Starving vermin would have left more."

"Keep looking," Drakis shouted, his voice echoing slightly and strangely amplified by the dome above. "We've got to find something to take back with us as a prize. Lord Timuran invested a great deal in this war."

"Yeah," Thuri said, "He invested us."

"For a House in the Provinces," Drakis said, "that was more than he could afford. Listen, the gleaners will be here soon and once they arrive nothing will be left. We've got to find whatever we can quickly to bring honor to the House."

"Honor?" Belag snarled. "Where is the honor in this? Honor is in battle and the blood of our enemies—not the blood of our own traitorous allies or these pretty pieces of metal and stone." The manticore threw down the broken jewelry he had just picked up.

"Hey," Ethis called out. "We need that for a prize!"

Drakis was finding it difficult to breath.

The last dwarven king . . . My death-knell did bring . . .

The dwarves have no doors . . . the dwarves are no more . . .

"We *had* the prize," Belag shouted, his deep voice resonating through the hall. "Drakis took it from the Dwarven King and stood with it . . . held it in his hands right there"—he pointed up to the platform where the dead dwarf still slumped on the throne—"and then he threw it away!"

Drakis squeezed his eyes closed, pressing the palm of his hand against his forehead.

I fight for a life . . . I fight for my life . . .

Weep for the pain and the loss . . .
The past is our sorrow . . . The past is our shame . . .

"He saved your life, Belag," Thuri said simply as he pushed over yet another dwarf corpse. "He saved all our lives."

"Not all," Belag growled.

Drakis turned toward the manticore, fixing his eyes on the enormous creature. Several quick strides brought him to stand directly in front Belag looking upward into the angry yellow eyes set deep in the wide face a full foot above his own gaze. "No, not all. ChuKang's dead. KriChan's dead. Braun is gone, and your brother– and, yes, you see I *do* know all their names—Karag's dead, too."

The past is our sorrow . . . The past is our shame . . .

Drakis began to sweat. "Maybe *you* wanted to join them, but the *rest* of us are satisfied that we're still here."

We kill without cause. We kill without thought.
Five notes . . . Five notes . . .

His hand began to shake. "So either fall on your sword and get it over with or get back to your *job* and help us salvage something out of this . . . this . . ."

Belag's eyes narrowed. "Drakis?"

They eat here. They love here. They laugh here.
Better if left and forgotten . . .
Nine notes. Seven notes.

Drakis flinched.

Awaken the ghosts long forgotten . . .
Recall the loved dead . . .
Dead is the hero . . . Dead to all lament . . .
Buried past memory here below . . .

"LEAVE ME ALONE!" Drakis screamed as he bent over, pressing both his palms against his temples.

Belag drew his sword. Thuri and Ethis both began making their way toward Drakis, picking their path around the bodies that covered the floor everywhere around them.

"Drakis!" Ethis said, his upper two hands gripping the human by his shoulders. "What's wrong?"

Mala will forgive . . . Mala will forget . . .

"It's . . . it's nothing," Drakis said, shaking off a sudden chill. "I . . . I hear this . . . I don't know . . . this music . . . this song in my head . . ."

"Song?" Belag raised one heavy brow.

"It's . . . just a song," Drakis said, drawing in a deep breath. "I don't know where it came from, but I can't seem to be rid of it. It's just something in my mind."

Belag's head raised suddenly, his ears swiveling forward. "I think I hear it, too."

Drakis shot a questioning glance at the manticore. "Hear what?"

"Your song," Belag said in a low, rumbling voice, his heavy eyebrows knitting together. He moved closer to the stairs leading up to the throne. "It's coming from over here."

Belag drew his long, curved blade, the ringing of the metal singing softly as it cleared its scabbard.

"Where?" Drakis asked on a soft breath.

The manticore gestured with the tip of his sword toward the right side of the enormous cone of steps.

Drakis shook his head doubtfully but drew his own sword. He took a step toward the stairs, the melody still there. He was no longer certain whether the tune was in his mind or his ears.

One thing was certain. Something was moving in the shadows among the dead.

Drakis froze. His eyes suddenly opened wide.

It was singing. The words were indistinct, but the tune was unmistakably the same as the one that had haunted Drakis for days.

The refrain stopped, replaced by a voice.

"Is it over," asked the lilting voice coming from the squat figure. "Can I come out now?"

Drakis raised his sword again, the squat figure still remained in shadow. "Show yourself!"

The dark outline stopped and then emerged from the darkness as it held both hands open, its chubby palms in front of its wide body.

Belag curled his lips in loathing. "By all the gods of the House, what *is* that?"

That it was a dwarf was not in doubt, but its clothing was of such a bizarre nature as to leave Drakis to question his own vision. The dwarf had the requisite long beard of its kind, but instead of the usual bushy splay, it was split down the middle and each side was carefully braided. The ends of this bizarre affectation were tucked into pockets on the outside of—not the universal dwarven brown jacket—but an outlandishly colored and intricately embroidered doublet that seemed a bit too large for him. Colored hose—one green and one red—clung closely to the dwarf's stout legs, which were planted firmly in incongruously heavy boots. Topping it all was an enormous puffy hat of purple and orange nearly overwhelmed with long feathers, beads, and glass—all of which was pulled to one side by a single bell that had no clapper and, therefore, could not ring unless struck.

Ethis shook his head with a smirk. "That, Belag, is a joke!"

"Very nearly on the mark, although it would be better to say a great many jokes!" the dwarf said cheerily. He reached up with his right hand and tugged at the hat. It proved momentarily reluctant to let go of the dwarf's brow.

"Sorry—bad entrance," the dwarf spoke with embarrassment as he finally pulled the cap free. Drakis could at last see clearly the broad face with the high, round cheekbones. The dwarf had thick, bushy eyebrows above twinkling, pale blue eyes—all of which was difficult to see behind a prominent, bulbous nose. His long, white hair looked as though it was usually combed straight back from his high forehead, but the reluctant hat had pulled it all into a rather messy nimbus. "I am Jugar, King of Dwarven Jesters—and Jester to Dwarven Kings!"

"You're . . . the fool?" Drakis said incredulously.

"Well, to be sure, we prefer the appellation 'court jester' or 'professional idiot,' but, I think you've got the concept at its core," the dwarf said, smiling patiently. He took a few more cautious steps toward Drakis and then stopped. He looked around the hall, his smile falling slightly as he gazed across the field of fallen warriors in the hall. "So, he said carefully, "how goes the war?"

"It's over," Belag grunted. "You lost."

"Ah," Jugar took in a deep breath, and then turned to Drakis. "Well, then I guess there's nothing left to do but surrender. Where's the king? I don't mean to brag, mind you, but I could probably smooth things over for you . . . put in a good word . . ."

Drakis gestured up to the top of the stairs. Jugar looked up at the obviously still figure on the throne.

"I see," he said slowly, then began to speak more quickly. "Say, how about if I surrender, eh? There doesn't seem to be anyone else around here to do it. I can offer you the whole dwarven kingdom—well, except for this hall. I like this venue, did some of my best work here. The ability of sound to carry in this space is phenomenal. Take, for example, that tune I was just . . ."

Drakis leaped forward, grabbing the dwarf by his thick throat. The dwarf stumbled backward and fell, slamming down against the steps. Drakis pressed his face closer to the dwarf, sweat breaking on his brow as he spoke through clenched teeth.

"*What were you singing*-+" he hissed at the dwarf.

A tense silence descended in the hall.

Ethis gazed questioningly at the human. "Drakis?"

But the dwarf was suddenly still. His eyes were shifting quickly, searching Drakis' face, but the rest of him lay absolutely still. "I thought . . . just some old song, really," Jugar said quietly at last. "It's very old. Very old indeed. I can't recall right now where it is from."

Drakis' hands began to shake once more.

"Can you?" the dwarf finished quietly.

Drakis slowly released his grip on the dwarf.

Jugar slowly sat up. "Look, I couldn't help but overhear your predicament. You need a treasure, and it appears," Jugar said looking about at the slaughter surrounding them, "that I am out of a job. Could we strike a bargain? I ducked into a little gopher hole to stay out of the way of this war of yours. It was well hidden, and there's still some pretty interesting loot in there—including . . ."

The dwarf paused for dramatic emphasis.

"The *Heart of Aer!*"

The Impress Warriors looked at each other and then back at the dwarf.

"The what?" Drakis asked at last.

"*The Heart of Aer!*" Jugar said, this time with as much exaggerated drama as he could muster, his hands quivering as he held them out. He dropped them at once, seeing he did not impress his audience. "Oh, by Thel Gorfson! You've never heard of the Heart of Aer?"

"Who's Thel Gorfson?" Thuri asked, rubbing his forehead.

Jugar only glared at him. "The Heart of Aer is only the greatest, most secret treasure of the Nine Thrones! You could have named your price and still not come close to its value!"

"Where is it," Belag said flatly.

The dwarf kept his eyes on Drakis. "Do we have a deal—my life for the greatest treasure of the dwarves?"

The human considered the dwarf carefully.

"I'll throw myself into the bargain as well," the dwarf added. "Your master's new slave, eh?"

Belag rumbled deep in his throat. "Beware, Drakis. Dwarves never give a gift without being paid for it first."

Drakis flexed his grip on his sword.

Jugar swallowed then spoke carefully. "Maybe I could remember that song for you."

The human raised his chin.

"Drakis," Ethis said, shaking his head, "maybe we should just . . ."

"You have a deal, dwarf," Drakis said abruptly.

The other warriors of his Octian spoke up all at once.

"Are you mad? You don't have the authority . . ."

"You really believe that this fool, literally . . ."

"The Tribune will never allow . . ."

"Deal, dwarf!" Drakis repeated loudly, his voice cutting off further argument. "But if this is all part of your supposedly clever amusements, know that I'm a very picky audience—and that I'd just as soon take *your* heart to my master as any Heart of Aer. Now where is it?"

"You won't regret this," Jugar grinned as he reached out for the stairs, feeling about the surface for a moment before he found what he was searching for. "If you're looking for a treasure to take home to your master's fine estate in—didn't you say you were from the Western Provinces?—and prove how great warriors you are, then you couldn't do better than this!"

A loud hissing sound erupted from the stairs, blowing dust into the air as the carefully fitted stones of several steps suddenly descended into the floor. It was an opening, but all Drakis could see beyond the obscuring dust was a glowing light from a chamber within.

Drakis glanced skeptically at the dwarf, took in a deep breath, and then turned toward the opening in the stairs. The passage behind was wide enough, but he had to crouch down to pass under its low ceiling. It was only a few steps, however, before he entered a larger, vaulted chamber directly under the Nine Thrones.

Alcoves surrounded the room, each holding ancient dwarven armor wrought of gold, silver, and platinum and decorated with jewels. There were great tablets of gold carved with writing—the ancient laws of the mountain probably inscribed by the first Dwarven King, old Brok himself. Many other glistening things lay about the room, but Drakis' eyes were fixed on the central object.

It was difficult to look at. The black multifaceted onyx seemed to absorb the light that struck it. It floated between intricately carved white lattices of what appeared to be coral, one curving down from the ceiling and the other up from the floor beneath.

It was terrible and compelling all at once. Drakis hated it—and had to possess it.

"Drakis!"

It was Thuri. Drakis had almost forgotten entirely where he was. He shouted over his shoulder, "I'm here!"

"It looks like the Tribune came through at last. S'kagh has arrived with the Sixth Octian." Thuri's words seemed to come to him from a great distance though the chimerian could only be a few yards away. "They've got a Proxi from another Cohort, and Tribune Se'Djinka is demanding that we return at once!"

"And so we shall ... but first, get Ethis and Belag and come in here," Drakis shouted back. "And don't forget that dwarf."

The onyx Heart of Aer spun before him.

Drakis smiled. "Looks like we're not going back empty-handed after all."

CHAPTER 7

The Way Home

DRAKIS TUGGED SELF-CONSCIOUSLY at his tunic as he stepped from the command tent of Tribune Se'Djinka in one final, hopeless attempt to straighten it into a presentable state. He had managed to leave most of his badly mismatched armor with Thuri in the encampment, but three weeks of campaigning had left him looking very much the worse for wear. He also suspected that his smell had been increasingly offensive to the elven Tribune with each passing minute of his report—though after the numerous campaigns Drakis had fought down the years of his service he scarcely noticed it himself.

Still, when dealing with the elves it was best to remember such things—and to have a sense about when one's masters were pleased. Though nothing in the elven Tribune's words or countenance gave any sign of trouble, their orders were extraordinary.

It all felt wrong.

Now he stood once more outside the field tent of the Tribune, glowering at the cold, wet wind blowing from the west. A miserable storm had moved in earlier in the day. The Tribunes of the Imperial Legions made their encampment outside the enclosure of the common slave herd that made up their Legions, finding a location that was both dominant and secure, looking on the battle from afar and remaining untouched by it. For this last of the Dwarven Campaigns, they had found a place from which they could lord over their warriors from a comfortable distance. Each Tribune, for that matter, considered the placement of his personal command tent just another part of the strategy of war—a strategy that extended not only to the enemy but to the combative politics of the elves among their own kind. Se'Djinka, Tribune of House Timuran, had outmaneuvered the two hundred and forty-three other Tribunes, placing his great tent so that it sat at the crest of the rise on the Hyperian Plain, its entrance commanding a view that overlooked the seven league wide valley to the north that ended in the abrupt and spectacular rise of the Aerian Range—granite peaks that stabbed the sky eight thousand feet above their base in some places. It was an advantageous position, putting the other Tribunes—not to mention a great number of the tents of the various Guilds and Orders of the Imperium—at a disadvantage.

That a Tribune in charge of a single Centurai in such an obscure House as Timuran should be able to place his tent in such a position was just another of the numerous mysteries about Se'Djinka. It was best, Drakis thought, to not think too long on questions to which the answers might be both painful and dangerous.

He had trouble enough of his own without inviting more.

Standing beneath the leaden sky, Drakis watched as the dark clouds hid the tops of the distant mountains and spat chill, intermittent rain and mist at him. He had to admit that he preferred it to the oppressive opulence of Se'Djinka's tent. Perhaps it was something within the elves, he pondered, that caused them to always go beyond what was needed. Anything worth doing was worth over-doing was a creed that the elves followed with pride. They always seemed to press beyond all boundaries, he thought, whether those of good taste or those of their conquered territories.

Drakis preferred an honest, chill rain.

He looked down from his Tribune's tent onto the enclosure of the Legion. The rambling clusters of warriors huddled together against the constant cold drizzle or crowded into the few lean-tos they had hastily erected for themselves out of scavenged supply crates. Their misery extended well into the valley below, a panorama of spent fury, their fitful fires continuing to struggle against the drizzle.

All around the perimeter stood the encircling totems of the Iblisi—the crystalline Sentinels of the Imperial Legions.

Perhaps that is why I am uneasy, Drakis thought to himself. *I'm out where I don't belong.*

Nine notes . . . Seven notes . . .

The Dark Prize in sight . . . the Dark Prize is light . . .

Five notes . . . Five notes . . .

Drakis took a few gingerly placed paces down the slope, as much in an attempt to leave the song behind him as to bring himself to with a few steps of the twelve-foot-tall Sentinel. It was one thing to let loose the warrior horde on the enemy, but otherwise the herd must be controlled. The Sentinels were the totems that defined the boundaries of each slave's world. The face details were obscured by the soft, violet glow emanating from within the crystal, and there was something about each of them that grew more repellent and loathsome the closer one approached.

They marked the rightful limits of a slave's world, and each knew that to pass between Sentinels unbidden was to die.

Drakis took in a deep breath. "Drakis Sha-Timuran."

There passed an uncertain moment, and then the light within the Sentinel flashed from violet to pale yellow.

Drakis started breathing again and stepped quickly across the line between the Sentinels and continued down the slope.

It would take him half an hour just to make his way through the soaked army to his own Centurai. He knew he needed to get moving faster, but his audience with Se'Djinka made him uncertain and hesitant.

He shook with sudden violence in the rain.

It wasn't just that he had been outside the Sentinel's protection and control.

It was Se'Djinka's news that he and his Octian were being afforded a great honor.

Drakis shook again.

There was definitely something wrong.

"Hey, Drakis!" Thuri shouted, standing up slowly from where he squatted next to the sputtering fire. "How is life among members of the higher estates?"

"Better than it is down here," Drakis shot back as he slogged toward them through the ankle-deep mud between the tents, "but when was that ever any different?"

"Why the summons, Drakis?" Belag was sullen and testy. The lost of his brother weighed heavily on the towering manticore.

Drakis stopped and took a deep breath. His eye was caught by the wet flapping of the *Centurai's* battle flag from atop a tall pole planted angrily into the ground nearby; elven symbols intertwined around a pair of crossed swords. What had once seemed so bright and inspiring now looked tarnished and old.

He glanced around at the milling warriors all about him, then motioned Belag and the two chimera closer to him.

"We're going home," he said factually, keeping his voice low. "Se'Djinka has ordered us back to House Timuran. We have an hour to secure our gear, resupply the packs if you can, and get the dwarf ready for accounting at Hyperian Fold number four."

"An hour?" Thuri scoffed.

"Drakis," Ethis shrugged, "we can't possibly get the entire Centurai ready to leave that soon. We're still missing three Octia. We have heard that they came back from the dwarven halls, but they haven't reported . . ."

"They aren't coming with us," Drakis cut him off.

"What?"

"Only our Octian is going back right now," Drakis said, his eyes blinking.

"But what about our loot?" Ethis said. "It has to be accounted and credited . . . prepared for transport . . ."

"Already done, it seems," Drakis said

"Already? What about the crown . . . did Jerakh get away with it?"

"I don't know. All I was told is that all the prizes looted by every Octian of our Centurai have already been accounted, credited, and sent on to House Timuran."

"Well . . . well that's more like it!" Thuri said, the semblance of a smile forming on the featureless face of the chimerian. "A great honor! Perhaps that throwing the Dwarven Crown from the throne *did* connect with Jerakh after all!"

"Whatever the reason," Drakis said, clearing his throat, "we're leaving right away . . . and there will be no time for Devotions either . . ."

"Not even at the Field Altar?" Thuri groaned. "I'm getting headaches . . . I *need* Devotions!"

"There's not enough time," Drakis said emphatically. "Listen to me: We'll get our Devotions soon enough and not from some weak Field Altar but straight from the House Altar itself." He turned to the manticore standing next to him. "Belag, I need you to find Jerakh—he's the Second Octian leader—and the two of you to round up the other Cohort leaders of the Centurai. Bring them here in the next half hour."

Belag straightened, lifting his snout into the air. "Why should I?"

"Because I was third behind ChuKang and KriChan," Drakis hung his thumbs from his belt. "They're both dead, which now makes me the Centurai captain. That was true in battle, and it's still true here. You are welcome to argue the point with Se'Djinka. I'm sure it would give him great pleasure to explain it to you."

Belag's lips curled, but by the slow slump of the manticore's shoulders, Drakis knew he was still in charge. "Jerakh will be in charge of the Centurai after we've left; it will be his job to get them organized for transport over the next week—maybe twelve days depending on how crowded the Imperial Folds get. Every Cohort on the front is going to want to get home at the same time."

"Except for the four of us?" Thuri's voice was uncertain.

"I guess Lord Timuran must have really missed your face, Thuri," Drakis spoke as lightly as he could manage. "He arranged for our immediate passage, and, from what I gather, the Myrdin-dai who are mastering the folds are none too happy about it. So get moving and you may be back in time for House Devotions tonight!"

Belag nodded once in deference to Drakis before turning to run between the throngs of warriors milling about, his large feet kicking clumps of mud up behind him. Ethis quickly began to douse the already nearly dead fire as Thuri collected several weapons from where they lay wrapped in an oilskin tarpaulin.

Drakis stood for a moment, uncertain as to what to do next. The damnable song had returned again. He tried to push it out of his mind with thoughts of returning to his beloved Mala.

"What about him?" Thuri said, nodding in the direction of the House Standard.

A waterlogged dwarf in outlandish costume sat with his back to the pole, his hands tied around it behind him. Water drizzled down from the leaden Timuran battle standard and directly onto Jugar's once glorious hat. Now the dwarf's entire outfit seemed to sag right along with him. The soaked brim flopped down over the creature's eyes, making it impossible for him to see anything.

"Helloooo!" called the damp dwarf from under his badly sagging hat. "May I help you? I'd be delighted to direct you to the valuables, but there aren't any here. They took them all this morning—only this sorry dwarf remains!"

Drakis huffed with irritation and strode over to where the dwarf sat in the mud. He reached down to yank the hat off the dwarf's head, but a pool of water had gathered in its crown. As a result, the hat only came away after sending a sizable body of water splashing down on the miserable dwarf's head.

"Sorry," Drakis said.

The dwarf vigorously shook his head, spraying water about, which, given the conditions in the drenched field, made little difference. He blinked the water out of his eyes and then looked up. "Ah, Drakis! Splendid! As you can see, I've been working on a particularly remarkable escape trick for my new act. It's not quite finished yet, but I'm hoping to have the little problems worked out before my next engagement. So, please tell me, my victorious friend, where have you put all that glorious treasure to which I so generously led you?"

Drakis shook his head then squatted down, wet dwarven hat still in hand. "You dwarves; I'll never understand you! Here you are, tied up and sitting in the mud—a conquered slave of the Imperial Will—and all you want to know about is where we put some treasure that's no longer yours?"

"Yes," said the dwarf, a strange intensity behind his smile. "Exactly. So, tell me!"

Drakis leaned back casually but his eyes were fixed on the dwarf. "It's gone, as you already pointed out. Spoils of war are the first to be sent back through the Imperial Folds."

"I see," Jugar said quietly, his smile becoming more affected by the moment. "Slaves no doubt are not as valuable as dwarven plunder, eh?"

Drakis chuckled darkly. "The value of each House's slaves is already counted to them; but the spoils of war have to be tallied and accounted to the honor of each House. It's the elven way of power—this counting of honors. Your precious jeweled armor and Heart-stone . . ."

"Heart of Aer," Jugar corrected with quiet politeness.

"Whatever it is called," Drakis shrugged, "it all belongs to the Greater Glory of House Timuran now."

"But it *is* actually being sent to this House Timuran of yours, isn't it?" The dwarf's voice was urging—a strange pleading quality somewhere under all the words. "I understand that this has long been the elven way of it. This same House of your elven lord to which we all shall be going?"

"Of course," Drakis said evenly, his eyes narrowing slightly. "Why?"

"Oh, just a dwarf's curiosity," Jugar smiled back, his white beard sagging under the weight of the water it carried and what remained of his hair flat against his head. "I thought I might be able to work it somewhere into my act, you know, when you present your lord—pardon me, *our* lord—with all the glorious trophies you have secured in your battles. After all, I *am* one of those trophies, and I want to make a good impression—right there along with all the other treasures. Of course, it's going to be difficult making myself presentable tied as I am to this pole. I'm curious as to why you feel the need to bind me?"

"You're the one treasure we're bringing back with quick legs and a quicker tongue. I just want to make sure you stay with me."

The dwarf smiled again. "But where would I go? Your Iblisi totems keep you and me both safely confined to this damp and overcrowded field along with the rest of the slaves."

Drakis' eyes narrowed. "You know about the totems?"

"But of course." The dwarf shifted slightly around the pole so that he could better face the warrior. "We dwarves have something very like them, which we use to pen our livestock and hogs. I've often wondered why the slaves of the elves never escape their captivity . . . but as a vaunted warrior, such thoughts may never have come to you. Still, you should untie me; you see I don't *want* to escape. I just want to be a part of the glory of House Timuran and my . . . rather, its treasures."

"Uh-huh," Drakis was unconvinced. "Jugoo . . ."

"Jugar," the dwarf corrected helpfully.

"Jugar, then," Drakis continued, "I don't know what you think is going to happen, but there are two conditions for slaves of the Elven Empire . . . obedient and dead."

"Oh, I'm not worried," the dwarf grinned, showing wide-spaced teeth that were perfectly even. "Heroes die, kings die, monsters and villains . . . they all die. No one *ever* kills the fool!"

"That's where you're wrong," Drakis said quietly. "I watch fools die every day. For as long as I can remember . . ."

"Now *that* is an interesting point!" Jugar interrupted.

Drakis shook his head and tried again. "What I was saying—for as long as I can remember . . ."

"Exactly!" Jugar shouted enthusiastically. "You've been on this campaign for, what, one or two weeks?"

"Three, but that's not . . ."

"Three weeks? That's a long time without House Devotions," the dwarf sounded impressed. "And how long since Field Devotions at that portable altar of your most noble Tribune?"

"Four days," Drakis replied, squinting at the dwarf. "What is your point?"

"The point is that I can tell you a great secret that, I'm sure, is entirely new to your experience."

"There's nothing you can tell me, dwarf."

"Oh, but I can," smiled Jugar. "I can tell you about that song you have whirling about in your head. Better still, I can tell you with absolute certainty that everything you remember—every kiss, every hurt, every victory and every failure that happened to you prior to four days ago—is a lie."

"My entire life—a lie," Drakis scoffed.

"Up until four days ago," the dwarf said in a husky whisper, "none of it was real."

Drakis leaned down, his face so close that his breath shook the large drip forming at the end of the dwarf's nose. "The only lie here is your foolish stories—but you're about to learn how real your own life has become, Fool."

CHAPTER 8

Myths, Legends, & Nonsense

WHILE EVERY TRIBUNE WAS CAPABLE—indeed, required—to create folds during the battle for the warriors in their command, it was the Imperial Folds that brought the Tribunes and their armies to the battle itself. These networks of larger folds had the enormous power to compress distances leagues long and large enough to march the Centurai of the Legions through them four abreast and still never touch the sides. Five of these opened directly to the plain just to the east of the encampment, each one a major tributary to the nexus of Imperial military might.

Stepping through to the other side of these folds would take the warriors to one of many widely separated staging areas near the Hyperian and Chaenandrian borders. These marshaling fields had tributaries of their own, smaller folds each of which led to other smaller and smaller tributary rally points until the final, narrow warrior folds of individual elven neighborhoods or settlement communities. These final folds were always located in a small temple well outside the walls of the individual House strongholds—the last step in the long journey home.

For the War of the Ninth Throne, the honor of bringing these warriors into battle—of planning the placement of the folds, setting up the fold platforms, linking them to the magical conduits of the Aether Wells, and administering the folds through an organization of Foldmasters—had been granted by the Imperial Will to the Order of the Myrdin-dai. These "Guardians of the Well" vied with another Order, the Occuran, for control of the Aether—that magical force that was the foundation of the Rhonas Empire. Their appointment to this calling had set many tongues of the court to wagging, whispering in the halls of power that the Occuran may, at last, have fallen from the Imperial Favor.

The Myrdin-dai responded to the Imperial nod enthusiastically and erected a network of folds that drew Impress Warriors from each House of the Rhonas Empire and delivered them to the field of battle with swift efficiency.

Returning them *from* the field of battle, however, was another matter.

"I don't care who you are, what your orders say, or who gave them," snorted the manticore standing in front of Drakis. A weathered sash that once may have been red was draped across his broad, furry chest. He thumped his big fist against the sash once more for emphasis. "I'm the field marshal here, and I've got seven Centurai to process before I can even think about letting you near one of my folds. Get back with your Centurai and wait to be called!"

"Marshal Korang," Drakis said, his patience nearly spent, "As I told you before, our Centurai is still at the front. We're just one Octian, but we've been ordered back to our master's House now. We've been through three folds already today just to get to this rally field, and we've got four more to go before we get back to House Timuran. The Myrdin-dai approved it, and the Foldmasters know all about it. All we need is to bring five of us through the Stellamir Fold—not an entire Centurai—just *five* of us through and we'll be no further problem for you."

"It's irregular," Korang rumbled.

"I agree," Drakis replied. "Nevertheless, those are the orders."

"I'm warning you," Korang said, his eyes narrowing. "I'm going to check on all this with the Foldmasters! They won't like it if you're lying."

"Fine!" Drakis shot back. "Just get it done!"

"Oh, I will!" the manticore roared. "And until I have, you go back and wait with the rest of your Centurai until I return!"

"But I'm not *with* my . . . oh, just go and ask the Fold-masters!" Drakis snapped. "Then you come and find me. I'll be on the east side of the clearing—you *do* know which way is east, don't you?"

Korang growled menacingly but only turned away.

Drakis turned as well, stalking off through the crowded field. The sun had vanished beyond the western horizon, leaving only a rich twilight illuminating the clear skies overhead. Jolnar, the wandering Star of Destiny, was just appearing in the sky. Drakis considered it for a moment.

Jolnar is seen from woeful lands of pain
But also from far-off shores.
Where call seas of sand . . .
Where winds of soft lament . . .

The music filling his mind now seemed to come from a place far away and barely imagined; a better and softer place. He hated the star in that moment—because in its al-luring promise he felt a vague sadness and dissatisfaction with his life that he had not felt before.

Drakis lowered his eyes to the more immediate con-cerns of picking his way through the milling warriors crowding the large meadow, each one waiting his turn to pass through the next fold and come closer to home. This place, he thought, may have actually been beautiful once: a great grassy expanse surrounded by tall, beautiful trees. He could imagine it a quiet place filled only with soft sounds in a gentle breeze.

The coming of the marshaling field changed all that. The Myrdin-dai had decided on this place as a rally point, the confluence of several smaller folds to bring Impress

Warriors from other marshaling fields together, consolidating their force to move into a single fold to the next field. Since then an army had trodden down the once-soft grasses and the delicate flowers as first they came and now they left. The leaving may even have been the worst of it, for masses of troops were coming through the large fold, and it was taking time to sort them into the appropriate smaller folds to send them correctly on the next part of their journey. Unfortunately, the Myrdin-dai had underestimated the area required for this marshaling field and had placed their totems in too small a circle. Worse yet, earlier mistakes required sending units *back* through the folds, which caused further delays. The result was that many of the warriors had settled into crowded encampments awaiting their turn to move on, filling what had once been a meadow with listless, uncomfortable, and quarrelsome warriors.

At last he came to the edge of the meadow and a small hollow just short of the tree line and the ever watchful crystal Sentinel totems. A campfire burned in the center of a circle of stones, illuminating the small group gathered around it.

"Well, it's going to be a while, my brothers *Sha-Timuran*," Drakis said as he approached.

"Why?" Belag asked, straightening up from tending the blaze. "What is it *this* time?"

"Would you be surprised to hear I found someone incompetent in charge?"

Belag laughed deeply. "Among the Legions of the Emperor? I'd have been surprised if you *hadn't*!"

Drakis smiled back at the manticore. "The field marshal has gone off to find one of the Myrdin-dai to ask about our special arrangement—and he's the second one today to do that. With four more folds ahead of us, I don't know how long this is going to take. It might have been faster just to come back with the rest of the Centurai."

"Maybe they'll pass us on their way home?" Belag shrugged.

Drakis nodded with a laugh and then turned toward

the chimera. Both were leaning comfortably against small stacks of their field packs. Drakis pointed toward the dwarf sitting between them on the ground. "Uh, don't you think that's a bit much?"

Thuri and Ethis each held separate ropes around the bound hands and feet of the dwarf. A gag was tied tightly over his mouth.

Ethis considered the prisoner for a moment before replying. "No, it seems a reasonable precaution."

"Why? What did he do?" Drakis said.

The chimera looked at each other, their blank faces considering for a moment.

"He kept promising not to escape," Thuri answered at last.

"He promised *not* to escape," Drakis asked, his brow furrowed with the puzzle, "and so you tied him up?"

"He wouldn't shut up about it," Ethis replied, his large eyes blinking indignantly. "He kept going on and on about how we could trust him and how he had nowhere to run and how he was glad it was us who took him as a slave captive of the war."

"It was unnerving," Thuri finished.

Drakis shook his head. "Fine, keep his hands and feet bound if you must but we've got to feed him. We need him alive—if only to explain to Lord Timuran why the prize we sent to him is a valuable treasure."

Thuri shrugged and reached over with his second right hand to tug at the knot. After a few moments struggle—the knot had been tied rather tightly—it gave way. Thuri yanked the gag clear.

"Oh, thank you, Master Drakis . . ."

"No master," Drakis replied flatly. "Just Drakis. We're all slaves here—and you had best remember that includes you."

"Of course, forgive me," Jugar nodded vigorously. "Brothers together, bound in war and circumstance—slaves are we all to the fates. Jolnar himself looks down upon us, does he not . . . an omen of our merging destinies?"

Belag and the chimera all glanced up into the deepening blue of the sky, the wandering star shining above the darkened silhouette of the treetops.

Drakis did not look up, but considered the dwarf. "You know of the gods?"

"Oh, I know much of the gods," Jugar smiled, his eyes shining. "We are on good terms; all fools are watched over by the gods. Jolnar, Tsajera, Mnera . . . even Rhon himself look favorably upon fools. But most of all Qin."

"The Wise One?" Ethis scoffed. "Why would Qin favor a fool?"

"Oh, Qin values fools most of all," Jugar said, tilting his head to one side as he spoke. "He trusts the fools to live and learn. In them he holds his trust to remember the things that were forgotten. Of the time when the plains of all Chaenandria shook beneath the mighty armies of the manticores, the armor of their fathers and their father's fathers shining in the bright sun as they ran to war, singing to the spirits that ran with them and made their armor bright and their weapons keen. Their manes were long, flying behind them, and they ran into glory in defense of their clan-prides. Their might was great and the prides were free to make war as they saw it. Their ships sailed the Sea of Benis and their justice was feared. This was long ago—long before the Rhonas elves came to Palandria and made it their own."

Belag snorted. "You are a fool; Rhonas conquered Chaenandria to civilize the manticores. We were a backward, violent race, destroying everything we touched. Becoming a part of the greater Rhonas Imperium brought justice to my race."

Jugar considered the manticore before he spoke. "Of course, so say the Rhonas, and thus it must be so. I am only a fool telling the tales of a fool, but that is how the gods have made me and so I must be. Qin himself would tell you of an ancient time—long before the elves had formed more than tribes—when manticores, chimera, and dwarves . . ."

"Dwarves?!" Thuri laughed in surprise.

"Yes, and *dwarves*," Jugar nodded earnestly as he con-

tinued. "Together they built a great civilization of their
own. Its name is difficult for us to pronounce and lost to
the knowledge of the Rhonas, but its name meant 'the
peace of reasoned thought,' and it ruled in glory for nearly
three hundred years. The Rhonas have torn down its towers and walls until all evidence of its existence has vanished
from its conquered lands, but in the wild lands beyond the
Rhonas Imperium its glories are said to be found still!"

"An ancient lost empire of invisible buildings?"
Ethis scoffed, poking at the fire with a long stick. "How
convenient."

"Yet that was nothing compared to the humans," Jugar
said in hushed tones, leaning forward toward the fire, its
light playing on its ancient, craggy face. "It was the humans
who created the greatest empire ever seen on the face of
the world. It was they who fought the dragons of the north
and won their respect. They alone stood up against the ex-
pansion of Rhonas, for their empire was mightier than the
dwarves, manticores, and chimera combined!"

Jugar paused for effect, taking in a deep breath.

The silence was broken suddenly by outraged laughter.

"Humans? A great empire?" Belag roared, his large
hands grasping at his belly as he laughed uncontrollably.

"Ooh! Fear the terrible two-armed beast!" Ethis hooted,
throwing his four arms up in mock alarm. "The brittle-
boned warrior in his might!"

"Hey, stop it," Thuri said through an irrepressible grin
that broke into laughter as well. "It's not . . . it's not that
funny."

"Their empire is probably invisible, too," Belag snorted
loudly, his side beginning to hurt. "The gods know their
hordes of humans are not to be seen!"

"No, you don't understand," Jugar shouted into the
hilarity that swirled around him. "I can prove it to you! I
can show you . . ."

"Show us your invisible kingdom?" Ethis nearly choked.

"We're probably *in* it right now, eh, Thuri?" Belag shook
with laughter. "What a fool!"

Jugar sighed and caught sight of Drakis.

The human was not laughing, but rather staring angrily back at the dwarf.

"I can *show* you," Jugar said emphatically to Drakis, his words nearly buried by the laugher that still rang around him. "Believe me, I can *show* you!"

But Drakis just turned and walked into the complete darkness that had finally fallen over the meadow.

CHAPTER 9

Mala

THE LIGHTNING EDGES of the fold flashed as Drakis stepped through onto the floor of the small temple. It was a minor community fold that served the local Houses of the Icaran Frontier—the farthest reaches of the Imperial Western Provinces. Three weeks and a lifetime ago, Drakis had marched into this same fold with over eighty of the House Timuran Centurai.

Now he stepped down the wide treads again onto the same tall grasses and low undulating hills. The gentle, early morning breeze drifted across the slopes, rustling the young wheat in the fields that surrounded him. Drakis drew in a deep breath, taking in the familiar smells of the dewy earth and the faint tang of the seashore to the south that lingered in the air. His field pack was suddenly lighter.

He longed to hold onto the peace he felt and linger in its embrace for a few moments more.

"So this is where you are kept a slave, then?" the dwarf said quietly, his voice sounding harsh in the morning stillness.

"No, dwarf," Drakis sighed with contentment. "This is my home."

He looked back at his companions. As chimera, Ethis and Thuri had no real faces for him to read, but Belag held his head high, the furrows of his broad brow now relaxed. The manticore, too, was glad to be home.

So few, Drakis thought, would return to share that joy. Less than half of his own Octian had survived, and the rest of their Centurai had fared little better. Part of him longed to return to the camps at the foot of the Aerian Mountains, to see to the Impress Warriors of his Centurai and bring what remained of them back to these same fields. But his orders from the Tribune were unequivocal—and in the morning air he was satisfied that it was so.

Drakis glanced back through the fold. The liquid image of the previous marshaling field—a small plaza surrounding the crystal pillar of an Imperial Aether Well—still had several Centurai trying to sort themselves out through the various folds around the open courtyard.

Drakis turned his back on the war and smiled again. It was easy to discern the sets of parallel House totems—planted by the House mages and much smaller than the Imperial versions—marking the paths from the temple to the various dispersed Houses of the settlement. Drakis did not hesitate, choosing one of the paths and starting between the fields of knee-deep green blades of the young wheat toward the top of one of the low, undulating hills surrounding them.

The dwarf frowned, struggling to keep up as well as peer over the sea of stalks that suddenly surrounded him. "Are you sure this is the right path?"

"Yes, dwarf, I'm sure. I could walk these hills blind, totem or no," Drakis said, pointing off to his right. "Over there is where I received my first field training when I was young . . . and there," he pointed off to the left, "those are the fields where I labored with my father and mother for the glory of the House until I was of age to train for war."

A low-lying morning mist stretched across the shallow tide pools of an inlet to the south, draping the shoreline in subdued hues of blue and gray. Tall reeds slept in the shadows that ran up the undulating slope from the shoreline, quickly giving way to the curving lengths of field that filled the gentle rising of the hills with ordered patterns. Here the colors were awakening under a salmon-colored sky of low-lying clouds set ablaze by the sun that was only now breaking over the eastern hills.

Drakis reveled in it all. "Belag, do you remember our first encampment?"

"The Chronasis campaigns?" the manticore asked.

"No . . . I mean during our first training." Drakis shook his head. "Down in the hollow below the orchard."

Jugar jumped nervously at the deafening trumpet-sound coming from the amused Belag. He glanced up at the human next to him. "I take it our manticore friend was amused by something?"

"Drakis and Belag made the mistake of making their camp on the wrong side of the lake," said Thuri, shrugging all four of his shoulders. "An easy enough mistake in the darkness, but when they awoke the next morning, they found themselves surrounded by their opposing warriors."

"By Thorgrin's beard!" the dwarf swore in awe. "However did you survive?"

Drakis laughed. "It wasn't a real battle, dwarf! We were just in training. Half the Centurai were to engage the other half in one of the fallow fields. Mostly it was about teaching us Centurai discipline, how to form Octia into a force of Centurai, that sort of thing."

"So what did you do?" Jugar urged.

"He and Belag stood up and demanded the opposing warriors surrender," Ethis answered for the chuckling human. "Fortunately Se'Djinka pulled them out before any real damage was done."

"To either side," Belag grunted.

Drakis smiled again. They were nearly to the crest of the one hill he had looked forward to above all others. "Here, dwarf," he said with quiet ease. "We are home."

Rising on the next hilltop, the glorious edifice of House Timuran pierced the sky, blocking the rays of the newly risen sun. The magnificent structure was cast in stark contrast, its purple-shadowed face outlined in a blaze of new day.

The avatria of House Timuran—the towering central

structure of all elven homes—was enormous. Rising almost fifty feet above the ground, its form resembled the graceful shape of an unopened rosebud floating freely above the subatria buildings on the ground beneath it. The avatria's curving petals swept upward from its rounded base to rise to a slight flare at its pinnacle. Ornate latticework between the petals framed the panes of crystal from which the elven family could look out upon their domain and know it was their own. Causing the avatria of an elven House to float in the air in such a manner was a common architectural feat among the elves, an ostentatious display meant to show that the House was of such wealth and prominence that it could use the mystical power of its Aether on extravagance. Of course, as all elves coveted ostentatious behavior, every elven House regardless of its size had long ago adopted the form.

Beneath the avatria and seeming to support but never touch it with its sweeping curves and surrounding minarets was the subatria, the ground buildings of the servants and slaves. In ancient times, the subatria was a warrior's fortification, a curtain wall of defense against enemies while the elven lords sat secure and separate in their avatria stronghold. There still remained many of the features of the warrior's battlements, though distance from the wars of conquest had long ago softened the lines.

Drakis raised his eyes to the top of the fifteen-foot-tall subatria walls.

A lone human figure stood there, silhouetted against the dawn-lit enormity of the avatria and looked longingly to the west . . .

. . . Looking for him.

"Mala," he murmured.

"Drakis!" she called as he came through the Warrior's Gate.

The high, curving interior of the curtain wall cast shadows onto the packed dirt of the narrow passage within the subatria even during the midpoint of the day. It was known in all elven structures as the chakrilya—the Warrior's Way—and its path curving around the center of the building led to the cells, mess halls, kitchens, and practice arenas where the Impress Warriors were kept. Drakis had marched out through this canyonlike passage five days before, its breadth filled shoulder to shoulder with his fellow warriors. Now he felt small with so few of them standing in its cavernous expanse.

But the sound of her voice cast all the loss, the pain, and the loneliness from his thoughts.

She was reaching for him through the crossed iron bands of the closed portcullis separating the Centurai wing from the other areas of the subatria. Drakis swung his field pack off his shoulders and tossed it quickly toward the base of the wall where Belag and the others were already setting theirs down. He ran over to her, casting a quick, worried glance down the length of the chakrilya as he took her hand.

"You're not supposed to be here," he said.

"And you've grown hair." Mala Shei-Timuran gazed up at him through her large, emerald eyes as Drakis pressed her palm to his cheek. She leaned forward against the bars, the sinque mark of the household easily read on the crown of her shaved head. She was half a foot shorter than he, her waist narrow but her hips full and desirable, achingly beyond his reach.

"Yes," he laughed. "But no doubt I'll be properly shaved and cleaned up before long."

"So you *did* return to me after all," she said, turning her face up to look into his eyes again. "I prayed to all the gods each day that they would bring you back to me."

"All of the gods?" Drakis smiled at her through the squared openings of the portcullis.

"Well," she admitted, her small mouth twisting mischievously, "perhaps not *all* of them—but certainly each of the House gods. You pray to all the gods and you're bound to offend one of them. So . . . are we to be paired?"

Drakis choked slightly. "What? I just came through the gate and . . ."

"You said before you left that if the campaign was successful, Lord Timuran would look favorably on mating the two of us," Mala said matter-of-factly, her eyes taking on a look that Drakis always considered dangerous. "The plunder was brought by the caravan porters yesterday, and you're here before any of the rest of the Cohort so—you must have honored the House, am I right?"

"Mala," Drakis said, pulling back a little as he spoke. "I don't think that's why we're here."

"Oh, but wouldn't it be wonderful if it were?" she said with a gentle smile. "You, honored by Lord Timuran and the two of us paired? Maybe even ascending to the Sixth Estate. We'd no longer be slaves and could contribute to the Imperium on our own!"

"Yes, it would be wonderful, but I don't think . . ."

"I'm not saying that it *will* happen, you know that, don't you, Drakis?"

"Of course, beloved, but . . ."

"It's just that it's such a wonderful dream."

Drakis held her hand tightly for a few moments, uncertain what to say as he looked into her eyes. She had a lovely heart-shaped face with a small chin. Her cheekbones gave her face a sharp beauty. Everything about her he found desirable, but it was her eyes in which he always lost his thoughts and his heart to her. How could he tell her that things had gone terribly wrong in the campaign . . . that he was not even certain whether he had won the prized crown or not.

"Yes, they are wonderful dreams, Mala—and I'm very pleased to hear that the plunder arrived," Drakis reluctantly let her go. "The Tribune has sent us back here to present the treasures to . . ."

"What is *that?*" Mala interrupted, pointing toward the somewhat worse-for-wear pile of flamboyant clothing shuffling toward her.

"Oh," Drakis said. "This is a dwarven fool—in more ways than one, I suspect. He's part of our spoils. We'll present him tonight for House Devotions."

"Greetings, good woman," Jugar said, bowing as deeply as his restraints would allow. "My new companion, Drakis, has given me only the most glowing reports of your beauty and your sagacious and erudite conversational skills, and I see now that he has portrayed them to me with crystalline accuracy! I am charmed and gratified to make your acquaintance."

Mala stared at the dwarf.

The dwarf answered her with a broad-toothed smile.

"Does he always talk like this?" Mala said to Drakis from the corner of her mouth.

"Only when he's quiet," Drakis sighed.

In the distance above them, a chime sounded twice.

"I must go," Mala said at once, pulling her hands back through the bars and quickly moving down the sweeping curve of the corridor that led from the chakrilya toward the central garden of the subatria. "Will they pair us tonight? After Devotions?"

Drakis smiled and called after her. "If it is the Emperor's Will."

"And why should it not be?" Mala said brightly before dashing down the polished stones on her bare feet. "What should the Emperor have against me?"

Drakis smiled and turned, to find the dwarf gazing up at him thoughtfully.

"You have a problem, dwarf?" Drakis was feeling suddenly annoyed with his diminutive trophy.

"Oh, not at all, not at all," Jugar replied thoughtfully. "She seems like the absolutely perfect woman."

"She is perfect," Drakis said with pride.

"Then I'm very sorry for you," Jugar said.

"What did you say?"

"Ah, well," the dwarf continued, "you can't make a country without cracking a few heads, eh? Perhaps you should tell me something about this ceremony tonight. I wouldn't want to make a mistake and embarrass you. That reminds me, how are you feeling now, Drakis?"

"Fine," the human shrugged and then stopped.

He did feel fine.

The song was completely gone from his head.

CHAPTER 10

Cleansing

"SO HOW LONG did they say it would take?" Jugar asked nervously through chattering teeth. The naked dwarf squatted with his back wedged into the corner of the dim room, holding a large, brass ladle firmly in front of his manhood and appearing resolved never to move it. An iron grating overhead allowed square columns of light to fall into the room, casting the dwarf and the human in shadows of stark relief.

Drakis stood naked on the stone platform surrounding the circular trough in the center of the room. Clear water constantly overflowed its edges, splashing down over the stones before falling through a metal grating in the floor. He held his own ladle in one hand, scooping water from the trough and, pouring it over his head, cascading it down his powerful body. He then set the ladle down and picked up a pumice stone from the floor, lightly scraping at the dirt on his broad chest and forearms.

"How long for what?" Drakis asked casually.

"You know for what!" the dwarf's voice almost broke in his nervous exasperation. "How long before that woman brings our clothes back!"

"Oh, that?" Drakis smiled to himself. He did not know much about dwarves beyond the easiest way to kill them and how they reacted in battle. He had imagined a great many things about them, but being prudish was not one of them. He was finding this fool of a dwarf to be most entertaining. "Essenia said that she would have them cleaned at once and bring them when they were fit to wear—although she appeared to have her doubts about getting your costume presentable. But, then, she had her doubts about *you* getting presentable either."

Jugar glowered back at the human in silence for a time, then his features softened slightly. "Wait! Hold still for a moment."

Drakis turned toward the dwarf. "What is it?"

"Turn back around . . . a little more," the dwarf murmured, his eyes fixed intently on Drakis. "Now lean forward just a little . . . there."

"What are you up to, dwarf?"

"Hold still, please."

The sound of the water murmured across the silence.

"May I finish now?" Drakis ask impatiently.

"Yes," the dwarf responded thoughtfully. Several heartbeats passed before he spoke again. "Those scars on your back . . . how did you get those?"

Drakis poured another ladle of water over his head, brushing the remaining grains of pumice from his skin as he spoke. "Which scars?"

"Those rather nasty looking scars on your back," Jugar replied. "Who gave those to you?"

"I'm an Impress Warrior, dwarf," Drakis scoffed. "We *all* have scars."

"So I have observed," Jugar continued. "But these are particularly nasty looking. I would venture to say that such scars would be most memorable indeed. So, when did you get them?"

Drakis absently reached his right hand around his side, running his fingers along the ridges of his skin. "Why, I . . . isn't that something? I don't remember."

"Have you ever seen them?" Jugar said through his still chattering teeth.

"Seen them? Now how would I see them? They're on my back."

"You don't know your own past, Drakis, my friend." Jugar's eyes squinted as he considered them. "So perhaps you'll believe me if I tell you something about your future. Your beloved Lord Timuran has not called you back to gratefully accept your bountiful conquest but to take out his rage on you."

Drakis set the ladle down slowly, the features of his face hidden in shadows. "That is no prophecy, dwarf. I could have told you that. I will be shamed before him."

"You will be more than shamed, Drakis," the dwarf continued, his gruff voice firm and sure. "He will strike you, lay open your flesh to agonizing pain and all your tears, and protest, and pleadings of your love for him will be soundless in his ears. He will not stop."

Drakis stalked over toward Jugar, the silhouette of his muscular frame looming over where the dwarf crouched. "The foolish curse of a dwarven fool! My master has never so much as touched me in anger!"

The dwarf looked up, the softened look of his eyes framed in the square of light from above.

"He would kill you if he could, Drakis, this very afternoon. But someone will intervene on your behalf—and will save your life, though in doing so you will wish that you had died."

"Only gods can know the future," Drakis said flatly.

The dwarf shrugged. "That which has happened before will happen again. You've only forgotten. Remember my words, Drakis, and maybe then, my friend, you will come to me and know the truth."

Drakis thought for a moment and then shook his head violently, sending particles flying from his shaved head. "So you're back to that again. Now I'm supposed to have forgotten nearly dying. Well, one thing *you* should not forget: that Essenia and I will throw you into this trough personally if you don't get over here and scrape off some of that dwarven stench."

"Dwarves do *not* bathe!" Jugar grumbled emphatically.

"That I most certainly believe," Drakis replied easily, "but in this case you may want to make an exception. We're being summoned before Lord Timuran himself, and he takes no more delight in the smell of dwarven slaves than any other conquered race."

Drakis and Jugar stepped into the Warrior's Courtyard. The Impress Warrior felt renewed after the bath despite the dwarf's bizarre and gloomy predictions; bathing was a ritual that was so basic among the elves that it made him feel a part of the Empire that he so fervently wished to join. The tunic that he wore was that of a slave, but it was clean, and in that he felt a sort of purity, elevated somehow above the commonplace.

He strode quickly across the packed dirt floor and through the open portcullis with the garishly dressed dwarf struggling to keep up. They passed under the tall archway and onto the darkly stained sands of the small arena floor.

"Our lives to the Imperial Will!" came the echoing call from across the arena floor.

Drakis smiled as he looked to the far side of the arena. "Jerakh! How did you get back so soon?"

"I have you to thank, brother warrior," the manticore replied as he crossed toward the human. "Our master's eagerness to see you has left the folds in complete disarray. The Foldmasters in their haste to comply have been moving any units from House Timuran they can find."

Drakis could see warriors straggling in behind Jerakh. He shook his head. "So the victorious Centurai of House Timuran is home at last, eh?"

"Hardly," Jerakh said with disdain. "I managed to come through with three Octia, but the rest of the Centurai is spread all through the fold system. It's a mess that will take days to unravel."

"I'm sure you'll manage it," Drakis said.

"I'm sure the only thing I'm going to manage is a bath," the manticore returned, a playful edge to his smile as he passed the human. "*You* can straighten out the Octian ... you're the Centurai Master now."

"Well, if that is so, then I'm turning over this dwarf to you," Drakis said, gesturing toward Jugar.

"Excuse me, Captain Drakis," the dwarf sputtered, "but I'm ..."

"Drakis, just Drakis," he sighed. "I've not been appointed captain yet, dwarf."

"But, Drakis, I've not been presented to your master as yet! As part of your rightful treasure which you so valiantly liberated from the dwarven realms ..."

"You'll be presented with the rest of the prize treasure tonight at House Devotions," Drakis said, interrupting the dwarf. "Before then, Jerakh here is going to see that you get properly shaved and branded for the slave you have become."

"He's full of words," Jerakh said with disdain.

"Which is why I'm turning him over to you," Drakis said flashing a tight grin. "I've been summoned."

Jerakh gripped Jugar's shoulder tightly enough to elicit a grunt from the dwarf. "I'll see it's done."

Drakis turned away, taking several steps before he stopped and turned back toward the manticore. "Oh, Jerakh ... I was glad to see you at the Ninth Throne. It was getting a little close up there, and I needed a friendly face in the mob. We'd have never gotten away with the prize without you. You saved our honor."

"I don't know what you mean," the manticore replied with a shrug of his great shoulders. "We were stuck on that pillar of rock you left us on for another six hours before a Proxi showed up to get us out. It must have been some other incredibly handsome Warrior you saw at the throne."

Drakis' smile waned at the thought. He turned instinctively to look up at the avatria towering above them. He pushed Jugar's predictions out of his mind and crossed the arena to the chakrilya and his audience with his master.

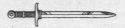

Sha-Timuran sat upon the elevated throne and glared down through his black, pupilless eyes.

Drakis kept as still as the cold, marble stone on which he knelt. Since he had been ushered into the large, oval room by the house slaves, he had waited on his knees, his head bent over in submission. Even so, he felt the chill stare of his master's blank, onyx-eyes. No slave spoke in the presence of his or her master until specifically bidden to do so. No slave looked upon the master until directly addressed.

So he had remained, with increasing pain shooting up his legs as the moments dragged into eternity.

He was keenly aware of his surroundings. The audience hall was situated within the floating avatria, its arching walls rising upward in the shape of wide, alabaster leaves whose tips cradled crystal panes, each casting columns of light from a delicate lattice overhead. Curved stairs led down into the room from two archways situated between the leaves while the throne itself floated at the far end of the oval floor.

Standing still as statues at the perimeter of the room were a number of the elves from the household, paid servants who worked in the avatria or as overseers in the subatria below. These were pressed against the curved walls well away from their master's position in the hall. One slave, the Lyric, had little choice in the matter. A waiflike human woman clad in a loose fitting, translucent robe, she was chained by a golden collar to the throne of the master. Drakis vaguely remembered seeing her, though if she had a name, he did not know it. The Lyric squatted as far from the throne as the chain would allow. Only Tsi-Timuri, Timuran's wife, and their daughter, Tsi-Shebin, stood next to the throne with any affectation of desire.

Everyone waited.

At long last, Sha-Timuran spoke.

"Drakisssssss," he said, his grating, high-pitched voice

hanging onto the last syllable, drawing it out like the sound of a snake.

"My Master," Drakis answered, his words sounding too loud in his own ears. He looked up.

Sha-Timuran was tall even by elven standards, making even more pronounced the narrow features of his race. His sharp, narrow chin jutted out from the angular features of his face. The back of his head was elongated compared to the other creatures of the world, a protuberance that the Imperial Will had pronounced at once as unquestioned evidence of both the physical and mental superiority of their race. His elegantly elongated ears framed his face, and the hair that rimmed his protruding crown fell back in long, white strands. He still wore a common lime-colored work tunic beneath the mantle of his House. The mantle was a required sign of his authority whenever formally holding audience, though today it had apparently been hastily donned. He held his long baton restlessly in his hands, the Imperial medallion fixed to its head turning repeatedly, flashing occasionally in the column of light cast down from overhead.

But it was the featureless, black eyes staring down the thin, hooked nose that held Drakis in such awe that he forgot to answer.

"Drakis," Sha-Timuran repeated from behind a thin veil of patience.

"By your will, my Lord!"

"So you have returned to us from the war," the elven lord said with quiet detachment. "My great warrior—now leader of my Centurai, it seems. ChuKang has fallen, and yet somehow—somehow—you managed to survive."

Drakis swallowed. "My Lord! My brother warrior ChuKang was great, indeed, and led the Centurai of your House to great honor. We followed him into the heart of the Dwarven Throne and . . ."

Sha-Timuran held up his long-fingered left hand, his right still gripping the baton. His voice wheezed with the sound of rusted blades sliding together. "We have heard the stories of that final battle—indeed, all the elven world, it seems, is talking about the fall of the dwarves, news of it having reached the Imperial ear itself. How could it be helped since the House of Tajeran has insured it to be impossible *not* to hear the tale?"

Sha-Timuran's long, pale fingers twitched along the handle of the baton.

"Tajeran . . . ah, that noble House of my neighbor." Sha-Timuran stood now from his throne, his voice rising with each step of his bare, narrow feet, "A neighbor who shall never let me forget that a warrior of my own House . . . *my own House* . . . held the crown of the dwarves in his hands and tossed it into *HIS hands!*"

"But, my Lord," Drakis blinked in confusion. Lord Timuran was a kind master who prized him. Lord Timuran had never spoken harshly with him in all the years of his life. "If you will but hear me . . . you will understand . . ."

"*THREW IT TO HIM!*" Lord Timuran screamed, his voice squealing with a sound like scraping glass. "Tossed it to my *neighbor's* warriors as if it were scraps from the table!"

Instinctively, Drakis leaned back from the onslaught, catching himself with one hand behind him before he could fall to the floor. Sha-Timuran stood over the startled warrior, his hands shaking with fury. "But, my Lord, your warriors . . . we *saved* them for you, and I thought I was throwing the crown to . . ."

"*Saved* them?" Sha-Timuran's lips twitched into a hideous grimace. "You *thought?*"

In a sudden eruption of rage, the elf lord's baton slammed against Drakis' face, its medallion cracking his jaw. The sharp edges of its ornamental wings cut furrows across his cheeks and nose that instantly erupted with welling blood. Drakis' head pitched sideways with the blow, its power twisting him around until he fell with his face against the marble.

Through the haze enveloping his mind, Drakis saw his blood staining the marble beneath him.

Marble, he noticed only now, that had been deeply stained before.

The pain of his broken face was nothing compared to the confusion that overwhelmed his mind. Drakis had fought and killed many creatures—human and otherwise—who had done him far less harm. Yet all he could think was that Timuran was good. Timuran was kind. Timuran was father to them all. Surely there had been some mistake. His master, he thought, did not understand. He pushed himself up, kneeling on the floor, his hands clasped together as he turned to grovel before the elf lord.

"I didn't want them *saved* you stupid, thoughtless *hoo-mani!* I wanted the crown! But now my *neighbor* has the crown, and in his appreciation of your 'gift,' he arranged to have you delivered to me at once—so that all the Myrdin-dai would know which House of the Western Provinces *gave away* the greatest prize of the war!" Sha-Timuran shouted through a rage that seemed boundless, beyond control or thought. His hands were working the length of the baton handle now, twisting it and pulling at it. "You embarrass my House, you embarrass my name, you make me the heart of every citizen's laughter from one end of the Empire to the other, and you think that is worth saving the pointless, worthless lives of a few slaves! You will pay for the insult—someone always has to pay, Drakis— someone always has to pay. *Hoo-mani always* have to *pay!*"

The baton handle separated under Sha-Timuran's hands, revealing as they pulled apart the long strands of a living firereed. The nine fronds of the plant extended nearly six feet in length, a whip waving menacingly in the air as Timuran raised his arm above his head.

Drakis' eyes went wide. His speech was slurred by the sudden swelling of his cracked jaw but he spoke past the pain. "My Lord! The bounty we brought you! The greatest treasure of the dwarves . . ."

"Bounty?" Sha-Timuran snapped. "You bring me a dwarven fool and an ugly piece of rock and call it 'bounty'?"

Sha-Timuran's arm swung. The fronds flashed suddenly through the columns of light, wrapping around Drakis' back. The razor-sharp hooks of the firereed cut through his tunic, burrowing down into the flesh of his back. Searing

pain engulfed the human as Sha-Timuran pulled, raking
the fronds across his back, their barbs tearing his flesh and
leaving his nerve endings raw and exposed.

Drakis' tears mixed with the blood flowing from his
face. "Please," he choked. "I'll do anything for you! Tell me
and it shall be done!"

Sha-Timuran, his hand raised for another blow, gazed
for a moment at Drakis through the solid blackness of his
eyes.

Then, with a coldness Drakis had never known, Sha-
Timuran slowly smiled.

The firereed whip cracked again through the hall, ripping at Drakis' back and tearing new furrows in his skin
and muscles.

"Master! Please!" Drakis sobbed like the confused child
he was, "Tell me what you want!"

The blows rained down on him faster now, the pain
becoming an overwhelming, encompassing reality. Drakis panicked within himself, repeating the same words
over and over again through the cries and sobs that were
wrenched from his soul.

"Please . . . I'll do anything . . . tell me what you want!"

The last thing Drakis knew was the sound of the whip
grating against his own bones . . .

. . . And the sound of Sha-Timuran's angry laughter.

CHAPTER 11

Taboo

"TRULY, DRAKI, I'm finding this tiresome," spoke the reedy, high voice, calling him back from oblivion.

Drakis' sight returned to him slowly along with his awareness. He was staring up into a hazy, dim green fog as pungent, conflicting smells assaulted his nostrils.

I'm not dead, he thought. *But I should have been.*

"I thought perhaps you had finally managed to anger Father enough to butcher you at last," the voice spoke once more with its dangerous, high-pitched purr. "I'll admit that I was tempted to just let him kill you—trouble that you are—but after all the effort I've put into you, I just couldn't let you go. Not yet."

Drakis seemed to float in a misty, emerald void. He tried to move, but his muscles refused to respond to his mind in even the smallest degree; his eyelids remained open, and his burning eyes were relieved only by the flow of tears that welled up in a constant and unbidden cascade. Panic threatened to pull his mind back into the abyss from which he had just emerged, but he thought of Mala and pushed the horror back down.

He ached everywhere, and his back felt as though it were burned raw; but it was a more general pain, he realized, than the deep cuts that had nearly stolen his breath for the last time. Sha-Timuran's unbridled rage still hurt and confused Drakis—in all Drakis' long memories of his enslavement not once could he remember Lord Timuran striking him in anger. Yet Drakis had seen enough war to know the meaning and intent behind those black, featureless eyes. It was unmistakable; Sha-Timuran meant not just to punish Drakis, not to teach him discipline, but to beat him to death for the simple pleasure of doing it.

"What are you thinking of, slave?" the voice whispered into his ear. "Are you thinking of your little slave girl *hoo-mani*? Does it excite you to think of her?"

Drakis felt the black panic rising inside him once more. *Where am I? What happened to me? Why, after all these years, would Sha-Timuran wish me dead today? If he wants me dead, what is to stop him?*

As he struggled to keep his fears at bay, the words of the dwarf came back to him, and he clung to them for a time like the last bit of rope before the fall into a bottomless chasm.

"He would kill you if he could, Drakis, this very afternoon. But someone will intervene on your behalf—and will save your life, though in doing so you will wish that you had died."

"Are you listening to me, Draki?" The voice was murmuring in his other ear now. He could feel the hot breath on his ear as she spoke and would have pulled away if he could. "We've shared so much over the years. I've always kept our dark little secret, haven't I? But you . . . you've been bad to me, *hoo-mani*. Very bad, indeed."

The dim ceiling overhead was coming into focus now and again through his tear-blurred vision: the outline of arches converging in a dome above him with frescos of vines set between the columns. It was useless. He did not recognize the room at all. It followed the elven pattern of design, but what its purpose was or even *where* it was he could not say.

But the voice . . . he knew that voice.

Tsi-Shebin's voice.

"You left me here with nothing to comfort me," the

elven princess pouted, "and nothing with which to occupy my time in this forsaken frontier."

Drakis felt the brush of silk against his right arm. The pinched face of the elf woman drifted into view as she sat next to him, leaning across him as she rested her weight on her hand.

Tsi-Shebin was young for an elf woman . . . impossible to guess in actual time but easily placed as equal to human females of sixteen or seventeen years. She was far from a child and yet not quite acceptable in elven adult company—an age of being between. Her head had the characteristic elongation of her race, though the back of her skull had a gentle taper to it that other elves found quite becoming. She wore her long, silver-white hair up after the royal fashion, exposing her shoulders while at the same time covering the baldness of the female elven crown with carefully pinned curls. Indeed, her angular features, narrow face and long, tapered ear tips were, Drakis had heard, considered stunningly beautiful by elfkind.

She looked revolting to Drakis.

"So, I suppose you're wondering what you always wonder about now," Shebin said through a crooked smile. She had been in a flowing household dress when he had last seen her in the throne room. Now she wore a vibrant blue silk robe wrapped with a wide sash about her narrow waist. She sat upright and placed her bony hand on Drakis' chest. "There isn't much time, so I'll just tell you."

Drakis was suddenly, horrifyingly aware that he was completely naked.

"We are in the healing room in the avatria," Shebin continued in languid tones. "You're lying on a bed of Healer's Blade, and thanks to the Aether Well of my father, your wounds are being bound back together. I managed to stop Father's little self-indulgent rage before you were of no further use to anyone ever again. I had the servants bring you here, and I dismissed them so that I might tend to your healing myself. They've never told on us before . . . so they certainly won't now."

She moved her hand lightly up his chest. "The door is barred, so no one will bother us."

His breaths came more quickly. He tried to think; Shebin was Timuran's only child, a pampered young woman whom he could only recall having seen watching the combats from the wall around the training arena. She had applauded him once some years ago—this much he could recall—but beyond seeing her smiling at him as she stood next to Sha-Timuran at court for the presentation of each bounty, he had no recollection of her at all.

"You were always my favorite," Shebin said, the long, carefully manicured fingernail of her right hand scraping across the skin of his wide chest. "Tsi-Narusin—she's that insufferable girl over in House Tajeran—she always used to brag about her little games with a *hoo-mani* from her father's stables. Her father found out about it, though, and burned that slave to ash right on the spot.

"Narusin was devastated about it for weeks." Shebin giggled to herself with a strange gurgling sound. "It still galls her that I've got you to play with—and I remind her of it every chance I get."

By the gods! Drakis thought. *This can't be happening to me! Mala!* He had to get away, but he could not. His body remained unresponsive to his mind, the nerves working, his heart beating, his lungs dragging in air, but he could not willfully move. None of this made sense to him—it was a bad dream from which he could not awaken.

The dwarf! His world had turned upside down ever since they found the dwarf. Perhaps the dwarf was the key to ending this horrible nightmare. Maybe the dwarf was cursed or was a wizard or a deity or demon who came into the world to plague him.

"I know you'll come to me tonight when you're better healed—it takes time to knit the tissue back together properly," Shebin cooed. The young elven woman reached down and began to unwrap the sash at her waist. "But we have a little time right now . . . and you've been away too long."

The sash fluttered down out of her hand. The silken

robe parted slightly, revealing the skin of the young elf female from her narrow neck down past the hollow of her stomach.

"I know I should have waited until after House Devotions," she said through a sigh. "But why wait?"

Shebin pulled her knees up under her, kneeling next to the human warrior's immobile form. She unpinned her hair, which fell down around her shoulders, revealing the long bald strip typical of her race between her forehead and the back of her elongated crown. Shebin laughed darkly, then slipped the robe from her shoulders.

Drakis drew in a sharp breath.

Shebin was easily numbered among the greatest elven beauties in all the Western Provinces.

To Drakis, her wraithlike, angular, and bony form appeared hideously cadaverous—a living corpse whose fingers now lightly stroked his chest and body.

"Tell you what, Draki," she murmured. "Why don't you just think of that *hoo-mani* woman you're always going on about—that precious Mala of yours—and know that *I* was the first to have you . . . that I am *always* the first to have you!"

Drakis could not—*dared* not—scream.

CHAPTER 12

Hall of the Past

DRAKIS STEPPED FURTIVELY through the archway and into the ornate hallway beyond. He noted with shocking clarity the pastel-colored walls curving upward from the polished stone floor. He felt the stones cool beneath his feet. Drakis concentrated on each of these aspects in turn with fierce single-minded determination, because if he did not, he would start to think . . .

"Has she quite finished with you?"

Drakis looked up into the face of Tsi-Timuri, Timuran's wife and the mother of Tsi-Shebin. He shook at the sight of her.

"Answer me, slave!"

"Yes, Mistress," Drakis mumbled.

The older elven woman folded her narrow arms across her chest, her long fingernails, filed to sharp points, digging slightly into the flesh of her upper arms. She leaned back slightly, her face all angular plains of displeasure around tight lips and glistening, featureless eyes of black. Her iron-gray hair may have been luxuriously long, but it was tightly constrained into an almost rigid form close to her long head.

"Can you walk?" she asked at last.

"Yes . . . no . . . I think I can, Mistress."

"Go on, then. Walk," she said, nodding down a long, curving hallway.

The elderly elf woman gave him a shove, pushing him down the curve of the hallway. He saw clearly the disdainful curl of her withered lips and her accusing eyes. He tried to navigate the hall, but his legs were still weak and required his full attention to remain under him. The best he could manage was a staggering gait as he moved painfully before the contemptuous elf prodding him forward.

"That was worse than usual," Timuri said behind him. "You should stay out of his way until Devotions. For now, try to remain as unnoticeable as possible."

"Thank you, Mistress," Drakis managed to say. "That is most kind of you."

"Kindness has nothing to do with it," Timuri snapped. "I will have order in my House. If that means pandering to my daughter's sick perversions—or my husband's for that matter—so be it. Someone has to pay for these indulgences for the sake of this House, and better you than me, slave . . . better you than me."

Tsi-Timuri's voice trailed off behind him, but Drakis did not mind; the words had only been spoken to fill an empty place and never meant for him at all.

"Now, get out of my sight until Devotions, or I will kill you with my own hands," Timuri hissed, "no matter how much my daughter considers you her personal pet."

He realized with a start that he had come to the end of the hall and was staring out from the framework of the Servant's Portal.

"Go!"

"Yes, Mistress."

There were four portals that accessed the avatria as it floated above the walled garden, each one connected by a delicate and ornate bridge to four matching towers that rose up from the walls of the subatria below. These towers were of varying heights, the two tallest reserved exclusively for the use of Sha-Timuran's family and the third for elven guests or officials as well as the elven servants of the avatria. These were each comprised of smooth, vertical shafts and relied on the small pedestal fountains at their bases—small Aether springs linked to the House Well—to levitate or descend according to the blessings of the elven gods whose powers they invoked. The fourth—and lowest—of the towers contained the only physical staircase between the avatria and the subatria.

This was the same staircase, he suddenly recalled, that he had bounded up so hopefully just a few hours before, the same rope-woven bridge that he had crossed gladly into the lower floors of the floating elven home with dreams of a better future bright in his mind.

He placed one foot in front of the other and then frantically gripped the railing of the bridge. The cedar planks that had been roped together to form the suspended bridge had once passed so surely under his feet, but now they felt shifting and treacherous. He swallowed hard, closing his eyes for a few moments, hoping for a momentary respite in the darkness within himself; then he opened them and peered over the side.

The Servant's Bridge was just over thirty feet above the floor of the garden below, he judged. Surely that was sufficient room to insure his death. All he had to do was vault the flimsy railings of the rope bridge. It would all be so easy and so quick. Mala would never have to know why he had done it.

Mala.

The thought of her gave him pause. She would not know why, indeed—and the not knowing would hurt her, too. So he looked away from the siren call of oblivion and made his way on unsure feet the rest of the way across the bridge.

He would have to find a way to keep his shame from Mala—because he would rather bear the pain of it himself than be the cause of pain to her.

Somehow, he made his way down the long, interminable circles of the spiral stairs until they ended at one side of the House Garden. He turned at once, keeping his watering eyes fixed on the curve of the garden wall, his left hand reaching up to feel its surface as he made his way quickly around its perimeter.

He bumped suddenly into the hulking form of a manticorian gardener—a fat brute he remembered as RuuKag—who snarled at him. Drakis mumbled his apologies and ducked past the lion-man quickly.

He had to get out of the garden. Mala often was assigned to work here, and he could not bear to see her, not yet at any rate. He had to think through this, figure out how it was that his good life and prospects for a better one had suddenly turned to ash in a single day.

No, he realized: not in a single day. Things had been going wrong ever since he had departed for the Battle of the Ninth Throne three weeks before. The terrible losses in the battle—friends and comrades with whom he had shared innumerable campaigns—as well as the loss of their Proxi at the climax of the battle itself and the subsequent loss of the crown. Then there was the bizarre dwarf whose endless prattle had suddenly, terribly come true and turned his blessed life into a cursed one . . .

"Hail Drakis!"

Drakis snapped his head toward the sound. The wall of the House Garden had ended abruptly at a long, vaulted hallway curving back around to his left. The walls were covered with the picture-writing of the elves and lined with enormous elven statues of each of the previous masters of the line of Timuran. The figures looked down with disapproval on the two figures coming toward Drakis from its far end: a short, squat figure and a manticore.

Drakis did not immediately recognize the dwarf, for he was shaven after the fashion of slaves. His once long and luxurious beard was gone, as was his mane of hair. His jowly and receding chin gave his face an almost infantile appearance, like a fat human baby who had been too well fed. His extravagant clothing was replaced with the common tunic, and his newly shaved head now bore the tattooed mark of a House slave.

"It is good to see you again, Drakis," the dwarf said with careful lightness in his voice, his eyes fixed on the human. "I have been worried about you, you know."

Drakis could only stare at the dwarf.

"Drakis? Are you well?"

Only then did he realize that the manticore was Belag. Drakis took in a long, shuddering breath and looked up into the face of the towering manticore.

The creature's yellow eyes narrowed suspiciously. "Is there something wrong?"

He doesn't know, Drakis realized. *Sha-Timuran has not told any of the Impress Warriors about my beating ... no one has told them. Perhaps Mala doesn't know either ...*

"No, everything is fine," he lied. "Sha-Timuran was ... was pretty upset about losing the crown, especially to his neighbor ... but everything is fine."

Belag considered this for a time and then nodded with a grunt. "You are square, then?"

"Yes—I am square," Drakis replied, but he looked away as he spoke. "What are you doing with the dwarf?"

"Jerakh told me to bring him for shearing and branding."

"Ah," Drakis nodded. "I see. So he couldn't stand him either. Where are you taking him now?"

They both turned to look at Jugar. He had wandered back down the long curve of the great hall, staring up at the wall above him with both of his thick hands clasped tightly behind his back.

"It's back to the barracks with him until he is impressed this evening at Devotions," Belag said although his furry brows were knitted in thought. "I don't like him, Drakis. There's something unsettling about him."

He can see the future, Drakis thought. *Yes, that is unsettling.*

"Just another conquest to the glory of the House Timuran," Drakis said. "Look, if you don't mind, I'll take the dwarf back—there are some questions I need to ask him."

The manticore looked suddenly relieved. "Gladly. How the gods put so many words into so short a soul, I'll never know. Better you listen to him than me."

"Then off with you ... I'll see you at Devotions."

The manticore was already padding quickly back around the garden toward the north hall and the chakrilya beyond.

Drakis kept his eye on the dwarf. His figure seemed

almost comical now that it was shaved and branded. This short, ugly creature had done more than bring them back to a world that was horrifying; he had predicted its horrors long before they had become fact. Drakis knew that the ways of the gods were strange and unfathomable to the mortals with whose fates they played, but he could not deny that this dwarf had conjured questions in his mind that he had to ask and have answered.

Drakis stepped up to the dwarf, and with a quick glance down the hall, spoke rapidly in hushed tones.

"Are you a god?"

The dwarf turned his chubby face toward the human. "What did you say?"

"I said," Drakis spoke with only a slightly raised volume, "are you a god?"

The dwarf smiled in return, "Ah . . . you want to know if I am a god?"

"Yes," Drakis replied.

"I see . . . well, that depends," the dwarf said, turning back once more to examine the picture-writing carved into the wall in front of him.

Drakis stammered for a moment before he could continue. "What is that supposed to mean?"

Jugar turned back to the human, his pleasant smile still fixed between his round cheeks. "Oh, Drakis, my dear friend . . . if someone ever asks you if you are a god, the only appropriate answer is—that depends!"

Drakis felt the warmth of his frustration rising into his face.

"Here, come walk with me for a while and I'll explain," Jugar said, turning to face back down the hall away from the garden. Drakis straightened slightly and fell into slow step next to the dwarf who still had his hands clasped in thought behind his back. "Let us assume that someone asks you, Drakis, if you are a god. If you were to answer them at once with a 'no,' then you would disappoint anyone who might have supported you, and, being embarrassed at their mistake and suddenly feeling you are much less than they expected of you . . . well they would lose respect for you and not follow you at all. If they are your enemies and ask that question, then saying 'no' is just an invitation to have your land invaded and your people slaughtered. You follow me so far?"

"I think so," Drakis said anxiously, "but I don't see what this has to do with . . ."

"On the other hand, if you were to answer 'yes' right away and all your supporters were following you based on your word that you were a god—and then it turned out that you *weren't* a god but just some fellow who didn't want to disappoint everyone by *not* being a god . . . well, they'd probably stone you right there on the spot and end your career rather abruptly. Then your enemies would come in and invade your land anyway and slaughter your people, so the result would be much the same, right?"

"Yes, but . . ."

"So the only reasonable answer is, 'that depends,'" the dwarf concluded. "It doesn't commit you to performing like a deity and lets anyone who might follow you do so with a clear conscience. It also keeps your enemies guessing . . . an altogether reasonable outcome for everyone involved."

"But you see the future . . . know it before it happens," Drakis said under his breath. "Or do you cause it to happen—determining my fate?"

Jugar stopped, looking up earnestly into Drakis' face. "No! No one determines your fate but you!"

"But you . . . you *knew!*"

The dwarf let out a great sigh. "Yes, I knew, Drakis— and I am sorry for it, my boy."

"But how? How did you know?"

The dwarf looked around them once more, gesturing as he did. "Have you ever been here, Drakis? Do you recognize the place?"

Drakis glanced around. "Of course. It is the Hall of the Past."

"Do you know what it is for?"

Drakis shook his head, "Why can't you just answer my question?"

"I *am* answering your question," the dwarf continued. "Do you know what it is for?"

Drakis looked around him. Pictographs and hieroglyphics ornamented the walls, each set in various sized framing cuts making a mosaic on the wall. There were the figures of elves, larger than the rest and more prominent. There were smaller figures of manticores and chimera as well as humans. There were other creatures, too, which he thought mystical for he had never seen them in battle. "They are the histories and honors of the House of Timuran after the manner of the elven language."

"That is right," Jugar nodded. "Can you read them?"

"Read them?" Drakis scoffed. "You are a fool!"

"I may be a fool," the dwarf replied, "but I *can* read these. Here, for example," and he pointed three-quarters of the way up the slope of the wall, "here is where a Timuran participated in the expedition to the God's Wall and slaughtered ten thousand humans in their native kingdom. And here," his fat finger pointed a little to the left of the previous frame, "is where two brothers of the Timuran line were killed as they fought a dragon."

"A what?" Drakis asked.

"A dragon," the dwarf continued. "It is a creature of power and majesty not seen among breathing dwarves or men in three hundred years. They are, in fact, the source of the song that has troubled you of late. See, over here," and the dwarf once more shifted the direction of his pointing finger, "is where the humans of the royal line were all called to their doom by the betrayal of the dragons that once had served them so well. It is written here that they sing this song now in lament."

"Foolish nonsense," Drakis spat.

"And this wisdom from a slave who cannot read." Jugar sighed once more, shaking his head. "I knew your fate today, Drakis, because I could read you as I read the markings on these walls."

Drakis shook his head in disbelief.

"Your back, Drakis . . . I read your back," Jugar continued sadly. "When we were in the baths. Those scars were too deep and the markings too regular to be anything but the firereed whip of an elven House Master. Combat scars would have been more varied and, truthfully, would have killed you had they come on the field. But they were also knitted back together with both elven skill and the power of Aether. That meant that someone in this household had saved you from death before and many times."

"Many times?" Drakis shook his head. "This is the first time my master has *ever* beaten me!"

"This is the first time you have ever *remembered* your master beating you," Jugar corrected.

Drakis paused. "Then how did you know about . . . about . . ."

"About your House mistress?"

Drakis glanced shamefully away once again.

"Those same scars—they were healed with elven powers of the Aether, too clean and regular to have been otherwise . . . and it had to be someone who cared not only about how you healed but how you *looked*." Jugar shrugged. "It happens in elven households—especially those of the higher estates. It is forbidden, of course, but the practice has gotten about among the younger generation of the elves that a warrior's—well, attentions—will bring more power to their use of the Aether. So now it has become a common, dirty little secret practiced in most households between elven youth who have too little else to occupy their time and the warrior slaves who have no choice but to submit or die and be forgotten. Elven society goes on turning its blind eye to the practice and is content to pretend it does not exist. By the looks of your back, this has been a cycle going on for some time."

"Shebin . . . Timuran . . . I don't remember anything like this."

"But you *can* remember," Jugar said earnestly. He reached up and grabbed Drakis by the shoulders. "You can know the truth for yourself! You don't need the word of an old dwarf or anyone else for that matter. You want to know about the gods—I'll tell you about the gods! The gods know the future because they understand the past.

You cannot see where you're going if you forget where you've been. You can be *like* the gods—you can come to know who you truly are, who you've truly been, and you can shape your own destiny. All you have to do is *not* participate in Devotions tonight."

"That's insane," Drakis said, pulling back. "Everything that has gone wrong in my life lately has been because I *haven't* been able to perform my Devotions."

"House Devotions *are* your problem, Drakis," Jugar growled in frustration. "It's how they keep you the happy little slave! They make you forget the pain and the suffering and the loss and the agony of your existence every night. But if that's what you want—if you *want* to remain the blissful slave-boy who *wants* to forget that his master regularly beats him into the shadow of death just for the pleasure it brings him, whose daughter plays with him like her personal filthy toy . . . if you *want* to be the slave who just dreams of a better life that will forever be *promised* and never *delivered* . . . if that is what you want, then take House Devotions tonight and go back to sleep, Drakis!"

The dwarf spat on the polished floor.

"But if you do . . . you'll condemn all of us to sleep forever."

CHAPTER 13

The Altar

HOUSE DEVOTIONS were the touchstone of every elven household. Each evening—from the over five thousand elves of the First and Second Estates assembled to see and be seen in the glowing courts of the Imperial Cloud Palace to the handful of Fourth and Fifth Estate elves gathered in a humble garden on the farthest frontiers of the Empire—every citizen and slave of Rhonas gathered about their respective altars to offer their Devotions.

The ceremony was universal and unerringly prescribed. At the House Altar, usually situated in the subatria garden although any large space where the House Aether Well was located would suffice, every member of the household would gather. Each would arrange themselves according to their estate—those of highest rank nearest the altar with lesser estates in successive groups behind them ending with those of the Seventh Estate—the slaves of the Empire.

The rites were conducted by the Lord of the House and began with the invoking of the Emperor's blessing on the proceedings and rededicating the household to bring its actions and thoughts in accord with the Emperor's Will. This was followed by beseeching the blessing of the particular gods worshiped by that family upon the House and its servants, each god placated in turn, their praises lauded and then chorused in turn by the assembly. Then, the glories of the House were praised, and, in the case of recent battles, its treasures were displayed to the House as evidence of their power and entitled rank in the Empire. Only when the status of the House had been thus properly accounted did the Devotions proper begin.

It was the ranking member of the highest Estate who first knelt before the altar, placed his hands on its surface, and murmured his Devotions. Occasionally, a House might be blessed with the visit of a member of a higher Estate, and in such rare instances, he would take precedence in the ceremony; but in nearly all cases the Lord of the House was first to offer Devotions, and such was true of House Timuran. His words and thoughts were thus communicated through the medium of the altar and its connected Aether Well to the realms of both the gods and the blessed Emperor. The words of the supplication were always in the ancient elven tongue and conjured the Aether magic, filling the House Aether Well with light during the Lord's Devotions. Then, by turns, each subsequent member of the household knelt before the altar, pressed their hands against the stone, and paid homage to the gods and the Emperor whom the gods had chosen.

For the slaves of the Empire, who were the last to approach the altar and universally the greatest in numbers, it was always a moment of rest and hope. To touch the altar was to touch—for the briefest of moments—the power of the Empire and the gods. It left them with the profound feeling of being bound to something greater than themselves and, during the long days of their servitude, granted them each night a sublime rest beyond anything else in their experience.

It was this thought that carried every slave through the day—the anticipation of the ecstasy that came with the Devotions each night. It was the embodiment of their hope to rise in status and someday become citizens themselves.

No slave *ever* willingly missed Devotions.

Drakis could not keep his hands still. Standing against the curving wall around the central garden, he was uncomfortable inside his own skin. Though he could no longer feel the scars on his back, they still burned in his mind, causing his back muscles to spasm involuntarily, flinching again with each imagined strike of the firereed.

"What's wrong with you?" Belag rumbled under his breath. It was as close to a whisper as the manticore could manage as he stood next to the human. "You look as though you were about to die."

Drakis shook his head quickly. His eyes were locked on the altar. It stood at the bottom of the great curved bowl that formed the central garden of House Timuran, just at the base of the towering crystalline facets of the Aether Well. The Well plunged into the earth below like a dagger, anchoring the entire household with the land on which it rested and connected it with the House Wells around them. Those, in turn, were connected to the Wells of the Houses beyond—in theory—until all the Wells of the Empire connected to the great Well of the Emperor in the heart of Rhonas itself. He glanced above the garden to where the towering avatria—supported by the force of the Aether emanating from the Well—floated just clear of the upper reaches of the subatria's garden wall. The underside of the avatria was a hemisphere of fitted alabaster carved with intricate patterns of inlaid blue sapphire. It was achingly beautiful and cold as a tomb.

His tomb.

"You can live, if you choose," the dwarf urged from Drakis' left. "You can know the truth ... the truth about the elves ... the truth about yourself ..."

Drakis shot the dwarf a withering look and then turned back to face the altar. Timuran was in the ceremonial robes that he wore each night, though he looked far less resplendent than Drakis remembered him in his mind's eye. He was just finishing his invocation of the Emperor's Will.

Now, with his hands reaching above him—toward the base of the avatria it seemed—he called upon the gods Jolnar and Rhon for their blessings upon his House in bringing to it the power of destiny and victory in battle.

He looked away. Timuran had always been like a father to him—a demanding yet benevolent and wise master. He could barely conceive of the cruelty that he had experienced at his master's hand, and yet it *had* happened, and, according to the dwarf, from the evidence on his own back it had happened many times before.

He suddenly realized that he had not actually *seen* his own back—nor was he likely to do so. All he had was the word of this dwarf who, so far, had been filled only with words. Jugar had made a lot of promises and had not truly delivered yet on a single one. Perhaps, he considered, it was all an elaborate trick by the dwarf.

But the beating the dwarf had predicted had been no trick. His near death had been no trick. And his healing and what happened afterward . . .

Drakis glanced at Tsi-Shebin where she stood next to her father. Her black eyes were featureless, and yet he was sure they were staring directly at him. He shuddered again, forcing the memories out of his mind and looking away.

His eyes settled on the members of the household arrayed about the garden for the Devotion. The garden was largely empty, due in no small part to the fact that most of the Centurai were still spread out among the folds between here and the battlefield nearly one hundred and thirty leagues to the north. Nearest to the center of the garden were the elven guild overseers of the Fourth Estate, craftsmen who were in charge of the various divisions within the household. Se'Djinka stood among them, his patched eye giving him a more sinister look than the rest of the overseers. Drakis realized that he must have arrived that same afternoon—had he come to watch the human die? He didn't remember him being at his audience with Sha-Timuran, but he could easily have not noticed him.

Behind them stood the Fifth Estate elves, the free workers of the household. These primarily included those who served in the avatria—since slaves were not welcome in those confines—but also included a number of Free Guardians, elves who took care of the safety of House Timuran while the Centurai was fighting for its greater honor. Drakis' practiced eye considered them at a glance: Their stance was practiced ease, but they moved well and touched their sheathed weapons with familiarity. The seasoned warrior in Drakis measured the Guardians as worthy opponents.

There were no Sixth Estate in the Timuran House—a fact that only now bothered Drakis—so the last, arrayed around the edge of the garden, were the lowest of the Seven Estates: the slaves. The household slaves of the subatria stood apart from the warriors of the Centurai. Drakis looked down the rows arrayed to their right and quickly caught sight of a familiar face smiling back at him.

Mala, he thought. *How can I tell her what has happened to me? How can I pretend that it did not happen at all?*

She must have seen something in his face, for her smile fell at once into an expression of question and concern. He looked away again, focusing once more on the altar and the ritual of the Devotion in its relentless and prescribed cycle of words, gestures, and chanted phrases.

There, arrayed about the altar, were the treasures that he had sent back as their bounty from the war. The pieces of armor that had been so impressive in their original setting now seemed short and comical when placed at the feet of the elves. One of the suits of armor had been carefully arranged to be holding out the black, onyx shard that Jugar had called the Heart of Aer. Here, in the glorious garden of his master, it seemed like a pitiful offering, and it had nearly cost him his life.

How could his entire world have turned so terribly wrong? The dwarf had prophesied it with frightening, fated accuracy—or possibly caused it. And yet all along the dwarf had insisted that Drakis could know the truth of it for himself, that he didn't have to take the dwarf's word or believe in anything but himself.

Drakis stared at the altar.

He didn't want to know the truth.

He wanted to embrace his ignorance.

Drakis wanted to just forget everything that had happened. There was comfort in that, he thought. The memories of what had happened to him over the last few days—of the senseless slaughter of friends and enemy alike, of the horrific violence done just to capture a crown of a kingdom that had already been conquered, not to even consider the violence done to both his body and his spirit that very afternoon—all these things had caused him to wonder how he could possibly ever sleep again, let alone face Mala. That the altar might offer him blissful forgetfulness of all of that was deeply alluring to him. He knew he could not live with the truth of his memories—so perhaps it was better to live a lie without them.

Lord Timuran had finished his Devotions as had his family. The overseers were passing the altar now, each in turn kneeling and making their Devotion as Timuran looked on. Those who were finished moved up the carefully manicured path out of the bowl of the garden and waited patiently for the rest of the household to join them.

"Drakis," the dwarf muttered behind him. "All our lives are in your hands! You don't have to be a slave . . . you can be free! You can know the truth . . ."

"I don't want to know the truth," Drakis said with a shuddering breath. He turned with Belag as the Centurai was preparing to take its turn at the Devotions. "I want to forget the truth."

"Forget the truth?!" the dwarf sputtered. They began moving forward, slowly. The Free Guardians had already finished their Devotions. The slaves of the subatria were approaching the altar. "I cannot believe I'm hearing this! You, of all humans, giving up your future . . . your great destiny . . . just to save yourself a little pain?"

Drakis snorted. He looked again to the altar. Mala was kneeling, her bald head bowing down before the altar as her hands pressed down into its surface. *A little pain?* he thought. *You have no idea how much pain I'm giving up.*

The dwarf had followed his gaze. "Ah, yes, and what about that girl of yours?"

He watched as Mala walked up the path to join the other House slaves waiting at the base of the garden wall. She turned and her eyes met his.

She looked back at him without expression.

"What or *who* will they make her forget?" Jugar urged, a vicious edge to his voice. "You could die tomorrow, Drakis, and she would *never* remember that you existed let alone that you ..."

"SHUT UP!" Drakis shouted, wheeling suddenly on the dwarf. In an instant, he grasped the dwarf by his tunic with his left hand, slamming his right fist into Jugar's face.

From behind a nose that was bleeding and most probably broken, Jugar smiled.

Drakis looked up. The entire assembly was staring at him in shocked astonishment. Sha-Timuran raised his head slightly and frowned.

Drakis released his grip on the dwarf, his breathing coming heavily. He turned from his astonished comrades and stepped to his right toward the delicately arched opening leading back toward the chakrilya and the Warrior pens beyond. Even as he did, however, a tall elven Guardian stepped in front of him.

"You are disturbing the Devotions," the Guardian said in a reedy voice. "Calm yourself and return to your place."

"I ... I'm not well," Drakis replied. It was true enough; he felt overwhelmingly nauseated. "I just ... I just need a few minutes ... I just need to breathe ..."

The Guardian reached down, his hand fingering the grip on his sheathed sword. "You will feel better after your Devotions, slave. Just return to your place and everything will be better soon."

"Please ... just give me a few minutes," Drakis hissed through clenched teeth. He could see the chakrilya beyond the Guardian, its anonymous space and emptiness inviting to his eyes and beckoning him. "I'll be right back ... I can't ... I just need to *breathe* ..."

"Do as you're told and everything will be right again." The Guardian said forcefully, gripping the human's arm.

"NO!" Drakis shouted. Training overcame thought as

the Impress Warrior suddenly stepped into the Guardian, forcing the elf to release his grip. He reached for the handle of the sword, but the elf was too quick, clasping his own hand over the human's and keeping the blade firmly sheathed in the scabbard.

A gasp rushed through the crowd of servants. Belag, Thuri, and Ethis all remained in their places, astonished at the sight of their Centurai commander striking one of their elven masters and uncertain as to what to do.

The elves, however, reacted quickly and surely. Guardians from around the room converged on the disturbance. One of them gripped Drakis from behind, pulling him away from the first Guardian while a third immediately reached to restrain his left arm.

Drakis would not relent. He flailed with his free arm, kicking as they tried to drag him down the path toward the altar. He kept yelling throughout. "Let me go! I just need a moment . . . I don't want to hurt anyone . . . just let me go!"

Several more Guardians were rushing in his direction. Out of the corner of his eye, he caught sight of Sha-Timuran striding up the path toward him, a grim smile fixed on his face as he drew the long, curving blade from its sheath.

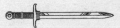

Unnoticed in the spectacle unfolding at the base of the subatria wall, Jugar the Jester slipped between the bushes of the garden.

No eyes witnessed him deftly remove the armored glove from the dwarven armor or, having donned it, use it to remove the Heart of Aer from where it was displayed.

Only Se'Djinka, embroiled in subduing the berserk Drakis saw the danger as the dwarf leaped up onto the altar, but he was too late.

The dwarf swung the Heart of Aer with all his strength. It struck against the crystalline structure of the House Aether Well with the precision that only a dwarf, knowing minerals, could achieve. The interior lattice of the Well fractured in an instant, the power of the Aether contained by it released a moment later. The Aether Well exploded into a million shards.

In that instant, every slave of House Timuran ... from the lowest scullery maid to the most fearless gladiator ... suddenly and horribly *REMEMBERED*.

CHAPTER 14

The Fall

DRAKIS COULD NOT stop screaming.

The garden of Timuran spun uncontrollably down into madness as each slave reacted at once to the flood of suppressed memories surging raw and unbidden into their conscious minds. A sudden, terrifying discord of anguished shrieks filled the air, an agonized chorus of despair and pain. In panic, most of the slaves bolted from their ordered ranks, running blindly about the garden chased by the ghosts of their own remembrance.

Drakis noticed none of this. He arched his back so hard that the Guardian Elves nearly dropped him from their iron grip. The sound continued from his gaping mouth, animalistic and unbidden. His eyes were wide, focused not on the elven Guardians or their rising panic and uncertainty but on visions from his own past suddenly confronting him like phantoms escaping from the prison of his thoughts.

Mother ... first mother, real mother ... stories of father and the Time Before ... running with mother and brother ... brother! Recaptured and enslaved ...

Outrage and fear surged through him, blasting strength again into his muscles. He snatched his right arm free and began flailing blindly about.

Mother dead in the wars ... her body never returned ...

*New mother and new father ... false family remembered ...
brother ... where is my brother?*

The Guardians released him, their hands reaching at
once for their weapons. Drakis fell heavily to the floor.

*Beaten ... sold ... beaten ... sold ... no lesson taught in
each beating, the point being not to teach him but for the
sheer joy of inflicting pain and humiliation on the human
boy ... sold again to Sha-Timuran because the elf girl was
spoiled by her father and thought the human boy was pretty
and Sha-Timuran could use another warrior ...*

He rolled over, kneeling on the ground, curling tighter
into a ball.

*Tenicia ... his first betrothal ... his first wife ... he had
forgotten her ... he had forgotten so many ...*

The sound of blades crashing together cut through his
avalanche of thoughts, replacing them with the single, clear
voice of the dead ChuKang come back to him.

*"To stand still on a field of battle is to invite death to
find you."*

Drakis pushed himself up, leaping to his feet, and
closing at once with the nearest of the elven Guardians.
Instinct and training took over, pushing the maddening
thoughts to the side as he concentrated on the moment
before him and the enemy that he barely recognized as
one of his own household. He gave himself to his instincts,
not wanting to think or consider the consequences of his
attack. He blocked the elf's frantic blow, arrested his sword
arm, and, in a single, fluid move, wrested the blade from
the horrified elf's grasp.

Drakis swung the blade, rotating the grip with his wrist.
The elf backed up, baring his teeth beneath his blank, black
eyes.

Drakis did not hesitate. He feigned a blow to the right
and then, with lightning skill, curled the blade over his
head and sliced it into his opponent on the left. He drew
the blade back and then thrust it forward, burying it deep
into the elf's gut and then turning it with a violent rotation
of both hands on the hilt.

Blood gushed over his hands from the gaping wound,

but Drakis maintained his grip on the hilt, jerking it free and reeling backward slightly from the effort.

It saved his life. A blade flashed downward in front of his face. He stepped back on his right foot, planting it for balance as he raised his own blade to deflect the downward cut away from him. He spun to confront his next attacker.

Don't think . . . just survive.

He locked his eyes with those of a taller Guardian for a moment, but it was enough. A massive fist, its fur already caked with blood connected with the elf's head from the left, driving it with such force into the garden wall next to them that Drakis heard the skull crack over the screaming chorus around them.

"Help me!" roared Belag. "Help me!"

Drakis turned to look at Belag. His golden eyes were fixed open, darting suddenly here and there. The human saw something he had never seen in any manticore before: fear filled the flat feline features of his countenance. He reached out with his bloodied, huge hand, feeling toward Drakis as though he could not see him.

A terrible sound, like a thunder that would never end, surged down around them. Drakis looked up.

The avatria was falling. Bereft of the power of the Aether Well, the elegant floating home of the Timurans first leaned to one side and then dropped straight down, smashing down onto the tall garden wall of the subatria with crushing force. Hundreds of alabaster tiles crashed down into the garden from the hemispherical underside of the structure, knocking many of the terrified household members to the ground. Several of the braziers lighting the garden fell over, their coals igniting a fire. Drakis watched in amazement as several subatria slaves, cackling as they danced, began pouring oil from amphorae on the fire, causing it to erupt robustly, its smoke obscuring the scene. As Drakis watched, an enormous crack opened up along the curved foundation that threatened to collapse the entire structure on them at any moment.

Training and instinct. Training and instinct.

The human grabbed Belag's forearm.

"Gather the Warriors," Drakis heard himself say, although his own voice sounded detached from him—a thing apart. "Tell those who can to meet outside at the totem hilltop southwest of the House ..."

"Outside!" Panic rose in the manticore's voice. "We've no permission to ..."

"Belag! I am Master of the Centurai now," Drakis shouted, his face pressed close, filling the vision of the manticore. In the back of his mind he knew how utterly ridiculous his words were. There were no masters any more ... no Centurai. "Get any warriors you can and meet me outside ... west of the Warrior Gate at the hilltop totem!"

Overhead, an overwhelming cracking sound shook the hall. Drakis glanced up fearfully. The amount of debris from the collapsing avatria above them was increasing at an alarming rate.

"Belag!" Drakis shouted. "Obey!"

The manticore's eye slits suddenly narrowed into focus. "Aye!"

Drakis glanced around as the huge lion-man turned and bolted off to his right. The garden was barely recognizable. Flames shot up from several large fires, their flickering light illuminating the shattered base of the avatria that threatened imminent collapse. Silhouetted or illuminated, everywhere there seemed to be figures moving through the haze of the smoke.

A single name came to him.

"Mala," he murmured.

He felt panic rise within him again. She had been on the other side of the garden watching him just moments ago.

Drakis leaped over the body of an elf Guardian, trying to circle the garden around to the right, but almost at once he ran into a group of slaves who blocked the way. Several of them lay still in a spreading pool of their own blood, but more than a dozen others—wild eyed and screaming—were tearing at something they had dragged to the ground. Their hands and arms were covered in blood as they pulled away chunks of flesh, tossing it behind them.

He turned at once down one of the garden paths. It took him farther under the ominous rain of wreckage from the shattered structure above, but he dared not stop as he ran past insane tableaus: An old servant he recognized from the House knelt on the ground, his eyes fixed as he gathered up shards of the shattered Aether Well and tried to piece them back together in his badly lacerated hands; Jerakh, his own Octian brother, standing in the midst of several elven overseers, his short sword in his hand as he screamed joyfully and gave chase to a fleeing overseer who had previously escaped his attentions; several slaves pressing their hands against the broken altar, desperate in their own way to forget the nightmare around them.

A tall chimerian leaped into his path, its four arms brandishing a senseless assortment of weapons: a broken branch, a bent brazier stand, and a pair of cooking ladles. The fact that all four were bloodied made less of an impression on Drakis than the look on the creature's face.

"Thuri!" Drakis said. "Come with us! Join us outside . . ."

The chimerian charged at once, shouting as he did. "Freedom! Vengeance and Justice!"

Drakis parried the first two blows in quick succession. "No, Thuri! Stop!"

But the chimerian did not hear or see him. He seemed to be fighting a battle in some other place or time. "I won't go back," he cried out. "You can't make me go back!"

One of the ladles connected solidly with the side of Drakis' head, driving him to the ground. He rolled quickly, the brazier slamming into the dark ground where moments before his head had been. Then he struck out with the sword, slicing at the back of the chimerian's foot.

Thuri howled with pain and toppled backward to the ground as Drakis got to his feet. White slabs of polished ceramic tile fell around him, shattering into dust as they smashed against the stones of the garden. He turned again and saw the path clear before him to the far side of the garden. He lunged forward.

"You cannot kill us all!" he heard Thuri's voice receding behind him. "You cannot kill . . ." Then the words were cut short by the sound of a massive foundation stone slamming into the ground.

Drakis did not look back. Impress Warriors were fighting everywhere—some with each other, some with a group of Guardians who had somehow managed to form a circle near the Hall of the Past to defend themselves, while others methodically moved among the slaves and overseers, slaying both indiscriminately. Drakis felt as though his legs were pushing him through water, that time itself was flowing against him and somehow he would not reach his beloved before his world fell completely down upon him.

Then, with a suddenness that shocked him, she was there.

Mala knelt on the ground before him, her eyes fixed forward. Tears streamed down her cheeks, cutting long, dark furrows in the dust-caked skin.

Drakis crouched down in front of her. A great groaning sound was coming from the stones above them. The foundation was giving way. He took her by both shoulders and stared into her eyes.

Training and instinct.

"Mala," he said firmly.

She did not move at all. Her eyes remained unfocused. A small trickle of blood stained her lips.

"Come with me," he said as kindly as he could. "I'll take you somewhere safe."

She shivered under his touch.

She had shivered at his touch before . . . or was that another woman? Stop! Was she dying? Don't think . . . act!

"Please," he said shaking her slightly. "I'll take care of you."

Her eyes suddenly focused on him and she blinked.

She started to giggle. "Take me?"

Drakis drew back. Sanity had left the woman's eyes.

"Take me?" Mala began to laugh. She threw her head back and started howling with laughter, hysterical and uncontrolled.

Don't think . . . just act!

He drew her up with him to stand, but her legs were

unsteady beneath her. He leaned over and picked her up, draping her over his shoulder as he considered the way back toward the chakrilya portcullis and the Warrior's Gate beyond. He adjusted the grip on his sword one last time and then charged forward, trying to concentrate on getting free, on getting out into the open air and then, maybe then, he could try to make sense of the terrible nightmare his own memories had suddenly become.

At his back, the hysterical laughter had changed to dreadful, soul-shattering sobs.

Drakis now knew the truth—but he did not know how he would live with the knowledge.

CHAPTER 15

Flight

DRAKIS STRUGGLED to reach the crest of the hill, then, stumbling, fell to the ground. Mala tumbled from over his shoulder, falling heavily onto the grass of the knoll with a groan. The totem at the crest of the hill was dark, its inner glow vanished and its ever-watchful eyes now dark and useless.

Don't stop ... don't look ...

But he did look. He dragged his feet back under him and, standing on quivering legs, turned to gaze on the House of Sha-Timuran.

It was twilight, and the ruin stood out harshly against the dim glow of the horizon beyond. Flames had engulfed nearly all of the subatria, the brilliant tongues of orange and yellow boiling up around the fallen avatria. The once-floating structure had fallen and was now leaning obscenely to one side, the petals of its exterior curves now broken and crumbling under their own weight. A great crack split the structure from the flames about the subatria wall to the shattered lattice of its peak. The avatria itself was burning, too ... the ornate polished woods of its interior quickly giving themselves over to the flames. Black, greasy smoke rolled upward, staining the deep blue of the evening sky and blotting out the stars as they tried to appear.

Drakis' gaze was drawn across the horizon. Other columns of smoke drifted into the sky.

The House of Timuran was not alone in its fall. Tajeran, too, was burning and at least a half dozen other Houses beyond.

Someone behind him spoke. "They'll be coming soon."

Drakis started at the sound, wheeling around as he instinctively readied his blade.

The shapeshifter held up two of his hands, their palms out in a sign of submission. "Relax, Drakis . . . I'm Ethis."

Drakis squinted. A tall chimerian stood facing him, his blank features lit by the orange, shifting light of the burning mansion.

"Who?" Drakis blurted.

"Ethis," the chimerian continued, his voice sounding oddly calm against the chaos of the burning ruins beyond. "We fought together—I was in your Octian."

"Yes . . . Ethis," Drakis repeated the name as though trying to convince himself that he knew it. Part of him recalled the chimerian as a trusted and valiant comrade in arms who had served with him for many years—but he also knew that was a lie. Drakis had no real memory of Ethis before three weeks ago. Yesterday he had trusted this creature with his life—now he knew him a stranger he could barely trust at all.

"How did you know where . . . ?"

"Belag," the chimerian answered quickly. "He told me where we were to meet." Ethis held a squat figure firmly by its collar with a third hand. "I also found an old friend of ours that I thought you might want to talk to before he skulked off—but I would not recommend spending a lot of time in conversation."

Ethis shoved the dwarf forward, his newly shaved skull glistening with sweat by the light of the conflagration.

"Jugar." Drakis spat the name as though it carried its own venom.

"This most noble chimerian warrior is certainly correct, Drakis," Jugar began talking at once with an earnestness that left Drakis feeling both amazed and disgusted at the same time. "Our lives depend upon staying ahead of the news of our escape. As soon as those most dreaded hunters of the Empire—the Iblisi—learn of what happened here, they will descend upon us like winged death. We must travel far and fast . . ."

Nine notes . . . Seven notes . . .

Children hear the calling song of dreams.

Return to past longings . . .

Then, pushing through the song, other voices and visions, too, from inside his head rising suddenly into his conscious mind, drowning out the music in his mind.

. . . Se'Djinka's face snarled at him. "You're barely worth the food to keep you alive . . ."

". . . Sure, Drakis, your father came from the northlands beyond the dwarves," his mother said as they washed their master's clothes. His feet dangled from the edge of the stone shelf. "Must I tell you again of how we were freeborn in the wilds . . . ?"

". . . Run!" screamed the voice behind him. "Run or we're all dead! . . ."

". . . Hello, Mother . . ." he heard his younger self say, but now he could see it was a different place and a different mother . . .

". . . Forget it, Dre," the tall boy said smiling down at him as they worked under the sunshine in the fields. "It's too far to walk no matter how long . . ."

Drakis let go of his sword, pressing his hands hard against his ears. The blade dug into the earth then fell onto its side. Drakis growled at the ghosts suddenly occupying his head. "Go away! Stop it!"

He thought that he might be going mad. He was certain that others had—he had seen it in the hall; slaves from all the races suddenly plunged into a living insanity in which they had experienced things, seen things, and said things that . . .

"Drakis, my Lord!"

The human opened his eyes at the roaring of his name, uncertain he had heard the words properly.

Belag, his slave's tunic shredded and his fur matted in

places with both his own blood and that of others, now lay prostrate on the ground before Drakis, face against the ground with his massive hands laid out wide in front of him. Different races, Drakis had heard Se'Djinka say time and again, show their submission in different ways. Humans usually kneel facedown and bow before their conqueror. Chimera show their open hands and sit back on their haunches. Manticores, however, were said to submit when they lay facedown, exposing their back to attack. Drakis thought it only a lie as no manticore he had ever known would allowed himself to live long enough to submit to anyone. Yet now tears streamed from Belag's eyes as he lay prone, gazing with a fixed, wondering stare at Drakis.

It shocked the human to see his fellow warrior in such a state. Nor was he alone in his astonishment as a human and another manticore were standing behind Belag gaping at the humbled lion-man as well.

"Please . . . Belag, in the name of all the gods, get up, will you?"

The manticore quickly got to his feet, towering a full head above the human. Drakis remained stunned; was Belag actually smiling?

"I have brought two more to join us," Belag said, his words rushed with excitement. "I hope that I honor you by presenting them in your service."

Drakis stared at the two newcomers. One was a small human female whom he recognized at once as the Lyric. She still wore the gold collar around her neck although it was now stained with dried blood—whether her own or someone else's Drakis could not say. The manticore he knew: Ruukag, the former gardener of House Timuran, stood quivering in the evening air, his massive fingers clenching and unclenching at the air around them.

Drakis shook his head. "Belag, I told you to gather the warriors!"

The manticore turned his head, gazing at the burning household as he spoke. "They were all that were left, Drakis . . . all that would come. We're the only warriors who have kept our minds. But now that I see who you are . . . I knew we would need a Lyric to chronicle your deeds and a second manticore to witness your coming to the manticorian elders in Chaenandria."

Kept our minds? Drakis thought, staring at the manticore. *How does one cope with a manticore warrior who has so obviously lost his wits?* Drakis took in a long breath, then spoke quietly. "I . . . I don't understand, Belag."

"We . . . my brother and I . . . we searched for you," Belag huffed through quick, excited breaths. "We had learned the stories from the Wise Ones deep in the forgotten wilds of Chaenandria. They spoke of you—of the day of your coming and of the power you would bring to the justice of the world!"

Drakis stared back at him.

"I know it all by heart," the lion-man spoke with pleading tones. "'He will come with power to throw down the pillars of the oppressor's might . . .' and you *did*, Drakis, you released us from our bondage."

"Wait, Belag," Drakis said, shaking his head, "that's not true, *I* didn't . . ."

"The Northern Prophecies?" Jugar interrupted, stepping in front of Drakis as he spoke. "Those legends of the masters of the Desolation who once commanded the monsters of the world and would return again?"

"Aye!" Belag replied quickly. "In the final days of the world, when hope was lost and darkness held the plains of Chaenandria in their grip, a warrior-king—a *hoo-mani* of the ancient days—would come again out of the north country, beyond the Straits of Erebus, a living man from the land of the dead. He would walk the face of the world for a time, hidden from the eyes of the sharpest watchers, and then—then he would make his great journey of conquest in the name of light, bring down the darkness, and usher in ten thousand years of peace!"

Five notes . . . Five notes . . .

Your fate you will loom . . . the weave of your doom . . .

"I hate to disturb this reverent scene," Ethis said with both sets of hands folded across his chest, "but unless we get far from here very quickly, we won't be enjoying anything *like* ten thousand years of peace. The dwarf is right about one thing—we have to stay a step ahead of what happened here or it's all over for us."

Drakis pulled his gaze away from the wild-eyed manticore with difficulty. "Yes . . . we have to get away from here. The quickest way would be to use the folds . . . with most of the Centurai not yet returned, we may be able to get through some of them."

"And then what?" Ethis asked at once. "Do you have a plan, or do we just wander about the countryside pillaging until the odds catch up with us?"

Drakis considered the chimerian for a moment before he answered. He suddenly realized that while he was surrounded by those he knew . . . several of whom he had this morning counted as more dear to him than his own life . . . he really didn't know any of them at all.

"*. . . Sure, Drakis, your father came from the northlands beyond the dwarves," his mother said as they washed their master's clothes. His feet dangled from the edge of the stone shelf. "Must I tell you again of how we were freeborn in the wilds . . . ?*"

"We go north," Drakis said, his words defying anyone to contradict him. "We make our way as far as we can passing through the folds, and then we set off on foot."

"Such a wise choice, Master Drakis, a wise choice indeed," chirped the dwarf. "I know those lands well. and, leaving all modesty aside . . ."

"An easy task," Ethis sniffed.

". . . I can tell you that no creature who breathes today can help you pass through those wide, untamed lands safer than Jugar Dregas, King of Jesters and Jester to kings! You won't regret it . . . not one bit!"

"I'm already regretting it," Drakis replied, "but as none of the rest of us have any idea about the world beyond the totems of Timuran, we'll just have to bring you with us."

"North?" Ethis said, raising one hairless brow. "Why north?"

Hear the call of the song whispering . . .

Follow the Northern Wind's call . . .
Training and instinct.

"Because it pleases me," Drakis replied.

"How far north?" Ethis pressed.

". . . Forget it, Dre," the tall boy said smiling down at him as they worked under the sunshine in the fields. "It's too far to walk no matter how long . . ."

"As far north as we must," Drakis snapped, then turned to Belag. "So this is all there is then?"

"Aye," Belag nodded his great head. "Many are dead . . . many more have lost their minds . . . others deny their own thoughts and can imagine no other life. We are all who have come."

"Then it will have to be enough," Drakis turned, but the large hand of the manticore turned him back around.

"Please," Belag said, his huge, yellow eyes peering into Drakis' face. "Tell me . . . I have to know . . ."

"Belag, we've got to move now while . . ."

"Please," the manticore said, gripping the human by both shoulders. "I have to *know* . . . are you the One?"

Drakis let out a quick, short breath.

Jugar spoke from behind somewhere at his back.

"Yes," the dwarf said with words deliberate and carefully spoken. "Tell us: Are you the warrior-king of the prophecy?"

The Hall of the Past soared above him, not yet fallen to flame and rubble but as it stood just hours before.

"Are you a god?"

The dwarf smiled in return, "Ah . . . you want to know if I am a god?"

Drakis glanced at the flaming ruin across the hilltop.

"Belag," he said, his mouth suddenly dry. "That depends."

The manticore gazed at him, his eyes puzzled for a time, and then he nodded slowly as he turned away. Belag gathered the still-shaken RuuKag and the Lyric to him and then moved with them down the hill following the line of darkened totems. Ethis considered for a moment and then gathered the cloth at the back of the dwarf's neck into one of his strong hands. The two of them followed the manticore and his charges down the slope.

Drakis watched them for a moment and then turned and bent down, offering his hand to the woman with whom he had hoped for so much earlier that same morning.

"Mala, it's time to go."

The young human woman sat on the ground, her face turned toward the flames. She spoke, but it was not for anyone's ears. "I liked it here. It was . . . terrible and . . . unspeakable . . . but at least I didn't have to know about it. Now I'll have to carry it with me . . . and I don't want the burden. Was it so bad, really, just to love you and hope for something better . . . even if it would never come . . . rather than to *know* it could never be?"

"It was a lie, Mala," he said softly.

"But it was a lovely lie," she sighed.

He drew her up from the ground. The others had already started down the slope, following the now-dead totems, their lights extinguished, back toward the Fold Temple. He turned away from the ruin of his former life and led her by her hand down the slope.

Mala followed, her eyes looking back all the way.

Book 2:

THE PREY

CHAPTER 16

Heart of the Empire

SOEN TJEN-REI, Inquisitor of the elven Order of the Iblisi, stepped through the delicately inlaid twenty-foot tall doors, grateful for the warmth of the radiant sun that thawed his chill bones. The grand reception hall had been unbelievably cold—undoubtedly someone's interpretation of the Emperor's Will—which even his layers of ceremonial robes were of little help in keeping at bay. It might have felt warmer to him, he reflected, if he had had any real interest in the proceedings. Imperial audiences were, it was true, generally convoluted and complex as the centerpiece of the game of Imperial politics should be. And yes, there was an occasional death and even moments of honest surprise to be had, but this was a game for the Ministers and Masters of the Orders to play . . . not an elf like him.

He was an Inquisitor of the Iblisi, and his province was the truth—something generally unknown and unwanted in the Imperial audiences.

He stood at the railed edge of the Emperor's Cloud Palace and surveyed the enormous city arrayed below him. The palace was currently facing west toward the setting sun. Its rays reflected off the thousands of gleaming avatrium that hung over the city like glorious lilies floating on an invisible pond. Many of those closest to the Emperor's own floating palace were of extraordinary grace and size, an obvious display of power and wealth that required no further word to be spoken on the subject. That they grew smaller and, in his eye, more reasonable the farther they were situated toward the horizon was yet another indication that he was standing at the very center around which the entire world revolved.

At least for today, he thought with a frown. *For today.*

Below him and between the forest of avatrium, Soen caught sight of the Coliseum and the northern edge of the great Circus. Several gladiators were practicing on the Coliseum floor, smaller than ants to his eye at this distance. Almost overshadowing them was the towering avatria of Myrdin-dai—the center of that Order's mystical power and teachings. The Myrdin-dai were currently basking in the glory of their contribution to the victory over the last of the Dwarven Kings. Their planning, execution, and management of the folds had been publicly recognized as a contributing factor in the conquest, and the grace of the Imperial thanks rested with them. This praise went down very hard with the Occuran, the Order that was in constant competition with the Myrdin-dai for control of the Aether and the network of folds that it powered. The Myrdin-dai's recent management of the fold system for the war seemed to be a shift in the Imperial favor—and the Occuran were forced to offer their respects with as much dignity as society demanded. His own Order, the Iblisi, was closely tied to the Occuran. Soen's presence at the audience today was intended to demonstrate to the Myrdin-dai that the Iblisi would not be diminished in the eyes of the Emperor despite their ties to the Occuran.

He sighed and looked west down the curving length of the wide avenue known as the Vira Rhonas until his gaze drifted to the horizon and the setting sun.

How did I come to this? he thought as he shifted uncomfortably in the layered, exquisite robes. *An Inquisitor of the Iblisi whose very name has been whispered with dread and awe in the farthest outposts of the Empire, and now I stand here as an errand boy fawning to the Imperial Will.*

He had seen more of the Empire than any other living elf, so far as he knew, and at that it was only a fraction of the glory that rested under the sure hand of the Emperor. He had stalked rebel manticores across their own rolling plains in the Chaenandria Reaches. He had sailed in war galleys against the separatists of the Benis Isles and infiltrated the conspiracy of the Aergus Coast Barons.

That was what had done him in; the fall of the Barons had whispered his name in the Imperial ear. He was no longer an Inquisitor but had somehow transcended that to become a symbol—the incarnation of Iblisi fealty to the Emperor and his damnable Will. That Soen's original mission had been merely to investigate whether the Iblisi should give covert aid to the Barons was conveniently washed away in a sea of sophistry, and he emerged from the cleansing a pure hero and loyal servant of the Empire.

Such was his fate—a comedy for the enjoyment of the gods while he languished in the cold heart of Imperial Glory.

Soen turned from the railing. Such melancholy did not become him, he decided, as he stepped across the polished granite, rounding the path that circumnavigated the base of the Cloud Palace's enormous avatria. Though the way was broad, it quickly became crowded with petitioners, guildmasters, clerks, cagistrates and ministers, not to mention the ubiquitous Cloud Guardians.

Soen knew from the chevrons on their breastplates that the Guardians were of the Order of the Vash—one of three separate military orders who vied for Imperial favor in the Empire. Each maintained their headquarters within the boundaries of Tsujen's Wall, the demarcation of the older part of the city and romantically considered the most blessed by the gods. The Iblisi had a number of agreements in place with the Vash and often supported them in their dealings with the Ministry of Conquest. Their being entrusted as the Cloud Guardians—replacing the Order of the Krish—should have worked to his advantage.

But no advantage, it seemed, could get him off of the Cloud Palace any faster. There were seven towers rising from the perimeter of the garden far below and surrounding the great palace's hovering avatria. Each tower represented one of the Seven Estates of elven society, and each provided ascending and descending shaft access to the palace ... limited, of course, to those of a specified Estate or higher. That he would mix at all with the Sixth or Fifth Estate traffic was unthinkable, and though he could see the Fourth Tower entrance, the very thought of packing himself in with the rest of the lowing herd of guild traffic made his skin crawl. He could, he knew, turn and reenter the palace itself, but that held the danger of encountering someone that he either knew or should know and thereby being trapped in yet another round of favor trading, positioning, and influence bargaining, all delivered in subtext, context, and always from behind a smile.

Though he personally had an intense dislike of being touched by anyone, he would rather push his way through a mob than deal with another politician. He managed to cut his own path through the throng and was relieved to see the wide walkway beyond leading to the Tower of the Third Estate free of all but a handful of masters and ministers. He quickly followed the gleaming path as it continued around the base of the Cloud Palace until it came at last to a nearly deserted platform and its bridge to the Third Tower.

Soen had long ago set aside the privileges associated with being a descendant of a noble House ... but at times like this, he reflected, it had its convenient uses. He quickly crossed the bridge with its crystal lattice railings and ornate renderings of the crests of those Houses that had donated to its construction. Then he passed through the archway into the tower itself.

Soen stood on a wide platform opening onto one of two shafts that plunged down the full height of the towers. This one was the descending shaft and was filled with a blue swirling light. He stepped out over the precipice without hesitation and began his slow drift downward through the air.

It was a fine defensive mechanism, he thought, as he drifted down past the occasional window cut into the curved wall. You had to have access to the Aether to use the shaft—and the only ones who had access to the Aether were the elves.

Soen frowned. The elves had not always been the only ones to command the power of Aether, he knew, but that fact was only one grain of sand in the mountain of secrets that he and all of the Iblisi kept.

Keeping the truth safe was the essence of their work.

The Iblisi's feet touched softly on the fitted stones at the base of the Third Tower, and he stepped quickly through the arch opening into the evening air. The Garden of Kuchen spread before him, teaming with elves as was common at this time late in the day. The setting sun cast a warm glow across the wide garden. It was a beautiful place, carefully manicured and maintained in honor of the Emperor's wife, for whom it was currently named, and shaded over all by the titanic bulk of the Cloud Palace directly overhead. It smelled green and alive and called to the souls of the elves who came to it each day that they might forget the walls they had built to enclose themselves and the desperation of their spirits that longed for open space but had compromised themselves into servitude to the Will of the Emperor in all its incarnations.

Soen hated it, for it reminded him of the true fields and green spaces that were far from this place. Having tasted of its truth, it was hard for him to endure the lie. So he walked around the edge of the garden as quickly as he could on the south side, following the fitted cobblestones of the Vira Rhonas past where they intersected with the Vira Condemnis to the south. He barely glanced in the direction of the Forums of the Estates, which stood behind rows of standing columns down the arcade to his left. Both the Circus and the Coliseum could be found in that direction, but he had little use for the games and no time for them in any event. Beyond the forums the Vira Rhonas widened, cutting a broad curving path through the heart of the Imperial City that was nearly as old as the Empire itself.

The Vira was just beginning to come to life with the evening revels. Litters supported by teams of manticorian

slaves quickly jogged up and down the street, bearing
their masters to and fro at their whim. A number of Fifth
Estate hawkers served their guild Orders by calling out
their wares to the growing crowd. As he walked down the
street, Soen saw a dwarf—a rare enough sight even in the
Imperial City—dancing nervously before a group of jeer-
ing elven youth. They prodded the stumpy creature with
their ornamental swords.

Soen shook his head. Poor dwarf. The youth today had
taken to wearing these next-to-useless engraved blades as
a fashion. Now, with the news of the victory over the Last
Kingdom, that dwarf was almost certain not to live through
the night of celebrations.

Next his eye was caught by a string of Muserian
slaves—orange-hewed barbarian elves from the southern
Aergus Coast—being pulled wide-eyed behind a manticorian overseer. He walked beside them, eyeing them
with mild curiosity before the overseer turned southward
down the Vira Coliseum. They were destined for one of the
newer noble Houses that had sprung up on the west side of
the River Jolnar against the Mnerian Hills, Soen thought
idly. Poor fools.

But poor fools aren't we all, he reflected as he continued
between the buildings on either side of the paved stones.
The structures on his right were known collectively as
The Ministries. There were no fewer than thirteen separate main ministries and more than an equal number of
subministries making up each of those. The mandates of
the various ministries overlapped each other in the most
confusing of ways, and yet it was the Emperor's Will not
only that this mess *not* be straightened out but that it reflected a wonderful redundancy in the government—that
should one ministry fail to work toward the Imperial Will,
then another would surely do so. The jurisdictional battles
among the separate ministries of Health, Nutrition and—
for reasons beyond Soen's understanding—Caravans were
perennial. The Ministry of War and the Ministry of Security, it was said, fought more battles between them as allies
in the Emperor's Will than in the field against any enemy.

This was further complicated by the strict caste system of the Estates, which dated back to the founding of the Empire by Rhonas and which had since those ancient days been so carefully codified that progression between the estates was, by Imperial decree, to rest only in the hands of the Emperor personally.

Then there were the Orders of the Empire: guilds, elite military Orders, wizardry unions, and other specialized clans that vied to force their own agendas and ascendancy in power on the Emperor's Will. Each had its own combination of gods they worshiped and unique pacts with other Orders, allegiances and enmities. Membership in the orders transcended castes, at least in theory. Any caste could be a member of any Order by application, but the vagaries and secrecy in the selection process were such that each Order had effective control over the makeup of its membership. The Orders were diverse—but only so far as their strength and power were supported.

None of which accounted for the rather public and often bloody conflicts of the vaunted Forums—one for the Estate Lords and the other the "voice of the common elf"—whatever that was supposed to mean.

Soen shook his head and smiled. *By the Emperor's Will, it all works perfectly.*

The Inquisitor came to the end of the Vira Rhonas and stepped onto the Gods' Bridge. It was one of the oldest bridges of the nine crossing the Jolnar and led to the oldest part of the city, the Isle of the Gods. It was not a terribly impressive island, as such; it sat as a rocky spit of ground between two branches of the River Jolnar that obligingly flowed around it. Still, as legend would have it, it was the place where Rhonas drove his spear into the ground and declared this spot to be where he would found his Empire. The first temples were built here. There were newer and more spacious temples in the districts beyond Tsujen's Wall, but the temples on this sliver of land were still the most revered by the Rhonasians. Soen crossed the bridge and passed among the ancient buildings. The Occuran made their home here, a privilege granted them by the

Emperor just short of one hundred years ago, but now their favor was waning, and Soen wondered just how long it would be before the Imperial Will got around to evicting the Occuran as neighbors to the gods and just what the Occuran would do about it.

Soen crossed the small island and came to the North Bridge. On the other side of the river rose the squat, angular walls of the Old Keep. They were designed in a time before the Aether, when war was waged as it should be: with hand on steel. It was the oldest structure in the city and the home of his own Order.

Soen took in a deep breath. Ministries, Orders, Estates ... by the Emperor's Will, all worked perfectly because it *was* the Emperor's will that it be so. To say otherwise was treason. To think otherwise was disloyal. To *be* otherwise was unacceptable.

So the perfection was maintained not in practice but in perception. The knowledge that the current Emperor ascended to the throne by murdering the previous Emperor as he was distracted by his lust for the wife of a recently assassinated Guild Master was not "working toward the Imperial Will." Indeed, that the entire history of the Rhonas Empire was filled with such unpleasant, vicious, horrifying events was also seen as "not working toward the Imperial Will." This concern for the solidarity, security, and loyalty of the greatest elven nation in all history extended itself down through every ministry, Order, and Estate as well. Anything unpleasant need not be true if it is not known. So their own histories were constantly rewritten for the sake of "working toward the Imperial Will."

Each part of the body politic played a vital role but, to Soen, none so important as the role his own Order played nor so dangerous.

The Iblisi alone existed to know the truth ... and it was their task to make sure that no one discovered it.

CHAPTER 17

The Keeper

THE OLD KEEP was a misnomer; it was more of a fortress than a keep proper. The angular path of its massive outer walls combined with those of matching trenches designed to both stop the enemy and inflict as much damage on them as possible. It was the oldest remaining structure in the city, said by many to have been built by the hand of the first emperor, Rhon Sah-Tseu himself. The Keep's antiquity was apparent at a single glance, for it lacked the grace and fine, curving lines of the more recent structures of the Empire. To the critical elven eye it was vaguely offensive as a brutish, massive, and graceless pile of carefully fitted stones that was an unpleasant reminder of dark origins best forgotten.

Soen never failed to smile at the irony of the thought each time he crossed the courtyard of the Keep, for now the building itself fulfilled that same function which its visage inspired. Within its walls, Soen knew, were kept all the "unpleasant reminders" of their dark origins safely hidden from view.

The Inquisitor stepped through the dark archway of an angular tower and with rapid steps made his way down a worn circular staircase. Under any other circumstances he would have already been removing the ceremonial trappings of his official robes. There were books, scrolls, maps, and tapestries in the Forbidden Grotto that were calling to him. He longed to lose the present in the writings of the past but he had one final duty to perform before he could comfortably claim some time for himself.

So, he turned off the staircase—how marvelous to have to use stairs, he thought—and made his way down the long central corridor. Several of his fellow Inquisitors passed him, though none acknowledged him in any way. It was just another sign in a long and seemingly endless series of signs that his presence here was considered unearned and unwelcome. It was of no real concern to him if they didn't want him here. He didn't want to be here either.

The corridor opened into a large antechamber, but waiting was not Soen's intention. He turned at once to the black doors of oiled wood and pulled them open.

"Ah, Inquisitor Soen Tjen-rei." The raspy, alto voice came from the far end of the chamber, dark as the polished slate of the floor over which it rolled.

"Keeper Ch'drei," Soen replied, bowing deeply. "I have come to report on the proceedings of today's audience between the Emperor and . . ."

"No." Ch'drei held up her pale hand. "Close the doors behind you. There are too many ears who prey on my words."

Soen stopped speaking at once. He was a trained observer and knew when it was time to talk, when it was time to listen. "You learn more when you stop speaking" was a motto that had served him well.

He quietly closed the heavy doors, then turned back to face into the hall again. The room did not have the vaulted ceilings so prized in later architecture. Like the fortress surrounding it, the Keeper's Hall was oppressive, its ceiling hanging low overhead and supported by thick, squat pillars. The walls of the room were dark so that the glowing light from the globe sconces on each pillar was swallowed up in the blackness. At the end of the hall, opposite the entrance doors, sat the throne of the Keeper atop three steps of a dais. Three steps were all it could afford without forcing the Keeper to strike her head on the low ceiling whenever she stood.

On that throne, Ch'drei pressed the long fingers of her hands together. The Keeper was old, even among elves. The skin of her face and long forehead looked almost transparent. It sagged in places and seemed to have been pulled too tightly in others. The mane of her hair seemed to float around her skull like a fine mist. Her lips were drawn back in her age, exposing her teeth in what might too easily have been mistaken for a grin. She stooped over as she sat on the Throne of the Oracle, her body curling forward around her arching spine. She looked frail, but Soen knew better. The Keeper's featureless eyes were still shining and as black as a grave. Soen knew that there were those who had thought it was time for the Keeper to ... well, relinquish her position in favor of younger, more dynamic individuals such as they themselves presented. Those who had sought the Keeper's forced retirement were no longer available to testify regarding how they were stopped in their assassination plots; they had simply disappeared.

"Soen, my son," Ch'drei said with bored detachment, "you are a most talented servant of the Iblisi Mandate and demonstrably a loyal servant of the Imperial Will."

She is not interested in my report on the court, Soen thought. *Something has changed.*

The Keeper shifted slightly in her throne. The words needed to be said, and so she was saying them although both Ch'drei and Soen were fully aware that they were only preliminary and without substance. "Indeed, your abilities have brought your name to be whispered with both glory and honor in the ears of many of the Orders even here in the capital of the world."

In change there is danger, Soen thought, *and profit. Which will it be this time?*

"The Keeper is most generous in her words," Soen replied evenly.

A hint of a smile pulled at the corner of the old elf woman's lips. "I can afford to be generous with words, my son, but the position of our Order among the powers that rule requires more circumspect frugality."

"And may I dare presume that I might assist the Order in some meaningful way?"

"Can you leave within the hour?"

Soen's heart jumped, but he maintained his outward calm. "I serve at the pleasure of the Keeper—I can leave at your word."

Ch'drei nodded, then straightened slightly. "The Myrdin-dai have asked for the assistance of the Iblisi— more particularly, *your* assistance."

"They asked for me?"

"By name," Ch'drei replied. "Had you not been at court, they would have demanded that you go with them at once." The old woman reached out with her bent hand, gesturing him closer. "Come, my boy, I'll bandy niceties with the primping fools of the other Orders but let's have some plain talk between us."

Soen smiled, the points of his ears quivering as he shook his head. "Who among us ever has 'plain talk'?"

"Oh, nonsense," Ch'drei spat the words with disdain, "If I were fifty years younger, I'd throw this at you, and you'd be dropping dead before you could utter another word!"

"*That*," Soen said as he casually walked the length of the hall, "is the Baton Seal of the Iblisi Keeper, and you shouldn't be throwing it at anyone."

"I'll throw it at whomever I please," Ch'drei said, her featureless eyes squinting at him. "I'm especially fond of hitting insolent young boys with it."

"I have heard that the Keeper might have found *better* uses for insolent, young boys," Soen said with a lightness in his words.

"Perhaps," Ch'drei said through a dark chuckle; then she paused. "Soen, the Myrdin-dai have a problem on the Icaran Frontier. They need it silenced, and they want you to do it for them."

The Icaran Frontier! The farthest western reaches of the Empire and about as far from the Imperial Court as one might hope to be assigned. Even if it were only briefly . . .

"What is the problem?"

"Something happened in the folds," Ch'drei spoke softly. "The Myrdin-dai have been basking in the glory of their handling of the folds in this last war against the dwarves. They've even gone so far as to make something of a public spectacle of themselves, using this as an opportunity to rub the noses of the Occuran in their success. Now something has happened in the folds of the frontier that has them worried—worried enough that they insist that *you*, the favored Iblisi of the Emperor himself, take care of it discreetly. They want it silenced, and they want it done by someone close to the Emperor. And they're willing to promise anything and *pay* anything to make it happen quickly. You're to be given complete access to the folds controlled by the Myrdin-dai throughout the Empire to serve this purpose. You'll be given a commission and seal specifically for this purpose."

"Generous of them to provide transport," Soen considered, "especially since it will allow them to follow my movements."

"Who trusts anyone anymore?"

"And they would not tell you what actually happened in the folds?" Soen asked.

"They didn't even try to lie to me," Ch'drei said with a shrug. "That was the most insulting—that they didn't even bother to make something up for me. I tell you, elves today have no respect for their elders."

Soen drew in a deep breath and nodded, his own black eyes looking at the Keeper from under his heavy brows. "So it is in the service of the Emperor's Will that the Keeper of the Iblisi is commissioning me to travel the Myrdin-dai folds to the Icaran Frontier to silence an unspecified matter that is currently distressing a companion Order of the Empire?"

"Oh, what nonsense!"

Both Ch'drei and Soen laughed heartily.

"I too soon forget why I like you, Soen," Ch'drei said through her grinning smile. "You have such a charmingly dry sense of humor. No, of course that isn't why I'm sending you. I wouldn't mind currying a little favor with the Myrdin-dai right now, but, no, that's not why you're going."

Peril or profit? Which will it be?

"The Myrdin-dai were not my only urgent audience today. Their rivals, the Occuran, visited me this morning," Ch'drei said, her voice softening. "Something has gone very wrong with the Aether Wells of the Icaran Frontier."

"*Twin* trouble in the Western Provinces?"

"Yes. It has caused disturbance patterns resonating all through the Aether links throughout the Empire. The Occuran tell me the Aether Wells have failed on the frontier."

Soen raised his eyebrows. "Failed?"

"Yes . . . failed."

Soen straightened to stand upright, considering the implications of what he had just heard. "It's been a long time since a well failed. Some of these Fourth Estate lords go to the frontier without knowing what is required to survive. Still, I don't see why you need *me* to . . ."

"It wasn't just one well that failed, Soen," Ch'drei said. "This wasn't just some mistake made by a careless House Lord. The Aether in the entire region collapsed, and a number of Houses in the Province have fallen completely."

"Fallen?" Soen's left brow rose in surprise. "One House falling is a potential catastrophe . . . but the fall of multiple Houses at once is unimaginable."

"The warding glyphs that link the Wells are meant to prevent such a cascading failure—severing the connection to the collapsed Well before any damage is done," Soen mused. "How could they fail in multiple Wells at once?

"According to the Occuran, the Wells all across the Western Provinces not only collapsed completely but inverted for a time, but we do not know enough," the Keeper continued. "Communication from the Frontier has failed both from the Occuran and the Myrdin-dai, but from the little we know as many as a dozen Houses could have fallen—and that could be an optimistic number. The glyphs must have worked eventually or the entire Empire would have gone dark."

"What about containment?" Soen asked, his mind still racing through the possibilities.

"Again, we don't know—and that is why you must depart at once. You have to discover the cause of this and secure its truth. If knowledge of any vulnerability to the system of Aether Wells were to become commonly known . . ."

"I agree," Soen mused with a frown, "but if even a dozen or so Houses have fallen, the number of slaves released from their Devotions alone . . ."

"I'm only interested in the cause of this collapse—not a few 'bolters.' If any slaves have something to do with this, then, of course, hunt them down."

"And the problems of the Occuran and the Myrdin-dai are related?"

Ch'drei shrugged. "Beyond doubt—but that is for you to discover."

Soen nodded. "How do you want the rest of the slaves handled?"

"If they can be usefully enthralled again, then ship them here for new Devotions; otherwise kill the broken ones," Ch'drei said though she was not really interested. "I'll leave that to your discretion. It is good policy, makes us a profit on the resale of the slaves, and maintains our rather ruthless image."

"I'll need a Quorum."

"You may take two Codexia of your choice."

"Qinsei and Phang, then, if the choice is mine," Soen nodded as he thought. "And the four Assesia?"

"I should think that Yarou, Shonoc and Wreth would be honored by the task. Perhaps you could also take young Jukung as your fourth?"

Soen smiled once more. He knew Jukung was a spy for Ch'drei. This assignment was important enough that the Keeper wanted a second set of eyes to report to her.

Who trusts anyone anymore . . .

"So the Myrdin-dai provide the transport and means to allow us to solve a mystery for their rivals, the Occuran,"

Soen chuckled. "We garner favor with *both* and neither is the wiser."

"Everyone profits," Ch'drei smiled. "Especially *us*."

"Thank you, Keeper." Soen bowed. "I am honored to serve with such a Quorum . . . and may I add my personal thanks as it will be good to serve under an open sky again."

"Do not thank me so quickly," Ch'drei returned. "You do not know what awaits you in the Western Provinces—and many a truth has left its Inquisitor buried beneath that same open sky."

CHAPTER 18

Tracks

THE EVENING HAD DEEPENED into a purple twilight around the horizon by the time Assesia Jukung joined the rest of the Quorum in the courtyard of the Keep. The globe-torches mounted on the inner walls of the Keep had just flickered to life in the gathering night, illuminating the ancient flagstones beneath their feet. Above the walls to the east, the towering subatria of the Imperial City shone in the night with a soft incandescence, the Cloud Palace itself shining above them all.

Soen saw none of its beauty; his eyes were focused on the Quorum that had formed before him. Each of them was clothed in much the same manner as himself, in a dull reddish-brown hooded robe with a black sash closure at the waist. They also, he was pleased to note, appeared prepared for an extended absence as all were shouldering backpacks bulging with their field goods.

Each also held the unique staff of their Order—the Matei—which was simultaneously the tool of their protection, the symbol of their office, and the means by which they measured out their often final, deadly judgments regarding the lives of those whom fate caused to cross their path. Just over six feet in length, the smooth wood of the staff had a polished steel cap with a diamond-edged spike at one end. The upper third of the staff was carved with intricate patterns and ended with an ornate headpiece representing the Eye of Qin—symbol of the god worshiped by their Order—fitted with a large crystal. Soen noted with satisfaction that within each one the power of the Aether shone; their staffs were fully charged for the journey ahead.

"I am Soen Tjen-rei," he said to the assembly without preamble. "We serve the Will of the Emperor tonight by journeying to the Icaran Frontier. It will be a long road but one that you are well prepared to face. We travel the folds of the Myrdin-dai with their blessing and should, with the favor of the gods, arrive at our area of need quickly. Where we are needed, we do not yet know, but when we arrive, it will be with death staring into our faces. Be prepared to stare back and spit in its eye."

Dark chuckles rolled among the members of the Quorum.

"Qinsei, you will be my first . . . Phang, my second," Soen nodded to each of them. It was necessary to make clear the order of command in case Soen somehow got himself in over his head. His death was unimportant; continuing the mission was. Qinsei was female and Phang was male. It made some difference in terms of their abilities, but generally he liked the idea of the balance it represented. "Watch each other. Trust in the Order—trust no one else. We are the Iblisi . . . and we serve the Imperial Will!"

"We serve the Imperial Will," they answered back in unison.

"We are one!" Soen shouted.

"We are one!" the Quorum shouted in reply.

Soen turned and pulled the deep hood up over his head until its forward edge hung low over his sloping forehead. He shifted his own Matei into his right hand and took his first step on a journey whose end he did not yet see.

"Where are we?" Wreth asked quietly.

"An Iblisi always knows where he is," Phang replied in

the same voice. "Even when he's lost. Did they teach you nothing in the Lyceum?"

Soen allowed himself a rueful smile, then said in a voice that carried throughout the Quorum, "How many folds is that, Qinsei?"

"Eleven, Master Inquisitor," she replied.

"Three more, then, and we should be within the borders of Ibania," Soen said.

Soen stepped off the fold platform. The Myrdin-dai priest who was managing the portal was watching them closely but always glanced away whenever Soen turned in his direction. It was the expected reaction. The Iblisi were, by Imperial decree, their own justice.

Soen gazed out over the assembly area. This one was in a hollow rimmed with tree-covered hills. It was the same sort of undulating geography that typified much of the lands northwest of Rhonas proper. The last four folds had been into similar terrain.

And each was similarly boring, Soen thought.

The weary slave armies of the Empire were being herded home once more. Most of these were from the Army of the Emperor's Blade heading back in the direction from which Soen's Quorum had just come. The Impress Warriors of the various Legions, Centurais, Cohorts and Octia were emptying into the holding pen of the surrounding totems from the fold at the far side of the hollow. They wandered about listlessly until their group was sorted out by the Myrdin-dai and their various Tribunes and then meekly filed through their respective folds on their own journeys homeward. He had seen it all before; these weary slaves with different faces had been shuffling out of every fold portal he and his Quorum had entered since the central junction in the subatria of the Myrdin-dai temple in the Imperial City. If there were a problem here, Soen had not yet found its edges and did not expect to do so for another six folds. It was a long way to the frontier, and even utilizing the folds it had taken them four hours to get this far.

"Phang, you know what to do," Soen said, tugging at his gloves.

"Find the Field Marshal, show him the baton, secure our passage, and report." Phang's words reflected Soen's own boredom. "Aye, Master Inquisitor."

The Codexia turned to make his way around the hollow. but Qinsei, standing behind Soen, called out. "One moment more, Phang."

Soen turned a curious eye on his First. "Yes, Codexia Qinsei?"

"The road is long before us," Qinsei said, her voice smooth and unusually deep, "and it is late. Our problems lie ahead of us, and wisdom might be found in resting mind and body to prepare for them when they are discovered. Might the Inquisitor consider camping here for the night?"

Soen considered for a moment. "You make an entire argument in a single breath, Codexia Qinsei."

The Codexia only smiled back and bowed slightly.

"Still, few words often carry the greatest merit," Soen continued. They had been traveling against the tide of warriors flowing through the gates since they left the capital. He was beginning to feel the weariness of the journey as well. "The question in my mind is whether to camp here or continue a few folds farther on . . . wait!"

A scream cut once more across the herd from the fold portal on the far side of the hollow. A chimerian stood on the platform before the shimmering fold and howled such a terrible sound that the Myrdin-dai and others on the platform scattered at once, stumbling over each other as they tried to get as far away from the mad creature as possible.

The chimerian was a horrifying sight. His skin was streaked with blood, glistening in the light of the globe-torches hung around the fold platform. He had extended his body to its full height, and all four arms stretched out from its sides, each holding a different type of sword. The chain mail vest he wore was ragged and broken, pierced in several places where the creature's own blood oozed out. But it was the eyes—fixed wide open and unblinking—that were windows into a torment without depth and a mind lost to its merciless ravages.

"*Run!*" the chimerian screamed. "*Run from your lives!*"

The mad creature lunged forward, leaping from the platform, its blades slicing with soft ringing sounds through the evening air. Heedless, the chimerian dashed forward into the herd, sword blades churning. The surprised warriors leaped back, several of them reacting instinctively to face their opponent, but the chimerian continued to dash across the base of the hollow, deftly slipping past one, slicing into the side of another, rolling around a third. The sound of the Impress Warriors rose to a thunderous roar, and still the chimerian continued its pell-mell charge across the field, its eyes fixed on one thing.

An exit portal . . . and Soen's Quorum alone stood in its path.

Soen stepped forward, spinning his Matei staff deftly in front of him, then gripping it in both hands. The headpiece suddenly flared with brilliant light, an incandescent blade forming outward from the top of the staff into the shape of a razor-edged scythe. At the bottom of the staff, a globe of crackling blue light was forming at the same time.

Soen kept his eyes on the mad chimerian, widened his stance and waited.

The chimerian plunged directly toward the Inquisitor, its mind fixed on reaching the exit portal beyond, its blades whirling so as to obliterate anyone or anything that stood between it and its next passage.

The young Assesia Wreth took a step forward, brandishing his own Matei . . . but Qinsei held up a cautioning hand to restrain him.

"*Run from the dreams!*" it babbled as it charged. "*They're coming! They're right behind! Run!*"

The chimerian lunged at Soen.

The Inquisitor rolled backward, his Matei spinning in his hands. Soen planted the headpiece in the ground next to him just as the glowing ball at the bottom of the staff discharged.

The chimerian soared straight up into the air, its body bent double by the force of the Aether discharged into its abdomen. The mad creature screamed horribly, and its arms—still gripping the blades in its hands—twisted angrily in the air. Soen held firm to the staff, his arms shaking with the effort. The glowing blade at the head of the staff was now against the ground, Soen using its force for leverage against the chimerian as the creature continued to writhe, now suspended over the staff in the air.

Soen looked up, his black elven eyes fixed on the chimerian. "I am Iblisi; I am the Emperor's Will . . . you are commanded to obey!"

The chimerian fixed his hateful gaze on the Inquisitor and then, screaming, slashed at the air with all four of the blades in his hands. "*Death to the Emperor! Death to his dreams!*"

Soen's eyes widened.

The chimerian's back arched impossibly backward, and then its entire body suddenly contracted and thickened. The tall lithe form was replaced by a stocky short one. "I'm awake now!" the creature said with a dangerous edge in its voice. "I won't sleep ever again . . . not for you or any of your bastard brothers!"

Soen nodded, then yelled, "*Death to the Emperor!*"

Assesia Wreth gasped.

A shocked silence filled the space around them. Jukung stepped forward, an angry frown on his face but Phang placed a restraining hand against the young elf's chest.

"*Death to his dreams!*" Soen shouted. His eyes were fixed on the chimerian above him.

The mad warrior suddenly relaxed.

"What is your name, friend," Soen asked quietly.

"My . . . name?" came the whimpering reply.

"I've come to end your dreams, friend," Soen said in even tones. "But I must know your name."

The chimerian blinked at him, unsure.

"What was your name in the dream?"

The chimerian curled his lips back in loathing. "Chentas—that is what *they* called me."

"And your House, Chentas," Soen's voice was calm, his eyes fixed on the chimerian. "What was your House in the dream?"

Chentas began giggling, blood running down from the corner of his mouth. "I won't tell you! You're going to put me back to sleep—send me back to those dreams!"

"No, Chentas, I can't do that," Soen replied. "I've come to *end* your dreams." The Inquisitor was beginning to sweat with the effort of keeping the chimerian suspended above him in the air. "I promise you . . . tell me your House in the dreams, and I will end them for you forever."

"Forever?"

"Forever."

Chentas shuddered.

"TELL ME!" Soen yelled at the chimerian hovering ten feet above him in the air.

"I dreamed of a slave named Chentas, of the House . . . of the House of Acheran," the chimerian sneered. "Now keep your bargain, Iblisi!"

Soen frowned and then nodded. The magic holding the chimerian collapsed at the Inquisitor's command. Chentas fell, but before he reached the ground, Soen whirled with the Matei, the scythe blade flashing through the air. In a single deft stroke, the wheeling Soen drove the long, mystical blade across the neck of the chimerian.

Chentas' head rolled a few feet across the ground, coming to rest at the feet of Assesia Wreth.

Four swords rang against the ground, falling from the limp hands of Chentas' body just as Soen finished his turn, planted his feet in a wide stance, and swung the blade down from above his head, driving it through the back of the chimerian and out the front of its chest.

Only then did Soen hear the thunderous shouts of the Impress Warriors around him. The Tribunes were quickly sorting them back into their units and regaining order, as Soen knew they would. He whispered to his Matei, and the glowing blade vanished, leaving only the blood to emerge from the wound.

"Master Inquisitor," Qinsei spoke as she approached him. "What does it mean?"

Soen knelt next to the body, considering it for a time, and then stood up, shifting his gaze to the fold portal at the other end of the marshaling field. *We have not even crossed the Ibanian borders,* he thought. *It is worse than the Keeper believes ... worse than even I could imagine.*

Soen turned back to his First. "It means that the trouble has found us. We will not be camping here or, I suspect, anywhere else tonight. Phang, have Assesia Yarou make a sketch of the Devotional tattoo on the chimerian's head—he's got a talent for that sort of thing—then prepare the Quorum for battle."

"Battle, Master?" Phang asked in surprise.

"Yes, battle, Phang," Soen said, placing his long hands on his hips as he thought. "We're going to follow the trail back to its source, and if this Chentas is an example of what we have ahead of us, our best course will be following a trail of murderous, insane slaves attacking everyone in sight to their source."

Qinsei's eyes narrowed. "Back to this ... this House Acheran?"

"Yes, if there is such a House," Soen said. "Have you ever heard of it?"

"No, Master."

"Phang?"

"No, Master."

"Neither have I," Soen said, fingering his Matei staff as he thought.

"It must be a minor House nearby," Phang said. "Some Fifth Estate fool who lost control of a handful of slaves."

"No, Qinsei," Soen said, looking down at the body of the dead chimerian. "The Keeper tells me this trouble started in Icara—and that more than a dozen Houses are involved."

"Icara!" Qinsei's voice rose in tone. "That's at the edge of the Western Provinces ... it would take us another day just to get there."

"Longer if we have to fight our way through some of the marshaling fields," Soen agreed, "which we almost certainly will have to do. But it is the Will of the Emperor ... the Will of the Keeper ... and *my* will that we find this—this House Acheran or whatever House is responsible—

and secure its truth for the good of the Empire and the glory of our Order. Gather the Quorum—we leave at once."

"Aye, Master Inquisitor," Qinsei said as she straightened her back with pride.

Soen watched his Codexia as they moved back to instruct the rest of the Quorum. He reflected for a moment that Jukung would no doubt find some way to report back to Ch'drei and he wondered what the old woman would think of all this.

He turned and gazed once more toward the fold portal at the far end of the hollow

House Acheran, he thought, struggling to recall anything in his vast memory about the name. *Who in all the gods of the Void knows ANY House Acheran?*

CHAPTER 19

Loose Ends

"IS THIS ALL OF THEM?" Soen demanded of the manticorian warrior standing next to him.

The evening breeze was rising behind the elven Inquisitor as he surveyed the scene. He would have enjoyed drinking in the freshness of the air as it flowed around him, still damp from the sea beyond his sight to the south. The sunset was deepening into a rich, vibrant salmon color, marred only by the black smoke still curling up from the ruin on the hilltop, its pall rising to join those of a number of surrounding Houses. He would have preferred to turn his back on the carnage, bask in the rays of the setting sun, and breathe deeply of the fresh evening. Such luxuries, however, would have to wait.

"Yes, Master," the manticore rumbled. "Fifteen of the House servants survived. Two warriors of the House Centurai were alive, but they engaged us on our arrival, and we were forced to kill them ... and it appears impossible to account for the full Centurai."

Soen turned his head slowly toward the manticore, his gaze itself a question.

The manticore was an old one, golden streaks running through his shorn mane. He shifted uncomfortably. "The Impress Warriors were still returning from the war. The majority of the warriors of this House appear to still have been in transit through the folds."

"We will deal with one disaster at a time," Soen said in clipped tones. "You were the first to arrive?"

"Yes, Master."

"And what is your name?"

"Gradek, Master ... Centurai Captain of House Megnara."

"Megnara?" Soen said with studied casualness. The names of these petty frontier Houses were only now, after four days into this investigation, starting to make sense to him. House Acheran was only one of the many Houses that had fallen on the frontier, and that name had quickly led them to a host of others within what Soen had come to call the Dark Frontier. It was not until Codexia Qinsei brought him a report of a messenger from the House Megnara Centurai that he had even heard of House Timuran. "Oh, yes, House Megnara. That's about fifty leagues from here, isn't it?"

"Yes, Master."

"So how does a Centurai Captain of a House many days' journey away end up at the door of *this* fallen House?"

The manticore's eyes narrowed, but he gave no other sign of his anger at his embarrassment. "By accident, Master. We were set upon by the mad warriors when they hit during our return from the war. We fed through whatever folds were convenient and available, trusting that the Myrdin-dai would sort out our transportation home after the mad warriors were killed. After several folds, we arrived here and sent a runner at once back through the fold to report to the Myrdin-dai what we had seen."

Soen nodded. "What of Lord Timuran and his family?"

The manticore gave a quick grunt to show his discomfort before he spoke. "The remains of Lord Timuran were found just inside the main doors. The fire had not reached the body, but there was little left nevertheless. He was only identified by the baton still in his grip, his signet rings, and what little remained of his clothing. We have not yet found his head."

"It was expected," Soen thought. "Anyone else?"

"We actually found Lady Timuran first," Gradek continued, the bile in his stomach apparently settling as he spoke. "We saw her above the subatria wall, impaled on one of the House standards. My Octian Leader Jatuh believes she was dead before the fire reached her body. He is the one who brought her down.

"Go on," Soen urged.

"Beyond that, the overseers and the Guardians were undoubtedly all slaughtered."

"All of them . . . you're sure?"

"The moment we arrived, Master," Gradek said, "I specifically ordered each of my Octian commanders to secure the House and protect any elves they encountered. None were reported."

"Still, they will have to be accounted for in any event." Soen turned back to examine the huddled group sitting on the ground before him, the smoking ruins of their former life behind them. "These slaves are all that's left, then. Any of them broken?"

"I do not understand," the manticore replied, shaking his wide head.

"No, of course not," Soen muttered under his breath, then spoke more clearly to the monster beside him. "A broken slave is one who has fallen outside the discipline of House Devotions, Gradek. Their souls no longer yearn for the peace and glory of the Imperial Gods—and as such they are dangerous to both the body and the spirit of the state. I'll need to examine each of them. You will stay close to me throughout, and I will tell you which are broken and which are not. If I tell you that one of them is broken, you are to kill him or her at once—at once, you understand, without further question or thought."

The manticore nodded and then looked up at the sky, searching for stars, perhaps, that could not yet be seen. "Yes, Master . . . I believe that four of them . . . perhaps five . . . are broken."

"Very well," Soen said, drawing in one last, deep breath of the sweet evening air before setting about the grim task before him. "Your Lord Megnara shall garner much favor this night because of your sure action in his name."

"Master," Gradek said, his wide, flat face gazing down at the elven Inquisitor. "We have not slept in nearly two days. It is nearly the hour of House Devotions. Many of my warriors are anxious to return to our Field Altar so that they might . . ."

"NO!" Soen barked. "Not a single Impress Warrior is to leave until I have questioned them to my satisfaction—*especially* for House Devotions! Is that absolutely clear?"

Gradek drew himself up erect with great effort. "Yes, Master Soen!"

The old human woman had stubbly, gray hair barely emerging from her head, but she was stroking it with her fingers like a brush. "There were flowers in the fields then. Such beautiful flowers. The smell of them was overwhelming in the bright sun. Patches of red and yellow and brown and blue. We ran and ran and ran through the field with the flowers rushing past us. How I laughed!"

"What is your name?" Soen asked in soft tones.

The old human woman's eyes came into focus again on the Inquisitor's face, but she didn't seem to actually see him. "She always called me Essie. I never much liked Essenia though Mama told me she named me after her grandmother. It's strange, in a way, because I can remember Mama telling me I was named after her sister, too. She called to me, 'Run, Essie! Run!' and we ran through the flowers in the fields. What a game we played, with the elves chasing us, but we were so fast that they couldn't catch us! Not Mama and me!"

"Essie," Soen said. "Do you know where you are?"

"Yes!" the woman said as her fingers caught on an imagined snag in her hair. "Are you looking for Mama, too? She fell into the flowers of the field—I think she was playing a trick on us. She fell among the red flowers, so bright and still wet. She said to keep running, but I can't remember to where. I've looked and looked for her, but she's hiding in the field, I know she is. There were flowers in the fields, then, you know. Such beautiful flowers!"

"Perhaps I can help you find your mother," Soen said, patting the woman on the hand.

"Thank you, sir," Essenia smiled childlike through her weathered, ancient face.

Soen stood and spoke to Gradek.

"She is broken."

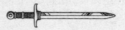

"Please, sire, I need help . . . I'm sick . . . something is terribly wrong!"

Soen nodded as he gazed into what passed as the face of the chimerian. It was difficult to look at because its shape kept shifting, the plates of its bones sliding beneath the skin as the creature struggled with his own inner monsters tearing at his memories.

"We can help you," Soen said with measured words, his black gaze trying to lock with the shifting, feverish eyes of the chimerian. "What is your name?"

"My name? My name is . . . I don't know!" The chimerian's voice rose to a panicked pitch. "I have *too many* names!"

"It's all right," Soen reassured the quivering being, the tips of his own ears starting to twitch. "Just tell me what happened here and we can help you."

"What happened? What *happened?*" The chimerian worked his hands nervously until the fingers on each hand had lengthened to nearly a foot in length. "Didn't you *see* it?"

"Yes, but tell me anyway," Soen said, licking his sharp teeth. "What was happening right before . . . when everything was still right."

The chimerian blinked, calming as he concentrated on the single memory. "We were at House Devotions. Lord Timuran was beside the altar with the Lady and his daughter."

Soen nodded. *At last we're getting somewhere*, he

thought. *Everything appeared fine up to the House Devotions.* "And then . . ."

The chimerian was blinking faster now, struggling to organize his memories into words. "Then there was some trouble on the other side of the garden. One of the warriors just returned. I didn't recognize him, but he must have arrived earlier in the day."

"The day of the trouble, you mean."

"Yes . . . there was a shout . . . that's what got my attention . . . and when I looked up, the Guardians were moving toward this warrior. He was fighting them, too. I remember thinking he was frighteningly strong for a human."

"A human?" Soen asked in mild surprise.

"That's right! I remember now; somehow he had a blade. Lord Timuran drew his own sword and was charging toward him. This human saw him coming, I'm sure of it. Guardians were all around him but I saw him turn and . . . and . . ."

"What happened next?" Soen urged. "One thing after the other . . . what happened next."

"The Well . . ."

"The Aether Well?"

"Yes, the Aether Well . . . it, I don't know, it . . . *shattered* . . . outward, away from the center . . ."

Soen leaned back. "It exploded?"

"I don't understand."

Soen shook his head. "You mean it cracked . . . it broke."

"No, sire," the chimerian's large eyes filled with tears. "It was suddenly no more at all . . . not a piece of it larger than the smallest finger on your hand, sire."

Soen shook his head in disbelief.

"I think it was that human who did it," the chimerian moaned. "I think he's the one that made me sick. Please, sire . . . my head is full of bad spirits . . . ghosts of the dead . . . please, I want to be well again."

"Rest easy. I know how to get rid of such ghosts," Soen said; then he stood and turned again to Gradek. "Check with your Octian Commanders. Find out if any of them saw a human male slave any time since all this began."

"Master," Gradek protested. "We were running through the folds for days ... we've probably seen a number of *hoo-mani* slaves ..."

"Just ask them!" Soen snapped.

"Sire! By the Will of the Emperor, I live to serve!"

Soen considered the young human warrior. Perhaps seventeen years of age, if he was any judge of human growth. The ears seemed to push straight out of the sides of his bald head, but the youth had a strong jaw. The scar across his forehead told the Inquisitor that he had already seen battle, but he was still young.

"You are an Octian commander?" Soen asked, his black eyes narrowed.

The boy flushed. "No, sire! That honor is not yet within my grasp. Perhaps one day, sire."

"Why, then, am I speaking to you?"

"Sire! My Octian commander ordered me to report to you on my observations during the time of our approach as we ran through the folds before our approach to House Timuran."

Soen smiled slightly as he folded his arms across his chest. *They really take themselves seriously at House Megnara. This slave acts as though he were in the Imperial Legions.* "And your name is?"

"Mellis, sire!"

"Then let us have your report, Warrior Mellis, by all means."

"Sire! This was four folds before we arrived at House Timuran. We had exited from the previous fold from the riverbank marshaling field and had arrived at the canyon marshaling field with the objective of surviving the mad warrior onslaught and finding another fold by which we could return to our quarters in House Megnara. We had nearly completed our crossing toward that objective when I realized that I had neglected to secure an important item of my field gear."

Soen glanced sideways toward Gradek.

The manticore leaned over slightly as he explained. "He dropped his sword."

Mellis flushed once again.

"Go on," Soen urged.

"I was rapidly approaching the fold from which we had just arrived when I saw several figures approaching outside the line of totems surrounding the marshaling field."

"*Several* figures, Mellis?" Soen leaned forward. "How many are 'several'?"

"Three humans, a pair of manticores and a chimerian, sire," Mellis said, straightening his back at once. "Oh, and a dwarf . . . I remember wondering about the dwarf. They passed right between the totems as they were making their way to the fold, sire."

"Fold? Which fold?"

"The fold we had just exited."

"You mean they were going *toward* the chaos?" Soen asked.

"Yes," Mellis replied at once. "That's what caught my attention. Everyone was trying to get away from the mad warriors—and these were trying to go *toward* them."

Bolters, Soen thought with a grimace. *Seven of them.*

Dawn broke with agonizing slowness over the eastern horizon. Soen was impatient for its illumination, for he needed to examine the garden of the fallen House Timuran and could not do so properly without the aid of its light.

At last the sky brightened enough that he dared risk entering the shattered remains of the House itself. The main doors stood slightly open, shadowed from the sun by the remaining bulk of the House. Soen stood there for a time considering them.

"Master Soen." The words were soft, deferential.

"Yes, Assesia Jukung," Soen responded without looking at the assassin.

"The remaining slaves are ready for transport."

The sound of flies filled the space of a breath.

"The Centurai of House Megnara has been returned, and a special Devotion has been arranged for each of their warriors . . . as you directed. None of them will remember this."

"Thank you, Assesia," Soen said but did not move. "Have you considered these doors, Jukung? The delicate and intricate carvings crafted no doubt in the Imperial City itself by skilled artisans of the Fifth Estate. What must it have cost old Timuran to have them brought to this remote place? Now they look tired to me, as though they feel the weight of what is behind them."

"Master," Jukung urged, an impatient edge to his voice, "Keeper Ch'drei is awaiting our report."

"Then we had best give her a complete one," Soen responded as he stepped quickly through the gap between the main doors. "We do not yet know *who* this House Timuran is . . . or why its fall brought down nearly the entire frontier. But I know where to look for at least some of the answers. Coming?"

It was the smell that was worst, Soen decided. The sights of the blood and carnage, torn limbs and broken, jutting bones one could analyze from a safer, more objective position of the mind, but the putrid, cloying smell of rotting flesh could never be put at a distance. He choked back his bile and took a single step into the garden.

Or what little remained of the garden. The avatria had crashed down into it before the structure folded sideways, collapsing into the northeast wall, slicing down through the subatria curtain wall and buildings, burying them in a hopeless pile of unrecognizable rubble. It was there, Soen noted with detachment, that the fire had burned most fiercely, but the off-shore winds of the evening must have kept the flames burning away from the southern and western sections of the subatria.

"What happened here, Master?" Jukung's words were heavy, as though he were having difficulty speaking.

"The House fell ... quite literally it seems. Here it is, Jukung; this is the center—the root. Everything that fell on the frontier—every Well that failed—started with this event." Soen turned to face Jukung. "The answer is here, Assesia. Have Qinsei and Phang discovered what I sent them to find?"

"I am only an Assesia, Master. I am not privy to ..."

"Have they or not?" There was no question in Soen's voice.

"Phang reports that the Impress Scrolls are lost—apparently burned and scattered beyond recovery," Jukung answered though his eyes were fixed anywhere but on Soen.

"And Qinsei?"

"She has recovered most of the Devotion Ledger for the last eight months."

"Well, that's something that may prove useful." Soen began picking his way around the southern edge of the garden wall. Here the debris was minimal although it was also unfortunately easier to pick out individual bodies or their parts. Soen dutifully noted a large concentration of warrior and Guardian bodies choking the hall that led back to the Hall of the Past on the far side of the ruined garden. In his mind, Soen pictured the Guardians gathering for their mutual defense against a suddenly insane and desperate enemy, trying to back into the corridor and find a more defensible position.

Just before this pile of dead, a glint caught his eye near the base of the curving wall. Soen looked up again at the smoldering mass of the avatria that loomed above him. He could make out only a handful of plates from the underside of the structure; it was unstable to say the least. Soen hoped to the gods that it would hold long enough to satisfy his curiosity.

Soen moved quickly around the remaining southern wall of the garden. There were more slave bodies here;

some had been crushed under the debris from the collapse while others had died from sword and dagger wounds. Their blood had mixed with the dust in dark, solid stains. Still he kept his eye on his prize, moving as quickly as he dared.

At last he stopped. He stood under the archway that opened into the Hall of the Past, but that history did not interest him just yet. He reached down and plucked the shining object from the dust.

It was a crystalline shard—barely more than a sliver—that fit neatly in the palm of his hand.

"What is it?" Jukung asked in a hoarse voice.

"That, my young Assesia," Soen said through a rueful smile, "is part of an Aether Well."

"You are mistaken," Jukung said. "It cannot be."

"And yet it is," Soen replied. "Aether Wells might crack or they might split, but the power of the Aether itself binds the crystals together. It is impossible for them to shatter once they are forged—*and yet*," he held the crystal within inches of the young elf's face, "here is it. In the face of the impossible we find ourselves holding it in our hand."

Soen turned and looked up. "And there *it* is."

"What, Master?"

"The story of the House," Soen said as he stepped carefully across the debris and strewn bodies into the Hall of the Past. Soen followed the broken wall, reading it for a few moments until he summarized for the young Assesia. "Sha-Timuran was an elf of the Third Estate," Soen said, mulling his own words. "His name apparently did rank among the noble Houses of the Empire. Two generations before it had been ranked only in the Fourth Estate, but due to a series of favors looked kindly on by the Imperial Eye, House Timuran was allowed to prove itself in the Third Estate by taking up residence in the Western Provinces. And this, it seems, was the result of all his efforts. He had grand hopes of garnering honor through battle. His single little Centurai had participated in nearly every battle against the Nine Dwarven . . ."

Soen suddenly stopped.

A long stain ran down the length of the Hall of the Past.

Soen moved quickly, running around the bend of the hall as he pursued the path of the blood on the floor. Within a few strides he could see its source—a single, elven body slumped backward against the wall at the far end of the corridor. The face was bloated and discolored, but Soen recognized at once the uniform of the House Tribune, a patch remaining over his left eye. His blade was broken, but the grip was still in his hand.

Soen straightened, considering the figure before him.

"I *know* this elf," he murmured in awe.

Jukung slid to a stop next to the Inquisitor, eyeing the dead Tribune. The smell of rotting flesh was overpowering. "Master, we must be going . . ."

"Pause for a moment, Jukung, and honor a fallen hero," the Inquisitor said, gesturing toward the dead elf sagging against the wall before him. "This is Se'Djinka—hero of the Benis Isles Campaigns among a dozen others. He was a general back then, and I only personally saw him twice. He lost favor in the Imperial Courts, however, and vanished from the official histories. Now we find him as a dead Tribune in this obscure, ambitious House."

"This place is unsafe, Master," Jukung urged, gagging even as he spoke. "We must hurry . . ."

"Don't you think this is odd, Jukung?"

"I . . . what, Master?"

"That the Guardians of the House had all formed together in the entrance to *this* hall," Soen said, speaking aloud his thoughts as he considered them, his eyes fixed on the corpse before them. "It doesn't lead anywhere except to one of the access towers, but the avatria had no doubt fallen by the time they made their defense. This hall would have been a dead end. Yet here we see their Tribune. Why would a Tribune—and especially a successful and brilliant tactician by all accounts—put himself and his force in such a precarious position unless . . ."

Soen reached forward, gripping the Tribune's armor behind his neck and pulling the body suddenly forward. It made a sticky, ripping sound as it separated from the wall and collapsed to the floor. Soen stepped over the body to the wall, gave it a cursory look, and then pressed against it.

The flat stonework shifted inward slightly and then swung back toward the elven Inquisitor. At once, Soen stepped back, pulling open the hidden door.

"Unless he was protecting something," Soen finished as he stepped into the doorway and then stopped.

The room was uncomfortably small and completely devoid of decoration or furniture. It had never really been intended for use but had been part of the original plans, and no one had bothered to make the alterations necessary to delete it. Yet the Tribune knew it was there—and so, at last it had served its purpose.

A single figure stooped shivering in the corner of the room.

Soen reached his hand out with care.

"Tsi-Shebin?" he asked softly.

The elven girl looked up, her black eyes wide, though whether with anger or fear, Soen was not sure. She remained as she was, however, her arms locked around her knees. The room stank of her.

Soen knelt down with agonizing slowness, then spoke. "Shebin . . . my name is Soen. We are here to help you. We will take you away from here. You will be safe again. Do you hear me?"

The girl jerked her head in two short nods.

Soen drew in a deep breath, watching her carefully.

"Who did this, Shebin?" he asked.

She blinked and then her eyes narrowed. She opened her mouth, and when she spoke, her words came in croaking sounds so harsh that he was unsure he understood her.

"Did you say a slave?"

"Yes," she rasped. "A slave . . . a *hoo-mani* slave! You have to catch him . . . bring him back to me . . . let me kill him . . . I have to kill him."

"What slave?" Soen asked. "What is his name?"

"DRAKIS!" she screamed.

CHAPTER 20

Bolters

"BY ALL THE GODS! It's getting worse!" Belag bellowed, raising his sword instinctively.

Drakis grimaced, setting his teeth, and pressed forward, gripping his cutlass until the blood fled from his knuckles. The curved blade of the sword was thick and strong, but the edge was already starting to dull.

He heard Mala moan behind him. She had long since grown weary of her own screaming and had subsided into a shocked daze. She now stayed behind Drakis, trying desperately to avoid any and all weapons with murderous intent that came anywhere near her. Her presence distracted Drakis, who found himself trying not only to maneuver against his attackers but simultaneously to protect her as well. He realized that he had been foolish: Because he had been trained in the arts of combat, he had blithely believed that every other slave had been as well. Now, as they were once again pressed to defend themselves, he felt how ill-prepared they were as a group. Of the six he had brought with him, only two were warriors, not counting the gods-cursed dwarf.

It didn't help that they were often fighting warriors of their own former Centurai.

Every fold they had passed through led to another

marshaling field filled with unique forms of horror and
chaos. The first had been bad enough—two members of
their own Cohort had gone mad when Timuran's Well was
destroyed and the Devotion Spell—or whatever it was
called—collapsed. By the time Drakis and his companions
passed through the fold, the Myrdin-dai had already abandoned their posts beside the portals and were fleeing the
murderous warriors from a host of Houses. The warriors of
the Houses who remained enthralled by their own Devotions were slow to take up arms without the direction of
their own Tribunes and were scattering as well either to the
limits of the totems that contained the herd or through any
convenient fold portal that offered escape. The Guardians
who remained engaged the newly murderous warriors in
direct combat, and the phosphorescent blasts in the center
of the carnage were accompanied by the screams of both
the rebellious and the loyal caught in the blasts.

Combat was not Drakis' objective; flight was. He led
his companions around the perimeter of the totems and
soon discovered that they were no longer bound by any of
them. They quickly circumnavigated the marshaling field,
ducked back inside the totem perimeter near the fold
portal from which warriors were still passing, and slipped
unnoticed through the portal to the next marshaling field.

Each subsequent passage through the next fold portal
brought them farther from their home and deeper into
the breaking madness and death. By the sixth portal they
passed through, the Tribunes were reacting to the carnage,
releasing their warriors against these suddenly dangerous
and insane warriors from all across the Western Provinces.

Now Drakis and his companions had stepped through
the eleventh portal only to find themselves at the rear of
a defensive circle raggedly set up just a dozen yards from
the fold platform onto which they had just stepped. The
Tribunes—too few remaining for the number of warriors
present, Drakis noted at once—were nearly hoarse with
screaming at the Impress Warriors on the line. Beyond
them, in the darkness, Drakis could vaguely make out
movement, but everyone present could hear all too clearly,

and the sound sent a chill up his spine. His insane fallen brothers were wailing and banging their swords together in an increasing tempo.

"Where are we?" Belag bellowed.

"This is the third Ibanian marshaling field," Ethis answered, perhaps a little too quickly for Drakis' liking. "We're north of Lake Stellamir. It should look familiar; we were here only two days ago. Is that of any help?"

"None," Drakis spat the word sharply. There was something about the chimerian now that made the back of his neck itch. He was a stranger with far too great familiarity. "It doesn't matter yet where we are . . . what matters is where we find the way out!"

"What? Again?" RuuKag groaned. "You're supposed to be saving our lives, not leading us from one hopeless, bloody battle to the next hopeless . . ."

"Oh, please spare us yet another chorus of this same old song!" Jugar said in a booming voice as he exaggerated the rolling of his eyes. "Next, if you remain true to form, comes your plea for us to return to the embrace of the Imperial Will—may the gods put his Imperial Will where it would be the most discomforting."

"We haven't done anything . . ." RuuKag growled.

"That's true," Mala agreed, her words fast on the heels of RuuKag's. "Maybe we don't *have* to run . . ."

"The master and his family are dead and their home burned to the ground," Ethis said with a sniff that sounded almost bored. "I doubt that the Iblisi will care whether we were the ones who actually held the torch or not."

"Not if they have to hunt us down!" RuuKag said. "The longer we run, the worse it's going to get for us. Can't you see that this—this *hoo-mani*—is taking all of us for fools!"

"Shut up!" Drakis shouted, turning on the fat manticore, the tip of his sword causing a small indentation in the creature's abdomen. "You want to stay and wait for the Iblisi's renowned mercy, then stay—or come and have some hope of seeing another sunrise. But either way, shut up!"

"Drakis!" Jugar had been tugging at the hem of his tunic for some time. "We've no time for this!"

Drakis glanced across the defensive line. The screams from the darkness had reached a fevered pitch.

The human warrior shoved RuuKag back in exasperation, then turned to the other manticore. "Belag! I seem to remember a line of trees just outside the totems on the right side. The portal we want is closer on that side anyway. We've got to push through this defensive line from behind—they're not looking in this direction, and it should be easier to get out than in. Rush the line from behind, then down into the trees."

"Wasn't that ChuKang's plan to get the dwarven crown?" Ethis asked at once.

"What of it?" Belag snarled.

Ethis shrugged. "It didn't work out very well is all."

"So you have a better idea?" Drakis' head was beginning to pound again. So far the danger, constant activity, and adrenaline had kept the shadows of his mind at bay, but he could feel them lurking in the corners of his thoughts, ready to tear at his mind.

Ethis considered for a moment, and then his blank face split into a wide grin. "I believe I do."

The chimerian turned at once, jumping from the platform and striding toward the right side of the line. He raised one of his right arms and then started calling with loud insistence. "Tribune! Tribune!"

Belag's eyes went wild. "What is he doing? He'll get us all caught!"

Drakis jumped down off the platform, clearing all of its steps at once, his legs churning as he tried desperately to catch the chimerian and stop him. The human could hear the other members of their fugitive band scrambling after him as well.

It was too late; a Tribune had already heard his calls and turned her angry, grim countenance toward Ethis. Drakis, only steps away, raised his sword preparing to attack the Tribune, part of his mind knowing it was an act of suicidal insanity.

The chimerian reached back with one hand and pushed

the blow aside. With a free hand, Ethis formed a fist and slammed it into his chest in salute to the Tribune.

"Mistress Tribune!" Ethis said as he stood tall. "We are an Octian of House Tajeran. Our Lord commands us to answer the call of the Myrdin-dai to add to the glory of your Order by defending this fold portal against the enemy."

Drakis' feet slid across the loose dirt beneath his feet as he came to a halt. The rest of the fugitives fell in behind in disarray.

"House . . . Tajeran?" The Tribune's black eyes narrowed, whether in distrust or disdain Drakis could not tell.

"Aye!" yelled a squeaky voice from the back of the group. "We are the most fearsome warriors in all the Empire! Ogres tremble at the sound of our name, and the heathen elves of Museria dare but whisper it."

The rest of the fugitives had turned to stare in wonder at the Lyric. The lithe woman was standing tall in her tattered dress, a look of fierce determination in her eyes as she held a sword before her with conviction. Drakis could not imagine where she had gotten that blade.

"We are the Octian of Oblivion!" the Lyric said with conviction, her short, wispy hair standing away from her head in odd angles.

"The . . . what?" the Tribune demanded.

"Aye," Ethis said, turning back to the Tribune as he responded with confidence. "We are the, uh, Octian of Oblivion . . . specialized warriors in the service of Lord Tajeran. He asks only that, if possible, we be held in reserve . . . behind the main line of defense as he considers us valuable warriors of his Cohort and . . ."

"You'll serve where I tell you," the Tribune snarled in grating, dangerous tones. "You'll go to the front of the line at once!"

"But my Lord's instructions . . ."

"I take no instructions from 'your Lord,'" the Tribune bellowed. "Marquen!"

"Aye, Tribune," came the response from a squat manticore with a long scar running up from the corner of his mouth to his ear. He wore the chevrons of a Cohort master.

The Tribune smiled to herself as she spoke. "Get this—this Octian—up through to the front of the defensive line!"

"But, Tribune!" Ethis protested.

"Stick him if he gives you any trouble, Marquen," the Tribune continued. "Let's let someone *else* spill their blood for a change."

The short manitcore only grunted and then started shoving Ethis, Drakis, and the rest of their group forward.

"My master shall hear of this!" Ethis shouted back angrily at the Tribune as he walked toward the line, then turned and grinned smugly at Drakis walking next to him.

Marquen's bellows were sufficient to get the troops arrayed in front of them to reluctantly part, and within a few minutes they were standing at the front of the defensive line. In the darkness before them, the rhythmic chanting of their own former brothers in arms—now insane—was rising in tempo and sound.

"It will be by your word," Drakis said to the warrior manticore.

Belag nodded, then spoke to their companions, "When I shout, that's when we run." The manticore warrior drew in a deep breath and then crouched down, preparing to spring.

Drakis grabbed Mala's hand. "Jugar, you have the Lyric?"

"Aye," said the dwarf as he shot a worried glance at the woman next to him staring blissfully out over the field. "Are you ready, lass?"

Drakis noticed only then that she had dropped her sword somewhere. The girl looked down at him and smiled sweetly beneath her unfocused eyes.

"That will have to do," Jugar coughed as he spoke.

The manticorian warrior bellowed and then charged away from the line of warriors, angling directly toward the woods. Drakis ran after him with Mala behind him struggling to keep up. Jugar charged forward as well with the Lyric as Ethis and RuuKag followed behind.

Surprise won over discipline for only a few moments, but it was enough. By the time the astonished warriors realized what had happened, Drakis and his band were already crashing into the underbrush of the woods to the right of the line.

The darkness of the woods panicked Drakis for a moment. His eyes had been used to the globe-torches illuminating the fold platform and were not yet accustomed to the darkness. Mala fell behind him, and he stopped, picking her up.

Then the ground started to shake.

The mad warriors were charging at last in the clearing next to them. Drakis stood, holding Mala in the darkness as the sounds of crushing pain and agonizing death permeated the air around them. He wanted to shield her from it, protect her from the horror that was taking place only yards from where they stood. His arms enfolded her head, pulling it to his chest.

And he was again aware of the insistent tugging on his garments by the dwarf.

"Master Drakis," Jugar growled under his breath. "Follow me. We must get through the portal at once."

"Why?" Drakis said, his arms holding Mala tighter still.

"Because the battle here will soon be ending," Jugar said in the darkness. "And those left will be looking for something else to kill."

With each fold passage, the carnage increased. Thanks to the confused rush of the armies to return home, the warriors of the fallen Houses had been spread unevenly throughout the complex system of fold portals, a cancer that erupted suddenly seemingly everywhere at once. Where the greater concentrations of warriors were found, the destruction was even more savage. That the warrior madmen were no longer restricted by the totems became

an even greater problem as in some places they were able
to overwhelm the forces of the other Houses and spill into
the countryside.

In those places, death was the rule.

It was the silence that shocked them.

Not total silence. The Lyric was humming a tune whose
quiet notes drifted with the smoke that lay like a thin veil
over the field. Mala whimpered as she shook behind Drakis. The others were grim and silent.

RuuKag broke the crystal stillness, his voice dry and
cracking, startling them despite his care. "Which way do
we go now?"

"*Now* you're in a hurry?" Ethis whispered.

"Anything to get out of this place," RuuKag croaked.

Drakis held the sleeve of his tunic across his nose and
mouth, desperate to separate his senses from the stench
that permeated the air around them. There were several
portals that he could see still operating at the far perim-
eters of the marshaling field. He remembered this field as
being one of the largest—the nexus of seven portals originally although now only five of them were functioning. The
bulk of Timuran's forces must have been bottled up here
when everything changed. Now, two of the portals were
dark and useless ... but the others ...

"That one," Drakis said, pointing beyond a slight rise in
the center of the field. "That one leads farther on."

"How many more of these portals do we have to pass?"
Mala murmured, her voice shaking. She could not take her
eyes away from the moldering death blanketing her view
to the horizon. "Can't we ... can't we just leave?"

"We've got to keep going," Drakis insisted. "The portals
are the fastest path for us to get as far as possible."

"But for how long?" RuuKag asked through a sigh.
"The Emperor will not tolerate such rebellion. He will
bring the weight of his Imperial Will down with a ven-

geance to regain control of the folds for the Myrdin-dai. It isn't a question of if but when."

"He's right," Jugar nodded. "The Armies of the Emperor will return order and soon. Face it, lad; we *have* to get off this path at *some* point."

"Not yet!" Drakis shook his head. He knew the dwarf was right—that they were *all* right—but he could not yet face leaving the confusion and horror of the portals. The thought of turning from the roads previously so familiar to him and striking out into lands unknown terrified him worse than the carnage and battle of the portal road. Drakis, warrior of House Timuran, was afraid of getting lost.

More than that, he realized, he was afraid of being alone with his thoughts. Being driven from terror to terror had the advantage that there was no time to reflect on the raging animal of his own memories still kept at bay in the back of his mind.

But they were right. He could not run forever.

"Two ... maybe three ... more portals," Drakis said. "Then we'll abandon the portals and strike out on foot."

"Two," the dwarf said. "Two ... if we can make it."

"Why two?" Ethis asked through the inscrutable mask of his face.

"I know that place well," Jugar said. "There are friendly caverns not far from the gallant—if ultimately tragic— marshaling fields through which we have been touring. It should provide us respite and, might I add, comparative safety for a time. I might even be persuaded to perform one of my more cheery and delightsome tales, if it would help."

"It might," Drakis said as he once again surveyed the gore-laden field of fallen warriors, searching for a path through the piles of dead. He reached back for Mala's hand. She clasped his quickly. "Listen, there are field packs everywhere ... and no one here is going to ever need them again. Everyone keep an eye out for a pack—the more provisions the better—and follow my steps. Let's go."

They alone moved. Globe-torches lay scattered on the

ground illuminating ghastly tableaus of carnage, death, blood, and gore.

Drakis trod carefully among the dead, dreading what his tentative next footfall would find. He could see the fold portal on the far side of the field around the edge of a small knoll. If they could somehow manage to keep their sanity until then . . .

"DRAKIS!"

He froze. The sound had come from the top of the knoll.

A single figure struggled to its feet at the crest of the small mound. A globe-torch at its feet threw the ghastly, blood-coated figure into stark relief. As the hideous form stood shaking, it raised its hand above its head, clutching a circular band in its hand. It was human in form and size, but it was otherwise difficult to distinguish its features. The figure's face was swollen and its hair torn away from one side, but the voice could not be mistaken.

"Vashkar," Drakis murmured, barely believing the name that fell from his lips. He let go of Mala's hand, gesturing for her to stay at the base of the knoll, uncertain about his former comrade.

The former Cohort leader swayed slightly as he arched his back and howled at the stars overhead. "We're free, now, aren't we? Free!"

"Yes," Drakis responded, as he moved cautiously up the slope. His footing was slick and squishy. He dared not look down, keeping his eyes on his former brother in arms. "We're free after all, Vashkar."

Vashkar's eyes shone white all around the wide-open irises of his eyes. "We've showed them, Drakis! They weren't expecting us to do it, but we did!"

"That's right," Drakis said calmly as he took another step up the slope. "Come with us, and everything will be all right."

"I have it!" Vashkar giggled through the foam at his mouth. "The dwarven crown! I took it! Now Master will be so pleased. We'll be able to buy anything, Drakis! Imagine it . . . anything we want!"

Drakis took another step, but his mind was churning.

The dwarven crown! He must have taken it while it was still in transit to House Tajeran. Maybe they could go back . . . barter the crown for their freedom. Maybe they could . . .

"Maybe he'll give me back my sons that he sold, eh, Drakis?" Vashkar grinned. "I didn't remember them, Drakis, but I do now. I can see them both screaming at the slaver as he dragged them away. Such fighters! That slaver nearly clubbed one of them senseless he put up such a fight—and him only eight or so years along. What good boys! Surely old Timuran will give me my sons back for a dwarven crown!"

Drakis stopped. He was finding it hard to breathe. He glanced down the slope and saw the others had stopped, too, transfixed by the terrible image at the crest of the hill.

"No, no . . . I've got it!" Vashkar nodded as his eyes darted from side to side. "Maybe he can return my daughter. She had gone lame on the march to the Provinces. You should have seen her before, but she was always such a delicate flower."

Drakis took another step. "Please, Vaskhar . . ."

The blood-soaked warrior suddenly sat down, his weight pressing down on the chest of a fallen manticore, forcing blood out of a gaping wound. Vashkar took no notice, holding the crown in front of him with both hands as he spoke. "I tried to carry her, but Timuran caught on that she was lame. He had me butcher her right there by the side of the road. Is she worth a crown, Drakis? Could it buy back her breath? I felt it leave her body."

"I—I don't know," Drakis said softly.

"What do you think, Drakis?" Vashkar said, as he looked up with pleading eyes. "Do you think he will give me back my soul?"

He held the broken, bloody metal ring above his head.

Drakis took in a long, deep breath.

It was not the crown at all, he realized. It was a jagged-edged, metal hoop torn from a small cask. It was cut in places, slivers of metal sticking out from it.

Worthless.

"Come with me, Vashkar," Drakis said, extending his hand. "We'll take care of you. Figure this out . . ."

"THIEF!" Vashkar screamed, leaping to his feet with unholy speed, his hand reaching at once for the hilt of his blade. "You can't have it! It's mine! My life! Mine!"

Drakis barely managed to avoid the blow, leaping to the side. He rolled, his body flopping over the dead, their filth covering him. Drakis tried to regain his footing, but Vashkar's blade flashed in the light of the globe-torch. and Drakis could only scramble out of the way again. His hands reached down to stop his fall, sliding among the bodies, scraping against the broken armor . . . a small dagger handle suddenly pressing against his palm.

Vashkar screamed above him, raising his sword as he ran wild-eyed across the slain.

Drakis leaped toward the insane warrior, connecting so hard that it knocked the wind from his lungs, yet he held fast to the slick grip of the dagger, pressing it upward into Vashkar's ribs.

Both warriors collapsed atop the knoll. Drakis rolled away, pulling the dagger free but his hand was caught beneath the gasping human's head. He tried to pull away, but Vashkar reached across with his left hand, gripping Drakis at the back of the neck and pulling him toward himself.

"Please," Vashkar wheezed, his lungs filling quickly from the wound. "Please, Drakis, don't take it from me! Please . . . my sons . . ."

Drakis grimaced, then held still. His face was inches away from the dying man. "As you will," Drakis said. "You may keep it . . . for your sons."

"And my daughter . . ."

"Surely," Drakis looked away as he spoke. "Surely for your daughter."

Vashkar grinned, his teeth filling with his own blood. Then his chest fell one last time, and he was still.

Drakis pushed the body away from him and stood, alone, at the crest of the knoll. The silence was complete and suddenly unbearable.

"What are you staring at," he yelled at his companions.

"Everyone pick up a field pack and let's get through that portal *now*. We've got a long way to go."

"It's quiet, and the dead will not trouble us," Ethis suggested. "We could rest here a while."

"No," Drakis spoke, the words sticking in his dry throat. "No one will ever rest here again."

CHAPTER 21

The Hunt

"TWO DAYS!" Soen seethed. "Two days we've been going in the opposite direction of these bolters, we finally are on their trail and you want us to *wait*?"

The Master Iblisi stood to the side of the fold platform, his face inches from Jukung's long nose. His two Codexia stood to the side, their hands folded inside the sleeves of their robes, hoods drawn over their heads, leaving their faces in shadow from the late morning sun. Each watched the scene with detached amusement. Hazing the younger members of the Order was an old and established pastime ... but it could be a dangerous game when played with one of the Keeper's favorites.

Jukung blanched but did not back down. He had to give the young Assesia credit, Soen thought through his rage. Jukung was a young, green blade, but he stood his ground. Ch'drei would not have chosen the whelp to spy on the Iblisi if he could not stand up against Soen's occasional hot wind.

"It is her order that we remain here until she arrives," Jukung replied, his back stiffening.

"Here?" Soen scoffed, his left hand darting out to point at the blood-soaked mounds of the field behind them. Impress Warriors moved about the battlefield, dragging the dead toward the center of the clearing where a great pit had been dug. Several Tribunes and a handful of Proxis maintained a raging fire in the pit into which the dead were being cast. The greasy, black smoke curled upward, fanning over the surrounding trees in the still air. The stench of the bodies lying under the warm sun was overshadowed by that of burning flesh.

"I confess that I am at a loss to understand your disapproval, Master Iblisi. It is a great honor that the Keeper affords us as she rarely leaves the Keep of our Order for any purpose, let alone to travel as far as the Western Provinces."

"Then *you* wait around and receive her honors," Soen spat. "No doubt you've honored her enough times in the past."

Qinsei, standing next to the Inquisitor, covered her laugh with a cough.

Jukung set his sharp jaw against the hot words that had come to his mind and spoke more delicately than he would have liked. "It is nevertheless her will that we await her coming as she is most anxious for your report."

"Odd that her intention should be communicated so quickly over such a distance," Soen continued. "I should have sent you back to the Imperial City, herding slaves with the rest of the Assesia."

"The instructions of the Keeper were clear," Jukung stated. "Such an act would not have served the Will of the Emperor!"

"Don't talk to me about the 'Will of the Emperor,' boy," Soen spoke in a quiet, dangerous tone. "I've stood in the presence of the Emperor, and know his will far better than any of Ch'drei's pets."

"Master Soen," Phang said at once, injecting himself between the Iblisi and his Assesia before either was tempted to take their argument further. "I have spoken with the Tribunes and have something worthwhile to report."

Soen waited for a moment before responding. "I will hear your report, Phang."

Phang bowed slightly and then spoke. "Tribune Tsa'fei

reports that just prior to the battle joining last night, an Octian from House Tajeran reported to her."

"Let me guess," Soen said, looking down at the ground and nodding as he spoke. "Three humans—two of them female—two manticores, one chimerian, and . . ."

"And a dwarf, yes, Master," Phang said.

Soen shook his head in wonder. Why take the dwarf? The creature was so obvious. It made no sense; if they were bolting, they would want to remain as inconspicuous as possible. But, he reminded himself, just how sane were they after all?

"Did he say which way they went?" Soen asked.

"Yes, Master," Phang nodded. "Just after they were positioned at the front of the defending line, they ran off into the trees." The elven Codexia raised his hand, pointing with a pair of long fingers. "There . . . near where those two trees are grown together."

Soen was striding across the field before Phang had finished his sentence. He took little notice of the putrefying bodies over which he stepped beyond occasionally altering his course when their bulk was otherwise unavoidable. He assumed that the remaining members of his Quorum were following behind him. Soen's eyes remained fixed on the twin trees at the edge of the field and the forest of which they were a part.

Soen's pace quickened as he moved between the glowing crystal structures of the totems surrounding the field. Their magic had contained the slave herd of warriors as intended, so the bodies diminished at once as he passed them. Diminished, he noted grimly, but did not end entirely; there were other bodies beyond the totems, each of whose shaven heads bore the mark of one of the fallen Houses. The explosive failure of the Timuran Well had far-reaching effects indeed, he realized, for now they knew that the bolters that had caused all this—or any of the fallen warriors, for that matter—were no longer constrained to the strictly controlled channels of the totems and fold platforms.

He slowed as he approached the tree, his keen eyes

searching the ground. He took it all in quickly: a broken twig here, a bent blade there, patterns in the grasses around the base of the trees and the patches of exposed dirt on the slope falling away from him down toward a ravine. For him, tracking was a gift from the gods for which he was grateful each day. It had saved his life many times down the long and difficult years of his service—and brought an end to many more lives who threatened all that he served.

He drew in a deep breath, holding his hand up in warning as his Quorum joined him from behind. He could see it all in his mind's eye: the squat dwarf cutting a wide path across the grass, the small, deep footfalls of the chimerian and a pair of manticores crashing through the lower branches of the overhanging trees.

They moved down the slope, slightly to the left.

Soen followed it all in his head, moving with light, quick steps down the slope. He had the track now and knew what to look for.

He stepped through the trees, the dappled light falling on him as he passed, and then stopped, kneeling down and staring at the ground.

"What is it, Master?" Qinsei asked.

"Here," Soen pointed. "Note this. Human footprints. They stopped here, facing each other ... very close, too. One set is deeper and larger than the other—male—while the other is smaller and lighter—female, I believe."

"Mated then?" Jukung offered.

Soen stood up, placing his hands on his hips and he surveyed his surroundings once more. "Perhaps ... a good sign, for it will slow them up. Make them easier to capture or kill. The dwarf joined them here it seems—as well as the other human woman—then they all moved off along the ridge line."

"They were making for the fold portal again," Phang said with a sigh.

"Yes, again," Soen said.

They followed along the path of their quarry, weaving among the trees and down into a shallow ravine. They turned with the tracks through the tall grass, traveling upward until they emerged from the tree line, as predicted, at the far end of the marshaling field near the base of the fold portal.

Jukung trotted up the steps of the platform. The fold shimmered before him as he gazed into its rippling surface. Then the Assesia turned and sat down on the steps. He gestured back through the portal with his thumb. "More carnage, more dead. I believe it's getting worse."

"The scale of this—it is almost too great to comprehend," Qinsei said as she gazed out over the slaughter still scattered before them. "How is it possible that the fall of a single House Well could cause this much damage?"

"It's because the Myrdin-dai and the Occuran do not trust each other," Soen said as he, too, gazed over the gory field.

"*They* caused this?" Jukung scoffed.

Soen ignored the implied insult. "In part. The Occuran have basked in the Imperial mandate for over a hundred years ... maintaining the network of Aether Wells in the Provinces and the Imperial Trade Folds that held the Empire together. It has long been the center of their power—the force of Aether is diminished exponentially by distance, requiring a network of Wells and folds to maintain its strength across the Empire."

"You speak the obvious," Jukung said.

"Only because you seem to understand only the obvious," Soen replied. "All that was upset when the Myrdin-dai got the Imperial mandate to provide the folds for the Dwarven Campaigns. For the first time the Occuran were not to be trusted transporting the Legions into war, and the insult was not lost on anyone in the First Estate. The Myrdin-dai could not trust the Occuran to provide them with the required Aether from the established system of Wells, so they were required to build their own, separate, Aether conduits linking through each of their own fold platforms. It meant having to build twice the number of fold platforms because they could not rely on any Aether being available at the other end; they had to push their *own* Aether through as well.

"But when the Timuran Well shattered and caused all those House Wells across the frontier to fail—the Myrdin-dai folds were *powered separately* and remained functioning. And *that* was what caused the biggest problem. Since the Devotion spells and the Field Altars of all the Houses were passing through the still active Myrdin-dai open folds, the failure of their Wells was carried, too. The warriors of the fallen Houses fell with them wherever they were among the folds on their return home."

Qinsei drew in a deep breath. "The Myrdin-dai did their job too well."

"And that answers the question that the Myrdin-dai sent us to answer for them, but we still don't know why the House Timuran Well shattered and caused all this in the first place," Soen replied, walking around the base of the platform as he spoke, looking for more signs of his quarry's passing. "That, my fellow Quorum members, is precisely what we must find out. How is it possible that a handful of slaves could bring the Fist of the Imperial Will to such complete destruction . . ."

Soen stopped, his eyes widening.

It was too perfect, he thought. It was not possible that he should be so blessed by the gods, and yet there it lay next to the base of the fold. He reached down, allowing himself a slight smile as his fingers closed around the object tenderly, as though he were afraid that it might vanish like an apparition at his touch.

It was several long blades of grass. He recognized it as coming from the base of the ravine they had just passed through. The blades were woven together, folded and twisted around themselves until they formed an intricate knotted pattern.

"Master?" Phang asked. "What is it?"

Soen slipped the woven grass blades casually inside his belt. "Nothing . . . get moving. We've not a moment to lose."

"Master Iblisi," Jukung spoke with exaggerated patience. "Mistress Ch'drei . . ."

"Will have to catch up to us," Soen finished angrily. "Move!"

"By the gods!" Qinsei exclaimed, her hand pulling the sleeve of her robes up across her mouth and nose.

As though such a futile gesture would help, Soen thought, fighting the rebellion of his own stomach at the sights and smells everywhere around them. The flies were thick over the sea of rotting flesh stretching across the gentle undulations of the wide field. One knoll, rising above the rest, was piled high in death, difficult to see through the swarming insects.

"Their tracks lead directly into the dead," Soen said, nearly gagging on his words. He had seen the carnage of battle many times before and had both faced and dealt death in many forms, but nothing had prepared him for this. He glanced at Qinsei, who was trying to keep her eyes moving and focused on the distant, indistinct regions of the marshaling field. Phang was holding very still. Jukung had turned and was doubled over, contributing the contents of his stomach to the horrific aroma though its effect was negligible.

Soen slowly knelt down on the platform, his hands indolently picking at the debris marring its once polished surface.

Phang spoke with care. "How ... how are we going to track them in *that*?"

Soen's eye caught something on the platform, and the shadow of a smile tugged at this lips. He picked up a trampled flower and examined it carefully before he stood. Soen thought for a moment longer, then spoke.

"We can't."

Jukung managed to push himself upright again. "Then ... then that's it. We go back and report to Mistress Ch'drei."

"No," Soen said, shaking his head. "We continue."

"Continue?" Jukung repeated in disbelief. "You just said we cannot track them through ... through this."

"Look," Soen said, pointing with his first two fingers to the far limits of the enormous field. "There are four other portals functional. One of them leads farther up toward Hyperia, the other three back toward Ibania. So far our prey has continued farther from the heart of the Empire."

"But which one do we take?" Phang asked.

Soen considered then spoke.

"All of them."

Qinsei, Phang, and Jukung all stared at the Iblisi.

"We can't be sure which one they took, but if we explore each of them separately, we might choose the wrong path and set ourselves back more than we already are," Soen said. "But if we each follow a separate path on our own—each of us looking for signs of our prey—then we'll cover them all much more quickly. We'll each take a different fold, then return here before nightfall. If one of us does not return, then we'll all know which path to follow, and we'll take it and continue the hunt."

"It breaks the Quorum," Qinsei said, obviously disapproving.

"If we don't recover these bolters while we can," Soen said, "there may not be enough Quorums in the Empire to stop them."

CHAPTER 22

Togrun Fel

"TWO DAYS we've walked ... and *this* is our prize?" Mala sputtered, unable to decide whether to laugh or weep.

"Aye!" Jugar said with pride, his eyes flashing in the light of the setting sun. "Partake of the sanctuary offered by the dwarven gods and glory in its honor! Few mortals have been privileged to enter the confines of the Togrun Fel!"

Drakis looked again and remained unimpressed. The hill was no taller than any of the others extending to the southeast. It did, he had to admit, have a rather precipitous exposed face on its southern side, but the carvings in its surface were altogether worn and crumbling, in such bad states of deterioration that it was difficult to get any idea of what they were meant to depict. Indeed, he had not even noticed the carvings until they were nearly at the base of the cliff itself. Mossy grass overhung the top edge of the rock face, the gods of nature trying to hide the scars that the dwarves had made.

The tears of the Dead are of dust now ...
The breath of their life now stopped ...
Their voices though still ...
Are calling your will ...

Drakis reached back and rubbed at the aching in his neck. The field pack he was carrying was heavier than he expected. "It's a tomb."

"Aye," Jugar nodded, his widely spaced teeth grinning in appreciation.

RuuKag let out a great chuff of disapproval. "He wants us to hide . . . in a grave?"

"Better to hide temporarily in a tomb than to take up permanent residence," Ethis said, folding his four arms in front of him as he inspected the entrance. "Still, I would have expected better craftsmanship from the dwarves. Even the entrance looks more like an accident than an intention."

"Are you blind, sir?" The dwarf huffed. "But that *is* the craft! Togrun Fel is not a dwarven tomb, though it was constructed by them and, might I humbly add, with the greatest of their arts in stone. It was wrought in honor of the friendship once joined between the Fae Queens of the Hyperian Woods and the Nine Dwarven Kings and the great sacrifice they and their dryads made near this very spot. This was back in the Age of Fire, when all the world was set ablaze by the elven conquests and the humans stood shoulder to shoulder with the dwarves and the faery against their onslaught."

Drakis raised a questioning eyebrow at Jugar.

"Well," the dwarf sputtered. "Perhaps not *exactly* shoulder to shoulder as the dwarven shoulders were always considerably lower than those of the humans, but I speak metaphorically. Even so, this is a place of dreaded power for the elves. Were it not for the special keywords to which I alone am privy, this innocent looking portal would blast us with the power of the gods themselves were we but to dare pass its threshold unbidden! Fear not, my good companions, for though you would suffer the most painful of curses otherwise, I shall . . . I shall . . . where are you going?"

Drakis turned to follow the dwarf's gaze.

The Lyric stepped quickly through the portal, her lithe figure swallowed almost at once by the darkness. Peels of her bubbling laughter echoed from within.

"Nasty dwarven curse, that," Ethis said in flat tones.

The dwarf sputtered. "But I . . . I don't . . ."

Drakis reached down wearily behind him and pulled Mala up from where she had collapsed to the ground. The House tattoo on her beautiful bald head was already being obscured by a fuzz of rust-colored hair emerging from her scalp. Her smudged face accentuated the exhaustion in her eyes. She looked hard, resentful, as she shrugged her own field pack higher on her shoulders, and he wondered for a moment what had happened to the bright face and the easy smile that he had seen so often in his dreams and his waking hours as well. She was so different now, so much less than he remembered, so much pain and loss, so common, so . . . real.

Nine notes . . . Seven notes . . .
The heart of the warrior is not his . . .
It beats for another's soul . . .

They had awakened from both a dream and a nightmare all at once when the Aether Well fell with the House of Timuran. They had left their innocence behind and now, eyes opened, found the reality of their lives to be a nightmare, too. He no longer knew the woman whose hand he held with such unthinking devotion, but he held it just the same out of a hope for the shadows he had once believed were true. He was a creature of honor and of duty though he no longer understood what honor he pursued nor to whom his duty remained. All he knew with certainty was that he once loved Mala—if not the woman that he no longer knew, then the ideal of her—and that, for all he knew, was what his honor and duty were about.

They stepped through the opening and nearly ran at once into a stone wall. His eyes were still adjusting from the light of the setting sun, and he could make out a glow to his left. He felt along the rock face, his right hand in front of him as he pulled Mala behind him with his left. The wall ended abruptly beneath his fingers where the glow was, and Drakis turned the corner.

The warrior's grim face relaxed into awestruck wonder. The entire stone hill was hollowed into an enormous dome surrounding a magnificent central fountain. Luminous waters cascaded from the top of the ornate spout, fashioned from the purest white marble to resemble the branches of a tree. The skill of its artisans insured that the water splashed in its descent to appear as the foliage of the tree, ever living and moving as the water fell down to where its stone roots gripped the floor of a wide, shining pool. The shimmering light from the surface of the waters played across the detailed carvings of enormous trees, hewn in relief from the encircling stone with intricate detail, their own branches interlacing in the dome above them. The movement of the light occasionally revealed figures in the carvings: faeries and sprites that seemed to form just at the fringes of his vision, nymphs that danced for a moment and then vanished, dryads that smiled back at him and then could no longer be seen at all. There were the unmistakable marks of age in the cavern, for it had long been untended, yet its beauty remained.

Jugar stepped up next to Drakis, his head hung in dejection. "I wanted you to see it in all its glory. There were gems, lad . . . gems as big as your fist and more gold and silver than a soul could see in a lifetime. But the tomb has been despoiled and its riches taken by thieves . . . oh, lad, I'm so sorry."

"You're wrong, dwarf," Drakis said in a whisper.

"How then?"

"The riches are still here," he said with a gentle smile. Drakis stepped carefully into the enormous chamber, his eyes gazing in reverent joy at the wonders around him.

"Welcome, my brave friends!"

Drakis turned with some reluctance from the glorious, magical carvings on the walls toward the deep, sultry voice now carrying through the hall. It came from the shining fountain tree, and for a moment he wondered if the tree itself had spoken to them.

The soaked form of the Lyric emerged from the nimbus of water. She had abandoned her field pack next to the pool. Now her wet dress clung to her body as she moved, revealing a strong and beautiful form that Drakis would not have supposed her to possess. She was transformed; her narrow chin was raised in elegant poise, and she carried her chest high and shoulders back so that a regal curve formed down her spine. She held her arms away from her body and bowed gracefully until the tips of her fingers lingered near her strong thighs. Drops of the water sparkled and shone in the white bristles of her emerging hair.

"I thank you all," the Lyric said in a deep, sleepy voice. "Together we shall triumph. Together we shall be free!"

Mala stepped out from behind Drakis, her questioning eyes fixed on the majestic form standing in the water. "Lyric?"

"So you may have known me," the Lyric replied, her head nodding slightly in acknowledgment. "But you have awakened me from my long sleep and freed me. The grateful thanks of my kingdom shall be yours!"

"Kingdom?" RuuKag rumbled. "What kingdom?"

"I see, you do not understand," the Lyric said with slight condescension. "It is to be forgiven."

"Perhaps our good lady would humor us?" Jugar said with a smile although his eyes showed uncertainty.

The Lyric raised her face in statuesque magnificence.

"I am Murialis," she said, her deep tones resonating in the hall. "Fae Queen of the Hyperian Woodland, lost these many years to my native lands, lying in forgetfulness until you, good friends, have freed me from my awful captivity. To you I offer the protection of my kingdom, sanctuary from your pursuers, and the grateful thanks of the woodland realm."

RuuKag gasped. "You're . . . you're a queen?"

"I am, RuuKag of the manticores," the Lyric intoned solemnly, "Fae Queen of the Hyperian Woodland."

Belag nodded thoughtfully. "It is another sign from the gods. It begins, Drakis—do you not see it? It is spoken of old that 'he shall meet with commoners and kings that the works of his justice shall be wrought.'"

Drakis held up his hand before his maticorian companion could get any further with his religious discourse.

"Jugar, we . . . I've never heard of such a queen. Do you know what she is talking about?"

Jugar kept his eyes fixed on the imperious form of the Lyric in the water. "I . . . there *is* a faery queen that is said to rule in cold isolation in the great woods west of the Aerian Mountains. Her realm is closed to outsiders, however, and there are no tales—at least, none reliable—concerning the ruler of forest spirits and sprites. It is said that those who have ventured beyond her borders never return, having been ensnared by that mystical realm and brought into a sleep that lasts a thousand years."

"Who would have been awake, then, to tell the tale?" Ethis asked dryly.

Jugar rolled his eyes. "These are indeed but tales, and I am, after all, a fool who is telling them. Entertainment is my business, not the chronicle of the ages."

Five notes . . . Five notes . . .

A queen of the north . . .

In hope drawing forth . . .

"But such a queen," Drakis persisted. "Could it be possible that Timuran somehow captured her . . . enslaved her?"

Jugar screwed his left eye into a hard wink as he considered. "Stranger things have happened, lad . . . although I can't recall any of them at the moment."

Nine notes . . . Seven notes . . .

"But if she *is* who she says she is," Drakis persisted, "then we have a chance at a life. If we can make it to this kingdom of hers . . ."

"The Hyperian Woods?" Jugar laughed. "You *are* ambitious, lad! That's full well sixty—maybe seventy leagues from here!"

Five notes . . . Five notes . . .

"But it is to the north, isn't it?" Drakis pressed with urgency.

"Aye, well, more west than north it is . . . but that's more than two weeks on stout legs with nary a rest between. And it would be well to point out that most of that is open country—not settled land by any measure of the term."

"We're provisioned," Drakis countered as he unconsciously hooked his thumbs under the straps of his field pack, a plan forming quickly in his head.

"Aye, partial field packs but that's not for the length of two weeks!"

"It will get us far enough," Drakis continued. "We can take local game . . . we've done that before on the longer campaigns . . . and RuuKag, you weren't always a gardener. I remember you in the work sheds . . . didn't you work for the butcher for a time?"

RuuKag's eyes closed painfully, his long fangs bared. "Yes . . . I was a butcher once."

"There, then!" Drakis answered enthusiastically. "What about this water, Jugar . . . can we drink it?"

"These are the sacred waters of the . . ."

"Can we drink it?"

"Well . . . yes, but . . ."

"We'll take our fill, rest here tonight and then set out at first light," Drakis continued. "We'll ration what provisions we have and then forage for the rest."

"The Iblisi will come for us," the Lyric intoned ominously. "They will not give up a Queen of the Fae."

"Then all the more reason for us to travel quickly and to travel light . . ."

"Stop, Drakis!" Mala interjected. "Just think for a moment! The Lyric hasn't said one believable sentence since we fled the master's House, and *now* you're willing to believe she's a queen of some place we've never heard of?"

"Jugar has heard of it," Drakis replied, irritation creeping into his voice.

"Jugar said that anyone who went in never came back!"

"Look, if we're going to survive and make any kind of life for ourselves, we've got to go *somewhere!*" Drakis heard his own voice growing louder with his frustration. "And if this faery place offers us asylum from the Iblisi then maybe I'd rather *not* come back from it!"

Mala wheeled to Ethis for support. "And you! You haven't said anything for a while. What do you think of this insane plan?"

Ethis looked up as though returning his thoughts from a distant place. "What? Oh, I quite agree with Drakis. By all means, we should make for the Hyperian Woods."

"What?" Mala squeaked.

The chimerian spread his four arms, then clasped them in two sets before himself. "The Iblisi surely will come for us. We are now considered—what is their term?—ah, yes, 'bolters.' They will have enough problems for a few days sorting through many others like us that have escaped from the armies—at least those who remain alive after the slaughter we've witnessed so far—but ultimately they will search us out. They cannot let us go free—no matter whether we have a 'queen' with us or not."

Ethis turned and focused his eyes on the Lyric standing with regal grandeur in the light of the pool. "We have run and must keep running. It seems that our hopes now rest with the Queen of the Fae."

CHAPTER 23

Murialis

QINSEI KNELT with one knee on the steps leading up to the portal, her Matei staff held vertically at her side. The deepening sunset cast a deeply colored salmon pall over the dead carpeting the ground before her. Qinsei did not move, her eyes shifting from time to time to the other portals at the distant points around the field of death.

The carrion birds had come and were only mildly disturbed by her return. Indeed, the longer she knelt here watching the field, the more it appeared to move, undulating under the motion of the rats, carrion birds, and other vermin whose task in the world—ordained by the gods themselves—was to clean up after the violence of conflict, death, and destruction. The pulsing blue-white glow emanating from the headpiece of her Matei staff not only kept the elven Iblisi Codexia safe but also served to isolate her from the scavenging going on all around her.

It was quite beautiful, she thought, her dark reddish robes shifting in the wind. All the power of death brought down to its absolute and common simplicity. The dead flesh would be rendered, the bones would dry, the metal disintegrate into rust, and all the death and violence would fall back into rich earth in time, smoothed over until even this blood-soaked field would be leveled not by the will of the Emperor but by the small things of creation. Elven children would one day walk this field and never know that the horrifying visage and overwhelming stench of death had ever troubled the grass beneath their feet.

Not that the any elves would pass this way for a very long time. The Myrdin-dai would very quickly and quietly reroute their fold system so that such embarrassing places would no longer be anywhere near where anyone might discover them. Fields of the dead like this would be abandoned and forgotten—along with their dead.

Qinsei alone would remember.

So she waited under the darkening skies as she had been told to do—as the Inquisitor expected her to do.

A ripple rebounded across the surface of the portal to the far south. Qinsei slowly stood as a figure in a robe matching her own emerged from the shimmering, vertical pool, Matei staff held with both hands across his chest.

"Phang," Qinsei murmured.

She could see her brother gazing at her and then stepping down from the platform. Qinsei understood; Phang had found no trace of their bolter prey just as she, too, had failed. But then, neither of them had expected to do otherwise. Wordlessly, Qinsei stood and lifted her Matei from the ground. Both Iblisi moved quickly across the carrion field, their light footfalls scattering the rats wherever they trod. They were both Codexia, well trained and experienced in performing their duties far from the eyes of the Emperor.

They both approached the third portal where the young Assesia—Jukung—had entered earlier in the day. They reached the portal at the same time, climbed the steps together, and stared through its rippled surface to the marshaling field beyond. Battle had been joined there too, but at least they could see movement on the other side. Whose movement and whether the survivors were still under control of the Imperial Will they could not see.

Crows cawed angrily behind them, then subsided.

The wind rose slightly, then fell.

"We should kill him," Phang observed.

Qinsei glanced casually at her companion. "He is young and foolish."

Phang was unmoved. "He is a spy."

"Yes, but whose? He may only be Keeper Ch'drei's spy," Qinsei noted with emphasis. "Had Inquisitor Soen wanted him dead, he would have slipped him among the rest of these corpses earlier in the day."

"You do not believe he has a mandate, then?" Phang asked.

"From the Emperor or one of the other Orders? I don't know," Qinsei spoke with a casual air though both Codexia knew that each of their words was chosen with the utmost care. "I believe that Soen does not know either, which is why both we and the Assesia have spent the day chasing shadows while our Master Inquisitor proceeds ahead of us."

The vague, shifting form of a dark-robed figure was approaching the portal from the other side.

"Then we'll not kill the Assesia," Phang agreed, folding his arms in front of him as he cradled his Matei in the crook of his arm. "With a full day's lead on us, will we be able to overtake the Inquisitor?"

Phang was surprised by her response. It was a rare and noteworthy occasion when Qinsei smiled.

"Only if he wants us to."

Togrun Fel, as Jugar explained with the enormous surety that comes when no one else present can possibly challenge one's facts, stood at the northernmost end of the Sejra Hills, a range of round-topped mountains that formed the northwestern boundary of the Ibania region. Beyond it stretched the plains of Western Hyperia.

None of these names were of any use to Drakis. Standing with the sun rising at his back, all he saw was a grassy plain that stretched to a hazy, indistinct horizon whose line was broken only by a single vertical finger of mountain so indistinctly blending its purple form with the dark horizon that he could almost doubt its existence. Even the dark line of the Aerian Mountains far to the north seemed more real than the single pillar to the west.

"What is that?" Drakis asked Jugar.

"That? . . . Oh, *that*. Well, uh," Jugar said, then spat on the ground suddenly. "It's nothing, really, just a big pillar of rock. We won't be going anywhere near it, I assure you."

"It's called the Hecariat," Ethis said, walking quietly up to join them. "A place which the dwarves considered both cursed by their gods and haunted by the restless dead—if my memory serves me well."

"The Hecariat is not a place to be spoken of," Jugar said and then spat quickly on the ground once more. "That sad tale and its tragic end is best left within the blasted stones of its lost glory. It is an abomination towering over the Hyperian Plains . . ."

"And it is our only landmark by which we may guide our steps across those same plains," Ethis said to Drakis. "We'll need it to get across, but the dwarf is right; we should endeavor to keep it on our left and pass as well to the north of it as we dare without running into the Occupied Lands to the north. The Emperor, I suspect, still has a large contingent looting the Mountain Halls of the Nine Kings, and they would make a quick end to us all if we ran into them."

"I've got to stop!" Mala dropped down among the tall blades of grass suddenly, her arms folded across her chest.

The stretching plain had proved to be both difficult to navigate and, at the same time, filled with an incredible, dull sameness. For the three days they had trekked across its expanse, the grim dark finger of stone on the horizon by which they fixed their path seemed to grow no closer. Everything now seemed to come with a mixture of both blessing and curse. Streams winding their way around the hills and ponds that accumulated in their hollows brought the welcome, life-giving water that they needed to sustain their march to the northwest, yet their advent was unpredictable, always bringing into question whether this was the last river or lake; moreover, each presented a diversion from their path as they searched for a crossing or way around its shores. Copses and even forests of trees offered the promise of cool shade and rest during the day but in so doing also offered the threat of wild beasts that took such places for their lairs. The rations they had secured as they passed through the portal system had thus far sustained them and kept them largely clear of any dangers the woods presented, but most of Drakis' companions knew that they would not last them the full measure of their journey. Within the week entering the cool shade of the woods and confronting the creatures there would become imperative. Even the stretches of flat grasslands that made the going much faster and easier also gave in their ease time to think, question, and, worst of all, remember.

"Now is not the time," Drakis responded with mounting frustration. "There is a copse of trees just atop that far slope. It does not appear large enough to be threatening. We can all rest there in the shade."

Mala looked up at him with such hatred in her eyes that it took Drakis aback. It was all so confusing. He was smart enough to realize that he had just said something that terribly angered the woman but could not possibly know what it was he had said that should provoke her. Something in their past—some memory he had just tripped on by accident.

It was a hazard whose avoidance he had not mastered, nor did he see, to his additional frustration, how he possibly *could* master it. A sound, a smell, or some otherwise meaningless, simple thing passing before his eyes would trigger a cascade of thoughts, experiences, and impressions that threatened to overwhelm him and, he knew, had completely overwhelmed others. In those moments he retreated to his training, occupying himself with repetitive tasks of his warrior calling until he beat back those unwelcome memories. Even then he could not avoid collapsing to the ground from time to time, fighting to control his thoughts and cope with the monstrous past that threatened to engulf him. Each night he awakened both screaming and weeping, his heart pounding at the nightmares that filled his sleep.

And he was not alone, for Belag and RuuKag both were doing the same. Each of them seemed to be clinging to something else that kept their individual monsters at bay.

Then there was Mala.

His perfect companion had become sullen, angry, moody, and argumentative, all while generally complaining to the point of distraction. She cried often and the rest of the time eyed him with such contempt as to make him feel shame without telling him why she hated him.

Part of his confusion was that he also *knew* why; there were memories of harsh words, snubs, slights, insults, fights, and far worse in his treatment of her that were roiling around in his memory. That he had been manipulated by Timuran and each of his masters—he realized now that there had been many different masters—made little difference to him since he had no connection between the memories to judge whether they were cruelties to Mala that had been manipulated by either Timuran or his daughter or terrible acts of his own volition. He flushed as he remembered the many nights when Shebin had called him to her rooms, disgracing him before her lusts, only to discover that the elven whore had arranged for Mala to discover them. Shebin took particular sadistic delight in breaking Mala night after night until she tired of that monstrous game.

Shebin was gone—dead more than likely at the hands of the very slaves she despised—and yet Drakis and Mala were left to deal with the horrors of the memories that now flooded into their minds.

How were they to have a future after such a past?

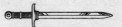

Drakis awoke with a start, a massive hand covering his mouth. His body tensed for a struggle but a great weight pressed on his chest, pinning him to the ground and making it impossible for him to move.

A huge silhouette crouched over him, its outline framed by the brilliant stars of the night sky. The pressure on his chest let up gently, and the hand came away from his mouth.

"You were crying out," Belag's deep voice whispered over him. "I thought it best to quiet you. It is not good to attract the attention of the night."

Drakis lay still for a moment, then sat up in the darkness. The nightmare still hovered around his thoughts as he struggled to awaken fully.

The manticore warrior moved silently away from him and the others of their group lying close together at the top of a small hill. He stood apart, tall and proud, his eyes searching the horizon as he watched over them.

Drakis stood up and moved to stand next to the lion-man. The manticorian clans hailed from Chaenandria, a land far to the north and east of the Rhonas Empire. Drakis wondered if Belag had ever walked its legendary plains and then realized that Chaenandrian lands might look remarkably like the land over which they traveled now.

The human turned to gaze at the Hecariat. The strange obelisk of mountain stone lay to the southwest still; it seemed to be at a great distance, but Drakis could make out details of its cliffs during the day. In the dark of night, however . . .

"What do you suppose that strange light is at the summit," Drakis asked idly.

Belag frowned. "I do not know. It shifts about the peak. It is an ill omen. We pass well to its north. I shall see that you are kept safe from its curse."

"Thank you," Drakis said, his smile unseen in the darkness.

"It is my honor, Drakis," the manticore replied solemnly. "You are the chosen one, the incarnation of our hope and the prophesied savior of us all. You shall unite the clans—bring to pass the restored Empire of the north and cast doom upon the elven oppressors."

The great warrior turned toward him in the darkness. "You are meaning to our existence."

Drakis said nothing but kept his eyes fixed on the strange lights dancing about the crest of the Hecariat. Belag, it seemed, was clinging to his faith in Drakis as some sort of hero of the gods. It was not true—or, at least, Drakis had to admit that he didn't *remember* it being true—but the one thing the human warrior *was* certain of was that an insane manticore would easily spell the death of them all. Better to let him believe whatever kept him calm for the time being.

"By Thorgrin's beard and all the jewels of Bardak," Jugar muttered in a tone more nervous than angry. "Where do you think you're leading us, lass?"

Murialis, Queen of the Fae, looked down her nose at the fuming dwarf. "Your impertinence shall be forgiven, master dwarf, but I must warn you against trying my patience. We are not amused by your antics, fool, and your disrespect in this hallowed place. We have come to pay homage to your betters, and I would thank you not to interfere in that which you do not fully comprehend!"

Drakis cleared his throat. They were much closer to the Hecariat than he had hoped, but the Queen had insisted that they divert more southerly and could not be persuaded otherwise. The tower of rock itself was still perhaps three or four leagues to the south, but its brooding presence unnerved him.

Worse, the plain surrounding the Hecariat was strewn with rock, blasted with great black stains. Most of the stones were nondescript pieces of shattered granite, but occasionally one side of the boulders showed carvings of strange, winged animals or of figures in warrior pose.

The Lyric—or Queen or whoever she was—had not given them any trouble since they had left Togrun Fel, but that in itself gave Drakis cause for worry. The woman had walked for over a week now westward across the plains with regal step and imperious demeanor. However, for someone, who claimed to have been a slave of the Empire for many years she showed no signs whatsoever of the same memory trauma from which the rest of them were suffering. Perhaps it was an effect of her being of the faery—if, in fact she even *was* faery—but her very lack of problems troubled him.

The Lyric turned from the dwarf and strode with casual step among the boulders. From time to time she would stop, stoop slightly and examine the rock before straightening back up and moving on.

"What is she looking for?" RuuKag snarled, his eyes darting about.

"I don't know," Drakis answered in exasperation. "We've been wandering this stone field for most of the morning and I *still* don't know."

"I cannot exhort you in stronger terms," the dwarf spoke with emphasis but was careful to pitch his voice so that the Queen would not hear him. "The Hecariat—that very mountainous pillar to which we have unwisely turned our backs—never sleeps. The lights that play upon its summit herald the doom of any who awaken the spirits that still strive within its cursed halls. I am but a humble dwarven fool, but wise would be the soul who could convince this 'Queen' to move her royal court to a safer distance . . . where is she?"

Drakis, distracted by the anxious Jugar, looked up.

The Lyric had vanished.

The Lyric lay asleep under a twilight sky.

The stones of the Hecariat stood about her, the carved faces all turned toward her. The air lay gentle as a blanket about her. No blade of grass moved. No cloud shifted in the sky above. The world was silent and watchful.

An enormous woman stepped from behind a broken stone, crossing the grass with silent steps as she approached the lithe form lying beneath the frozen sky. The hem of her turquoise robe brushed across the blades without disturbing them. Brown hair fell in waves around her cherubic face. She stopped and watched the sleeping human with a deep sympathy in her eyes.

A second figure stepped from behind a shattered pillar. This one was a broad-shouldered human woman with powerful arm muscles and a narrow, determined jaw. She wore armor of leather tooled with ancient symbols and carried a scimitar with practiced ease. Her dark eyes, too, were on the Lyric.

"Murialis," the human warrior-woman spoke in hushed tones as she nodded in acknowledgment to the large woman.

"It is good to see you as well, Felicia," said Murialis in a whisper.

"Does she sleep still?" asked Felicia of the Mists, leaning closer over the Lyric.

"She does," Murialis nodded, "and so she must remain."

A new figure—a chimerian in mismatched armor—stepped hesitantly from behind a jumble of rocks, its four hands shaking slightly as they gripped four blood-soaked swords. The chimerian spoke warily as it approached. "Who are you?"

"I am Murialis, Queen of the Faery," the enormous woman answered. "This is Felicia of the Mists—Raider of the Nordesian Coast. And who are you?"

"I am ... I am Dyan, assassin warrior of the Shadow-clan," the chimerian answered, slowly returning all four sword blades to their scabbards crossing its back.

"You are new here?" Felicia asked.

"Yes," Dyan answered then nodded toward the Lyric, still sleeping on the large flat slab before them. "Is *she* the reason we are here?"

"Yes," Murialis answered. "We have come for her."

A ghostly man, transparent down to his long, flowing hair drifted through a stone to meet with the three females in their observations. These were joined almost at once by four more figures stepping from behind even more stones—a towering female manticore in ancient battle armor, a sad elven woman in tattered robes, a pinch-faced human woman in an elaborate black-mantled robe, and a small, female gnome carrying a sack over her shoulder. These joined with the others, forming a circle about the sleeping form of the Lyric, all gazing down upon her.

"Who is she?" asked Dyan, the chimerian.

"She is all of us now," said the black-robed woman.

"Better to ask who she was," spoke the ghostly man.

"Who was she then?" Dyan said as she gazed down on the sleeping figure.

"She was loving," the gnome said sadly.

"She was an incomparable talent," said the black-robed woman.

"She was powerful," agreed Murialis.

"She was fragile," said the sad elf.

"She is fragile still," said Felicia. "We are all she has to protect her. She has seen too much, heard too much. She cannot protect herself from the truth of her past. Without us to watch over her, her mind would be forever broken, and she would cease to exist."

"And we would no longer exist along with her," the ghostly man added.

"I have protected her," Murialis said, stretching out her hand and brushing it gently across the stubble of her growing hair. "I shall live in her and for her. I shall continue to stand between her and the truth that would destroy her and all of us. And each of us must be prepared to do the same."

"But we are only characters from the stories she has told," Felicia said, frustration evident in her quiet voice. "We are only dreams."

"Then we shall be made real through her," Murialis replied. "We shall stand between her and the truth of the world, and within our circle she will be safe."

"Will she not feel *our* pains, too?" the sad elven female asked with concern.

"Yes," Murialis responded. "And we shall bear them, too."

"Lyric?" Drakis called carefully. "Uh, Murialis?"

Mala nudged him, then whispered. "Listen!"

Weeping.

They found her lying across a great stone half buried in the plain. A carving of a woman, her face broken and now missing, lay beneath the Lyric's embrace. The Lyric sobbed, tears running down her cheeks and washing streaks across the blasted stone.

"Tianya!" she cried. "My sister and darling! That your tragic love should have brought this doom upon all your people! Was it not enough to break your heart? Did you have to break the hearts of the mothers and daughters of your ruined kingdom, too! May the woodland spirits curse a passion that should cause such pain!"

Drakis leaned toward the dwarf. "What is she talking about?"

Jugar shook his head. "Lad, I have no idea."

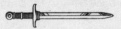

The sky was dark. Rain clouds had gathered in the afternoon. Lightning flashed to the south, rolling thunder in their direction.

Drakis, his beard thickening along with the ragged hair on his head, stepped wearily toward the chimerian, who squatted on the ridge at the top of a narrow hill. They had left the Hecariat and its terrible pillar five days behind them, and yet still his gaze was drawn to it off to the southeast. He felt sometimes that it was calling him back to his death.

"How much farther do you think we have to go?" he asked.

Ethis didn't look back, didn't turn. "We can't stop and rest, Drakis. We have to continue the march tonight."

Drakis blinked. "What?"

Chimera were difficult for Drakis to read even in the

best of times. Their pliable faces and shape-altering bodies and limbs made it impossible to judge their moods. Still, there was something in the way Ethis spoke—those few times he *did* speak—that stood the hairs up on the back of Drakis' neck. Something was different about Ethis, and, as every warrior knew, what a fighter doesn't understand can kill him.

"We're within fifteen—perhaps twenty—leagues southeast of the border," Ethis said casually. "We can pick up the River Galaran to the north and follow it all the way up to the Weeping Pool."

"Wait," Drakis said, cocking his head to one side. "How do *you* know about . . ."

"The banks of the river will be our guide in the darkness," Ethis continued. "It's the surest way we have of getting there, and we haven't a moment to spare."

"That's not possible," Drakis felt his anger rising. "Mala was a House slave. She's in no way prepared or trained for the rigors of a forced march. Besides, we all need rest. We're nearly there now, why not just . . ."

Ethis turned his head toward the human. "We are being followed, Drakis."

"We're . . . followed?"

"For a week now, perhaps longer," Ethis replied.

"And you didn't tell . . ."

"There was only one of them then. I could keep track of him. But now there are four, and we are in real danger," Ethis continued. "Our best hope now is to run—all night and tomorrow—as far and as fast as we can toward Murialis' realm."

"What do I tell them?" Drakis asked. "What can I say that will get them moving again?"

"Tell them they are being hunted."

CHAPTER 24

Hyperian Trap

THE GRASSLANDS ROSE STEADILY before them as they moved northward, making the going more difficult. A growing black belt of trees—the fringes of the Hyperian Forest—split the horizon to the northwest, a dark line growing wider with each step. Yet it was not so much the hope beckoning before them as the fear at their backs that drove Drakis and his companions on.

It was an hour past sunset when they reached the steep banks of the River Galaran that Ethis had promised would guide them. Belag bounded down the ten-foot embankment, reaching the riverbed first, his keen eyes reconnoitering both up and down the length of the dark, murmuring water before him.

"You call this a river?" Drakis said to Ethis, his voice hoarse with exertion as he hurriedly made his way down the precarious slope, struggling to steady both himself and Mala at the same time. He had seen many of the great rivers in his time—including, he suddenly recalled, the majestic Jolnar, which ran through the heart of the Empire—but this shallow bed only twenty to thirty feet in width barely qualified as a stream by those standards. "A child could cross it! What good is it for defense?"

"It isn't a fortress, Master Drakis—it's our road," the

Lyric replied, her nose lifted in haughty displeasure as she stepped quickly across the smooth rocks and knelt next to the stream, the long fingers of her left hand scooping up the water and letting it run through her fingers. "This is the lifeblood of our nation that you so casually dismiss. You would be wise to remember that and be grateful for our largesse."

"How much farther," RuuKag groaned, rolling his wide head as he rubbed his neck.

"Not far," Ethis said, "Seven, maybe eight leagues."

"Eight leagues!" RuuKag bellowed.

Belag hung his head, shaking his growing mane.

Jugar coughed. "May I suggest that we take a different course? We must head north at once! This western track will plunge us into dangerous lands that can only . . ."

"We follow the river," Ethis asserted as though to a child. "That is the plan."

"*You* follow the river, chimerian," RuuKag snarled, his large, furry hand sweeping in a dismissive gesture before him. "It's all well and good for you grand warriors! You're no doubt used to walking your feet off crossing the length and breadth of the Empire and all its conquests, but *some* of us are House slaves! By the gods, look around you; you're wearing campaign sandals of the Legions and we've been crossing open country in these household sandals. Have you even taken time to notice that Mala's feet are blistered—that she's had to repair her sandals every day for the last three days and wrap her feet in whatever cloth she can tear from the hem of her wrap? No . . . you've been too busy looking to the sunset to see what's at your own feet. Well, that may be *your* life, warrior, but it isn't *mine*, and I'm not taking another step until . . ."

Drakis turned from Mala, his short sword ringing slightly as he deftly pulled it from the scabbard at his side. In two quick steps he closed the distance between himself and RuuKag. With his left hand, he reached up and, before RuuKag could react, closed his fingers in an iron grip on the manticore's right ear.

RuuKag howled in pain, rearing back, but Drakis, jaw

set, held fast and twisted the manticore's ear farther backward. RuuKag's head moved involuntarily back with it, trying desperately to relieve the pressure and the pain that so suddenly overwhelmed him.

Drakis pressed forward, the sword pointing upward between the two of them, its tip centered on the exposed throat of the lion-man still in his grip. RuuKag staggered backward, falling at last against the wall of the embankment. RuuKag clawed at Drakis, but the warrior responded at once by twisting the ear harder and sliding the tip of his sword up to rest against the manticore's throat.

RuuKag suddenly held very still.

"That may have *been* your life, RuuKag, but not any more!" Drakis said in as definite tones as his raw throat could muster. "Yours was a proud race who ran as such a tide across the Chaenandrian Plains that their war cries and footfalls brought fear to the thunder itself—but you, *you've* become a pet of the elves, tamed and groomed, fed and obedient so that you might be patted on your shaved head by your masters. Well, not any more, RuuKag! That may have been your life before, but you're in *my* life now! No one is going to carry you, coax you, coddle you, or drag you—least of all me. So, you've got just two choices: die right here and now by my hand or say 'Yes, sire,' and *move*."

"I swear, *hoo-mani*, one day I'll . . ."

Drakis tensed, the sword tip cutting slightly into the soft throat before him.

"Yes . . . sire," RuuKag said.

Drakis shot a steel-cold glance at the dwarf. "And you?"

Jugar looked down intently at the ground.

Drakis relaxed slightly, stepping back. He extended his hand to Mala. Tears were streaming down her cheeks, but she took his hand and stood painfully.

"Let's go," Drakis said.

He kept his sword drawn.

Three robed figures stood next to the River Galaran looking on as a fourth knelt inspecting the riverbank.

"How long?" Jukung asked.

"One hour, certainly no longer," Soen said as he stood.
"So, they're following the river. They are impatient and
prone to mistakes. We must trap our prey while we can."

"Surely they cannot escape us," Jukung boasted. "The
glory of their capture shall be ours."

"We are far indeed from the Imperial Majesty where
such glory is tallied, Assesia," Soen observed in dry tones.
"There is a border not far from here which few of our Order have trod and fewer still have returned to report. The
faeries occupy that forest. Our prey has no doubt decided
it is better to hope for life in a place from which no soul has
ever returned than to face our justice. We must take them
before they can find such dubious sanctuary."

"Then we shall return to the Keeper, as agreed," Jukung
said with an oily arrogance that he no longer bothered to
disguise. "You have much to answer for, Inquisitor."

Phang cleared his throat.

"Indeed," Soen replied with serenity. This boy was a
fool after all, he thought. Soen knew with calm surety that
he could plant this boy's cold body just about anywhere
in this wilderness and live the rest of his life in absolute
confidence that Jukung would never be found. Still, there
was something about the youth's overconfidence coupled
with so little prudence that he found entertaining in a sad,
tragic way. Perhaps that was why he let him live; it amused
him to do so. "Perhaps, I could answer for it now and save
you the trouble later."

"This is not the appropriate time or place to . . ."

"Oh, but I think it is," Soen said through a sharp-
toothed smile. He started pacing in a circle around the
Assesia as he spoke. "Let me anticipate you, young Jukung.
You would ask before the Council of the Iblisi Disciplines
why I broke up the Quorum. Answer: It was necessary—in
order to secure the Timuran household—to assign most
of the Assesia of the Quorum to continue the work in the
Western Provinces while the remainder of the Quorum

pressed the pursuit of the bolters who caused the fall of the Aether Well. No, you assert; you meant why did I break up the Quorum at the Field of the Dead and send each of us through separate folds? Because, as I said at the time, we needed to pursue all four directions at once. But, you will counter, I did not return. Of course, I will reply; I found evidence that our bolters were fleeing our justice, could not risk losing their trail, and knew that the rest of my Quorum would follow. And I will point out that I *did* leave a trail of fold glyphs that brought you all to my location when the prey were cornered at last . . . saving *you*, my little Assesia, the trouble of having to walk for weeks across the Hyperian wilderness."

Soen stopped his circular stroll in front of Jukung, his face barely a handbreadth away from the Assesia's. "I can't wait for the Tribunal. Let me know when it starts."

"Yes, Master Inquisitor," Jukung answered as he turned his head away.

"Qinsei and Phang," Soen said. "You will take opposite sides of the riverbank. Stay on the high ground and get ahead of our prey. When you find a suitable site for an ambush, mark it and position yourselves on the far side. Our young Assesia—now so eager to learn—will come with me up the riverbed. We'll drive the prey to you, and then you take them. There aren't enough of us to do this properly, so Jukung and I will have to kill the manticores and the chimerian and dwarf outright. You capture the human male. Once he's secure, kill the females."

"Why keep the male alive?" Phang asked.

"I have my reasons," Soen answered. "Do not disappoint me."

When no further explanation was offered, Phang nodded then set out.

Qinsei and Phang, with quick and silent footfalls, outdistanced their squabbling quarry with little trouble. Qinsei followed the left bank with Phang on the right. They had worked together often down the uncounted years, and this part of their job had become a matter of routine. Their target was in sight—all that remained was to answer the questions of where and when the trap would be sprung.

Wordlessly, the two Codexia closed again on the river. Their prey was now behind them, coming in their direction. They remained on the high ground of the steep, sheer banks, following its curves and undulations farther, Qinsei thought, than she would have preferred. But it was Soen who was their Inquisitor, and Qinsei wanted to find the perfect place for them to bring this sorry business to its inevitable close.

"Ah," Qinsei sighed with satisfaction as she stopped at the crest of the bank where the river turned sharply. "Soen will be pleased."

It was a steep banked bowl surrounding a pool at the base of a waterfall. The river had cut a narrow passage that was the only way in or out. It would be slow climbing out of such a bowl. Qinsei saw it all in her mind: their prey walking into the bowl, Soen and Jukung closing off their only escape out of it, while she and Phang stood atop the edge of the bowl, capturing them all before their prey was even aware they were caught.

Qinsei reached over next to her. She grabbed a branch and deftly twisted it back, locking it among the other branches in an awkward bend. The sign set, she looked across the ravine to Phang and made hand signs to him as to her instructions. He responded silently with signs of his own that he would do as she suggested, circle the top of the bowl to the northern quarter and prepare to spring the trap.

Qinsei moved around the southern edge of the bowl. All that was left for them to do would be to wait until . . .

Sobbing.

Qinsei froze at once, her Matei staff readied.

She could hear quiet sobbing just through the trees to the south.

Qinsei frowned. It would not do to have someone unknown at her back. She stepped cautiously through the trees, weaving a careful path to be as silent and unseen as possible. She halted at the tree line, her breath carefully slow and her black eyes dappled by the afternoon light through the shifting leaves of the trees.

A long clearing ran up a slope between the trees on either side. The clearing itself remained in the shadow of the surrounding trees under a bright sky. Qinsei waited patiently for a moment, her eyes searching the trees and the tall grasses for a time before her gaze fixed on the small head whose back was turned toward her just past the crest of the hillside meadow.

A child—an elven child sat at the crest of the hill weeping in this lost and forsaken wilderness.

Qinsei frowned. She was more puzzled than concerned. There were no Rhonas settlements this far west—certainly none so near the Murialis Woods. It might be rebel elves out of Museria somehow come this far north. Whoever they were, her maternal instincts were not aroused; she meant to question this elf child and get answers quickly regardless of the cost.

Qinsei stepped into the tall grass and smiled. The ground was soft and spongelike beneath her feet. Her footfalls would go unheard.

She remained unaware of the long line of stones that she had stepped over as she crossed into the meadow.

Phang's eyes searched quickly along the northern rim of the pool's box canyon for the best point where he might lie in wait until Soen came and sprang their trap. This was his favorite part of the hunt; the prey were coming toward him, their fate irrevocably fixed and held in his hands and those of his fellow Iblisi. There was something about watching their approach—seeing their faces completely unaware of the doom that he knew was about to descend upon them. He relished their lives in that moment—that they were still dreaming of another tomorrow and making plans that would never be. Such a moment deserved a well-chosen position from which to view the show.

He soon saw the perfect spot from which to observe the last moments of his prey's freedom. It was a collection of large boulders at the top edge of the steep northern slope overlooking the waterfall and the pool. He could see and not be seen there. He smiled and was about to move up to the rim of the canyon . . .

Then he heard the piercing scream.

Qinsei, he thought at once. He raised his Matei staff and, drawing from its Aether, leaped twenty feet to the top of the river's steep southern bank. The scream had come from the south where his Codexia companion had just gone. He saw the careful, subtle marks of her passage— marks only another Codexia could follow—as he moved with swift yet silent steps among the trees.

The trees ended at the edge of a meadow running up the hillside between the trees. He could see Qinsei kneeling at the top of the ridge, her hooded head bent over as though she were examining something in the grass before her. Phang watched for a moment but was satisfied; whatever had happened to her, Qinsei had the problem well in hand. It would be best if he returned to the northern ridge and took up his position among the boulders, he thought and was turning to do so when some movement caught his eye.

It was Qinsei. She was motioning for him to come and join her on the ridge.

Phang grasped his Matei staff in both hands and ran easily up the slope. The ground under his feet was soft and had a spring to it that he found pleasant. The grasses around him were nearly up to his knees. He would not mind staying here to rest a while once the butcher-business of their calling was finished.

"Qinsei," Phang called as he approached. "We must be in position soon. What is so urgent that . . ."

Phang stopped at the sight of Qinsei's face, raising his Matei staff at once.

Qinsei gazed up at him with the dull eyes that were

shared by all elven dead. Thin green vines riddled her face, neck, and hands, shifting and writhing just beneath the surface of her skin.

Phang commanded the Aether of the staff to discharge at once into the hideous apparition that had been his companion, but the Matei staff did not respond at all, its powers vanished. Instead, the wood of the staff came alive, coiling like a snake around Phang's arm as it slithered toward his head.

Tendrils running through the grass wound their way up Phang's legs, but it was Qinsei's dead face that fixed Phang's vision. The vines in her lifeless muscles contracted and forced the dead Codexia's features to smile.

The winding course of the stream had cut down into the sloping plain, leaving banks on either side of its curves sometimes as low as three feet, occasionally rising as high as twenty. Soen envied Phang and Qinsei; they were making good time across the open ground, paralleling the river, while the Inquisitor was forced to make his way along the meandering streambed with the sulking Jukung at his side. He could not afford the luxury of speed, for he was closing on his prey and dared not lose their track should they for any reason decide to defy his expectations and leave the watercourse. Still, he took satisfaction that with each twist of the River Galaran, his two Codexia were getting farther ahead, better positioning themselves to spring their trap on the bolters.

Jukung had crossed the river at a shallow ford nearly half a league downstream and remained on the opposite side. It was just as well, Soen mused. The young Assesia had been something of a concern early on, but Soen was convinced now that Jukung was only a pawn of the Keeper, a much easier problem than Soen had thought he was facing. The Inquisitor had been concerned that Jukung was working for one of the myriad other Orders, Houses or lords who were constantly scheming against the Iblisi, but the youth's actions had dispelled most of Soen's apprehensions. The youth was still dangerous—both to the Inquisitor and to himself—but apparently not with any darker purpose than his own aggrandizement.

A power-hungry youth was something Soen could manage.

They moved quickly, their Matei staffs held either across their bodies or parallel to the ground in their hands. Their soft boots pushed them soundlessly up the crooked path of the riverbed. He knew their tracks by heart, having followed them across the Hyperian plain when few others could have made out their mark. Now, fresh and deep, he had no trouble making them out even in the predawn light: two sets heavy and wide of the manticores, one lighter and longer of the chimerian, the heavy footfalls of a dwarf, and the three humans—two females and the male. One of the female tracks wandered slightly along the river's edge.

Soen smiled, baring his sharp teeth. *The woman is tired. She slows them down.*

The banks of the river were steep now and tall, vertical precipices on either side. Just above their edge, Soen could see the tops of trees.

The Inquisitor continued his silent run, but he was troubled. They should have caught up to the bolters by now—or at least the Codexia should have stopped them before they reached the sanctuary of the woods. There were foul things lurking in those trees, for it was the realm of Murialis, Queen of the Woodland Nymphs and Dryads. All elves hated the woods but especially the forbidding trees of the dryad realm.

Soen was about to quicken his pace when he heard them: voices arguing around the turn of the gully.

The elf slowed his pace and saw what he had been looking for high on the riverbank. The twisted branch pinned back against the trunk of the tree. Qinsei and Phang had marked the spot as just around the bend in the river.

The prey were already in the trap.

Soen signaled to Jukung with his Matei staff to stop. The young *Assesia* obeyed at once from the opposite side of the river, his black eyes narrowing as he strained to look beyond the angled slope.

Soen crept forward, his Matei staff held firmly across him with both his long hands. He slid with gliding step behind a large boulder that had, in some age long past, tumbled down the slope just, he fancied, to provide him cover right now.

Such was the way of the gods.

Soen peered around the edge of the stone.

The steep "V" of the gully opened just a few yards beyond onto the wide oval of a pool. The waters of the river cascaded down a rock face into the pool on the far side. Soen could see the tree line of the woods running just atop the crest of the rise at the other side of the pool.

Soen frowned. Qinsei and Phang seemed to be cutting this a bit close. The location was ideal for their ambush, but there were several other locations farther downstream that would have served just as well. His concerns, however, were drowned out almost at once by the arguing voices on the left side of the pool.

"...just leave him here!" one of the manticores was saying. "If he's so upset by these woods, then he doesn't have to enter them!"

"We can't leave him here," the human male shouted. *Drakis*, Soen realized with a shiver. "The Iblisi are on our heels. The gods alone can conceive of what they would do to him!"

"All the more reason to leave him behind," the manticore roared back. "If we toss them a morsel, then maybe the rest of us will have a chance. He's not coming unless we hit him over the head with a rock, and he's slowing us down more than that woman of yours."

Five separate voices erupted at once, arguing among themselves by the side of the idyllic pool without a thought of the black eyes watching them from the shadows.

All too easy, Soen thought.

He frowned again.

It *was* too easy, he realized, and the hair at the back of his elongated skull stood on end. Something inside told him that there was something wrong with what he was seeing—that his eyes were being fooled in dangerous ways. It was a sense that he had, an unexplained inner knowledge that seldom failed him and that had saved his life more times than he cared to remember. It was never the danger you anticipated that bit you, he remembered, but always something you didn't see coming and could not have anticipated.

He glanced across the river. Jukung was moving forward, a vicious smile curling his lips back from his sharp teeth. His eyes were on the prey, the predator about to spring.

His eyes were fixed on the prey.

Soen's eyes shifted around him. The walls of the gully they were in . . . the waters rushing past him . . . the stones of the riverbank.

The Inquisitor's black eyes widened.

The stones under the water formed a pattern. Nature had not placed them there, rather the hand of design, thought, and intention. It was subtle and would have escaped the most casual glance, but now his mind was fixed on it. His eyes followed it up the near side of the river where it wound purposefully into the placement of the stones and boulders just in front of him. It wove its pattern up the embankment, disappearing over its crest. It was formed of stones, pebbles, roots, and dirt, but it was unmistakable. He turned quickly, his eyes following its line beneath the waters of the river to where it emerged on the other side among the boulders where Jukung was carefully moving forward.

"No!" Soen whispered as loudly as he dared. "Jukung, stop!"

Whether the Assesia heard him or not, Jukung continued forward, intent on garnering his prize and honor to his name. The Matei staff shifted in his hands. Jukung stopped just short of the line and pointed toward the crest of the ridge on the other side of the pool.

Soen turned and gaped. Two robed figures—Qin and Phang—rose up along the crest on the far side of the pool and began moving toward the rock face, their own Matei staffs swinging unnaturally before them—as though they were marionettes whose strings were being badly pulled.

"NO!" Soen shouted, springing out from behind the boulder, running toward Jukung.

The bolters at the edge of the pool leaped back in alarm. The human woman screamed, her shrill voice echoing off the rocks of the cascade.

Jukung leaped toward his prey, his Matei staff thrust in front of him, its crystal flaring with power. "By the Will of the Emperor, I command you to . . ."

Jukung stepped across the line before Soen could reach him.

The waters of the river exploded upward with a crashing like ocean waves, but the water did not fall back into the riverbed; instead, it shifted and broke into hands, arms, fingers, and bodies. Hair of froth cascaded off of heads of incredible beauty whose transparency gelled more solidly by the moment.

Jukung stepped back, turning toward the monstrous multitude rising from the water at his side. The Matei stick flared, pulsing in waves at the onrushing tide of horror. The figures were battered by its force, twisted, wrenched, and shattered, only to re-form.

Soen stopped at the edge of the patterned line, his own Matei staff held uselessly in front of him.

The bolters backed away into the pool. They, too, could see the robes of the Codexia on either side of the waterfall's crest. The human male held his sword at the ready, but even from here Soen could sense the panic of the surrounded and cornered prey.

Soen opened his mouth and raged in anger, his howl tearing through the air around the pool. There was nothing he could do. Too late he had seen the faery line—the pattern in the ground demarking the unquestioned realm of the fae and their power. Murialis had been busy on the frontier and had claimed more land than the Emperor had taken notice of.

Jukung screamed. The water nymphs had reached him

at last, tearing the Matei staff from his hands. They pulled him over the pool, clawing at his robes, his hair, his flesh. They twisted him back and forth as though he were being tossed upon the waves of some unseen storm at sea.

The Assesia tumbled through the air. Tossed by the water nymphs, he slammed back-first against the ragged stones that formed the wall of the ravine. His body fell heavily to the ground. Jukung lay screaming incoherently just at the edge of the faery line.

For a moment, Soen moved to stretch his own Matei staff in to where Jukung lay but, cursing, stopped himself. The faery line would almost certainly discharge his staff the moment he pushed it across the line just as it had rendered Jukung's staff useless.

Soen gazed down at the screaming Assesia. He could see terrible welts ballooning on Jukung's tortured face: acid burns from the touch of the angered nymphs. Unchecked, it would literally melt the face from the Iblisi.

Soen frantically looked about him and then saw it: a thick branch jutting out from the tree growing at the upper edge of the ravine. At once, he pointed his Matei staff upward and uttered the words. A column of brilliant light flared upward, severing the branch. It crashed downward, nearly knocking the Inquisitor off his feet.

The nymphs had regrouped in the water and were surging again toward where Jukung lay.

Soen wrapped his arms around the thick branch, thrusting it past the faery line as he yelled. "Jukung! Take it! Hold on!"

The Assesia felt the hands of the nymphs wrap around his feet and ankles. His hands flailed in panic, falling on the branch and gripping it fiercely.

Soen braced his feet where he squatted and then in a single motion used his legs to push away from the faery line, applying all the strength he had to pull Jukung free.

The nymphs were not prepared. Their prey slipped from their grasp in a single lurch, tumbling back over the faery line and falling atop the now prone Inquisitor. Soen rolled the elf off of him, the cloying smell of sizzling flesh filling his nostrils. He quickly picked up his staff and pointed it at the Assesia.

The agonized Iblisi fell with sudden silence into a deep and gratefully dreamless sleep.

Soen lowered his staff and stood upright just short of the faery line, turning to stare at the man he knew was called Drakis.

The human stared back at the elven Inquisitor as he crouched uncertainly with his sword in hand and a human woman behind him. *He protects her,* Soen observed. *He has something to fight for.*

At the top of the falls, the bodies of Qinsei and Phang tumbled forward, rebounding off the stone face of the falls before falling among the wet rocks. Neither moved. Soen had no doubt that they had been dead since before he arrived at the pool.

The manticore and the chimerian fled first up the far slope. The two women followed them, urged on at last by the dwarf as all disappeared among the dark trees of the Murialis Woods. Only the tall manticore remained, pulling at the human to follow.

"Drakis," Soen called as cold and still as death. "Wait."

The human stopped in shock and turned.

Soen spoke in a calm voice that carried across the waters.

"Do you still hear the song . . . the song in your mind?" the elf asked casually.

Drakis blinked. "How did you know?"

But then the tall manticore pulled forcefully at the human, and they both fled into the woods.

Soen, standing at the edge of the faery realm, took in a deep breath under his dark glare, turned, and picked up the tortured form of the Assesia called Jukung and made his way back down the stream.

CHAPTER 25

The Glade

RUUKAG SLID TO A STOP, his wide feet skidding across the rotting leaves that blanketed the forest floor. He fell at once into a crouch, his head swiveling quickly around as his wide eyes tried desperately to pierce the mist-laden spaces between the vertical tree trunks surrounding him like bars. The manticore could not take in enough air, could not rein in his fear. Panic circled around him like a predator that he could not see or smell but knew was waiting to pounce upon him if given the slightest opportunity.

RuuKag bared his fangs, growling at his own panic even as he shivered. He wanted to go back; was desperate to go back to the blissfully forgetful life that had been his comfort and his redemption.

Now he was alone, and he hated that more than anything. He had fled into the woods along with the others, but somehow they had all gotten separated in the mists. He knew that he should call out to them, find the reassuring sound of their voices regardless of who it was, and find some comfort in numbers, but he feared that the circling panic would hear his call and take him down under its terrible darkness.

A bush shook behind him. RuuKag spun about.

Another manticore stood before him, his wide paws open and extended out to the side.

RuuKag relaxed slightly.

"I couldn't find you," Belag said, his voice a low rumble among the trees. "Are you injured?"

"No . . . no thanks to that *hoo-mani*." RuuKag shuddered and then stood upright. "Where has he led us now?"

Belag raised his furry chin, his feline face looking slowly about. "The Murialis Woods . . . a magical forest and a dangerous one by all accounts. It is not wise for us to be alone. Follow me and I'll take you to the others."

"We should leave them," RuuKag sneered. "They are unworthy of us."

"You do not believe in the Drakis Prophecies?" Belag asked in a steady voice.

"Stories told to cubs so that they might sleep at night," RuuKag replied at once. "Lies perpetrated by the elders to keep themselves in power."

Belag accepted the remark casually then turned, making his way between the mist-shrouded trees. RuuKag followed a moment later, his own steps close on the heels of his brother manticore.

"I was of the Khadush Clan," Belag said as he pushed aside a thick fern in his path.

They were descending a gentle slope. RuuKag could hear the murmur of a brook somewhere nearby.

"Khadush?" RuuKag said. "I'm of Shakash Clan."

"Then we both are brothers in a greater cause," Belag said in conversation, though he never turned his head from the path before them.

The mists seemed to be thickening, making it difficult for RuuKag to see his companion. He quickened his steps to close the distance between them. "What greater cause?"

Belag stepped around a moss-covered tree whose trunk stretched above them to vanish in the gloom. "We are both from clans in rebellion against the Manticas Assembly. We have broken with the Chaenandrian Lords to continue the war against the traitorous Rhonas elves."

RuuKag gave a single, derisive guffaw. "They *called* it a

rebellion! Our elders fled the just decrees of the Assembly and dragged their women and children out onto the Northern Steppes. They filled our heads with songs and stories of the old days and promised us glorious futures of honor and strength ... but we were nothing more than raiders and thieves."

"So how is it you know of the old days?" Belag asked, still walking ahead and not turning his head as he spoke. They were climbing again now, the obscuring mists growing thicker with each step up the densely wooded hillside.

"Know of them? I was *there*," RuuKag spat the vile words with distaste. "I stood at the front in the Battle of the Red Fields with the rest of the fools."

"You must have been young then," Belag spoke in quiet, even tones.

"Too young," RuuKag said. He was finding it difficult to breathe again. His arms felt heavy, and his feet felt as though they were lifting stone weights. He followed Belag between a pair of trees and stopped.

With breathtaking suddenness, they had come upon a forest glade of magnificent beauty. Light filtered down through an opening in the forest canopy, its dappled rays illuminating the clearing with soft light. Gentle grasses carpeted the soft soil on either side of a clear brook that cut through its center as it danced across the rounded stones of its bed. It was a place of peace and warmth in the midst of the gloom, and RuuKag longed to lay down on its verdant expanse.

"Too young indeed," Belag said as he stepped to the center of the glade and turned to face RuuKag. "I know the Battle of the Red Fields, RuuKag. The story has been carried far of the young manticore warriors—untrained children—who were shamed into joining the desperate battle. Even I have heard of the charge that day and the ..."

"Stop!" RuuKag said, stepping into the glade. The warm soil beneath his feet felt more luxurious than anything he had known before.

Belag stooped down, scooping up some of the clear, cold

water from the brook and tasting it. "It's all right, RuuKag. I understand. It was a foolish, prideful order that called for the charge that day. Every manticore that heeded that command died that day, cut down by the Rhonas Legions and the terrible power of their Aether weapons. Thousands of them, tens of thousands, charging across the Northern Steppes, and none of them . . . not one survived to claim their honor or victory."

"No, some lived," RuuKag said though his voice sounded hollow.

"Yes, some lived," Belag agreed, reaching down again with his cupped paw and feeling the water fall between his fingers. "But the story is that only those who fled the battle . . . who did not charge when the order was given but turned and ran . . ."

"No, that's not true," RuuKag said too loudly. "You can't know. You weren't there!"

Belag stood up and faced RuuKag. "It's all right, RuuKag. We've all remembered things we want to forget. Come, you're tired. Lie down here in this clearing. The others have gone upstream in search of food, but they will be back shortly. I'll watch over you."

RuuKag stepped farther into the glade. They had run through the night, and he was so tired. He could barely lift his legs now. He gratefully lowered himself to the ground, pressed his body against the warm, soft grass and sighed.

"You won't leave me?" RuuKag asked.

"No, I won't leave you," Belag replied.

RuuKag closed his eyes and slept.

"Drakis!" Belag called out between his cupped paws. His voice was nearly hoarse from shouting the past hour. He stopped and tried to be as still as possible for the expected reply.

"Here, Belag!" came the distant reply. "We're over here! Where are you?"

The manticore drove both fists upward and roared in

frustration; then he turned in the direction he believed he had heard the voice and charged again through the mist-obscured tree trunks. Ever since he had pushed Drakis ahead of him into the trees, the gods had seemingly deserted him. He had stepped around a tree expecting to find Drakis on the other side, but he had vanished—swallowed, it would seem, by the strange morning fog that permeated these woods. He had called out to him, tentatively at first and then with increasing fervor as the voice in reply seemed to his ears to get farther away each time he called out.

He was tired. The forced march the night before had taken much out of him, and he knew it. He had somehow believed that all they had to do was to cross the border into the faery lands and they could rest, recover, and prepare for whatever else lay ahead of them. But now he had lost everyone—even Drakis, who had been barely an arm's length away from him when they entered these cursed woods.

Belag bent over, placing his paws on his wide knees and closing his eyes. He had failed again . . . as he had so often failed before.

"Belag?"

The manticore looked up, a wide smile splitting his feline face. "Drakis! At last."

"Are you all right?" Drakis stepped up to Belag and lay a hand on his shoulder.

"I am now," Belag replied straightening up. "Where are the others?"

"Not far from here," Drakis answered. "Come, I'll show you."

The human turned and started walking back among the trunks and undergrowth. Belag quickly followed, determined not to lose Drakis for a second time.

"Belag, we've got to talk—while it's just the two of us," Drakis said as he walked though he spoke without turning his head. "We've been through a great deal together, old friend. I've fought by your side through many campaigns—many of which I am only now starting to remember and appreciate."

"It is the same with me," Belag agreed as he followed behind. The human seemed unusually spry for having traveled such a great distance the night before. "I, too, am having to deal with the thoughts and remembrances that are both new and old to me at once. Much is still confusion in my mind."

"To all of us," Drakis agreed as he continued to walk ahead, apparently intent on the trail before them. They were following the bottom of a gully now with a clear stream running beneath their feet. "But there's been something I've wanted to ask you, Belag, if you don't mind."

"I serve you, Drakis," Belag intoned, though he was beginning to wonder why it was so hard to breathe in this small canyon.

Drakis did not look back but spoke clearly. "Belag, how do you know that I'm the one who was prophesied to return?"

Belag replied at once, "Because I know it. My heart speaks the truth of it to me. I know it because I believe."

Quite suddenly, they stepped out of the mists. Belag caught his breath.

Before them was the most beautiful glade the manticore had ever seen. Sunlight shone across the surface of a small pool situated at the edge of the clearing. The pool was fed by the gentle cascade of water down a small rock face, and its water was so clear that Belag could make out the shapes of the smooth rocks that lined the bottom of the pond. At the edge of the pond, soft sand rose in a bank up to the grasses of the glade, warmed by a shaft of sunlight shining down through an opening in the forest canopy overhead.

Belag longed to warm himself on the sands next to the pool, to close his eyes under the sun and find a moment's peace.

Drakis stepped into the glade and sat down in the grass, crossing his legs under him. "It's all right, Belag ... we're safe here."

Belag took a hesitant step into the glade.

"What is it?" Drakis asked, concerned.

"I ... where are the others?"

"Others?"

"The Lyric . . . Mala . . . RuuKag . . ."

Drakis laughed. "Are you sure you *really* want to know where RuuKag is?"

"I won't be heartsick if he gets himself lost . . . or that dwarf . . . or the chimerian for that matter . . . but where are . . ."

"You needn't worry," Drakis said, leaning back on his elbows in the sunlight. "They've gone upstream to forage for our lunch. They wanted me to stay behind to make sure you got here."

Belag smiled and stepped across the soft grasses of the glade to the pool. He stretched out on the sands, feeling their warmth soak into his muscles and bones.

"So, tell me," Drakis continued. "What led you to me?"

Belag's eyes closed, and he frowned slightly as he spoke. "I was raised Khadush Clan, both me and my . . ."

The manticore paused.

"What is it, Belag?" Drakis asked.

"My brother." He sighed the last word as though with a final breath. "We both believed strongly in your legend— the prophesied return of the Northern Lords. Our clan holds that all manticores are cursed for their betrayal of the Drakosian Kings of the *hoo-mani* and that only by offering our lives to the rightful heir of the human empire will we absolve ourselves of our complicity in their downfall. We were so sure—both of us—in our faith that we vowed to find you. We became pilgrims, Karag and I, devoted to finding you and freeing our race from its shame and curse. We set out west across the northern slopes of the Aerian Mountains, hoping to make our way into Vestasia to the northwest. We heard there were humans in that region and thought that they might be able to direct us to you."

Belag rolled over in the warm sand and thought for a moment before continuing. "We were taken before we reached the border by an elven slaver party though we put up quite a fight and cost them the lives of three of their group before we were taken. Everything after that ... well, you know too well. We were forced to forget it all ... everything that made us who we truly were ... we even forgot why we had come in the first place as we were passed from Rhonas House to Rhonas House as Impress Warriors. I have thought much on this since, Drakis, and I know that it was the wisdom of the gods, because by enslaving us—even in our forgetfulness—we were brought to you. And even when my brother ..."

Belag turned his face away, lying back on the sand once more.

"Go on, friend," Drakis encouraged.

Belag closed his eyes again, basking in the warmth of the sun shining down on him from above. When he spoke, his voice was unusually heavy. "Even when my brother died that day on the Ninth Dwarven Throne defending you ... even though he did not know who you were because of the terrible veil of forgetfulness cast by the evil of the elves ... even then the gods smiled down on my brother and showed him how his death would have meaning."

"I understand," Drakis said in words barely heard above the splashing water nearby. "It's my turn to watch over you, now. Rest for a while ... and I'll watch out for both of us."

With a great sigh, Belag relaxed into the warm sands and drifted into a deep and contented sleep.

Drakis, sword drawn, walked with cautious step between the towering trunks of trees stretching above him into the mists. He had thought Belag was right behind him, but, impossibly, the huge manticore had vanished into the dim, fog-blurred shadows of the forest, and he found himself quite alone.

A sobbing sound caught his ear off to his left. Drakis adjusted the grip on his sword and followed the weeping as it grew louder with each step.

He rounded a tree and stopped, letting his sword arm swing down to his side.

"Mala?"

The human woman turned toward him, tears still cutting marks down the smudges on her face. She ran to him, her arms quickly wrapping around him as she buried her face in his chest.

A smile flashed across Drakis' face. He felt suddenly awkward. With the sword in his right hand and the scabbard on his left side he was left to comfort Mala by putting his left arm around her and trying not to nick her with the blade he still held in his right. "Mala . . . I'm here now, it will be all right."

"I didn't think I'd find you," she said, looking up into his face, her eyes large and still watery. "I was so worried . . ."

"I'm fine," Drakis said, pulling away from her. "Have you seen anyone else?"

"Oh, yes!" she smiled. "They're not far from here . . . they're waiting for us. They're all out looking for you now, but I found you and we'll be together again soon."

Drakis smiled again. "That's excellent, Mala. If we are going to have any hope of getting through the madness of this wood, we'll have to stay together. Where are we meeting?"

"It's not far from here, just down a nearby stream a bit," she said, taking his hand. "I can show you. Belag says we can rest, replenish, and get our bearings—whatever that means. And . . . and . . ."

"And what, Mala?"

"Oh, Drakis, I'm so frightened and tired," Mala said. "Will you please just tell me where we're going . . . and why we're going there?"

"I'm not sure it will make much sense, Mala," Drakis replied. "It's got something to do with a song."

"Really?" Mala said, puzzled, and then started pulling at his hand. "Then promise you'll tell me all about it when get there."

"Get where?"

"It's not far," she said without turning her head, "and it's the most peaceful glade you've ever seen."

CHAPTER 26

Three Truths

C H'DREI TSI-AURUUN, Keeper of the Iblisi, sat in stillness on her newly settled throne, now placed before
the fountain at the heart of Togrun Fel. Its beauties were,
for the moment, entirely ignored by her; Ch'drei's only
movement was a slight quivering of her hand as she
gripped the top of her staff with a pale fist.

Her acolytes, who had carried her heavy throne
through every fold gate from the Imperial City to the far
reaches of northern Ibania—a seemingly endless succession through increasing carnage—had never complained
about its weight or the length of the journey. Her personal guard had made no utterance regarding the open
danger to which the Keeper was exposed. Each of them
took their orders and performed their duties in unquestioning silence.

Now, her throne situated before the bone-white fountain inside the Togrun Fel—a pretty little dwarven tomb
about as far removed from every benefit of civilization as
could be found—Keeper Ch'drei alone could afford to be
as loud as she liked.

"How is it possible," Ch'drei barked in a shrill voice
that seemed to shake the very stones of the great, crafted
cavern around her, "that the Keepers of All Truth ... the

sharpest eyes and ears of the Imperial Will . . . cannot even find one of their own?"

"My Keeper," replied Master Indexia Charun from where he half bowed in front of the throne, "we followed the trail to a small fold gate to the west. That led us across the Hyperian Plain . . . beyond the Hecariat Pillar. We have eight Quorums searching now. It is only a matter of time before . . ."

"I do not care if it takes another *hundred* Quorums," Ch'drei yelled, spittle flying from between her long, sharp teeth. "I haven't traveled over two hundred leagues into the wilderness just to wait for three days in this . . . this *grave* for your report of a stunning lack of news."

"Keeper Ch'drei," Charun said, looking away from her as he spoke, "the Assesia who have returned to report tell us that the trail moves in the direction of the Murialis Woodlands. It is entirely possible that Soen and the rest of his Quorum may be dead."

Ch'drei nearly choked on her laugh. "Dead? Soen?"

"Yes, Keeper Ch'drei."

"He wouldn't *dare* die without asking my permission first!"

"That being true," came the raspy voice from the entrance to the tomb, "then perhaps . . . perhaps I might ask your permission now . . . in advance. I would hate to . . . disappoint you."

Ch'drei's head jerked up toward the voice. "Soen? Is that you, my son?"

Soen stepped from the dark opening onto the broad flagstone of the tomb's floor. The black of his robes was lost under layers of dust, mud, and stains. He swayed slightly, his balance uncertain. His narrow jaw hung open as he sucked in the moist air. "Yes, Keeper . . . your loyal servant has returned with news of a great victory . . . or, what *will* be a great victory once we deal with a few awkward realities."

Soen shuffled forward, casting a tired smile at the Indexia. "Ah, Charun is here to save me. How considerate of him to be so concerned about my welfare, but, as you can see, I am not so much lost as I am delayed."

"Soen," the Keeper said, trying unsuccessfully to keep the anger out of her voice. "I left the Citadel to meet you among the marshaling fields in Ibania."

"So your Assesia informed me." Soen stepped around the throne to the tree fountain in the center of the great hall. He sat at the edge of the pool and removed his boots. "Poor Jukung . . . so young and so ambitious. Also, sadly inexperienced although, in all honesty, even my own two Codexia didn't see the danger—no offense intended, Charun."

Soen eased his feet into the cool waters and closed his eyes with a sigh.

"You've lost them all, then?" the Keeper said with a dangerous purr in her voice.

Soen, ignoring the remark for the moment, turned to face Charun. "My deepest thanks for your concern, Master Indexia, and the efforts of all those under your charge on my behalf. Perhaps now, however, would be an excellent time for you to recall your searching Quorums as, clearly, I have been found."

Charun stiffened slightly, but one glance at the Keeper and he knew it was time to retreat. With a bow he turned and quickly stepped across the stones to the exiting tunnel and disappeared into its blackness.

Ch'drei waited a moment before she spoke again. "What happened, my son?"

Soen smiled to himself, then reached down with both long hands and scooped up water from the pool. He buried his face in his hands, rubbing the water vigorously over his face, then plunged his hands back into the water.

"Soen," Ch'drei spoke in dark tones, "there are limits to my love."

The Inquisitor stopped and then turned toward her. "So I have observed." He looked up at the cascading fountain. "It *is* rather magnificent, although its effect would be ever so much better were it moved out of this cave and into the light of day. When our Imperial Legions finally managed to break the seals on this place, I was one of the first called in to evaluate it. There was considerable discussion at the time about how we should dismantle the entire thing and transport it as a trophy back to the Imperial City, but ultimately the idea was abandoned . . . it was just too much effort. Rather fortunate for you, however, that we left it here. The sound of its waters rather conveniently obscures close conversations from more distant ears."

Ch'drei remained silent for a time, her black eyes fixed on him. "This is why you drew me to this place? You knew that I would choose it?"

"I think it much more pleasant to say, rather, that I counted on the tactical and political good sense that has made you a legendary Keeper of the Iblisi," Soen replied, leaning back on his elbows as he faced her.

Ch'drei spoke just loudly enough over the hiss and roar of the elaborate fountain for Soen to hear her words. "The Quorum then?"

Soen took in a long breath before he continued, his own voice pitched just for the Keeper's ears. "My two Codexia are dead—those that came with me, that is. The borders of Murialis have always been in some dispute with neither side pressing for exactly where to draw that line. It seems that Queen Murialis decided of late to expand her perception of what constitutes her territory. I expected the faery line but not nearly as soon as we came upon it. I had sent both Qinsei and Phang ahead to envelop our prey before the bolters reached the line, but they were both taken before they could get into position."

"And the Assesia?" Ch'drei asked quietly.

"I brought him back, but I do not know how much use he'll be to you now. Water Nymphs attacked him when he crossed the faery line. He may live, but I wonder if it wouldn't be better for him if he doesn't. I tried to warn Jukung when we came upon the line . . ."

"But he crossed anyway," Ch'drei sniffed and then shrugged. "Foolish boy. Well, I suppose that's the end of it then. Sorry to have put you to such trouble, Soen."

Soen stood up, stretching. "Who spoke of endings, my Lady?"

"You chased those bolters from one end of the Hyperian Plain to the other only to herd them all to their deaths," Ch'drei said. "It's over. Now we may never know what brought down those Wells in the Provinces . . . and it all seems like such a waste."

"Quite the contrary, Madam Keeper; this investigation grows more fascinating with each passing moment. We know three very important truths now—truths that are best kept to ourselves," Soen said, his black eyes shining. "First, I must report that while those august members of my Quorum who were with me at the time were, indeed, utterly destroyed by the denizens of the Murialis Woods . . . the bolters, on the other hand, were left entirely unscathed."

"What?" Ch'drei's outburst threatened to overwhelm the noise of the enormous fountain behind her.

"Rather interesting, isn't it? An entire living forest bent on the destruction of *anyone* invading its territory, and these seven bolters from an obscure and apparently unimportant elven House pass the faery line without so much as a hair out of place. It rather begs the question of why these particular seven are the exception to Queen Murialis' standing decree to kill all invaders first and then ask who they were later."

Ch'drei leaned forward on her throne. "You think Murialis is assisting them?"

"Certainly. Why else would they have survived the border crossing unless on her express instructions." Soen stepped in front of the throne and dropped down on the stones of the floor, crossing his legs under him as he sat facing the Keeper. "As for why Murialis would do such a thing—that part remains hidden to me. Murialis knows that harboring bolters would provide the Emperor with the very excuse he needs to declare open war on the faerylands—and she knows that he's looking for any such excuse now that the war with the dwarves is finished. The fact that she allows them to live means that she is aiding them somehow though she won't publicly admit to it. But suppose that rumors began circulating around the Imperial Houses that Murialis is not only harboring dangerous fugitives but even hinting that they may have been acting under her orders to destroy an elven House on the frontier? Were I Murialis in such a circumstance, I would be under increasing pressure to push these trouble-plagued bolters out of my kingdom as soon as possible. Murialis won't risk open confrontation; neutrality has worked too well for her thus far."

"So you want me to foment a war?"

"Just beat the drums loudly enough so that Murialis is uncomfortable."

Ch'drei nodded slowly. "I think I can manage that ... but why bother? Seven slaves escaping into the Murialis Woods are hardly ..."

"The reason to bother is, in fact, my second truth," Soen said, straightening his back. "You no doubt have the reports of our discoveries at House Timuran."

"Yes," Ch'drei nodded, her face thoughtful. "Great tragedy, that. Never happened officially, of course, but the explosive collapse of the Aether Well is still of considerable private concern—especially to the Occuran."

"You know, then, that one of the bolters is a human male by the name of Drakis?"

"Yes ... what of it?"

"The second truth I have discovered is that this human named Drakis also hears the Dragon Song."

Ch'drei looked up in disgust. "Oh, by all the gods! Do you actually *believe* this human to be the fulfillment of the Desolation Prophecies?"

"Of course not ... what kind of a fool do you take me for?" Soen snapped, his voice echoing off the walls of the domed chamber. The Inquisitor stood up quickly and moved closer to the Keeper. "One out of every ten human males of the Seventh Estate hear that same song in their heads—and since the humans still teach that prophecy to their young before they're impressed for Devotions, it seems hard to find a male child who *hasn't* been named 'Drakis' by their sires. Those prophecies are nothing but the cooling embers of a dead faith."

Soen's hand reached out, grasping the arm of the Keeper's throne and pulling him closer to her. "He may not be the Lost King come to destroy Rhonas and bring honor back to humanity...but he *could* be the one or, worse, mistaken for the one. We've got to find him before any of the ministries do...before the Legions and their generals...before the Emperor or any of his minions have any idea of his existence. We are the Keepers of Truth, Ch'drei, and this is one truth we would want within our control."

"You think he might be useful to us," Ch'drei nodded, her voice barely audible over the rushing waters behind her.

"He doesn't *have* to be the One," Soen smiled, his sharp teeth showing. "But in the *right* place he could *pass* for the One. He did cause the Aether Wells of nearly every House in the Western Provinces to fail—think of it, Ch'drei! To *fail!* The Well of House Timuran utterly destroyed: a feat beyond even the Grand Wizard of the Occuran, and yet this Drakis did it. In the wrong hands he could threaten the foundations of the Empire."

"And in the *right* hands." Ch'drei asked.

"In the *right* hands," Soen replied, "the Empire might still fall—but in a direction that could be to the *right* people's advantage."

"You propose a most dangerous game, my Inquisitor."

"But it is *my* game, Keeper," he replied, his lips parting into a wide smile revealing his pointed teeth. "The stakes are high—perhaps none higher—and yet in the end you know that you risk nothing at all."

Ch'drei nodded slowly and smiled back through her translucent, needlelike teeth. "I always liked you. I'd hate to have you killed."

"It might prove a difficult task to carry out, my Keeper," Soen nodded. "It's been tried before."

"Stay with the subject at hand," she snapped. "All of this might have proved useful...if you actually *had* this Drakis slave," Ch'drei pointed out, her long fingers uncurling into an open palm. "But as you have already said, this bolter is a guest of the vast kingdom of Murialis. Even if we flush this bird out of the forest, he could reappear anywhere along a thousand leagues of Murialis' border . . . back into Hyperia, Aeria, Chronasis . . ."

"This Drakis is currently about seventy-three leagues inside the border of Murialis," Soen said, standing upright and folding his arms across his chest.

Keeper Ch'drei eyed Soen in astonishment, momentarily unable to speak.

"And he will emerge in Vestasia to the north," Soen finished with a smirk.

"Are you a wizard, Soen," Ch'drei frowned.

"You can believe that if you wish, my Keeper," Soen said, reaching into the folds of his robe. "But the source of my knowledge is more mundane—and it is my third truth that I have brought to you."

He pulled out his fist, opening the fingers into a loose bowl. Cupped in his fingers were five round stones, each entwined with twigs or blades of grass.

"Beacon stones!" Ch'drei sighed in wonder.

"I found the first of them before the fold gate near the Timuran ruin," Soen said, his eyes wandering lovingly over the stones in his hand. "Once found, it was a simple matter to align my staff to their Aether emanations and follow them—and other signs—through each successive gate."

"The gods favor you, Soen," Ch'drei chuckled.

"If so, they did not see fit to favor me with the lives of Qinsei and Phang," Soen replied, closing his fist around the small stones.

"Do you think the other bolters know?" Ch'drei asked, her question merely curiosity.

"That they have a traitor among them who is giving away their every move to us?" Soen pondered for a moment. "No, this is a truth that is known to only three of us . . . you, myself . . . and the wretched creature that will deliver these slaves into my . . . forgive me, Keeper . . . our hands."

CHAPTER 27

Pretending

DRAKIS AWOKE WITH A START, sitting upright so quickly that he felt three vertebrae in his back crack back into place. He drew in a great gulp of air and then held it for a moment, his eyes blinking as he tried to make sense of his surroundings.

The walls of the circular space were a dark, rich brown color. The curve of their surface showed slick and glistening in the thin light that spilled down through a woven grating that capped the room ten feet or so above his head.

At length he let out his breath and stretched slowly. Every muscle in his body felt stiff and aching. It was to him as though he had slept for a thousand years, and yet he still longed for the bliss of unconsciousness. He rubbed his hand quickly over the bristles of his emerging hair and was surprised at how long it had gotten.

How long have I been in here? he wondered. For a while, he fingered the matted animal furs under him. He remembered running into the woods. Then something about Mala finding him . . . leading him somewhere . . .

He frowned at the thought of her, his mind tumbling through a cascade of memories. He loved her—*had* to love her—and yet the things he had done to her, had suffered because of her were shameful, painful, and unforgivable . . .

A small, quivering voice cut through his dark musings. "Drakis?"

He turned at once toward the sound. He sat on a slab of stone about the size of the tombs where the bones of the Rhonas dead were so often placed. There were two more of these slabs set around the floor of the curved room, but only one of them was likewise occupied.

"Mala," he replied as evenly as he could manage. "I'm here."

Mala sat with her legs pulled up tight against her chest as she rocked nervously back and forth. "Please, Drakis. Is it you?"

Drakis smiled ruefully, gripping the edge of the stone bier with his hands as he leaned forward. "I might ask the same of you. Are you all right?"

"I . . . I don't know." She raised her face toward the light. Her eyes were red from crying and still filled with tears. The beautiful shape of her head was now covered with a bristle of rust red hair, nearly obscuring the dark stains of the House tattoo. But there was something in the heart-shape of her dirt-streaked face and her wide mouth that called to his heart. And her eyes . . . those emerald eyes . . . called to him still.

"Where are we?" he asked.

"I . . . I don't know that either," she said, her voice quavering. "I'm frightened."

"There's nothing to be frightened about . . ."

"Have you seen the walls?"

Drakis turned his head around, pressing it closer to the reddish brown surface. "I don't see what . . ."

He stopped.

The wall was composed entirely of enormous cockroaches. Their legs were linked together, forming a thick pattern so dense that it was impossible for Drakis to tell if there was anything beyond the mass of roaches or whether they alone formed the wall. He reached out gingerly to touch it.

"No, Drakis! Don't . . ."

The wall of roaches reacted at once to his touch, a

clattering, chattering sound engulfing the cell as the walls around them contracted inward in a violent spasm. Drakis leaped off of the stone slab with a yelp, reaching without conscious thought for his weapon and only then realizing that it was no longer at his side.

Mala screamed hysterically, pulling herself into a tighter ball as the size of their confined space grew rapidly smaller.

Then, with equal swiftness, the surrounding cockroach wall stopped and receded, though, to Drakis' eyes, not quite so far back as it had been before.

Drakis concentrated on bringing himself under control. His breath was too quick, and he could feel the heat of his flushed face. He had no idea where they were nor how they had gotten here, but he was certain that anywhere else would be better for them. At once he turned his face toward the overhead grating and was again surprised. What had appeared to him to be a thick grillwork he now saw was constituted entirely of large snakes, their bodies woven to cover the opening. He could not discern much of anything in the light beyond the snakes, but he held little hope it was much better than where they were now.

Drakis looked down at the soft, fine-grained floor under his feet. Various skulls protruded from the deep white grains along the wall's peripheral base; the sand was composed of crushed bone.

"It will be all right," Drakis said, as much to himself as to Mala.

"How will . . . will this possibly . . . be all right?" Mala asked through gulping sobs.

Drakis turned. He longed to go to Mala, to take her in his arms and comfort her. He took a step toward her, and then he stopped and stood awkwardly in midstride, watching her.

She gazed at him, her tear-filled eyes narrowing on him, reflecting a world of pain, longing, hatred, hope, and despair. When she spoke, her words were more of an accusation than a question. "You *remember*, don't you?"

Drakis heard his own quickened breaths in his ears. His mouth had suddenly gone dry, and he was having trouble looking her in the eye. "Yes, Mala. I remember . . . I remember a great many things now . . . we all do . . ."

Her lips parted in contempt.

Drakis let out a harsh breath. "But, yes, I remember."

"How could you, Drakis," her voice shook as she spoke. "How could you do that to me? The servants who brought me to Shebin's rooms scorned me and tore at my clothes . . . all the while screeching that my *hoo-mani* body was too ugly to tempt them . . . and then they forced me to watch you . . . you . . . and that hideous, soulless elf bitch . . ."

Her voice trailed off to nothing.

Only now did he remember it all—how he had spurned Tsi-Shebin the day before because of his love of the garden slave called Mala and how her vengeance had taken its own cold course. So she had changed his Devotions that night to include erasing his memory of the woman he so tenderly loved so that she could arrange her horrific and unforgivable humiliation.

It was not the first time, Drakis knew, that Tsi-Shebin had played cruelly with him or with those he dared love other than her.

He shook with revulsion, feeling the urge to vomit and all the while knowing that it was he alone who made him sick . . . that it was himself whom he hated the most. Drakis was filled with unspeakable shame over what had happened and what he had done.

Yet his other memories of Mala persisted at the same time: of their yearning to touch softly through the bars that separated them, of the quiet talks they stole, and the warm smiles they shared.

He looked again into those emerald eyes and saw his own loathing and longing reflected back.

"Mala," he said quietly at last. "I am so terribly sorry—more sorry than I think there are words to tell. I wish there were a way that I could take it all back or change it all. I even sometimes wish that I could just forget it all and go back to being ignorant and happy."

Mala gave a short laugh, wiping her eyes against the soiled cloth covering her knees. "I'd settle for ignorant."

Drakis smiled slightly and nodded. "Well, if all you're looking for is ignorant, then here I am."

Mala gazed at him again, her face serious. "Drakis, I don't know how to forget. I look at you and I see so many different faces now all at the same time. So many of them I hate and so many of them I long for all at once. I can't make myself forget what I know. I *need* you, Drakis... I don't understand what is happening to us or where we are going... but I *need* to follow you, be with you and be comforted by you. But every time I see you I also see your *other* faces, and I just can't ..."

"Maybe," Drakis said. "Maybe we could just—pretend."

Mala looked away from him. "What?"

"Look, I—I don't know what happened to us, and we're all dealing with our own pasts," Drakis said, taking a step closer.

Mala tightened her grip around her knees.

"I know there are a lot of things in my own past that absolutely terrify me," he went on. "I've seen things ... *done* things ... you *know* that I have ... that are ..."

Drakis ran out of words, unable to express his self-loathing. "Up until now I've been able to push all these memories aside. I keep telling myself that I've got to take command, I've got to be in control and get everyone to safety—and that I'll think about my unthinkable past later. I haven't stopped—haven't really let any of us stop—long enough to deal with our own thoughts and memories. We've been running away from ourselves as fast as we could, dreading being caught by our own pasts as much as any Inquisitor the Empire has sent after us. Now we've stopped, and we have nowhere left to run from ourselves."

Mala turned her gaze back on him once more, her eyes both pleading and reserved.

Drakis offered his hand out in front of him. "Now all I know is that you are here ... and I am here ... and together we're stuck in this hole. You need someone to hold you, and I need someone to hold. So if we can't forgive our pasts or forget them, maybe we can just pretend—for a while at least—that I still love you and you still love me.

Let's pretend that all that happened before was just a bad dream and that all that matters is what's happening right here and now."

Mala did not move.

"We are who we are," Drakis said quietly extending his hand once more. "But for today, can we pretend to be those people we were before we remembered?"

Mala reached out her small, dirty hand slowly, taking his large hand in hers. He climbed up onto the stone bier next to her and slowly, carefully, put his arms around her. She turned into him, leaning against his body and turning her face into his chest.

He held her there for many hours, doing his best to pretend that she loved him.

All the while, she shrank from his touch.

Chapter 28

Eternal Halls

DRAKIS OPENED HIS EYES to a dream.

He sat facing walls that were the white of fine marble illuminated by soft balls of light floating in perfect stillness at set distances between narrow, fluted pillars. Carefully shaped trees and plants adorned the octagonal space in hues of green, augmented with brilliant flowers in orange, blue, yellow, and crimson. The pillars drew his eyes up toward a glorious and intricate ceiling twenty feet above him. Clouds drifted past the intricate latticework formed between the arches high overhead.

Somewhere in the distance, he could hear the soft echoes of musical pipes playing a gentle melody.

Mala was still at his side, though sleep had taken her at last, too. She leaned against him, quiet at last.

Drakis closed his eyes. *So this is what peace feels like,* he thought. Free from care or pain. Free from responsibilities. Free from your own past. He smiled and shifted slightly to relieve a muscle that was threatening to cramp in his lower back.

He seriously considered whether it might be possible to remain in this one spot forever. He supposed that eventually he would need to find water and food and other such bothersome necessities of life, but for now the relief that he felt in this one place was acute. He had been in pain for so long that it was not until now—when he let it go—that he realized just how large a burden it had been to him.

The hollow tones of the pipes continued to drift over him, carried from a distance on a gentle, sweet breeze.

Five notes ... Five notes ...

He wondered how he'd got here. He remembered finding Mala in the woods. He remembered following her into the glade, the rock fountain in the middle and drinking from it. His memories became more confused after that and it seemed like too much of an effort to remember. Then he remembered being in the terrible cell with Mala and ...

He shifted once more, frowning. He didn't know how he got from that horrible cell to this place, but he knew that he didn't care. For now, he thought, it is enough to just sit here, drink in the peace, rest, and listen to the sweet sounds of the ...

Nine notes ... Seven notes ...

He sat upright suddenly, his eyes open.

The song ... *that* song.

The distant pipes were playing the melody that had so often troubled his dreams and even his waking hours of late. He had tried so hard to push it from his thoughts for so long that he could scarcely mistake it now. It must be the dwarf, he thought. Jugar had been humming the tune around the Ninth Throne of the Dwarves when they first took him as a prize. It had to be him!

The peaceful, languid tones suddenly annoyed Drakis. That damnable little beast! He *would* be the one to spoil this.

Mala roused slowly, blinking as she awoke. "Drakis? What happened? Where are we?"

Drakis pushed himself off the stone—the same stone they had sat upon in the roach cell, he realized, as his bare feet landed on a soft green material that blanketed the floor. His practiced eye glanced around him, searching for something that might be used as a weapon, but other than the large stone bier itself in the middle of the tall room and the small trees that seemed to be growing right out of the flooring, there was nothing that presented itself to him as useful in combat.

He took in a deep breath and blew it out slowly. This was not a battlefield; indeed, there was something about this place that was so far removed from everything he knew about life that he found himself increasingly anxious in the midst of absolute peace.

"A land of peace and rest?" the young boy said. *"Even if there were such a place, you won't know what to do when you get there."*

"What do you know about it?" his brother whispered gruffly beside him as they pushed the wheel of the mill with a dozen other slaves. *"There is a land of peace and freedom . . ."*

"That's not what Drakosta says." I'm twelve, Drakis thought as he heard his young self speak. That young boy was me. Drakosta was still alive then and would not be beaten to death by Timuran for two years yet. *"He says that it's all a story someone made up."*

"Well that's not what Mom says," Polis answered back, sweat pouring from his forehead. *"It's north—in Vestasia maybe—beyond a sea of water and even a sea of sand. That's where we're going, Drak . . . you and me together. No one will ever make us work again. You wait and see."*

I had a brother, Polis. Which brother was that? And was that our mother who told those tales or was it someone we only thought was our mother because the elves always tried to make us believe we were in families even when our parents were dead, when several sets of parents were dead and our memories of each were successive lies . . .

"Drakis! What is it?"

Drakis shook himself back into the present. Mala stood in front of him. The soft tune continued to play.

"Come on," he said as he turned toward the tall arched doors of translucent glass and pushed them open with a violent shove.

The room beyond was a small, circular garden enclosed by a glass dome overhead. A fountain murmured in the center of the garden, whose appearance mildly shocked Drakis as it was identical to the one he remembered being in the glade just before his thoughts faded.

"This is it," Drakis said. "This is where you brought me when you found me in the Hyperian Woods."

Mala cocked her head, her eyes narrowing above her cheekbones. "What are you talking about? I couldn't find you in the woods . . ."

"This," Drakis said, stepping up to the fountain. "When we first entered the Hyperian Woods, we all got separated. You found me and brought me back to this fountain . . . it was in a glade then . . ."

"What glade, Drakis?" Mala asked. "I never found you . . . that dwarf of yours found me."

"Oh, that *dwarf*," Drakis growled and gritted his teeth. Drakis turned around, shouting up into the dome. "Jugar, you monstrous little snake! As soon as I find you playing those damned pipes I'm going to take them, break them and one by one insert them into your . . ."

"Silence, Master Drakis," came the imperious voice behind him. "These are my halls, and you will respect my home."

Drakis turned, his tirade cut short.

The Lyric stood before him, her narrow face uplifted in regal scorn. She still wore the same dress, now tattered to rags, that she had from the beginning of their ordeal, but now on the sparse and stubby golden hair sprouting from her head she wore a circlet fashioned of woven twigs. "You need not concern yourself with Jugar. He is with us, and his dwarven ways shall not trouble you while you are in my realm."

The Lyric gestured behind her, and a wide, familiar, and now troubled face came into view at about the level of her waist.

"Good friends are always well met in strange circumstances," Jugar said quietly, his mouth shaking beneath troubled eyes as he spoke. "You're a mighty man, Drakis, to live within the boundaries of the Murialis Woods."

The Lyric turned to face Drakis once more, her face

raised in defiance. "You stand within the Eternal Halls—my forest palace where you are, for now, my guests. But you may find what the dwarf, it seems, has lost the words to tell you: that it is far easier to enter the Eternal Halls than it is to leave them."

Drakis stared at the Lyric for a moment, then held up his hand. "Wait. Do you hear it?"

"Hear what?" Mala asked.

"Listen!"

In the immediate stillness, the tones of a set of pipes drifted through the garden.

Drakis stared down at the dwarf, who was trying to keep his oversized robe closed around him. Jugar shrugged, shaking his head in denial.

"If it isn't the dwarf, where is that music coming from?" Drakis asked.

"From your destiny, Drakis," the Lyric said. "Shall we find it together?"

The lithe woman walked with long, measured steps toward one of the arched doors. With elegant grace, she pulled the doors open and stepped into the enormous hall beyond.

Drakis took Mala's hand and pulled her along as he followed the Lyric with Jugar keeping so close behind that he stepped on Drakis' heel several times before the human's angry looks forced him farther away.

The hall was a magnificent space with galleries on both sides. Here the floor was polished stone, cool to their bare feet as they walked across its even and measured tiles. It was over a hundred feet in length, dizzying in size, and, to Drakis' mind, brain-numbing in its impracticality. It was opulent, glorious, and magnificent all at once and yet seemed to serve no purpose whatsoever. There were no audience chairs here for an assemblage nor artwork for display, nor did it appear to have anything to do with combat or training or any other function that Drakis could imagine.

They followed the Lyric through the enormous arch at the far end of the hall into a magnificent garden. In its center stood a raised dais platform with a wide, grand

throne. The back of the throne fanned up and over the seat
with sheltering branches and golden leaves. Three figures
stood before the throne and were at once recognized by
Drakis: Ethis the chimerian and both manticores, Belag
and RuuKag.

It was the fourth figure seated on the throne that
caught Drakis' attention, for she was the one who was
playing the pipes. She was an enormous human-appearing
woman who, Drakis judged, would be fully eight feet tall
when standing. She wore a robe of deep turquoise in color
though the exact shade seemed to shift as she swayed
with the rhythm of her song. She was a strange woman, to
Drakis' eye; her hips were disproportionately wide, and
she appeared heavy even for her height. Her breasts were
enormous and seemed barely kept in check by the closed
robe. She had a wide, fleshy face that tried unsuccessfully
to obscure two brightly twinkling eyes. Her mouse-brown
hair fell in wavy strands down as far as where her waist
should have been.

She looked up at once as they approached, her panpipes
dropping from the warm smile of her supple lips.

"So you *do* come when called," she said in a deep alto
voice filled with the warmth of late spring.

The Lyric stopped at the base of the dais, and Drakis,
Mala and the dwarf stopped just behind her.

The Lyric bowed deeply. When she spoke, her voice was
suddenly high-pitched and had a nasal quality to it that
Drakis had never heard before. "Queen Murialis! I am
Felicia of the Mists . . . Princess of the Erebusia Isles. I have
long traveled the paths of the sky and hidden my identity
from common men, but I lay myself bare before you, my
royal sister!"

Drakis gaped at the Lyric. "You're . . . who?"

Murialis, Queen of the Nymphs and Dryads, nodded
with a smile, then turned to Ethis. "Is *this* the Lyric you
were telling me about?"

"Yes, Your Majesty," Ethis replied.

Murialis turned back to the Lyric. "My sister, you are
most welcome here in the Eternal Halls. May you find

respite from your weary road and surcease for a time from your adventures. You honor us with your trust."

"Thank you, Murialis," the Lyric said imperiously. "Your kindness shall forever be remembered among my clan."

"Of course," Murialis said with a slight smile. "As a princess, perhaps you might rest for a time while I give audience to your companions? I understand that you— Felicia—are constantly weary."

The Lyric considered that for a time. "That is true, Murialis. I shall rest here in your garden for a time."

"You have my leave," Murialis replied.

The Lyric turned and strode across the grasses of the garden and settled to the ground almost at once.

Murialis turned to Ethis, laughter playing across her lips as she spoke. "She certainly takes her job seriously, doesn't she? How do you think she did as an impression of me?"

"She was but a shadow of your Imperial Presence, Your Majesty," Ethis answered with a slight bow.

"Flatterer! You must agree that even my shadow is so large that she can't even fill that!" Murialis laughed heartily and then turned her eyes on Drakis. "So this is the one, eh? He answers to the song well enough, I'll give you that."

"Yes, Your Majesty," Ethis nodded. "His name is . . ."

"Drakis, of course, I know . . . but then it would *have* to be, wouldn't it?" Murialis nodded, her eyes fixed on the human male. "So, are we standing in the presence of destined greatness? Is this the one of whom it is said that he will return the glory of the human age?"

Ethis began, "Your Majesty . . ."

"Let *him* speak," Murialis cut off Ethis' words. She rose from her throne, towering over them all. Drakis looked up into the wide face and realized that Murialis was in no way weak or even benevolent. There was malice and anger behind her eyes, and her body held power and strength that might easily break even a manticore in two. "What say you, Drakis? This manticore tells me that you are the human of prophesied destiny who will free us all from the tyranny of Rhonas and bring back the glories of the past. Are you this avatar of the gods?"

Drakis swallowed, the words forming with difficulty in his throat.

Jugar spoke into the silence. "He is, Your Majesty I can personally assure you without hesitation . . ."

"If I had wanted a lie, I would have asked you first, dwarf!" Murialis took a step closer toward Drakis. Clouds gathered with unnatural speed overhead. She towered over him as she spoke, her face pressing down close to his. "I am not some young wench who can be impressed by tales, human! Do you know why these are called the Eternal Halls? It is because there is no end to them. The halls, rooms, walls, floors, ceilings, furniture . . . everything . . . is constantly being built for me by the subjects of the forest. You cannot escape these halls because they never end . . . they are being renewed from moment to moment so that my palace surrounds me no matter where I go in my kingdom. You cannot find a way out because there *is* no way out until I decide there is! Your destiny is in my hands until I say otherwise, so tell me: Are you the prophesied one?"

"I . . . perhaps."

"A dwarven answer if I ever heard one!" Murialis shrieked. Lightning cut across the sky, its thunder shaking the garden. "I'll ask you once more, human! Are you . . ."

"I DON'T KNOW," Drakis yelled.

Murialis straightened up.

The sky began to brighten.

"Oh, Felicia?" Murialis called brightly.

"Yes, sister?" the Lyric said, sitting up at once on the grass nearby.

"Please take my friends through that door," the Queen said with a smile as she pointed to an opening on her right. "You will find a banquet prepared in your honor."

"Your courts honor us!" the Lyric replied with a firm nod.

"Yes, we do," Murialis nodded. "Just leave me with Ethis and this Drakis fellow for a time. We have a few more things to discuss."

CHAPTER 29

Unwelcome Guests

"HE'S A LOT SHORTER than I expected for a god," Murialis purred dangerously. "I must say I'm disappointed in what you have brought me, Ethis."

"I regret having been a disappointment, Your Majesty," Ethis responded at once.

"You're a chimerian of many words, my old friend, but I sincerely doubt that 'regret' is one of them." Murialis took two steps down from the dais as she peered at Drakis, then threw back her head and laughed. "Oh, look at him, Ethis! Have you ever seen such delightful puzzlement?"

"If I did, I do not recall it, Your Majesty," Ethis said with ease, his blank face gazing back at Drakis while he folded two sets of arms in front of himself.

"Ethis, what is going on?" Drakis said quietly to the chimerian. "Do you . . . you *work* for this woman?"

"This woman?" Murialis hooted. She stood on the ground directly in front of Drakis, towering over him. Her low voice started with a soft lilt and turned slowly to a keen edge as she spoke. "My dear, frail little human, your kind is such a wonder. You all have egos ever so much larger than any evidence would support. The embodiment of nature stands before you—the very same patient force that pushes mountains up from plains, cuts valleys from stone, and will surely outlast every single construct wrought by the hand of your fleeting race—and you have the effrontery to call me 'this woman'?"

The ground of the garden suddenly softened beneath his feet. His feet plunged down into the earth, which had suddenly turned into a worm-riddled mud that refused to support his weight. The worms churned in the mire, pulling him downward. Drakis struggled to pull his feet out of the mess, but he was already up to his knees.

"Ethis!" Drakis cried out. "Help! I can't . . ."

"Your most Glorious Majesty," Ethis intervened, "he is, as you yourself have noted, only a human and as such carries with him the follies of his race."

"He should show better manners," Murialis replied in tones devoid of compassion. "And know his place in the world."

"I should be delighted to instruct him on your behalf," Ethis replied. "But in Your Majesty's interest, may I point out that your august self only has a use for this human if he remains breathing."

Murialis considered for a moment and then nonchalantly raised her left hand. Two of the great ash trees that stood to either side of her throne bent over at once, their branches wrapping around Drakis' torso and pulling him from the mire. Drakis cried out from the crushing pain and then fell awkwardly to the now surprisingly firm ground beneath him as the branches sprang away from him and the trees returned to their stately positions.

"*This* is supposed to be the fulfillment of the Rhonas' Doom?" Murialis sneered as she climbed once more to her throne and sat down.

"So the dwarf says . . ."

Murialis gave a dismissive laugh.

". . . And so the manticore believes," Ethis continued. "He bears the name of prophecy, and the circumstances of his past fit the legend—or would with a little judicious revision. Your glorious self has proved that he answers to the Dragon Song."

"As one in any random dozen humans do," Murialis

mused. "Still, the possibilities are intriguing. You've questioned him ... what does he think of this prophecy he is supposed to fulfill?"

"Your Majesty, he is aware of ..."

"Questioned me?" Drakis interrupted but on seeing the look on the Queen's face struggled to think of more appropriate forms of address. "Forgive me, Queen Murialis. I am ... only a slave warrior ... but this chimerian never questioned me on any 'prophecy' or anything like it."

"Oh, this is too entertaining," Murialis' voice purred as she leaned back into her throne. "Ethis, indulge me! Show this human your marvelous trick."

"Your Majesty knows that I serve at the behest of the Lady Chythal, Mistress of the High Council in Exile," Ethis said, straightening slightly as he spoke, "It would be a betrayal of that trust if I were to reveal ..."

"I need no reminding of Chythal," Murialis spoke loud enough to cover the chimerian's words. "You and your vagabond traveling companions are still reveling in your tiresome mortal existence only because of the bonds between your Lady of the High Council and my most generous self. Show him, Ethis. I *will* be amused."

"Might I suggest ..."

"You may not," Murialis frowned, and as she spoke, storm clouds gathered over the transparent dome above their heads. "Oblige me."

Ethis paused and then bowed, spreading all four of his arms out graciously. "At your service."

Drakis wondered for a moment just what it was he was supposed to be impressed by; he had fought alongside chimera—and occasionally against them—for as long as he had gone to battle. His training in the arena had taught him all about their telescoping bone structure that allowed them to vary their size and, at the same time, made it nearly impossible to break their bones in combat. He knew, too, of their ability to alter the coloration of their skin so that they could blend into their surroundings and be more difficult to see on a battlefield. As he watched Ethis' form shift, it was all familiar to him, and he wondered if he would have to work up some feigned astonishment in order to please the mercurial Murialis.

But the transformation continued beyond anything Drakis had experienced before. The bone-plates of Ethis' face began to shift, and the muscles over the skeleton shifted their positions. The normally translucent skin began to change texture and color. Flaps appeared in the skin, seeming to shift with the chimerian's slightest move. Ethis grew shorter, his second set of arms disappeared as his shape became more human.

Drakis gasped, uncertain whether it was from horror or wonder.

Ethis stood before him . . . in the perfectly modeled form of Mala.

"By the . . . the gods!" Drakis sputtered.

The chimerian Mala walked up to him, speaking in a slightly husky rendition of the human woman's voice—an honest sadness in her expression. "I'm sorry, Drakis. It was the only way I could get us through alive."

Drakis kept his eyes fixed on the counterfeit woman as though seeing some terrible vision from which one cannot look away. "Ethis? How . . ."

"It's rare among our kind," the pseudo-Mala said with a rueful smile. "A very few of us can alter our shape radically and hold the new form for extended periods of time. It takes effort, a great deal of training and discipline. Hair is the hardest to form; clothing from skin folds is perhaps more challenging still. It's also a rather lonely existence—we are considered freakish by most of our own kind—but the High Council in Exile makes good use of turning our curse into their blessing. They call us the 'Shades of the Exile,' and we can go places in the world, perform the bidding of our Lady Chythal and . . ."

"And none would ever suspect the chimera?" Drakis finished.

"Something like that," the false-Mala said through a pout as she took another step toward Drakis, near enough now to touch him. "It does allow us to get far closer to our targets than they might otherwise allow. And anyone will tell any secret to the right companion. Still, I am glad that you and Mala were having problems when we arrived."

"Why?" Drakis said, finding himself leaning in toward the woman.

The false-Mala reached up with her hand and held Drakis back.

"Because you're a good friend, Drakis, and I'm not that kind of girl."

In a moment, Mala melted in front of him, expanded, faded, and became the four-armed Ethis.

Drakis leaped backward with a sharp cry.

"Oh, that was wonderful," Murialis clapped atop her throne. "We stage dramas for ourselves from time to time—just for our amusement—but that was far better than I could have produced. Bravo, Ethis! And your performance was refreshingly honest, Drakis of the Prophecy."

"Queen Murialis," Drakis said with growing exasperation, "I'm not this . . . this man of any prophecy!"

"Oh, I don't care whether you are or not, boy," Murialis said with delight. "It doesn't matter either way, really. All that matters is that *other* people think you *could* be this great legend destined to bring about the fall of the Rhonas Empire. Fear and doubt are like weeds growing between mortared stones; given enough time, they will destroy the strongest wall. If what Ethis tells me is true, then you've already planted those seeds whether you think it's your destiny or not. It is up to us, now, to help those seeds along a little."

"Your Majesty?" Ethis prompted.

Queen Murialis leaned forward on her throne as she spoke. "The Empire will know that you are here—that much is certain. Not all of the Iblisi who were hunting you were taken; one left to the east carrying a second who was badly damaged, and, it has been reported to me by my own operatives, has returned in great haste to Imperial lands. No doubt his report will be interpreted against me—they will claim that I am harboring you and threaten to use it as a pretext for invading my kingdom. Of course, they have never really *needed* an excuse to invade my lands, but that is one of the peculiarities of the elves—they feel compelled to justify themselves to some trumped-up morality before they commit an immoral war. I never could understand why they didn't just call it conquest without a lot of foolish justification and get it over with."

"Your Majesty, please," Ethis urged.

"It's a long, sorry process," Murialis lamented. "They will assume that I've granted you asylum. I'll tell them I didn't. They'll accuse me of lying, which is right enough, and I'll tell them I'm not—which is just another lie. Then they'll threaten to invade my land 'for my own good,' and I will in the end either capitulate and hand you over to them—in which case they will have beaten me—or I will rush you across my border and claim with feigned innocence that you aren't here at all—which, if they want you badly enough, may be what they're after all along."

"Then might I suggest," Ethis said, "that we could try to win the game before the elves know they are even playing. Don't wait for the elves . . . send us out of Hyperia now. You remove their pretext for war and upset their plans all in a single move."

"I always like the way you think, Ethis," Murialis mused. "Where would I send you? I'm on good terms with Chronasis to the southwest. You might make your way down to Mestophia."

"We might also go east," Ethis considered, "into the Mountains of Aeria and then into the chimerian lands of Ephindria. The dwarf might then be of considerable . . ."

"North," Drakis said.

"North?" Murialis asked with surprise. "Into Vestasia? Why would anyone want to go into that backward swamp?"

"Well." Drakis thought for a moment before continuing. "Isn't that what the legends say . . . that I'm supposed to go north?"

Ethis frowned. "That might be a good reason *not* to go north. The Rhonas know the legend well and would anticipate such a move."

Murialis slapped both her open palms down on her

knees at the same time and stood up. "So they might—but how can we resist twisting destiny's tail? North it shall be, but we shall best them with speed. They may expect a move to the north but never this quickly. I shall make the arrangements at once. Thank you, Ethis, for bringing me such amusement! I knew there was a reason that I let you live!"

"I am grateful, Your Majesty," Ethis replied. "But do you not think that the Rhonas may invade you whether we are here or not?"

"If they wish to invade my sovereign lands," Murialis replied with a quiet smile, "then they will have to invent a lie in order to do so. I will not provide them the satisfaction of an excuse. And if they *do* come—let them come! The land itself shall rise up against them. Let us see how their Legions fare when the rocks themselves rebel beneath their feet!"

Murialis stepped down to where Drakis stood and, leaning over slightly, extended her hand.

Drakis glanced at Ethis.

The chimerian nodded.

Drakis took the woman's large hand and kissed it.

Murialis straightened and smiled. "Drakis, I bid you farewell. Your journey is young. I go now to make arrangements for you and your companions to be tossed out of my kingdom at once. I trust you do not mind being such unwelcome guests?"

"Your . . . Majesty," Drakis said, "I believe I prefer it. Thank you."

Murialis smiled and with a nod vanished into fading embers and smoke.

Drakis paused for a moment and then turned slowly to face Ethis. "This—'trick' of yours—who else have you done this to?"

Ethis cocked his head to one side, his face once more the blank that was common to his kind. "Each in turn after we entered the woods. Murialis was long acquainted with me but did not trust the rest. It was the only way I could convince her—the only way she would spare your lives."

"Who are you?" Drakis asked. "Part of me remembers you as a faithful and long-standing comrade, but that I know is a lie placed in my mind by the Devotions. What *is* true is that I have no memory of you prior to three weeks ago. So, tell me: Who *are* you?"

"No one that need concern you . . ."

"But I *am* concerned," Drakis stood his ground. "How does a creature who has such incredible abilities—who could be *anyone*—allow himself to be enslaved? You could have taken the form of an elf and . . ."

"I did!" Ethis chuckled.

"Then how . . ."

"My own mistake," Ethis said then shrugged his four shoulders. "It matters little now. My mission was to find Thuri."

"Thuri?"

"Yes, the same Thuri you know from your *Octian*," Ethis continued. "He had been a rather prominent leader of a rebellion that threatened the security of the chimerian High Council in Exile. I had been hunting him for over a year when I found him as an Impress Warrior in House Timuran. He had forgotten his past, of course, but I knew if I could get him away from Devotions long enough, he would remember what I needed to know. I came in the guise of a Fourth Estate Elven Guardian and applied to the Tribune for an appointment as a House Guardian."

"Tribune Se'Djinka," Drakis urged.

"Yes," Ethis admitted. "I knew he had been a general some years back and hoped to use the story that I had served under him as means to gain his trust. He seemed to me, on our first meeting, to be ancient and feebleminded— and that was my mistake. It was all a game on his part. He laid a trap for me—literally a metal cage. The last thing he said to me before forcing Devotions on me was that he could remember the name of *every* warrior who had ever served with him. It seems he had never believed my story from the very beginning."

"And now you have told me a story, too," Drakis said. "And I still don't know you."

"How is that possible when each of us has barely had time enough to know ourselves?" Ethis replied. "Let's find the others. Murialis always puts a good meal on the table for her guests, and as we are apparently bound for Vestasia, we should avail ourselves of her hospitality as much as possible. Vestasia is a wild land, and that part of our journey will be difficult."

"I don't trust you."

"And you shouldn't," the chimerian went on, "but then I think that's sound advice in general—don't trust anybody."

CHAPTER 30

Shift in the Wind

CH'DREI SETTLED ONCE MORE on her throne in the heart of the Iblisi Keep and permitted herself a grateful sigh.

It was an entirely familiar place, and she was thankful to enjoy it again. In her younger days she, too, had been numbered among the Inquisitors who ranged across the wide lands and seas wherever the influence of the Rhonas was extended and often far beyond. But age and the politics of the Imperial City had eroded her enthusiasm for distant horizons and new vistas. She preferred that the reports of such places came to her here in the center of political life. Better to hear of the open sky than to experience it; rather the world be brought to her than she leave her lair to see it herself.

There were, however, those rare occasions when a journey beyond Tsujen's Wall was required . . . as when the truth to be learned needed to be kept to herself and as few others as possible. This business with Soen on the Western Frontier was one such time. Yet whenever she was required to travel, she was comforted along the road by thoughts of this place . . . that all her journeys would end back here in the quiet darkness of her court deep beneath the ancient stones of the Old Keep. The darkness better suited her purposes and the decisions that she was required to make for the good of the Empire.

It felt much like a tomb, she mused, and where better to bury the truth than with the dead?

Truth, after all, was the province of the Iblisi. The Imperial Will had from its inception altered the public perception of its past. Lie upon lie was told in the interest of the greater good and the Will of the Emperor until any concept of the actual truth was becoming lost. Even the Imperial Family of the Rhonas had begun to lose track of which lies it had told on top of other lies, and too often real truth would surface to the detriment of the state.

It was during the Age of Mists, Ch'drei recalled, that the Scrolls of Xathos came to the elves. The legends every elf knew by heart told of the great Rhonas, father of their Empire, wresting the scrolls from the gods in a challenge of wits and physical strength and founding the magic on which the Empire would be forged. Its epic tale made Rhonas the undisputed leader of the elves trying to conquer a land that was then called Palandria.

But the *truth* was that the Scrolls of Xathos were bartered from a group of manticores who had no concept of their worth as they were capable neither of reading the scrolls nor of reproducing the magic even if they could read. They had stolen those scrolls centuries before from the chimera in Ephindria who themselves had stolen them from the humans of Drakosia beyond the Erebus Straits to the north.

But the truth would not make Rhonas a mythic emperor.

So it was that early in the burgeoning Rhonas state nearly eighteen hundred years ago, it was decided that one group would be tasked with keeping the actual truth intact against those times when new lies had to be crafted in the face of reality. After all, a lie based on a truth is far more effective than one made up entirely of whole cloth. The truth—a powerful and dangerous thing—would be kept safely hidden from the general populace and often from the guilds and Orders of the Empire as well when it was in the interests of the Imperial Will.

The Guardians of the Imperial Family—the Iblisi—were originally charged with this task, and for nearly two millennia they labored tirelessly as Keepers of the Truth and the touchstones of the Imperial Will. The histories were written and rewritten, torn down and written once again to shape the minds of the Rhonas elves to support whatever the current political climate wished to be true in the public heart. Yet through it all, the Iblisi remained the keepers of the true past and the black, violent, and immoral bloody treacheries that were the constant tempo of the real Rhonas histories.

The Age of Frost, the Age of Mists, the Age of Fire ... all were chronicled in gory, terrible detail and then buried here; buried for the good of the citizens of every Estate and the welfare of the Imperial Rule.

Yet unbeknownst to the many guilds, Imperial Orders and ministries of the Empire—even to the Emperor's own thoughts—was the deepest truth of all: that for many years the Iblisi were not as concerned with safeguarding the past as they were with avoiding destiny.

The Empire was doomed; the Iblisi alone knew it, and they alone had any hope of preventing it.

Prevent it, Ch'drei thought as she sat on her throne, *at any cost.*

The doors opposite her opened with a terrible booming sound that echoed between the squat pillars of the hall. The Keeper smiled graciously at the figure approaching her with determined, quick strides.

"Inquisitor Soen," Ch'drei said through a smile. "How good of you to pay your ..."

"Keeper Ch'drei!" Soen angrily cut across the Keeper's words. "Why am I here?"

The Keeper drew in a breath before she lightly responded. "Why, my very question to you, Inquisitor ... why *are* you here?"

Soen ignored her attempt to blunt his anger. "Three weeks! Three weeks since we returned from the Hyperian Plain and still I'm kept in the Imperial City like some shackled animal!"

"Hardly shackled! I would have thought you might have taken more time to recover from your journey . . . or at least reacquaint yourself with the pleasures of Rhonas."

"You know that the city holds no interest for me. My duty lies in Vestasia—not behind these damp walls."

"Of course," Ch'drei said in purring tones. "But I have only begun to bend the Imperial Will over Murialis and your bolters. It could take weeks more before we can apply any real pressure on . . ."

"Keeper, we both know that I should have left weeks ago," Soen interrupted once more. "We cannot be certain that Murialis will hold them at all. I must leave at once. We dare not risk losing them."

"Calm yourself," the Keeper replied. "Haste breeds mistakes, Soen . . . you of all people know that."

Soen seemed about to make a sharp reply but hesitated, his face relaxing slightly. "Indeed, you are right, my Keeper, but the circumstances dictate haste. I should not have returned so far as the Imperial City in the first place."

"Have a care, Soen," Ch'drei said with an edge in her voice. "It was I that instructed you to return here."

"And in doing so have cost us both not only weeks of delay but the contact with the beacon stones that mark their path," Soen countered. "I could have been in Vestasia reacquiring them by now if you had . . ."

"If I had done what—bartered passage for you through the Imperial Folds? And just how would I have done that without giving the Occuran answers about the Provinces or the Myrdin-dai some report on the mess they are *still* cleaning up on the frontier? They only granted you and your Quorum access last time to find out why they had been made out as fools—they certainly would not have done so again without receiving their payment for your last adventure! You may be a great Inquisitor, Soen, but you know *nothing* about politics. One day you'll trip over your tongue once too often, boy, and fall where no amount of craft can save you."

"Forgive me, Keeper," Soen said carefully. "I serve at your pleasure."

"Yes, you do," Ch'drei said, her tone still sharp. "And you will continue to do so. Having been so adamant, I hesitate to tell you that I have indeed arranged passage with the Occuran through their Imperial Trade Folds as you requested. You have been granted an Imperial Charge that cannot be questioned and that leaves you free to pursue your target at any price—*any* price, you understand."

"Yes, my Keeper."

Ch'drei nodded with satisfaction. "Very well, Soen. How do you intend to proceed?"

"I must leave at once, Keeper," Soen said. "I'll follow the Trade Folds into occupied Chaenandria and then the old Northmarch Folds as far as Yurani Keep. Then I'll make my way southwest, to pick up their track once more. My Matei remains aligned to the traitor's beacon stones. It is only a matter of time after that."

The Keeper raised her brow over her glossy black eyes. "Time before what?"

"Before I track down this Drakis and find out who he really is," Soen said. "If he's worth your time, Ch'drei, then I'll bring him back to you as a gift."

Ch'drei smiled. She could imagine Soen thinking and rethinking this plan each day for the last three weeks. "Bring this Drakis back to us and we'll see if he is of any use. I am counting on your skill and your discretion. No one may know of this, you understand. I am sending you out alone and with no Quorum in support. This is against the laws of our Order, but under the circumstances I think it best you be left to act on your own."

"Wisdom indeed," Soen said with a smile. "For if I am discovered . . ."

"I will deny that this conversation ever took place," Ch'drei nodded. "I believe we are both clear on this subject?"

"Yes, Keeper," Soen nodded. "When may I leave?

"Within the hour," Ch'drei said. "You are expected at the Trade Folds of the Occuran before noon."

"Thank you. I shall bring honor to your name, Ch'drei," Soen said with a slight bow and a wry smile.

"I have every confidence in you, Soen," Ch'drei smiled in return.

The Keeper watched her Inquisitor as he backed a few steps from her and then turned, his strides carrying him across the floor back to the still open doors. He stopped and, flashing a sharp-toothed grin, pulled the doors closed as he bowed out of the room.

Ch'drei sat for a moment, waiting for the deep silence to once again permeate the room. She always thought of the silence as a physical thing that she both welcomed and respected. She reveled in it for a while longer until she was certain that it would not be disturbed by Soen again.

"You understand what you have heard?" Ch'drei whispered into the silence.

The silence whispered back. "Yes, Lady Ch'drei."

"And your Quorums? Are its members in place?"

"Yes, Lady Ch'drei," came the hushed response, barely echoing between the columns supporting the low ceiling overhead. "They are arranged among the Trade Portals as you requested. Everything lies in wait."

"And none of the Quorum members know your mission," the Keeper said, stressing each of the words as she spoke. "It is absolutely vital that you alone know your true mission—that you *alone* complete it."

"They know only that we serve the Iblisi," the voice replied. "They will obey me without question."

The Keeper allowed herself a sad smile. "He must never suspect you are tracking him—never have the notion so much as enter his head. If he so much as hears you breathing, you will be of no use to me."

"Yes, Lady Ch'drei."

The Keeper stood up from her throne and carefully descended the three steps to the floor of her audience hall. "Tell it to me once again . . . let me hear it in your own words. What is your first task?"

"Track the Inquisitor Soen wherever he may go. Leave no trace of our passage. Follow him to a human slave named Drakis—the Drakis who bolted from House Timuran in the Western Provinces."

"That is right," the Keeper purred. "What is your second task?"

"When we are assured of his identity, we are to capture this Drakis alive and kill any who may have associated with him. I am then to deliver this Drakis to you personally here in this room."

"That is right," Ch'drei said . . . and then, holding up her hand, she paused.

The Keeper had thought this through again and again since that day at Togrun Fel, tried to find a different course to take; but her first thought as she had sat on this same throne inside a tomb half a continent away remained her only answer.

Soen was right; this Drakis could easily be mistaken for the bringer of doom to the Rhonas Empire—especially because he was a weapon of untold destruction. The fall of the Empire *was* coming as Ch'drei, Soen, and a number of other Inquisitors were well aware. Soen wanted to control that fall and emerge victorious from the rubble with the Iblisi to rule.

Ch'drei shared that vision, but she also knew that such power was not something easily held in common with anyone—especially an Inquisitor with boundless ambition. Sooner or later, one of them—Ch'drei or Soen—would have to go.

Better sooner than later, Ch'drei sighed to herself. And better Soen than her.

"And finally?" Ch'drei spoke at last to the darkness.

"And then we are to track and kill Inquisitor Soen," the voice said, a rasping sound now apparent in its speech.

So it had been said, and having been said was now the will of the Keeper. Killing Soen would not be easy, she mused. For that she had needed someone who was personally motivated and committed to the Inquisitor's death.

Ch'drei smiled as she turned. From the shadows at the side of the hall, a robed figure emerged. It drew its hood back, revealing a face that would have caused even elven adults to blanch. A flap of damaged skin sagged down over the elf's right eye, which was now a dreadful and useless milky-gray in color. The skin of his face bore long scars and discoloration from slashing burns that ran up his long forehead to the elongated crown, but one particularly terrible scar pulled badly at the left corner of his mouth, lifting the lip on that side into an unnatural and perpetual snarl.

Ch'drei sighed at the sight of him. "I delayed as long as I dared. I had hoped that the healers of the Occuran could have done more for you, but there is no more time left to us. Are you ready, my son? Can you do this thing that the Order demands of you?"

"To follow Soen to this human, rob him of his glory, and then kill him?" the misshapen elf asked. After a slight pause, the figure fell to his knees. "Yes. Oh, yes, I can with the greatest of pleasure, Lady Ch'drei."

The Keeper laid her long, bony hand atop the burn-scared forehead of the elf kneeling before her. "Then go with the blessings of the gods and the Will of the Emperor, Inquisitor Jukung."

Jukung raised his face toward her, his effort at a grateful smile contorting his features into a grim mask.

Book 3:

THE FORGOTTEN

CHAPTER 31

Fool's Errand

THE DWARF STOOD on an outcropping of rock, survey-
ing his own mind as much as the landscape spread
before him.

There were two obvious paths in the morning light. One
lay northward into the broad, unknowable expanse of the
Vestasian Savanna that ran to a flat and hazy horizon. The
other path led eastward up into the foothill foundations
that formed the western end of the Aerian Mountains. He
could see the peaks in the distance now outlined in the
slowly warming twilight of the dawn.

Northward with Drakis . . . eastward with his heart.

In truth, back into the roots of the mountain had been
his original—if somewhat desperate—plan. When the Last
Throne had fallen, he was trapped with the Heart of Aer,
both of them hidden in the midst of the Rhonas Army occupying the caverns surrounding them on all sides. It was
only a matter of time before the entirely too predictable
elves would come with their gleaners and discover him and
his treasure. Then Drakis had come—a gift from the forge
of the gods—and the confused human became the means
of Jugar's escape.

That his "escape" involved placing himself into slavery
was, he chuckled to himself, the very foundation of its

brilliance. House Timuran was obviously just another of uncounted self-important and equally insignificant Imperial Houses of the Third Estate aspiring to grandeur in the grandeur-ridden Rhonas Imperium. A more important House—or perhaps one closer to the actual power of the Empire—might have recognized the Heart of Aer for what it truly was, and then Jugar would have been a fool indeed. But a backwater House of the Western Provinces . . . no, that was a place that would not recognize what they had until he had used its power against them, caused their hearts to be torn still beating from their chests, and freed himself and his prize.

That this human idiot heard the Song of the Northern Legends in his mind made it all the easier.

And it had all worked out so much better than he had planned. Jugar congratulated himself again on how well he had manipulated this Drakis fellow to the point where his distraction had allowed the dwarf to recover the Heart of Aer—and do all the damage that he had hoped to achieve. That Drakis and his companions had brought him north through the infernal elven folds had been a wonderful and happy accident that he had managed to steer toward Togrun Fel—his intended destination all along. The westward bend in their course across Hyperia had been necessitated by the Rhonas armies that remained encamped at the Southern Gates.

But then things began to go wrong. The Hecariat had been a close thing, and then, try as he might, he could not influence Drakis—who had grown unreasonably stubborn—to turn them back north toward the mountains. Somehow that madwoman Lyric had put that nonsense about Murialis in his head. Even then he might have managed to persuade Drakis to turn north toward the end of the mountains, but his back luck turned to worse. The Iblisi Inquisitor and his Quorum had shown up at the most inopportune moment and forced them all into the lands of the dreadful Murialis faery queen.

But the dice of the gods had not stopped rolling, and even that apparent disaster had turned to his advantage.

Murialis had bought into the Drakis legend—no wonder faeries are so fond of tales—and had not only spared their lives but had managed to whisk them through her kingdom and deposit them all at its northernmost boundaries almost exactly at the spot where—in his wildest dwarven dreams—he had hoped to come.

"So, you're leaving us?"

Jugar actually started at the voice behind him. He slipped the black, cold crystal stone back into his pocket. "Eh? Oh, Drakis!"

"My apologies," Drakis said, his own gaze fixed on the mountains in the distant east. "Still, I'd be sorry to see you go."

"Go?" The dwarf turned and smiled charmingly. "No, friend Drakis—I was but looking on the ancestral mountains of the lost dwarves. Just a fool lost in thought."

"Not so lost, I think," Drakis replied. "I've been doing some thinking of my own. Just before the last battle—before we met—Braun told me . . ."

"Who?" Jugar asked.

"Braun," Drakis answered with some annoyance. "Our Proxi . . . you don't know him. Anyway, he pointed out that there were no young nor old among the dwarven dead."

"Indeed?"

"Yes, indeed," Drakis continued. "So, I think they must have gone somewhere, Jugar. There must be dwarves somewhere—and a great many of them, I wouldn't doubt."

"This—Braun—friend of yours seems uncommonly clever," Jugar sniffed.

"My point is that you should go and find them," Drakis said, nodding toward the mountains. "You've done enough for us."

"Nonsense!" Jugar laughed. "We've only just started down our road!"

"My road, not yours," Drakis said. "Why have you even come with us this far? I half expected you to leave us at Togrun Fel . . ."

He nearly had, Jugar thought to himself.

But now he wavered.

Jugar gazed at the distant outline of the Aerian Range to the east and sighed with great satisfaction. He pulled the Heart of Aer from his pocket, fingering its cold facets as he tumbled it over and over with the fingers of his hand. There beneath the mountain, he thought, his people waited. There, deep in the dark roots and secret places farther below than elves or men ever suspected, his fellow dwarves waited for the return of the Heart of Aer and through it the healing of their race.

But healing was not what Jugar had in mind.

Vengeance, retribution, justice, pain—that is what filled his thoughts and schemes, along with the growing conviction in his soul that Drakis could be the means by which he could achieve all his dark and cold desires. Could Drakis be the real thing? If he was, then Drakis could be the means of spilling enough elven blood to satisfy even Jugar's thirst for revenge.

All he needed was for Jugar the Fool to guide his steps a little longer—and a little farther north.

"Sometimes it's a good idea to take a road you've never walked before and see where it leads, Drakis," Jugar said through a gap-toothed smile. "I'd like to walk yours a bit longer and see where it takes me."

"Drakis?"

The human warrior and the dwarf returned from the ridge to the small encampment. Ethis tended a cheery fire that was somehow almost entirely devoid of smoke. Jugar moved quickly to the flames, warming his hands. Drakis would have joined him, but the Lyric rushed up to him before he could take another step.

The pale face of the Lyric was staring at him. "Drakis, it is long past time you returned. There is a journey before us, and you are our guide."

Drakis took the Lyric's offered hand. "Thank you . . . and you are?"

The Lyric flashed a bright, roguish smile. Her emerging hair was almost white in its lightness, a fuzzy nimbus framing her pinched face. "You are still confused from the journey. You will remember me as Felicia of the Mists."

"Yes," Drakis nodded, trying to remember just who the Lyric last thought herself to be. "The . . . uh . . . Princess of the Isles."

"Princess of the Erebusian Isles," the Lyric corrected with a light laugh. "Fear not, good Drakis; we raiders of the Nordesian Coast are far more forgiving than our frightening legends make us out to be. When we reach the coast, our cousins who sail the Bay of Thetis will show you such hospitality that you will never again forget my true name!"

"I shall look forward to it," Drakis said, but his words seemed to fade toward the end as his eyes tried without success to take in the vista that lay just beyond the Lyric.

The morning sun cast long shadows across a low, jagged terrain that gave way quickly to a seemingly infinite plain of grassland marred only occasionally by a grouping of solitary trees or the flash of water through the shimmering waves of the warming air. To his right, distant purple peaks rose above the line of dense trees that ran from the east behind him and continued to form a great arch that vanished into a hazy and indistinct horizon to the west. The sky itself seemed larger to him stretched over such a vastness so flat that he felt he might almost fall off of it.

Ethis looked up, his face now the typical blankness that characterized most of the chimerian race. "Good morrow, Drakis."

Drakis ignored the chimerian. "Jugar, since you're determined to be here with us . . . perhaps you could tell us just where are we?"

"We are precisely where you asked that we should be," the dwarf said brightly. "We are beyond the northern border of the cursed Hyperian Woodland and now stand on the verge of Vestasia itself! We have traveled just short of eighty leagues and seemingly overnight."

"That far?" Drakis asked. "How is that possible?"

The dwarf looked up from the campfire and smiled. "My good Drakis, it is a miracle—nothing short of a miracle of the gods—that we have been brought here. Carried by the demons of Queen Murialis for reasons of her own and deposited as you yourself requested here across the northern boundaries of her most terrible and feared kingdom! I had hoped to skirt the western slopes of the Aerian Range and avoid any danger that her minions might present, and yet here we are and a week's journey the richer for it! And fortunate—fortunate indeed—for all our possessions remain with us with not a piece of lint nor thread subtracted from the lot as one might expect from the faery folk! A week's worth of travel in a single day—thanks to the capricious whim of the Faery Queen."

"Hardly capricious," Ethis added, his eyes fixed on Drakis. "Drakis negotiated our passage for us. It seems Murialis is a reasonable monarch after all."

The human warrior eyed Ethis critically for a moment but decided not to let the comment escalate into an argument. Drakis had done nothing that brought them through the strange woods of Murialis except to let the Faery Queen believe that he *might* be this mythical fulfillment of some ancient prophecy that everyone seemed to know about except him. Ethis had been the one who had saved them, bringing them into the faery realm and insuring that they weren't summarily killed. If Ethis had his reasons for letting the rest of the group think that Drakis had been the big hero, then an argument over who had actually saved them would have been foolish.

They were in enough trouble without fighting among themselves over anything; so Drakis turned his mind to other things.

Vestasia, Drakis thought. It felt different from the Hyperian Plain that they had crossed with such trepidation just the week before; though it had been deserted, Drakis felt it was a land where civilization had once flourished and could return again to tame the broad plain and cultivate its expanse. The overwhelming impression that the warrior had of the grass-and-rock choked flatlands before him was that it was entirely wild, forbidding and savage. It was a badlands with its own natural law that defied anyone from the outside who wished to impose any rule other than that of unstoppable, deadly nature.

"Beautiful, is it not?"

Drakis turned toward the deep voice. "You think it beautiful?"

Belag seemed to stand taller than ever. His great, flat snout was raised as though sniffing the wind for the scent of prey. RuuKag stood behind him but presented a completely different demeanor; his shoulders were hunched forward, lowering his head with the curve of his back as he looked over the plain.

"Yes, beautiful," Belag said, a smile pulling at the corners of his mouth and baring his fangs as he spoke. "This place is known among my race as the 'Land of the Shamed.' It is the place where cowards come to die in exile from their clans. It is supposed to be a cursed place ..."

"It *is* a cursed place," RuuKag said abruptly.

"Cursed? How is it cursed?"

"It does not matter. You are with us, Drakis," Belag continued. "It is sung of in the prophecy that where you walk, the cursed lands shall be made whole beneath your feet."

"You seem terribly pleased at the prospect of crossing this cursed place," Ethis observed.

"I find the open land calls me," Belag said drawing in a deep breath. "It brings into my mind the great plains of Chaenandria where my father and his father's fathers hunted our prey and fought our battles down through all our songs of glory. RuuKag and I can run in the open ..."

"I have no desire to run," RuuKag grumbled.

"Then I shall feel the wind pass through the hairs that are springing from my mane and the sun beat upon my back. The open sky shall be my temple and all the wild beasts shall flee from me in fear. I shall pit my speed and strength against them and bring them down in righteous sacrifice in your name. I shall hunt for you, Drakis, and for all of us. I shall taste the warm blood of my prey in my mouth once more as the star-gods intended from the beginning."

Drakis turned to Ethis. "What about you ... I can assume you've been here before."

"Here, yes," Ethis said then nodded toward the great plain to the north. "But there? No. That is a land that cannot be tamed, a land too wild and harsh even for the determined and cunning elves of Rhonas. The Empire has extended its influence farther to the north and east, but into this place they rarely bother to venture except on occasional slaving expeditions on the southern shores of the Bay of Thetis . . ."

Drakis was having trouble hearing what Ethis was saying. He had to remind himself that he could not trust the chimerian, a creature that a small part of his mind still told him was a trusted colleague and brother in arms but only, he reminded himself, because the Devotions had made him believe it. Drakis had no memory of Ethis before the battle for the Ninth Throne, and his actions since the fall of their Devotions—his alarming transformations in the faery kingdom and his use of them to trick Drakis into revealing so much of himself—had left the human hurt and suspicious.

Beyond his distrust, the song was running through his mind, and it distracted him once more. It was never far from his thoughts and was growing stronger with every step they took toward the north. In some ways, this was a comfort to him; before it had been a weak annoyance, like an itch that one could not quite reach. With its increasing prominence he was better able to tune it out and even ignore it from time to time. But occasionally it dislodged memories that rushed to the surface of his thoughts and broke upon his consciousness.

"Well that's not what Mom says," Polis answered back, sweat pouring from his forehead. "It's north—in Vestasia maybe—beyond a sea of water and even a sea of sand. That's where we're going, Drak . . . you and me together. No one will ever make us work again. You wait and see."

Drakis forced his attention back to Ethis as he spoke.

". . . no real knowledge of the nomadic tribes that manage to make their home here," Ethis concluded. "I took a very long road to avoid crossing that dangerous wasteland—no one enters the savanna of Vestasia lightly."

"All the more reason we should," Drakis answered. "What better place to hide than a place no one wishes to enter?"

Ethis raised both his hairless brows in surprise.

"It's north—in Vestasia," Drakis said with a thin smile. "You wait and see."

They walked for five days across the plain without feeling they were making any progress. Ethis insisted that they pick a point in the distance in the morning that appeared to be north and then keep their track fixed on that destination. This almost always amounted to finding a distant grouping of trees that could be spied across the seemingly endless grasses.

The terrain was far from entirely flat; undulations and occasional rock outcroppings gave some variety to what otherwise would have been a near tabletop flatness to the land. The grasses were yellowing and the ground beneath them parched. Their footfalls raised great clouds of gray dust that drifted upward, which greatly concerned Ethis as their movements could undoubtedly be seen for many leagues in any direction.

Mornings were the time that Drakis liked best, for each of them worked in harmony toward their common good. Belag, who had disappeared the previous night, would return exhausted in the morning—but always with a fresh kill. RuuKag would quarter the creature and properly butcher its meat so that it could be cooked. Jugar would busy himself finding or making a properly clear space while Ethis constructed a fire pit. Mala and Drakis would cook the meat for them, while the Lyric always seemed to appear with wild roots or berries though none of them could determine just how or where she came by them. Then, their meal concluded and the remaining cooked meats packed for use later in the day, everyone would see to cleaning up the camp before setting off.

Belag would remain behind and sleep in the early part

of the day, but he would always join them by afternoon, his deep-throated voice singing through the grasses as he approached.

By midday of the sixth day of their trek northward, they came upon a wide, meandering river that wound its twisted way across the plain. Wildebeest, antelope, and ibex appeared from time to time at the river's edge to drink . . . each one a sight that astonished the humans and even, Drakis noted with amusement, the chimerian. Jugar at each opportunity managed to spin a tapestry of knowledge about these beasts based entirely on stories he had heard or, Drakis was convinced, that the dwarf made up on the spot.

They followed the river for four additional days, but by the morning of the tenth day it was obvious that the river's course was leading more toward the west. When Belag reported that there were watering holes to be found on their northern course, Drakis determined to abandon the river, and once more they set off across the plain.

It was on the evening of the thirteenth day that they saw the great dust trail crossing the plains to the north. For three days they followed the long cloud of dust that seemed to precede them. By the end of the seventeenth day on the savanna, Drakis could see that the clouds of dust they had been following ended at a brown knob too distant for them to make out any detail.

When Belag left on his evening hunt, he promised to hunt in that direction and report on what he saw over their breakfast.

Drakis waited from dawn of the following day to hear Belag's report.

The manticore did not return.

CHAPTER 32

The Hak'kaarin

"**Y**OU'VE KILLED US, Drakis!" Mala screamed, her fists flailing against him as he tried desperately to restrain her without doing her any harm. He was finding it impossible to do either. "*You* did this! You killed Timuran . . . destroyed our home . . . destroyed our *lives!*"

All reason had fled from Mala. The despair and anger that she had pushed down behind a wall of apathy from the first step they had taken into Vestasia now exploded in a senseless rush of blind anger and rage focused on Drakis.

She shoved at him, pushing herself away and staggering back onto the trampled grass where they had all spent the night. Drakis was keenly aware of the audience around them. Ethis stood with both sets of arms folded across his chest, detached and observant. Jugar looked as though he were enjoying a play that was being enacted for his benefit, while RuuKag was openly enjoying Drakis being ridiculed and shamed by his supposed mate. The Lyric, at least, was paying no attention whatsoever.

Mala glared at Drakis. "I've walked for days . . . *days* . . . into this, this . . . this *nothing* . . . because *you* said we should. And now the one creature that provided for us . . . brought us our food and made it even possible to live in this . . . this *armpit* of the world has vanished because *you* sent him off to find out about something you know nothing about."

Drakis breathed in deeply, reining in his own rage and embarrassment. "Mala, this isn't the time for this. You just need to . . ."

"No!" Mala shouted back, running one hand in frustration back from her forehead through the red hair that was now nearly an inch long. "I do *not* 'just need to' do anything for you anymore! You ruined it all, Drakis! Ruined our lives and led us out here to die!"

Drakis let out his breath and gazed up into the sky.

He could feel their eyes on him, waiting.

"Fine," he said at last, a cheek muscle twitching as he spoke.

"What?" Mala said between clenched teeth.

"Fine. You're right." He was not looking at her, his gaze fixed on a horizon of his own choosing. "I did it all, Mala . . . just the way you said. I brought down House Timuran and woke us all up to the lie we were living. I brought us into this dangerous, barren place. If it makes you feel any better, I agree with you that it is *entirely* my fault." Then Drakis looked directly at Mala with the same cold stare through which he had often viewed his prey in battle. "But *you*, Mala, are *here*. All of us are *here*. How you got here or why isn't going to change the fact that you are here right now. So you have a choice to make. It's your choice, and you're going to be responsible for it."

He took a step toward the woman.

She stepped back. Drakis could not decide if her look was of fear or hate.

"You can either stay here, curse my name for as many days as you have left to you, and *die*," Drakis said. "Or you can *shut up*, come with us, and do something that might get us through another day."

Mala glowered back at him. "How *dare* you even . . ."

"It's up to you. You may not think I'm much," Drakis continued, "but right now I'm all you've got. I'm going to find my friend Belag . . . if he's still alive . . . and find some way to live another day. Come or stay—you decide."

Drakis turned to face the rest of his companions. "That goes for you, too. Die on your own or come with me now."

He gazed out over the tall grass and pointed toward the strange, brown mound to the north. "He went that way. Let's go."

Ethis smiled slightly and then, drawing his sword, walked in the direction Drakis was still indicating. The dwarf took his cue from the chimerian and followed closely behind. The Lyric jumped up from where she had been otherwise seemingly ignorant of the proceedings and, slapping Drakis on the shoulder in earnest support, quickly fell in line. RuuKag looked everywhere but in the direction of Drakis and lurched into movement after the Lyric.

Mala remained stone-still.

Drakis turned, drew his own sword and fell in line after RuuKag.

It was many long minutes before he heard Mala following behind him through the grass.

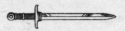

"What is it?" Drakis whispered as he crouched down in the grass.

Ethis knelt on one knee next to him. "I don't know . . . I've never seen anything like it."

The tall grasses ended abruptly just a few feet in front of them. Beyond was a barren ground completely denuded of any plant life perhaps a thousand feet wide surrounding a mound of sun-baked mud so enormous that neither Drakis nor Ethis could see the sides from where they watched.

"It looked smaller this morning," Drakis mused.

"It also looked a good deal closer," Ethis observed, gazing at the deepening hues of the horizon. "We've only got about an hour of daylight left now. What do you suggest?"

"I don't know!" Drakis sputtered. "It's . . . well, it's enormous! Someone or something must have built it here. Look there, see the way there's an overhang all around the bottom of the mound? It curves outward to keep predators off the top. The thing has openings all around it under that overhang, but they each seem to be blocked by a large stone. And we don't know what's on the other side of those stones either. The two of us are the only warriors left in a group whose remaining skills include butchering, storytelling, singing, and complaining."

"So you were planning on storming the defenses?" Ethis asked.

Drakis chuckled. "No . . . but we haven't seen any signs of movement out of the . . . wait! Did you hear that?"

"You *were* talking at the time and . . ."

"Quiet!" Drakis said, holding up his hand as he cocked his head to one side.

It was a strange, hollow sound, but in the silence around the mound it was unmistakable.

"Drakis . . . Come!"

Drakis turned to Ethis, but the chimerian was already craning his neck higher, straining toward the sound.

"Drakis . . . Ethis . . . come!"

"Where is it coming from?" Drakis whispered hoarsely.

"I don't see where . . . wait!" Ethis pointed with his upper right hand. "There . . . just to the right of center. I would swear that was closed just a moment ago!"

Drakis gazed closer in among the deepening shadows being cast by the overhang around the mound. One of the blocked openings was suddenly and inexplicably open. A tunnel ran backward and up into the mound. Two torches burned in sconces mounted on either wall.

"That's a little too accommodating," Ethis said.

The voice from within called once more. "Drakis . . . Ethis . . . night is falling. Come . . . RuuKag . . . Mala . . . Jugar . . . Lyric . . . come!"

"It's Belag," Drakis said as much for his own assurance as Ethis' benefit.

"No, it can't be," Ethis countered. "This makes no sense, Drakis!"

"Perhaps not, but I'm going to get a closer look," Drakis said, dropping his pack. He unstrapped the small shield and adjusted the sword at his hip. "You wait here and watch. If I don't come back, get everyone out of here and back to some more civilized place."

"North, I suppose?" Ethis quipped.

Drakis chuckled. "If I don't come back, I wouldn't advise following such an obviously flawed prophecy."

Drakis bounded from the cover of the grass straight onto the flat, open ground. He ran quickly across its surface, puzzled at the springy quality of the ground under his feet as he ran but too intent on the opening looming before him to stop. He flattened himself against the wall next to the opening and then slowly turned to look inside.

The tunnel floor rose upward. Pairs of torches fluttered in a breeze coming from inside the tunnel, emitting greasy smoke as they flagged, each pair lighting the way farther inside. The upward curve of the tunnel itself prevented him from seeing more than a hundred feet or so down its length. The closing mechanism was obvious to him now as a round, carved stone rolled out of its channel and into a space in the wall. Something had built this place.

"Drakis . . . I've got to explain something." The voice was unmistakably that of Belag, but there was an odd quality to it that Drakis could not identify.

Drakis ducked into the tunnel and, grabbing a torch, ran up the curving incline. He passed several pairs of torches along the way as the rough-walled tunnel first curved upward into an incline and then began to curve down away from him. There were no side passages nor openings that he could see. Each step carried him farther and deeper into the great mound.

The tunnel ended abruptly in a black void so large that the torch in his hand did not penetrate it.

Just over a hundred feet in front of him, illuminated by a single torch, sat a manticore on a woven throne.

"Belag?" Drakis called in a loud whisper.

The manticore stood. "Drakis! Thank the gods! I must beg your forgiveness . . . I would have come, but the Hak'kaarin would not permit me to leave."

Drakis did not wait but walked quickly toward his friend. "You are being held a prisoner, then?"

"No . . . not exactly . . . please, Drakis, I need to explain . . ."

"Explanations later," Drakis said. "First, let's get you out of here."

"No, you don't understand," Belag said, holding his huge hands out in front of him. "I need to warn you. The Hak'kaarin . . ."

"Warn me?" Drakis stopped at once, crouching down and turning slowly, his senses heightened. "What is it?"

"The Hak'kaarin," Belag started again. "They love to . . ."

In that instant, ten thousand torches flared into life; their light banished the blackness from the enormous chamber.

"WELCOME!!!"

Drakis screamed in shock, his body reacting at once in fear. When he came to his senses once more, he was crouching, his sword drawn and shield held high as he stared in wonder.

"The Hak'kaarin," Belag sighed, "love to surprise guests."

The torches illuminated hundreds of caves that honeycombed the walls of the mud cavern. Branching caverns could be seen in several directions, now completely visible in the bright light. But it was the eyes staring back at him that astonished him the most; each of the hundreds of caverns was filled with short, reddish brown creatures with enormous eyes and hooked noses. They wore hides, pelts, and tanned leathers for clothing, and each held a torch in large hands with long fingers.

Drakis was standing next to a great blackened pit filled with dried grass bundles and even a few dead trees. As he watched, two of the small creatures scurried forward and tossed their torches onto the pile. The pit erupted into a towering fire, and the thousands of creatures in the caverns lining the walls broke into an enormous cheer.

"Where in the abyss have you been?" Drakis yelled at Belag, trying to be heard over the noise.

"Here," Belag roared back. "They caught me last night

trying to get a better look at them. They have a rather impressive defensive plan that . . ."

"Not now," Drakis yelled back. "Why didn't you come back?"

"They wouldn't let me," Belag replied. "We need their help, and I didn't want to hurt any of them."

"So you just sat here?" Drakis barked.

"No," Belag shook his great head. "The Hak'kaarin are mud gnomes . . . wanderers of the wasteland. About the only thing they love better than surprising other creatures is hearing their stories."

Drakis was not sure he heard the manticore correctly over the noise. "Did you say 'stories'?"

"Yes!" the manticore bellowed in reply.

Drakis looked up, suddenly aware that the cheering had become rhythmic.

"Oh, no!" Drakis' murmured words were completely obscured by the chanting.

"DRAKIS! DRAKIS! DRAKIS! DRAKIS! . . ."

The human warrior turned to the manticore and smiled grimly as he yelled. "I think I can guess which story you've been telling!"

CHAPTER 33

Caliph

"SOEN TJEN-REI, Inquisitor of the Iblisi," the brilliantly robed gnome shouted from the far end of the Great House Hall, throwing his chubby arms wide. "My dear old friend! The sight of you fills my eyes with joy!"

Soen bowed deeply at the hall entrance, dust billowing from his robes as he quickly returned upright and threw his own arms wide, his narrow face split into a sharp-toothed smile. "Argos Helm, Caliph of the Dje'kaarin and my most honored citizen of the north! The burdens of my journey are lightened at your sight!"

Argos Helm slapped both his fat hands down on the top of his trouser-covered thighs with a resounding clap. This caused both his short legs to jerk forward slightly in reflex, his ornate silk shoes swinging away from the tall throne where they hung two full handbreadths above the floor.

Soen determinedly held his fixed smile, fingering his Matei staff in his right hand and mentally reviewing the many ways in which he might use it to most satisfactorily obliterate the pompous, scheming, slippery, and utterly corrupt gnome who sat so cheerfully before him. Argos was the latest in an unfortunately long line of Caliphs who had ruled the Stone Gnome tribes of the northern coastal regions of Vestasia since the Grand Army of the Emperor had come to a disappointing end to its march at these miserable shores three centuries before. Mortis Helm was only one of several dozen self-proclaimed warlords, but it was he alone who had both the shrewd foresight and unbridled pragmatic opportunism to ally himself and his family with the weary invaders. Mortis was in awe of the might and splendor of the Rhonas Imperium from the distant south—especially their stand against the humans who had, in his mind, long ignored and dismissed his people as unworthy of their attentions. He envisioned a day when all his people would be a part of that Empire, forever giving up the wandering ways of the tribes, living in one place in sheltering walls of stone while enjoying at their ease the luxurious splendors of a more civilized world. Of course, being the only visionary he knew, Mortis would rule them on behalf of the greater good. The Dje'kaarin would no longer govern themselves, but then governance was such a burden for the unworthy and unenlightened. Better that he should do their thinking for them.

Not all of the other warlords agreed with this view of the world, but Mortis Helm was not bound by such mundane considerations as ethics, and he had the support of the Rhonas Legions of Conquest. A little treachery went a long way, especially when it was coupled to an incredibly huge lie: He convinced the stone gnomes that he and his tribe had actually affected the *surrender* of the elven Legions to *him*. At the same time, Mortis offered to hand over the effective rule of the stone gnomes to the elves so long as they were discreet about their arrangement and supported his deception. Soon the elven commanders with smiles on their faces—not unlike the one which Soen now wore—fulfilled their promise and installed Mortis Helm as the first Caliph of the Dje'kaarin—master of all the stone gnomes of the Vestasian Coast.

Succeeding generations saw the dreadfully accurate fulfillment of Mortis Helm's original vision. With the establishment of an Occuran Trade Portal in Yurani Keep—the farthest portal of the northwest fold chain—trade goods from the heart of the Empire were soon flooding the village. The stone gnomes, once proud nomadic warriors, were enslaved at last not by chains or whips but by soft clothes, easily bartered meals, and their own complacency. The old stories were still told to their children, but with each generation it was harder to believe that gnomes had lived any other way than as a drone outpost of Rhonas civilization.

The one thing that never seemed to fade was the general hatred of the Dje'kaarin gnome citizens for their Helm Caliphate rulers. The Helm dynasty's treachery was by no means limited to the origins of the Caliphate and over time had become the stuff of legend among the Stone Gnomes. Down the centuries there had been repeated attempts by various factions—usually descendants of the ancient warlord families—to oust the contemporary Helm Caliph, install their own warlord, and foment a radical change in the Dje'kaarin government. Time and again, the Iblisi were called upon by the successive Caliphs to journey to this miserable outpost of the Empire and shore up the sagging fortunes of the Helm dynasty.

Soen's shining black eyes studied the Caliph even as he strained at his studied, pleasant grin. Argos was only the latest incarnation of the line of succession and, if anything, had proved himself as typical an example of his forbearers as possible. He was short even for a gnome, the top of his head—minus the ridiculous crown—barely coming to the midpoint of Soen's thigh. His gray beard was carefully groomed, coming to two separated points just below his waist. These he kept tucked inside a wide belt that he wore incongruously over an elven Imperial tunic. His skin was of a reddish brown color reminiscent of cherrywood. He had the large, hooked nose that was typical of his race and bright, narrow eyes with perpetual smile lines at the corners. The top of his head was bald—shaved, Soen suspected, so that he might look more like the elves with whom he did his most important business.

Indeed, the Great House Hall itself was a ridiculously bad imitation of the Emperor's audience hall in Rhonas. The great domed ceiling was reincarnated as a stick framework tied together with rawhide thongs. Even then it was not properly put together and sagged badly toward the eastern wall. Someone had shored it up with additional long poles inside the dome, which destroyed any marvelous architectural affect the dome might have presented in the first place, but at least it didn't look on the verge of collapse. The walls were entirely of native stone covered in a thick adobe mud, but the mud itself had been scratched at by gnome artists with sticks in an attempt to reproduce the delicate marble friezes of the Emperor's throne room. The mud had proved to be a poor medium for such reproductions, and Soen often had to remind himself not to look at them. The throne was bad enough—a vulgar and unintentionally sacrilegious copy of the Seat of the Empire that, were its existence generally known, might have been deemed sufficient to put an end to the Helm Caliph line once and for all. The throne was, like most things, entirely too big for Argos Helm.

The Caliph had to bounce twice on the cushion before he could gain enough momentum to hop down from his perch. "You honor me and all my people. For you the generous nature of my heart is laid open without reserve—but, how it is you have come to me in such a state? What long roads have brought my favorite son of the Empire to my humble self?"

"I regret that my mission requires urgency, oh great Caliph," Soen said, letting a hint of deference into his voice. "I would have made myself more presentable to you, but I am on the Emperor's errand and time is against me."

"The Emperor's errand!" Argos' rubbery face affected astonishment as he waved the Iblisi to approach him. "Perhaps from the Imperial City itself?"

"Yes, oh great Caliph," Soen began.

"Ah, to visit the heart of the Empire!" Argos opined. "To see its towers and walk its streets! I have heard of your citadels that float among the clouds and the magic of your Aether that flows like water from your Wells. I should dearly love one day to make the journey and stand among my fellow citizens!"

Soen gripped his staff until his fingers lost all color. Argos was a citizen of the Empire, but only just; he was considered to be of the Sixth Estate—technically a citizen by the laws of the Empire but devoid of any real rights. It was reserved largely for elves who had no social station whatever and was the last refuge of elven criminals. It was also a status held out as a reward to slaves who had performed some heinous deed for the Empire: betrayal, murder, assassination, spying, and the like. It was rarely granted to slaves—and was relatively meaningless when it was given.

"Perhaps the Caliph shall see it one day," Soen said as evenly as he could. "But the way is long and arduous. I myself had some trouble along the way . . ."

"No! May the gods forbid!"

"The Northmarch Folds can be treacherous," Soen advised. "And dusty, as you can see . . . but my need is great and my time short."

"Then come at once, my friend! I shall forgive at once your ill manners to the need of haste and history—for no doubt you are on a mission that impacts both!"

Soen tried for a moment to make sense out of Argos' words but realized it was pointless. The Caliph often misspoke—a problem that had been the root cause of several assassination attempts. The Inquisitor simply took in a long breath, nodded, and walked quickly toward the short ruler with his staff in hand. "Oh great Caliph, your words are as wise as they are meaningful. You have no doubt already divined that I have come to request a boon of your eminent self."

Argos frowned uncertainly.

"I need a favor," Soen urged.

"Ah!" The Caliph's face brightened. "Of course! I am most anxious to assist the Will of the Emperor in all things! You have but to ask, and Argos Helm shall grant all that is in my power to give! Please . . . sit with me as brothers and we shall discuss your needs."

The Caliph indicated three curved benches set at one side of the hall. Together they formed a broken circle— a *mychural* in the gnome tongue—which translated into "story circle." It was where gnomes traditionally gathered to converse, discuss, and listen to stories. It was, Soen noted, the only gnomish conceit in the entire hall.

The tall elven Inquisitor sat down on one of the benches. It was, unfortunately, built to gnome specifications. Soen was more stooping than sitting. Argos took no notice of his guest's discomfiture and plopped himself down on an opposite bench.

"There!" Argos leaned forward and spoke quietly. "What favor might I do for my good friend Soen?"

"I am looking for a man," Soen began.

"A man?" Argos interrupted, stroking his beard. "I don't know about a man. I can get you a woman—a good number of them, in fact, I should think—but ours is a backward people not as enlightened as the heart of the great Rhonas Imperium."

"No, Argos . . ."

"Just give me a moment, friend . . . I may be able to come up with a man for you . . ."

"No!" Soen began fingering his staff once more. "I am looking for a specific man . . . a human bolter."

Argos' eyes were losing focus. "Bolter . . . bolter . . ."

"A runaway slave," Soen continued. "A human male. We believe he and a number of fellow travelers left the Murialis Woods and were making their way into Vestasia."

"Murialis . . ." Argos repeated as he nodded his head vaguely. Suddenly his eyes focused, shifting to stare at the Iblisi. "Murialis? *That* Murialis? The witch west of the Southern Mountains?"

"Yes," Soen continued. "I believe they may have been traveling north."

"But that's over one hundred and seventy leagues from here!" Argos laughed incredulously.

"Yes," Soen agreed, "and it is land with which I am not familiar. What can you tell me about it?"

Argos leaned back, his face turned upward as he considered the question. He began stroking his beard with his left hand as though trying to pull some answer out of it. "Ah, you believe your quarry is in the Great Savanna."

Soen nodded. "If that is to the north of Murialis lands, then yes."

"Difficult place, that savanna," Argos mused. "You'll need to travel south around the edge of Gnevis Bay, then follow the Lynadio River inland until you cross at the confluence. West, beyond the river is the Great Savanna . . . filled with wild creatures and death. Perhaps you would like some men to accompany you—our finest warrior guards and at a most reasonable price! I could get you some women also, but that would be more difficult and, naturally, more expensive . . ."

"No," Soen said, his sharp teeth grinding slightly as he spoke. "I don't need an army—just your—your most excellent advice. Have you any news of my prey? There are three humans, a pair of manticores, and a chimerian who . . ."

"A chimerian?" Argos laughed. "That sounds like the beginning of a joke."

"I assure you it is not," Soen snapped then drew in a breath. "Have you any word of such strangers?"

"In the savanna?" Argos chuckled. "No one cares what happens in the savanna!"

"Isn't there anyone . . . any tribes who might have seen my prey?"

"Ah, perhaps the Hak'kaarin," Argos said with a disdainful sniff.

"Hak'kaarin?" Soen urged.

"Foolish creatures . . . you could barely call them gnomes really," Argos shrugged. "Mud gnomes of the great savanna. Backward savages that constantly wander the savanna wastes traveling from mudpile to mudpile. They have no appreciation for property, no understanding of the finer things of the world. Uncivilized and unworthy of your attentions, my friend. They cover the savanna like a river of idiots, never stopping long enough to build anything of value. But if anyone will have seen your . . . 'bolters' did you call them? . . . the savages of the Hak'kaarin will know of it."

The doors were closed, and at last, Argos pulled himself back up onto his throne and sat on it with satisfaction.

The gnome Caliph relished the moment. After all, he had a family tradition to uphold. All of his Helm ancestors had been brilliant politicians and strategists, he reasoned, otherwise how could they have stayed in power so long? So he, too, had to be as masterful and cunning as his forebears.

This time he was more cunning than them all—for he would outsmart an Iblisi.

"Fon!" the Caliph yelled, and at his word a gnome guard appeared from a side door, resplendent in his ridiculous armor.

"Yes, oh great Caliph!" Fon barked.

"There is an elf awaiting word from me in the Shadow Caves—do you know them? They're in the gully north of the city."

"I know them, oh great Caliph!"

"Tell him his friend journeys into the Great Savanna," the Caliph grinned. "And tell him to follow the trails of the Hak'kaarin."

The gnome bit his lower lip for a moment. "Oh great Caliph . . . how will I know I have the right elf?"

"You idiot!" Argos screamed. "How many elves are there in this province?"

"Sorry, my Caliph!" the gnome mumbled.

"Oh, very well," Argós grumbled. "His name is Jukung. He is an Inquisitor of the Empire and will reward us for our service."

"Yes, oh great Caliph!"

"And we must always be grateful to the Empire," Argos sighed, then, in a flash of inspiration, turned and put his hand in a semblance of benevolence on the helmeted head of the guard. "Quickly write this down so that we can have it written on our next wall. We must always be grateful to the Empire, for without it all the gnomes would be forced to endure terrible suffrage!"

CHAPTER 34

Traveler's Tales

"AYE! There he stood, Drakis the Just, atop the very throne of the dwarven kingdoms! His hands were stained with the blood of a thousand dwarves—the sworn enemies of his cruel masters—as he took the crown from the last of the Dwarven Kings!"

The dwarf's voice filled the cavernous space inside the mud gnomes' city adjacent to the main fire pit. He stood in the center of an enormous crowd of mud gnomes, all staring back at him in rapt attention. On the fringes of this congregation, however, a number of gnomes were talking excitedly and gesturing wildly. These would then fall away from the crowd and meld back into the constant stream of mud gnomes that swept past them in an unending river only to be immediately replaced with yet more gnomes who would chatter away at the fringes of the group, trying, it seemed, to catch up to events in the story before they arrived. A few of these would settle more toward the middle where the dwarf was blathering on while others fell back into the perpetual parade. It was an audience whose comings and goings seemed to have little reference to the story as it was being told. The mud gnomes might love stories, but Drakis could not be sure that any one of them had heard a single one of Jugar's tales from beginning to end.

They seemed to be perpetually in motion and unable to stay in any one spot long enough for a long joke, let alone an epic tale.

At the edge of the cavern, two additional figures watched in stillness as the river of gnomes swirled around them.

"Jugar is in rare form tonight," said Ethis, both pairs of his arms folded across his chest.

"Yes," Drakis said in disgust. "Rare . . . almost raw."

"You don't approve?" Ethis asked in a calm, droll manner.

"Is that meant to be a joke!" Drakis complained. "Just listen to him!"

Jugar stood, his thick arms raised above him, his head bent backward in the drama of his storytelling. The gnomes were leaning toward him now. "There Drakis stood, gazing upon the fabled crown of the dwarves—its jewels sparkling like all the stars of the winter sky—his mighty army arrayed about him, howling in their blood-crazed frenzy for *more* slaughter, *more* violence, *more* death to fill their empty souls! Drakis saw in that dwarven crown all the terrible sins of his elven masters—the pain of his fellow slaves, the loss of their dignity, and their life's blood all sacrificed on the altar of Rhonas ambition to take one more jeweled crown into the already burgeoning coffers of the elven state! What was this crown weighed in the balance against the thousands of lives he had taken to obtain it? What was this crown weighed in the balance of his own soul!"

"That's it," Drakis grumbled, taking a step forward. "I've got to put a stop to this."

"Just a moment," Ethis said, reaching out with one of his left hands and restraining Drakis by the shoulder. "I think he's nearly finished."

Jugar's voice dropped dramatically into hushed tones, drawing his eager audience even closer to him. "So what did Drakis do?"

The gnomes leaned closer still.

"He THREW the crown away from him!" Jugar shouted,

reenacting the moment by swinging his arm in a wide arc over the heads of the nearest gnomes.

The gnomes gasped in astonishment.

"That's the truth of it, and may the gods strike me down otherwise!" Jugar concluded. "Drakis tossed away the riches of the elven world—a crown whose wealth would have bought him power and position even among his evil elven masters—for he saw that wealth and power were meaningless if one pays for it with one's own soul! And from that day to this, Drakis the Just, Drakis the Wise, Drakis of the Prophecy, has wandered the face of the world seeking to fulfill his destiny, destroy evil, and bring lasting peace to all!

"And now," Jugar paused then pointed his finger directly toward the astonished Drakis. "Now he has come to YOU!"

The mud gnomes leaped up, cheering.

"Oh, no!" Drakis murmured, his eyes going wide. "No, no . . . !"

The gnomes rushed toward Drakis in a riotous wave of approval, sweeping the human off his feet.

"DRAKIS! DRAKIS! DRAKIS!"

"Put me down!" he insisted to no avail. He managed to twist in the mud gnomes' collective grasp as they lifted him over their heads. "Ethis! Where are they taking me?"

"I suspect back to the feast hall," Ethis replied through a perplexing smile splitting his malleable face.

"Again?"

"That seems to be their preferred way of showing their appreciation for a good story," Ethis replied, pushing gingerly away from the dried mud wall of the story-cavern. "Besides, we're leaving with them in the morning, and we'd all rather do so on a full stomach. I don't see the need for any complaint. The food here is quite good, and they seem perfectly content to share it with us."

"But it's a lie!"

"They don't seem to care," Ethis observed as the gnomes once again carried Drakis above their shoulders and down a ramp toward their common feast hall. "If anything, they seem to prefer it."

Early the next morning, Drakis stood outside the great mud city of the Hak'kaarin mud gnomes and waited in the cool dawn with Jugar, Ethis, Belag, and RuuKag with their traveling packs filled to overflowing in preparation for their journey.

"What are we waiting for?" RuuKag grumbled. "The sooner we get moving, the quicker we're out of this cursed plain."

"We're waiting for Mala and the Lyric," Drakis responded. "A pair of gnomes came with word that they would be late but would be along shortly."

"Where have they been for the last three days?" Ethis asked. "I've seen them at the feasts, but then they seemed to disappear."

"Oh, I know about that!" Jugar said brightly, his round cheeks bowed upward in a cheery smile. "I asked the Chief of the Day where they had taken the precious women in our company and . . .

"Chief of the Day?" Drakis asked.

"Oh, yes! I assure you that these Hak'kaarin have enacted a most fascinating form of governance, really," Jugar replied. "They have no permanent rulers but rather take turns directing things. They change out the chief pretty much whenever they feel like it. There is no set schedule, but a change in leadership usually takes place when the Chief of the Day gets tired of doing the job and gives someone else a chance. They have no interest in power or wealth as we understand it—indeed, they find the stories we tell of the acquisition of such things to be something like cautionary tales. Their civilization is entirely based on total community of property and pride taken in the whole rather than the individual. Individuals don't 'own' anything as we understand it but take ownership in the whole of their society. All these gnomes coming and going take whatever burrow is available to them when they arrive, use the things in it as though they were their own—because in a very real sense they *are* theirs as a community—and then just leave them behind when they travel to the next mud city. For that matter, it's one of the reasons the elves—or anyone else for that matter—have never bothered to conquer them: They don't have anything worth taking. They live relatively simple lives, journeying constantly from one mud city to the next. They have no desire for power— they even think that the great Aether magic of the elves and even the Aer magic of the dwarves is a 'crutch' that weakens the moral fiber of anyone who touches it. With no desire for power and no interest in wealth, they are a formidable group for anyone wanting to corrupt them."

"Fascinating," Ethis replied through a yawn, "but you were telling us about the women?"

"Oh, indeed I was!" Jugar nodded brightly. "The Chief of the Day told me—and in rather disappointed tones— that they have been keeping Mala and the Lyric separated from the males of our group and offered women of their own tribes to you in substitution."

Drakis blinked. "What?"

"The Chief of the Day had hopes that you might each mate with some of their women," Jugar concluded. "It would have been a great honor for their community."

Belag sniffed. "Barbarians!"

"Well, each of us has our different customs," Jugar replied with a shrug. "Strange as they may strike us as outsiders, it sometimes is to our credit to keep a more open mind about the traditions of other nations . . . ah, but here is the rest of our intrepid group now."

Drakis turned to see Mala running toward him, relief in her eyes. She threw her arms around him, nearly knocking him off his feet in her eagerness. "I've tried to find you! These little mud creatures kept pushing me off in other directions. Are you all right?"

Drakis looked down at her upturned face. The anger and the fear had for the moment evaporated from her countenance, freeing her once again to look like the Mala he had loved in that life before—and still loved in the jumble of memories that occasionally threatened to overwhelm his thoughts. Her skin was still smudged and tanned from the long journey, and her face was now framed in the rust-red hair that had sprouted from her head, nearly obscuring her slave brand tattoo, but in that moment she looked again like the woman he had so long loved—or believed he had loved—and he smiled warmly in return.

"Mala, I am fine," Drakis said. "Are you ready for the road?"

She stepped back, still smiling at him. "Three days' rest in a mud cave seems to have been quite enough. I've got my pack and, thanks to these gnomes, far better shoes for the journey."

She turned in front of him, raising her foot. Drakis laughed at the sight of the soft leather boots with their hard soles—indeed, perfect for the road but entirely incongruous with the rest of her tattered clothing.

"What's so funny?" she asked, a note of caution coloring her words.

"They are, indeed, perfect," Drakis laughed, letting go of his anxiety and fear seemingly for the first time in ages. It felt good to laugh again. "How is the Lyric today—or perhaps I should ask 'who' is the Lyric today?"

"You'll find out soon enough," Mala teased. "But one word of caution—duck right after you ask."

They were two days out from the third mud city. The trail of Hak'kaarin gnomes stretched across the savanna in a seemingly endless procession. The line heading northward, in which Drakis and his companions marched on the left side of the trail, was matched in kind by a second endless procession heading back the way they had come on the right side.

Drakis smiled as he marched along. There was something soothing in the rhythm of his strides, the wide sky above

him, and the warmth of the sun on his face. Mala and the
Lyric—now claiming to be Sheen-rhaq, Warrior-Queen of
the Manticores—were both riding on a large wagon being
pulled by scores of gnomes . . . an honor he had declined.
Ethis was arguing once more with RuuKag behind the
wagon while Belag tried to broker some peace between
them. Ahead of him, Drakis could see Jugar marching alongside the gnomes and decided he could use the sound of the
fool's prattle in his ears. He quickened his pace and shortly,
as they crossed a shallow river, caught up with the dwarf.

"We are making good time," Drakis said, gazing northward. "We'll make the next mud city before nightfall. The
Chief of the Day tells me that it's the farthest north of the
Hak'kaarin settlements. He also says that they often trade
with humans there—actual *free* humans from the forests
bordering the shore."

The dwarf's gaze remained downcast as he stumped
along in silence.

Drakis walked alongside Jugar for a few moments as
the silence stretched on.

"What? No long description of the wonderful customs
of free humans in the wild?" Drakis chided. "No half-
forgotten epic poem that will last us until sunset in its
recital? No made-up facts about an ancient civilization
from the past that is going to resurrect dragons from our
nightmares and save us all?"

The dwarf looked away as he marched.

"Well, isn't that my fate," Drakis said, shaking his head.
"As long as I've known you, I couldn't get you to shut
up, and the *one* time I want to talk to you, you lose your
tongue!"

Jugar turned his head and glared at the human. "We *do*
have a need to talk, my boy! But not so close to so many
ears!"

The dwarf gave Drakis a great shove, pushing him into
the tall grass bordering the trail and following in his wake.

"You dwarven fool," Drakis exclaimed, "what are you
up to now?"

"It's time for *you* to be quiet and do as I say," Jugar

said with menace in his voice. "Keep walking and keep the trail in sight. The grass is taller than I am and will keep my words between us alone."

"But I still don't . . ."

"Keep walking!" Jugar snapped. "Don't look at me, look at the trail."

"What's this, dwarf," Drakis said as he walked through the rustling grass. "What new game are you playing?"

"No game," Jugar replied, "but we are the ones who are being played. See this?"

Drakis glanced down. "In your hand? That round ball of mud with some grass stuck in it?"

"It's a good deal more than that, lad," Jugar explained, "although it's certainly meant to appear as innocent as you suggest. Only someone familiar with the magic involved would know its true purpose."

"And I suppose that someone would be you," Drakis said.

The dwarf spoke with pride. "I know a thing or two about magic."

Drakis nodded. "I've been meaning to ask you about that . . ."

"Soon enough, my boy," Jugar interrupted. "But we must speak of this first. This, lad, is a beacon stone."

"A beacon stone?" Drakis urged. He'd never had such trouble getting the dwarf to talk before. "What is a 'beacon stone?'"

"It's a device of the Iblisi," Jugar replied. "It is used by the Inquisitors to find anyone who drops them along the way. They have many uses, but it would seem they are now being used to track us. Wait! Did you hear something?"

Drakis stopped. "You mean beyond the marching feet of several thousand gnomes? No, I don't hear anything— and just what are you suggesting? That the Iblisi are still following us—all the way across the Vestasian Savanna?"

"More than that," Jugar said. "That they are still following us is now certain . . . but what we did not know before is that one of our trusted number is also helping them to do so."

CHAPTER 35

Preceding Reputations

THE SUN WAS SETTING by the time they reached the entrances to the mud city. Drakis wished as he forced his tired legs up the long sloping tunnel into the city that the Hak'kaarin would take the trouble to put different *names* to their settlements so that he could at least keep track of where they had been. For a time crossing the savanna he had occasion to wonder if the gnomes were somehow magically leading them back each night to the same mud city. A different name would have helped him at least feel some sense of progress. As it was, however, the Hak'kaarin's rather odd view of physical possessions— they didn't believe in them—led to an inability to distinguish any Hak'kaarin thing from another. They simply took whatever hovel-hole was unoccupied at the time in whatever mud city they found themselves, shared in the communal food, and worked at whatever job was needful at the time, and then, bidden by some inner impulse Drakis could only guess at, they would leave one mud city and make an arduous journey to the next. Some patterns in this chaotic life occasionally emerged; not all the gnomes were skilled at everything, and sometimes groups of them would gather who shared the same skills to teach each other what they had learned on their last pilgrimage. Yet such gatherings never seemed to last for very long and would dissolve just as quickly as they formed.

As to his own inner voices—the musical demons that seemed to torment his mind—they were making him increasingly uncomfortable on the road. Ever since the dwarf had told him that there was a traitor among them, he had not been able to shake the feeling that the sooner they left the beaten paths of the Hak'kaarin, the safer they would be. At least they would be in the wilderness again, and it might be easier to spot trouble as it approached and possibly catch this informer in the act of placing one of these beacon stones.

As to who that traitor might be, that was a painful thought that revolved in the music of his torment in every monotonous moment of walking whenever they moved between the mud cities.

manticore fanatic lunatic . . .
Breaks with a crystalline sin . . .
Never forgiven . . . ever deceiving . . .

Belag had evinced a near reverential attitude toward Drakis since the fall of House Timuran that was nothing short of fanatical, and yet there was something inside that fanaticism that Drakis did not and could not trust. He suspected that anyone so deeply committed to a single idea or person was probably likely to react just as strongly the other way if he felt betrayed in that commitment.

Lion-man hiding from shadows past . . .
Fleeing from lands he once loved . . .
Longing for lost homes . . . Longing for dead tombs . . .

Then there was RuuKag, a manticore whom he never liked even before his memories came flooding back. He had fought the group at every step, but recently he seemed more anxious than any of them to cross this savanna. He never explained himself either way, and his distrust seemed to breed it in everyone else.

Shifting the shapes of allegiances . . .
Nebulous is his own heart . . .
Constantly changing . . . Soul rearranging . . .

Ethis was demonstrably not only a manipulative and

deceptive creature at his heart but now appeared to be highly trained for it. Drakis still shuddered to think of how the chimerian had appeared to him in the form of Mala.

Hope of a past now a memory . . .
Love that was all just a game . . .
Where does her heart lie? When does her tongue lie?

Then there was Mala herself, of course. Things had improved with her, and recently she had become almost cheerful. Her face was tanned now by their long day journeys between mud cities, and there was an almost robust health to her that was, he had to admit, an improvement over her former self. Yet he knew resentment still smoldered beneath the surface like banked coals waiting to burst again into hot hatred. Their bargain in the faery kingdom to pretend their painful past did not exist had only buried it shallowly.

Everyone else but the girl herself . . .
Who is the woman within?
Masking her faces . . . and her dark places . . .

He had considered the Lyric, who was unquestionably insane and changed her personality as easily and as often as anyone else might change their mind. She could be the traitor among them and not even remember it from day to day. That, he thought, would be worst of all since she was the least accountable of any of them, and Drakis felt certain he would have to kill whoever it turned out to be.

Jesters all hide in the light and sound . . .
Plain in the face of our doom . . .
Watch for the fool . . . Laughter is cruel . . .

Finally, he had to admit that it could even be the dwarf, who had pointed all this out to him in the first place. The conniving little fool might have thought himself in danger of being caught and tipped his hand as a bluff just to throw suspicion off himself. The only thing Drakis was sure about regarding the dwarf was that he couldn't be sure about anything.

So he would journey through the day, receding more and more into the cycle of his siren song. Sometimes Mala would walk with him, chattering away about some innocuous memory she had of her life in the Timuran House or some previous House she had been a part of and only recently remembered. Such recollections studiously avoided the darker memories and were occasionally expurgated as she spoke—her voice stuttering slightly and stopping altogether only to restart on a completely different topic— light and breezy once more. Sometimes Belag would journey with him, speaking sonorously of the legends of the manticores regarding the afterlife, or Ethis would join him, respecting the human's silence with his own. Occasionally the dwarf would accompany him, rattling off some nonsense story he remembered that the shape of a bush they passed or some figure in a cloud above them brought to his memory.

But all along the way, the names of his companions would circle through his mind and soon merged with the cycle of the music—that dreadful music—that called to him and ran always in the back of his mind.

Nine notes . . . Seven notes . . . Five notes . . . Five . . .
Jugar, Lyric, Belag . . .
The smiles of each beguiling . . .
Whose is the false heart? Who plays the false part?
Ethis, Mala, RuuKag . . .
They swear their oath is telling . . .
One is more than willing . . .
All your lives they're selling . . .
Jugar, Lyric, Belag . . . Ethis, Mala, RuuKag . . .
The smiles of each beguiling . . .

"Drakis-ki?"

Drakis shook himself. He had nearly fallen asleep on his feet. His eyes were trying to focus on the short figure before him. Drakis thought that he had never seen this particular gnome before but could not be entirely sure. The only thing he was certain of was the orange vest and floppy hat that signified the gnome's august position in the mud city. Since which gnome was the Chief of the Day changed seemingly on a whim and each mud city had its own chief who was just as apt to pick up and wander to the next mud city as any other gnome, the only way to tell who was in charge was by which gnome wore this bizarre outfit. "Yes . . . uh, Chief of the Day . . . what is it?"

"Drakis-ki," the gnome bowed deeply as he repeated the name with respect. "You honor us with the stories of your people. We thank the gods of the sky that you have come among us to brighten our thoughts and dreams."

"Yes, thank you," Drakis spoke through a yawn. "I'm sorry, Chief of the Day . . . is there something you want?"

"Drakis-ki," the gnome bowed once more. "I have a story to tell you!"

"Ah," Drakis nodded, closing his eyes as he continued to trudge up the ramp. "Thank you, Chief of the Day. I would *love* to hear your story and I am certain that it is a really great story but . . ."

"It is! It *is* a great story," The Chief of the Day responded, enthusiastically following along next to the human. "It is the story of a human like yourself, a great warrior woman who journeys from the coastal forests, who moves in silence and shadow. She comes from a human tribe that is lost to the knowledge of the world and remains hidden from the knowledge of all except the Hak'kaarin! And most remarkable of all, in her story she is searching for *you*, Drakis!"

Drakis stopped and rubbed his eyes, not entirely certain of what he had just heard. "A human woman—and she's looking for me? Where did you hear such a tale?"

"Oh, of course," the Chief of the Day nodded with sage understanding. "My poor skills in the telling of the story would diminish it, and I will not do such a fine tale this injustice. Would it not be better if Drakis-ki heard it from its source?"

Drakis look at the gnome with a frown, his awareness sharpening as the words sank into his tired mind. "It would. Is this storyteller near? I may have some questions . . ."

"Not *near*," The Chief of the Day shook his head. "*Here*. The woman herself is here."

"What? Here?" Drakis blurted out.

"What is it?" Mala asked, concerned at the look on Drakis' face. She and the Lyric were walking up the ramp toward Drakis with Belag, RuuKag, Jugar and Ethis behind them.

Drakis did not answer her but continued speaking to the orange-clad gnome. "She's here? Where?"

The gnome grinned with all his wide-spaced teeth. "Why, Drakis-ki! She is there behind you!"

Drakis turned at once, his hand instinctively moving to the hilt of his sword.

Above him, at the top of the ramp, stood a tall, slender woman the likes of whom Drakis had never seen before. Her skin was a deep black—as deep a black as the middle of the night and as smooth and unblemished as pure silk. Her thick, black hair was pulled back from the high forehead of her oval face and gathered into an explosion of curls at the back of her head. Her large, brown eyes gazed at him above her pronounced cheekbones, their eyelids shuttered languidly in disdain. Her lips were thick and plump around her smallish mouth—drawn slightly up at one corner as though being amused by some secret thought. She stood with casual confidence, the long fingers of her right hand resting on her hip as her head tipped upward slightly atop her long, slender neck.

"So," the woman spoke in a deep, husky voice, "*this* is what a prophecy looks like."

"Who are you?" Drakis asked, his eyes narrowing.

The Chief of the Day, still standing behind Drakis, thought that was his cue for a formal introduction. "Oh, I sorrow over my lack of honor! Drakis-ki . . . I present to you Urulani-ku, Warrior of the Sondau!"

"Urulani will do," she replied with an amused smile. "I suppose Drakis will do for you . . . or do you have some rather more exalted title you prefer as the living fulfillment of a legend."

"How do you know who he is?" Mala demanded, moving smoothly to Drakis' right side and wrapping her arm around his. Drakis muttered a curse; she was holding his sword arm.

"How do *I* know who he is?" Urulani said through a hearty chuckle. She stepped toward them down the ramp, her athletic figure moving with ease. She wore an outer vest of cured leather over a loose, sleeveless shirt of homespun cloth. Drakis noted that she wore soft buckskin breeches laced tightly up both legs as well as matching boots that made no sound as she stepped. "How is it possible *not* to know of Drakis—the bolter from House Timuran—who is the professed harbinger of doom and salvation now sprung to life? It's a story that's being told and retold all across the Vestasian Savanna by every Hak'kaarin gnome with a tongue and, it now seems, by every Dje'kaarin opportunist looking to find you and turn you in for more Rhonas coin than they can possibly carry."

Urulani stopped just in front of Drakis, her eyes fixed coolly on him though her words were aimed at Mala. "No, I tell you, little slave princess, I'd be surprised if there were a blade of grass or a stone under all the sky from the Southern Mountains to the Nordesian Coast that doesn't *know* who this Drakis is by now."

Drakis could hear Belag's low growl rising behind him.

Urulani looked up at the manticorian warrior. "I'm not your problem, big cat. In fact, *I'm* here to help you all, so you might think again before you decide you'd like to try and eat me."

Drakis drew in a breath to speak, but Mala interrupted, gripping Drakis' arm tighter and pulling him possessively toward her. "I don't see how you can possibly help us."

Urulani turned her gaze on Mala for the first time and took her in through a long stare before she replied. "You may have weathered a bit on the road, princess, but your little cherry tan and cracked lips don't hide you. I see that the Rhonas pigs still prefer to stock their households with cloud-white, dainty human slaves who can blend in so invisibly into their marble walls." She turned her look back to Drakis. "Until that fashion changes, the Imperial hunters have no need to bother with us. We're 'the Forgotten Ones' and we prefer to keep it that way. As long as we're forgotten . . . well, you'll have a chance."

"Why should we trust you?" Drakis asked.

"Don't, if you'd rather not," Urulani said with a tilt of

her head. "I just happen to be the first to find you. If you like, you're welcome to refuse my help and wait for some bounty-crazed fool or an Iblisi to find you, although I suggest that they might not present terms quite as good as I have to offer."

Drakis shook his head and smiled. "And, uh, just what *are* your terms?"

Urulani took a step back and folded her arms across her chest. "Drakis . . . I don't believe in you. I was raised on the stories and the legends, and I gave up on believing in them years ago. No human is going to rise up and free us from the Rhonas oppression with a wave of his mystical fingers. The only freedom we'll ever have will be what we take for ourselves." Urulani shrugged. "But . . ."

"But?"

"But the Clan Elders *do* still believe," Urulani continued. "They sent me here to find you, hide you from the eyes of the Rhonas hunters, and bring you before the Elders to answer their questions about you."

Drakis nodded, his hand slipping slowly from the hilt of his sword. "And if they don't like my answers?"

Urulani looked up at the ceiling as she spoke. "You know, it's a hard thing when you're confronted with a legend and you discover that he's only a man after all. The faithful who are disappointed in their gods can be so unpredictable in how they will react."

"No," Drakis said. "I disagree. They are entirely *too* predictable. Very well, but you have to . . ."

"Drakis!" Mala said turning toward him. "You aren't actually considering going with this . . ."

Drakis ignored her. "But you have to take all of us. You must promise to extend your protection to all of our group, or we'll just continue on our own way."

Urulani nodded. "Done. Anything else?"

"One last thing."

"Yes?"

"Tell me that your clan is to the north."

CHAPTER 36

RuuKag

THE MUD CITY of the Hak'kaarin usually bustled with activity regardless of the time of day. The only exception was on the night of arrival, when most of the mud gnomes, exhausted from the day's journey, retired to their newly occupied warrens and slept through the night, leaving only a few hundred or so of their number to keep watch over the city and keep the fires stoked until the mound could properly be brought back to exuberant life the next morning.

The enormous central space of the city was, therefore, nearly deserted as RuuKag moved with contemplative, heavy steps onto the main floor space. His great head hung down from his hunched shoulders. The field pack—completely provisioned once more—did not weigh him down nearly as much as the burdens of his soul.

The manticore looked up. The open dome of the mud city was lined with the cavelike warrens of the gnomes almost to its very summit, lit now only dimly by the flickering flames in the great central pit that had earlier been a roaring bonfire. The curling smoke rose up to the full height of the chamber, escaping through the large hole in the ceiling.

RuuKag watched the smoke for a time. The hole through which it escaped the mud city was called the Oculei by the Hak'kaarin—the Eye of God. It watched over the mud gnomes in their pursuits and, for the most part, brought light into their lives.

RuuKag chortled to himself. The Hak'kaarin repaid their god by blowing smoke into its eye. Perhaps, he mused, that was why god's eye seemed so blind to the problems of the mortals in their care.

But then another thought came to RuuKag. The blaze of the great fire pit in the center of the mud city consumed the solid wood and sent it up to the gods. Through the Oculei he could see the stars of the night sky beyond—the very realm of the gods—welcoming the smoke and freeing it from the cares of the world.

"RuuKag-ki?"

The manticore, startled from his reveries, looked down into the face of a young gnome. By his reckoning the creature could not have seen more than twelve years in this world. "What do you want, gnome?"

The large, liquid eyes of the youth gazed up at him. "Your story, RuuKag-ki! I want to hear your story."

The manticore shrugged his field pack higher on his shoulders. "I have business to attend! Go away."

"You are leaving us, then?"

"Yes," RuuKag said at once. "I mean, no! I've just got to go outside for a while . . . I've just got something I have to do."

"Not with a field pack," the gnome replied, pointing up at the manticore's back. "You're leaving forever."

"I've business to attend to, boy!" RuuKag said, pushing past the small gnome.

"But you have to tell me your story!" the gnome said, the urgency in his voice making it louder.

RuuKag turned in frustration. "Quiet! You want to wake the entire city!"

"Just tell me your story," the young gnome urged. "Look! We're right next to the storytelling cavern, and there's no one there now."

"I don't *want* to tell you my story!" RuuKag growled.

"But you'll be lost!" the gnome wailed.

"Quiet!" RuuKag said quickly. "What are you bellowing about?"

"Your story," the gnome replied, his eyes tearing up. "If you don't tell someone your story, you'll be forgotten. No one will remember that you passed through the world. Your story will be lost, and your soul will not be recognized by the other souls in the sky!"

RuuKag looked up through the Oculei once more. The stars were looking back down on him. He felt their disapproval. "No one wants to hear my story," he said at last.

"I do," replied the gnome.

RuuKag sighed. He needed to get out of the mud city, and the last thing he needed was a whimpering, wailing gnome cub calling attention to what was supposed to be an unnoticed departure. "Fine! A short story and then I've got to leave."

"Your story," the young gnome insisted.

RuuKag sighed again. "Yes, *my* story. What's your name little cub?"

"Jith!" the gnome replied.

"Well—Jith—where do we get this sorry tale over with?"

Jith wrapped his small, long-fingered hands around the manticore's paw as best he could though even both hands failed to encompass it entirely. He tugged at the manticore, who dutifully followed him into a round, side cavern. In its center sat three curved benches that formed a circle. "Here, RuuKag-ki! This is the storytelling place. Sit! . . . Sit! Sit! Sit!"

The manticore squatted down on one of the benches most definitely not built for someone of his size. "Just a few minutes, Jith. I'm very busy!"

"Yes, of course, *very* busy," Jith nodded as he scampered over to one of the opposite benches and clambered onto it. He turned around, his own feet dangling from the edge of the bench and not quite reaching the floor. The young gnome leaned forward in anticipation. "But first you tell *your* story."

Yes," RuuKag said. "Well, once between a moon long ago there was a manticore named RuuKag . . ."

"No, that's no way to start a story!" Jith interrupted. "You start with, 'I, RuuKag.'"

The gnome milled his hands through the air, urging RuuKag to continue.

The manticore bared his canine teeth in frustration. "Very well then . . . 'I, RuuKag' . . . and then what?"

"Tell me about your family!" Jith suggested.

RuuKag closed his eyes. "I have no family."

Jith caught his breath in surprise and excitement. "What a wonderful beginning! 'I, RuuKag, have no family.' Why?"

"Why . . . why what?"

"*Why* do you have no family?" Jith asked. "You must have had one sometime—did you lose them?"

"No," RuuKag replied, looking at the wall. "They . . . well, my father threw me out of my clan. He proclaimed me dead and banished me into the savanna—the eastern edge of this same savanna, as a matter of fact."

"Banished!" Jith drew in a long breath. "How terrible for you!"

"It was . . . I was heartbroken at the time," RuuKag replied. "My father was a proud warrior who had joined the rebellion against the elven occupation, leading our clan out of our traditional lands and into the wilderness of the Northern Steppes. His name was KraChak, and his armor was ten generations old—very prestigious among our clans. He was the result of a long line of brave warriors with their own tales of bravery in battle and honors in their warfare. He taught me the use of the spear and the blade at an age when other cubs were still wrestling across the green. My mother—her name was Lyurna of Clan Khadush—was so upset with our father that day that he had to call a clan council just to get away from her for a few days! They were both proud manticores who were in a lot of pain now that I look back on it. They had lost everything in the Rhonas occupation—everything but their prideful resentment. My father had lost his ancestral lands, and that was a terrible thing for him to bear. My parents could not give up the life that they once had—maybe they didn't know how to live any other life . . ."

There was something about talking to this little gnome that felt good to RuuKag. He had been carrying the words around inside himself for so long, never daring to tell them to anyone. He had forgotten them entirely while under the elven Devotional enslavement magic, but their burden had returned to him in force with the fall of House Timuran. He wanted desperately to return to the mindless bliss of his enslavement and to rid himself of the weight of his own decisions and consequences. But here and now, in the quiet of the night of a far-off land, he could tell those bitter words to this little gnome and somehow be rid of them.

Soon the words started coming unbidden and in a rush, as though the story had been there all along waiting for him to tell it and be rid of it. He told of his life growing up in a clan exiled from their own nation. He spoke of the customs of the manticores and how disputes were most often settled in combat. He told of the wonders of getting up at dawn on the Northern Steppes and hunting at his father's side. He talked of lying under the canopy of the night and listening as his mother explained the lights in the sky and how they were his ancestors looking down on his honor from above.

As he spoke, another gnome happened by and stopped for a time. Then a third and a fourth came and sat down. RuuKag took little notice as he spoke, for he seemed lost in the telling of his tale to the large eyes of the enraptured Jith.

"All these wonders . . . all these beautiful stories," Jith said as RuuKag paused, "and your clan family, they are lost to you? Why?"

"The Battle of the Red Fields," RuuKag said, his voice breaking as he spoke the words for the first time in decades. "The Rhonas Legions were not satisfied with taking control of the government of Chaenandria, they wished to crush all possibility of rebellion once and for all. With the aid and assurances of the Chaenandrian Council, the elf Legions moved north to challenge our rebel clans directly."

"A war then?" Jith asked breathlessly.

"Barely even that. It had been a hard winter, and we

did not expect them to join us in battle so soon," RuuKag replied. The hall was now full of gnomes, but he no longer cared. To speak the words unburdened him. "When their Legions were reported, there were few that the rebel clans could field. Everyone who could hold a blade was pressed into service—many of them barely trained youths, and I counted myself among them."

Jith was in awe. "You joined the battle?"

"What choice did I have?" RuuKag snapped. "I was the son of the Clan Elder—an honored warrior with ancestors covered in glory for a hundred years! I had grown up on stories of fortune in battle. It was all such a fabulous game to me. Here was my chance to add to the name of my clan, to add to the glory of my ancestors, to . . . to . . ."

"To what?" Jith urged.

"To prove myself to my father," RuuKag roared. "To show the rest of the clan that I wasn't just a child of privilege but that I, too, could stand with my ancestors and lay claim to my father's armor."

"What happened?" Jith asked.

RuuKag sat back and lifted his head. He could see the field before him as though he were there once more. "We formed a line as we had been taught. None of us were tried in battle—we barely knew how to hold a sword much less use it against a cunning enemy. We were supposed to be in reserve—not to be used in the battle itself—but the lines before us broke. The Legions of Rhonas stormed into the gap, pushing back the lines to either side, trying to flank them. But our leader was an old warrior whose mind had grown brittle and his judgment stale. He saw the gap in the lines and ordered our unit to charge into the bloodiest part of the battle."

"And what happened?" Jith whispered.

"I . . . I couldn't move," RuuKag replied in a voice that felt detached for the images in his mind. "I saw the death and the blood and the slaughter in front of me, and I just couldn't move."

The room was filled with gnomes now, but only the sound of RuuKag's quiet voice was heard.

"The line closed again as the manticores fought back," RuuKag continued. "As it turned out, the charge was in vain; the line would have closed anyway, and all those young manticores who stood next to me and charged died for nothing. Yet there were a number of us who just didn't heed the call—and we lived. It would have been better for us to have died that day—we were branded as the cowards that we were. We lived—and that was our shame."

RuuKag paused and looked up. Gnomes filled the story-cavern and were standing at the entrances. Each was facing him in rapt attention, sadness in their eyes.

Sadness for him.

RuuKag was now intent on letting all the words come out. He had forgotten his urgent reasons for departing. He spoke of returning to his father's clan, his shame of a coward son. He told of his banishment and the tears and howls of his mother echoing in his ears as he departed into the Vestasian Savanna.

He spoke of his longing to die.

His words spilled from him throughout the night in one tale that was many tales: the tale of his enslavement to the Devotions of House Timuran; the tale of Drakis teaching him the pain of knowing the truth and RuuKag's longing for the peace of not knowing at all; and finally the tale of Belag and Drakis leading them across the savanna and how a dishonored manticore now stood on the edge of a knife trying to decide between the oblivion of the elves and the hope of a life at last.

At last, RuuKag stopped, all his words spent. He looked up into the eyes of the gnomes and settled at last on those of Jith.

The young gnome looked at the manticore with his large, watery eyes . . . and gently smiled.

RuuKag looked at the ground.

Jith stepped quickly over to the manticore, moving beneath his face and gazing up as he spoke. "Thank you, Ruu-Kag-ki. Thank you for your story. We understand now."

RuuKag took in a long, deep breath.

Jith took the manticore's huge paw with both his small

hands. The gnome then touched his forehead to the back of RuuKag's furry grip.

"Your story begins again," Jith said. "Now begin with 'I, RuuKag, of the family Hak'kaarin.'"

Then, each in turn, the mud gnomes stepped up to RuuKag and, taking the manticore's paw, placed their foreheads to the back of his grip.

The gnomes were still doing so when Drakis found him the next morning.

CHAPTER 37

Different Roads

"KEEP UP!" Urulani growled.

"What is your hurry?" Mala snapped. "You said it was less than half a day's walk, and the sun has barely risen."

"It's dangerous out here in the open, princess." If anything, Urulani quickened her own pace a little. "And can you see those peaks ahead of us?"

"Those hills?" Mala sniffed. "You call those peaks? I've climbed bigger hills just to get a good *look* at real peaks!"

"Really?" Urulani laughed. "Well, then, you won't mind climbing those. We call them the Sentinels, and those 'hills' have kept our clan free of elven interference since before your entire family was groveling and begging for scraps from the Rhonas table."

They had left the Hak'kaarin mud city only a short time before, just as the first hint of dawn lightened the eastern horizon. Urulani led them northward on a narrow path that occasionally vanished for long stretches. Still, the dark-skinned woman always picked up the trail again as it ran northward toward the Sentinel Peaks.

It was true, Drakis reflected, that these mountains were not as tall as the Aerian Range that they had left so far behind them to the south, but they were not that much shorter and were of a far more formidable aspect. The peaks looked like sharpened teeth that erupted from the ground at nearly vertical angles. Urulani said they would be crossing them, but from where he walked now on the savanna, even he was skeptical as to how they would manage it.

"Drakis! Did you hear that?" Mala turned to the warrior striding next to her under the early morning glow. "Did you hear what she said to me?"

Drakis drew in a deep breath as he strode next to her under the soft glow of early morning light. "Yes, Mala; I heard."

"Well?" Mala demanded. "What are you going to do about it?"

"Yes, pray tell," Urulani snarled. "Just what *are* you going to do about it?"

Drakis rolled his eyes upward in an appeal to the stars. He was no longer sure that he believed in the gods; the only gods that he knew were those of the Rhonas pantheon, which had been instilled in him by his slave masters, and now he questioned everything that they had taught him. Still, at this moment, he would have preferred some divine answers—or even an inspired lightning bolt or two—to help him find a way to keep Mala out of Urulani's way.

Thus far this morning, the gods had wisely stayed out of the fight as well.

"Please," Drakis urged. "We need to get into the safety of those mountains . . ."

"So you're siding with *her*?" Mala shouted, her voice squeaking at the end.

"No!" Drakis said quickly. "I'm not siding with anyone . . ."

"She said we groveled for scraps!" Mala fumed.

"Look, Mala," Drakis shrugged. "She just doesn't understand how it was or she wouldn't have . . ."

"*I* don't understand how it was?" Urulani had the voice of a commander that carried over everyone else when she chose to use it. This was one of those times. "Maybe I don't understand how it is that you 'cattle' managed to find your way out of your pens and wander out here into the world where people actually live and die for *something* more than their master's pleasure."

"Now, wait just a moment," Drakis said.

"See? Do you see what kind of a person you've entrusted our lives to?" Mala jabbed Drakis with her finger. "She has no respect for you or any of us!"

"Respect?" Urulani roared back. "And just what have you done, little pale princess, to earn my respect?"

"Ladies! Stop it! Please!" Drakis held up both his hands in exasperation. "Can we all just calm down and . . ."

"This," Urulani threw her head back in derision, "from the Domesticated Warrior!"

Drakis turned to appeal to the rest of their companions, but there was no help in sight. RuuKag seemed to be enjoying the row with deep amusement. Ethis, Belag, and even Jugar all walked behind him, keeping a distance that also kept them out of the argument.

Only the Lyric quickened her step toward him. She smiled and said, "Don't worry, Drakis! I'm only too glad to help."

"You are?" Drakis asked dubiously.

"Of course!" the Lyric said, her eyes bright. "They're both wrong and I'll be happy to tell them why."

Drakis looked again to the stars and offered a prayer. It was going to be a very long day.

"I have news, Inquisitor!"

Jukung looked up, his face shadowed by the deep hood pulled over his head. The new Inquisitor sat still beneath a great tree of the savanna as he had for two days awaiting just such news.

"Speak, Codexia Mendrath," Jukung said.

The robed newcomer bowed and then began. "Word comes from the savanna, west of Tempest Bay. There are several mud cities of the Hak'kaarin in the northern regions of the Vestasian Savanna."

"I do not need a geography lecture," Jukung snarled.

"Yes, Master Inquisitor," Mendrath responded at once. "There are stories now being circulated among the mud gnomes in that region about a man named Drakis who is traveling with the gnomes. He is said to possess great powers and to be the fulfillment of prophecy."

Jukung looked up sharply. "And his companions?"

"The story speaks of two women, manticores, a chimerian, and a dwarf."

Jukung smiled. "A dwarf! Yes, that is news, indeed! Where? Where are they?"

"The Hak'kaarin move a great deal," Mendrath replied. "There are a dozen or so of their cities across the region where they were last seen."

"And Inquisitor Soen?" Jukung asked quickly. "What news of him?"

"He is moving toward those same mud domes that the Hak'kaarin call their cities."

Jukung stood up at once. "Then we must get there before him so that we may greet him properly. Contact the Quorums wherever they are and have them journey at once to the mud dome cities of the northern Savanna. Have them determine if Drakis and his companions have been there."

"And what are their orders then?" Mendrath asked.

Jukung smiled once more. "Our orders are explicit, Codexia. Capture this Drakis and bring him to me."

"It will be done," Mendrath said and turned to move away.

Jukung's arm restrained him.

"There is more." Jukung removed his hood, exposing his hideously deformed face. "Anyone who has had contact with this Drakis—anyone at all—is to be killed at once."

"I . . . I am not sure that I understand the order, Master Inquisitor," Mendrath said. "There are entire cities of these gnomes who may have had some contact with this Drakis human . . ."

"And you will find them and kill them all," Jukung said quietly.

"That could be thousands of gnomes," Mendrath said, still uncertain he understood the order correctly.

"I do not care if it numbers in the tens of thousands," Jukung said, irritation rising in his voice. "Towns, cities, females, children . . . if they have had contact with this human pestilence, they are to die!"

"But, Master Inquisitor!"

"Do you question the Imperial Will?" Jukung screamed. "This is the order of the Keeper of our Order and the direct expression of the thoughts of the Emperor! Will you shirk your duty and forfeit your honor to his glorious ideal?"

"No, Master Inquisitor!" the Codexia stiffened.

"They will die!" Jukung said, his breathing labored as he spoke. He reached up with his right hand and ran his fingers lightly along the melted skin of his face. "They must pay for what they have done. The Emperor has declared them poisoned to his Will by this Drakis. Any creature that has any contact with him must die . . . they must *all* die!"

CHAPTER 38

Sondau Clans

"ELDERS OF THE SONDAU," Urulani said, dropping to one knee and placing her right hand against the floor as she bowed her head before the three older men. She knelt in the center of the lodge, the long building that served as the heart of the Sondau Clan's society. The walls were framed from wood hewn from the surrounding forests and carved intricately with the tales and legends that formed the foundation of their laws and beliefs. The vaulted ceiling was supported by thick beams, each carved with different and portentous figures overhead. The floor was planked from the same wood as the walls though this was scrubbed and sanded to a smooth and carefully maintained finish. Flaming torches mounted to the walls and angled out above the floor filled the space with guttering light. "I am Urulani, daughter of the Sondau Clan. I have done as the Elders have asked."

"The Elders praise the gods for your return—and are *astounded* that you should return, it seems, on the very heels of your departure," stated the balding Elder with the short cropped hair who sat in the middle of the three. "Thus said, we welcome you before the Elders' Council."

Urulani stood at once. "The Elders honor me."

"As apparently do the gods to an extent we had not

hoped possible," said the man with the long, iron-gray hair pulled into a ponytail at the nap of his neck.

"As you say, Elder Harku," Urulani replied, glancing toward the ceiling.

"You have returned with him so quickly?" asked the bearded man on the left who was sitting back in his chair.

"I have done as the Council has asked," Urulani responded. "I have the man and, I must also report, several of his companions with him. I thought it prudent to bring them as well—and not risk their tongues waggling once we had left."

"Wise, as always, is our Urulani," nodded the man with the iron-gray hair.

Urulani bowed slightly. "Elder Kintaro honors me once more."

The central, balding Elder leaned forward. "What is your report, Urulani?"

The tall black woman opened her mouth to speak, hesitated, and then began. "As instructed by you, Elder Shasa, I journeyed southward through the Cragsway Pass and onto the Vestasian Plain. I made my way southward to the first of the Hak'kaarin mud domes to begin my search."

"That was but three days ago," Elder Kintaro said, his eyebrows raised. "We had expected your journey to take many months to complete."

"I had not been in the mud dome a day when this man Drakis and his companions came to me."

Kintaro raised his eyebrows. "Indeed? You did not look for them then?"

"I had intended to search for them as instructed," Urulani corrected gently. "We had heard stories of their passing through the mud domes in the deep parts of the Vestasian Plain—indeed, it was impossible *not* to hear of it from the Hak'kaarin. But as it happened, they arrived at the same mud dome where I first began my search at nearly the same time I did."

"A miracle of the ancients!" Harku intoned, closing his eyes.

"Perhaps," Urulani said, again looking away toward the ceiling. "Or it may have been an accident. I cannot say."

"And so your journey is over before it has begun," Elder Shasa intoned. "You have done well, Urulani. You are among our most trusted sisters of our clan. Will you then assist us? We wish to begin our investigations at once."

"Direct me, Elders," Urulani replied.

"We will find the heart of the tree by starting with the leaves," Shasa said, pressing the fingers of his hands together and lightly touching his own lips. "Let us begin with his companions."

"Elders of the Sondau," Urulani said, bowing low. "I present to you Mala, an escaped slave from the House of Timuran in far Rhonas."

The man with the iron-colored gray hair leaned forward. "Mala . . . is that not a Merindau Clan name? Are you of the Merindau Clan?"

Mala stood shivering in the torchlight.

The gray-haired man glanced at Urulani. "Does she not understand our speech?"

"She understands, Elder Kintaro . . . I cannot explain her silence as she would hardly keep her words to herself during our return journey today. Indeed, I had soon begun to dread our rest periods as she was always so full of words after we stopped."

Mala shot an angry glance at the woman.

Urulani smiled in response. "Perhaps you might ask her again now, Elder Kintaro.

"I am not of any clan," Mala said at once then her eyes fell to gaze unfocused at the floor. "I was . . . I was born a slave and know of no clan but the Houses in which I served."

"But you are no longer a slave," said the balding man seated between the other two, his voice calm and quiet. "You no longer serve any 'House' as you call it. How it is that you have come to be free?"

"Free, Master?"

Shasa smiled. "I am not your master, Mala. No man is your master any longer ... do you understand?"

Mala nodded her head but kept her eyes fixed on the floor. "Yes, Master."

Shasa shook his head.

"What we want to know is how you came to no longer be a slave," said the older man with a beard.

"I do not remember it very well, sire," Mala replied.

"It is difficult," Harku pressed on, "but you must tell us."

Mala's lower lip began to quiver.

"Tell us!" Harku commanded in a firm voice.

Shasa's face was full of warning for his brother, but Mala suddenly began to speak.

"We were at House Devotions," she said, her words coming out in a rush. "Everything was happening just as it always had before. Lord Timuran and his wife and daughter were near the House altar. I had already had my Devotions from the altar and was standing to one side of the subatria. Then Drakis—I don't know what happened, but Drakis was yelling and fighting the House Guardians on the far side of the Aether Well. He didn't want to take his Devotions. I couldn't understand why ... we had just spoken earlier in the day, and we had such great hopes ... but there he was, fighting the Guardians, and ..."

Mala stopped talking, her eyes still fixed far away.

"And what, child?" Shasa urged.

"And then the Aether Well came apart ... like shattering crockery only so much quicker and with a terrible noise. That's when I knew."

"Knew what?" Kintaro asked.

"That's when my memories returned to me ... and I knew that my life was over."

"He is the fulfillment of a prophecy laid down in the most ancient of times." Belag stood tall in the center of the lodge, the crest of his growing mane nearly touching the rafters of the ceiling overhead. He spoke with conviction, his eyes bright in the torchlight. "He freed me from the enslavement of the Rhonas sorceries and showed me the way to life and peace. He is the embodiment of the promises made of old. He *will* journey to the north countries, commune with the gods, and return in power to wreak vengeance and doom upon the Rhonas Imperium. He is the one that my brother sought beside me . . . and for whom he gave his life."

"And how do you know this?" Harku demanded. "How do you know he is the one?"

"My brother gave his life for him," Belag affirmed. "He is the one!"

". . . now, Drakis, he knew that the Iblisi were after us after we had spent the night at Togrun Fel, and he was determined that those slippery elven bastards would not lay a hand on us. He also knew the Song of the Dragon that was calling him along, giving him the knowledge of what was to come, that if we had stayed there but another hour, those very demons of the Imperial Corruption would be upon us. So, he stood before us and led us westward through the entire length of the Hyperian Plain—where the gods favored him by laying all manner of food and drink in our path. I tell you, Elders of the honored Sondau Clan, that the gods themselves granted powers to that boy that are beyond explanation!"

"Thank you, Master Jugar," Shasa said for the fourth time.

"Wait! There's so much more to tell! Take, for example, that time when we were passing the Hecariat—that terrible, doomed tower on the plains of Hyperia! The spirits of the mountain came down among the stones as we passed . . ."

"We shall take your statements into account as we deliberate," Harku said emphatically. "You may go."

"Oh, but there is so much more!" the dwarf offered cheerfully. "The Miracle of the Faery Halls! The Miracle of the Hak'kaarin! The Miracle of the . . ."

Elder Kintaro groaned.

"THANK YOU!" Shasa said too loudly.

It was late by the time RuuKag was led out of the lodge. As the manticore was led from the room, Urulani moved to one of the guttering torches at the side of the room.

"He is hiding something," Kintaro said a few moments after the door closed behind RuuKag.

"He is afraid," Shasa replied. "Fear can make anyone do foolish things."

"He doesn't believe in Drakis," Kintaro said.

"He says he does not know, but, then, he doesn't really believe in anything," Harku observed. "Which is of no use to us."

Urulani pulled the fluttering torch from its mount and snuffed it out in the pot filled with sand sitting on the floor below it. "You will not need the others."

"How so?" Harku asked.

Urulani pulled a new torch from a second holding pot and lit it on one of the other torches. "Because one is a Lyric who no longer knows herself—or finds it too painful to be herself. In either case, examining her will not help you."

"And the other?" asked Kintaro.

"The other is a chimerian," Urulani answered as she placed the new torch in the wall bracket. "It has been rightly said that a chimerian once told the truth—and was executed on the spot for heresy."

"I do not like your tone," Shasa said, "but I agree that we cannot in this matter trust the word of a chimerian. They see the world through their own eyes . . . and have no love or regard for us."

"Then it is time we dealt with this prophecy directly," Kintaro said.

"I agree," Harku responded.

Shasa nodded. "Urulani?"

"Yes, Elder Shasa."

"Bring us this man Drakis."

"What is your name?"

"Drakis, my lords."

"Of what clan?"

"I do not recall. I may have been too young to remember—and my memories are still disjointed, especially of my youth. But I believe that my family came from one of the clans near here."

"The white clans were hunted to near extinction," spoke the gray-haired man.

"It was obviously many years ago," Drakis replied, "but I recall my . . . my mother . . . I believe it was my true mother . . . telling me about our family to the north. She always spoke of going north and family at the same time."

"And your father?"

"I do not recall my father, my lord."

"Any other family?" the balding man asked.

"I . . . I had a brother," Drakis paused, looking away briefly and then, blowing out a quick breath, continued. "I had a brother whom I recall as being quite close to me. He, uh, he died—beaten to death by one of our masters. I may have had a sister . . . but I cannot say with certainty whether she was my actual sister or some relationship our masters concocted for us."

The bearded one spoke next with impatience. "What caused you to rebel in your master's House?"

"I . . . I don't know what you . . ."

"Where did it start?" the balding man urged. "What brought you to the point of breaking the bonds of the Devotions?"

"Well," Drakis thought. "I guess it all started with the song."

The bearded man's eyebrows arched up. "What song?"

"Well, it's not really a song, I suppose . . . I'm sorry, my lords, let me answer your question. I suppose in a way it started with the dwarf . . ."

"Wait," the balding man said, holding up his hand. "Tell us about this song."

Drakis looked puzzled. "Well, it's something that seems to be running in my head all the time. It wasn't always there, but the dwarf calls it . . ."

"The Song of the Dragon," the bearded man finished.

."Well, the Dragon Song actually, but . . ."

"Enough. Drakis . . . come with me." Shasa stood up from his chair and stepped in front of Drakis, crossing to the right side of the room. He took a torch from the wall and then stepped down to the corner of the lodge, beckoning Drakis to follow.

"Look here," Shasa said, pushing the torch closer to the wall.

Drakis leaned forward, gazing at the relief carved into the wood planks. It was crude by elven standards—almost primitive—but the figures were unmistakably human.

"This is our story of what *will* be," Shasa said, as he moved slowly down the wall with the torch. "The other walls tell of our past and our present but this wall . . . here . . . tells us the story that is yet to come. It is the story of the man who will be a slave but will break his own bonds. It is the story of the man who will come out of the south and journey across the waters to the ancient home of our people now lost to us, hidden beyond the clouds. It is the story of the man who will bring back the glory of humanity that was lost and destroy the oppressors of the land. Look here!"

Drakis drew himself closer to the carvings, following Shasa's pointing finger.

"Here is this warrior-prophet being called home."

"What are those creatures calling him?" Drakis asked.

"Dragons, brother. They are dragons calling to the souls of the chosen to come to them and find their destiny. Many have heard the dragon song, but none before you have followed the path of the story."

"Are you a god?" the dwarf's words echoed in his mind.

Drakis looked into the face of the Elder.

"Are you this Drakis, son," the Elder asked. "Are you this warrior-prophet who will free us all?"

Drakis drew in several breaths before he responded.

"Elder Shasa . . . I truly do not know."

CHAPTER 39

Something of my Own

"WELL, DRAKIS, what are you thinking?"

Drakis smiled. "I was just thinking how beautiful this place is, Elder Shasa."

Drakis walked side by side with the large, balding Elder down the wide path on the right-hand side of the village square. Small children ran about their feet, chasing one another with concentration in their delight that was oblivious to the adults around them. The square itself was lined with stalls filled with a dizzying variety of goods—fruits and vegetables from the farms that terraced the hillsides surrounding the village as well as pottery, tools, weapons, shields, and any number of other crafts. Many of the goods were obviously made by the Sondau, while many others had quite obviously been looted during previous raids. Everywhere Drakis looked there were dark-skinned men and women, young and old, all freely engaged with one another. Three huge and powerful men stood together at the corner of the green speaking to each other in quiet tones but with large gestures, their eyes filled with the passion of their argument. Ahead of them, two women walked past, their arms filled with large fruits. They both turned to look at Drakis as they passed, then broke into giggling laughter as they walked on.

"Yes, son," Shasa said as he stopped at a stall filled with

a sweet-smelling, long yellow fruit and turned to face a woman with high, delicate cheekbones tending it. "There is no place more beautiful than Nothree ... wouldn't you agree, Khesai?"

"Far be disagreement from my door," the woman replied with a wide smile. "May the gods grant you a fair wind, Elder Shasa."

"Where is Durian today?" Shasa asked. "I would have thought he would be here on market day ... especially with such a fine crop."

"He is helping Moda repair a ship at the beach," Khesai replied. "Moda has offered to help us add a room to our home in exchange."

Shasa raised his eyebrows. "Another room? Then have the gods blessed your family, Khesai?"

"Soon enough," the woman smiled even more.

Shasa nodded. "Have you met our traveler, Drakis?"

"Fate smiles," Khesai bowed slightly with the traditional greeting.

"Fate smiles," Drakis bowed back.

"Your family shall be in our hearts, Khesai," Shasa said. "Forgive us our leaving. I must speak with Drakis."

Shasa turned and continued down the path with Drakis falling into step at his side.

"Elder," Drakis said, "I have only been here a week, and yet I feel more at home here than any other place I have ever been."

"This was not always so, Drakis," Shasa laughed deeply.

Drakis grinned. "No, Elder Shasa ... that is true. When we first arrived ... well, I had never seen any humans with skin nearly so dark as the Sondau."

"And this worried you?" Shasa asked.

"Well, no ... I just felt terribly conspicuous ... as though everyone was looking at me."

Shasa laughed again; warm and filled with humor. "Everyone *was* looking at you. It is easy to pick you out in a crowd ... your white face could be seen from two leagues in the darkest part of a cloud-covered night. Finding you is not a problem ... hiding you is."

Drakis nodded.

They passed the great house at the end of the square. The path under their feet now moved under the canopy of the tall, palm trees and the huts of the village families. The sounds of a mother yelling from inside the home for one of her children drifted past them as the path soon started to climb a winding trail up the steep slopes surrounding the village and its bay.

"There was one other thing," Drakis said after many steps in silence.

"Yes, Drakis."

"It's that I've never seen so many humans in one place before," he replied. "There have always been a few of us, of course, doing specialized jobs or kept around as curiosities. Timuran owned five or six of us, and that was considered an extravagance. But several hundred in one place? That could only happen when entire Legions were called into battle, and even then it would be hard to find them in the enormous press of so many other races. How did you get here? How have you survived?"

"The Sondau Clan settled Nothree during the Age of Fire, some seven hundred years ago by the counting of our lorekeepers," Shasa said. "In those days, it was an outpost of the Drakosian city-states; the human kingdoms of the north that ruled all the land of Armethia. They were still recovering from the War of Desolation—the first great conflict between the humans of the north and the Rhonas army of conquest from the south. It was an unsettled time, and the Clans of the Coast took it to be a sign of opportunity."

"Opportunity?" Drakis squinted in disbelief.

The path became steeper and more winding as they climbed.

"Certainly!" Shasa nodded. "In all change there is opportunity to benefit someone. So our ancestors came in their ships to what they saw as a land of promise. They found that the Forgotten Coast east of Point Kontantine was mountainous and lush, its ground fertile and mineral rich from the ancient volcanoes that had shaped it. Much of the coast was treacherous going for ships but there were choice harbors to be had if one knew where to find them along the arc of Sanctuary Bay. The Sondau captains were exceptional seafarers, and soon small settlements tucked in the back of hidden harbors like this one—accessed through all-but-impassable rock-strewn passages—dotted the great jagged shores of Sanctuary Bay."

As Shasa spoke, they stepped to the crest of a low hill overlooking the village. The thatched roofs of the huts below could barely be made out through the canopy of trees—lush broad-leafed hardwoods and tall, strange trees with great fanlike leaves spreading out from their tops. He had never seen their like in all the lands of Rhonas and wondered why. Surely, he thought, they would fetch a handsome price for so strange a thing as these trees Shasa called "palm."

The village was formed around a small, deep harbor surrounded entirely by steeply rising hills. The homes had to be built on the hillsides, and in many cases the roof of one butted up against the foundation of the next home higher up the hill. Communities here seemed to grow in clusters, like fruit springing somehow from the mountainside. The harbor itself was guarded by a narrow and winding passage that looked to Drakis to be entirely impossible to navigate although whenever he brought this up with the Sondau villagers, he was universally greeted with laughter.

Behind him, bright in the rising light of morning, stood the craggy peaks of the Sentinels, nearly vertical mountains whose slopes were covered in lush foliage and whose tops were always shrouded in clouds. Those peaks seemed to hold the outside world at bay and, Drakis reflected, perhaps that was truer than he knew.

"So they found their land of opportunity, then," Drakis said as he sat down and looked back out over the village spread below him.

"No, not nearly as easily as they had hoped ... for no dream comes without cost," Shasa mused, sitting next to him. "Many other settlements were established during that time as the Drakosians tried to extend their land holdings to include footholds in Nordesia and the Vestasian Coast. but each in turn failed. Only Nothree, Notwo, Nofor and a handful of others clung stubbornly to their existence through the tumult of war and shifting alliances that marked that age. Our fathers found themselves increasingly on their own. The Clans of the Coast, as they called themselves . . . Darakan, Phynig, Merindau, Sondau and Hakreb . . . struggled to survive as the ships from our homelands became increasingly infrequent, and our distant government drifted farther and farther removed from our lives."

Shasa picked up a stone from the hillside and tossed it lightly down the slope.

"Then, two centuries ago, when the dragons of Armethia betrayed their alliance with the Drakosian lords," he continued, "the ships stopped coming at all. We became 'The Forgotten' colonies, and here, in our little havens, we have been born, loved, lived, and died ever since."

Drakis thought about this for a moment, the silence resting easily between them. "Elder Shasa . . ."

"Yes, Drakis."

"Have you determined whether I am this 'prophet' everyone is looking for?"

"Drakis, what a strange question," Shasa said. "It seems to me that a prophet would know the answer to that question himself!"

"I don't know, Elder," Drakis replied. "Sometimes I believe it, and sometimes I think it's just nonsense. I hear the Dragon Song in my mind, but from what I understand so do many others. My name fits the prophecy, but then it's a common name . . . there is none *more* common among human slaves."

"There seem to be a lot of people who *want* you to be the Drakis of prophecy," Shasa replied. "Perhaps you should ask a different question."

"A different question?"

"Yes," Shasa said as he, too, gazed off across the harbor. "Perhaps you should ask yourself what *you* want. Do *you* want to be the Drakis of the prophecy . . . or do *you* want something else?"

Drakis stared at the balding man sitting next to him for a moment.

"Because if you're looking for something *else* . . . then you might consider looking down that upper path around the western hill," Shasa said casually. "I believe I saw Mala following that same path toward the Lace Pools not ten minutes ago."

Drakis smiled and stood up at once. "Thank you, Elder Shasa!"

"Write your own destiny, Drakis," Shasa called after the warrior as he sprinted down the path.

Drakis could hear the cascade of the Lace Falls before he saw it, a gentle, quiet roar of water tripping down a rock face. The warrior in him knew that it masked the sound of his approach, and almost without thought he softened his footfalls and stepped more gingerly down the beaten path that wound between the dense undergrowth and the tree canopy above. The stream ran down the slope next to him, its clear, cool water rushing down toward Nothree far below. Before him, the forest was brightening as he neared the clear area around the pool.

He stopped just short of the water's edge, holding his breath.

Mala.

She stood in the pool beneath the falls, the cascade of white water splashing around her shoulders and masking her body in tantalizing sheets. He could just make out the sweeping curve of her back above the surface of the pool, a hint of her breasts and the profile of her elegant neck as her face turned up into the tumbling water.

Mala turned toward the pool and dove, the momentary sight of her shoulders, waist, hips and legs shining in the morning sun taking his breath once more before the lacy foam on the surface that gave the pool its name hid her from him.

Her head surfaced near the center of the pool. She

reached up out of the water with her glistening arms, and pushed the water back from her short hair.

"Hello," he called gently across the water.

Mala turned suddenly toward him, but her startled, angry stare softened at once. "Oh, it's you."

"Yes, it's me."

"If you've come for a bath, you're too late," she said, her shoulders just above the surface as she moved her arms back and forth through the water. "I claimed this pool, and it is mine by right. I will not share my private little paradise with anyone else—no matter how badly they need bathing—and you, most certainly, are desperately in need of a bath."

"I didn't know you could swim," Drakis said, moving to the shore of the pool and sitting down.

Mala took in a luxurious breath. "Neither did I, but I must have learned at some point. It feels so right . . . and I've probably left so much of the road in this pool that it will probably foul the stream for several months. Oh, but it's good to be clean again! What do you think of my hair?"

Mala turned around. Her red hair was wet, but he could already tell it was shaped differently than he remembered. "That's a new look for you. When did that happen?"

Mala smiled and turned her head. "Several of the women from Nothree took it upon themselves to trim my ragged mop into this more pleasing form. Do you like it?"

"Yes," Drakis said as he reached down and removed his sandals, "I like it a great deal."

"Now, you can stop right there," Mala said, though there was a smile still playing at the edges of her pout. "I said this is *my* pool, and brutal warriors are not allowed to share it."

"I just want to put my feet in," Drakis complained. "Surely you cannot deny me the opportunity to wash these travel-weary feet?"

"You? Travel weary?" Mala said. "You've done nothing *but* travel, Drakis—and dragged us all along with you." She affected a serious look on her face, lowering her voice. "We go north! Keep going north! Don't know where it is . . . but it's north!"

"Fine, have your laugh," Drakis said, though he was chuckling as well. He slipped his feet into the water. "But it got us here, Mala . . . and here is not a bad place to be."

"No," she said softly. "Here is a good place."

Drakis paused for a moment and then, reaching up over his shoulders with both arms, grabbed the back of his tunic and pulled it off over his head.

"You can just stop right there, warrior-boy," Mala said sternly.

"It's a mess!" Drakis replied holding out the rumpled cloth. "Look at it! Hasn't been washed in weeks . . . I'll bet it would move on its own if I left it standing. People won't talk to me, Mala, for the stench of it. This shirt needs a cleaning . . . it's just a courtesy."

Mala giggled. "Those are the worst excuses I have ever heard! Can't you come up with something more creative?"

"'Warrior-boy?'" Drakis smirked.

"Very well, that wasn't my best either, but you have me at a disadvantage."

"So you need clothes to think?"

Mala smiled through her pout once more. "I don't seem to be thinking very clearly without them."

Drakis laughed again, plunging his shirt deep into the pool. Then he drew the wet cloth up, wrung it out and then stopped, just holding it.

"What is it, Draki?" Mala asked, her lithe arms making eddies in the surface of the pool.

He stopped. "It's good to hear you call me that again."

"So what is it?" she urged.

"I *am* weary of the road, Mala," he said in a voice that barely carried over the rushing sound of the waterfall. "I've been fighting all my life for things that meant nothing to me . . . for masters who thought of me as property and who didn't care if I lived or died. Now with all this 'prophecy' nonsense . . . it feels as though everyone wants me to be something or somebody *for* them again. I'm tired of living my life for everyone else's expectations . . . everyone *else's* life."

"What do you want, Draki?" Mala said quietly.

"I want . . ."

Drakis struggled for a moment. It was a new thought for him and he was having trouble even putting it into words.

"I want . . . something of my own."

"Something of your own?"

"Yes," Drakis said, his words forming with more conviction around the idea. "I want a place like this, a life that has nothing to do with the Iblisi or the Imperium, or mad dwarves, or prophecies, or this damn song that keeps calling me to a destiny I never asked for and certainly do not want. I want . . . I want *this* place, a small home in the village, cool water to drink, food to eat. I want children to raise and a life that is my own to share and . . ."

"And?" Mala asked, pushing backward through the water.

"And . . . and I want to know how to swim," he finished.

Mala laughed.

"What's so funny?"

"The great big warrior afraid of the water!"

"Yes," he sighed.

"Draki . . ."

"Yes, Mala?"

"You shouldn't be afraid," she said softly. "I'm standing on the bottom. It's not that deep."

Invisible to them both, Ethis the chimerian stood watching Drakis and Mala from the shore of the pool. His skin blended so perfectly with the foliage that had they known he was there, they would not have been able to see him even were they looking directly at the spot where he stood.

All they might have discerned was the movement of the cloth as he fingered Mala's gown where she had draped it over a bush.

But they would have had to look quickly . . . for in the next moment, he was gone.

CHAPTER 40

Without Doubts

BELAG CROUCHED DOWN in the lodge of the Elders, peering intently at the pictographs on the walls.

"Hmmm," he growled in a low voice, his great eyes narrowing as he looked more intently at the images carved into the wall. "They appear to have some of this wrong."

It was a perfectly reasonable assumption for the manticore—his faith was sure and unshakable.

As cubs pouncing and rolling through the tall grasses of the Chaenandrian borderlands, both he and his brother Karag had lived and breathed the legends, histories, and tales of the loremasters. In the fading light of a spent day, the two of them would gather with the rest of their pride as the stars appeared and listen as the ancient dead and their deeds were brought again to life in their imaginations. Stories of the old ways and the shattering empires of men, the fall of the dragons and the desperate charges of the Chaenandrian Guardians, whose numbers were so great that the earth trembled when they ran into battle.

But of all the legends told beneath the fading cobalt of the sky, none impressed his brother Karag more than that of Drakis Aerweaver and the Dragons of Armethia. Both of them would lie spellbound at the sound of the loremaster's voice as he wove the tale from memory. Belag could still see in his mind's eye those dragons that flew in their imaginations just beyond reach, weaving in and out between the stars as they appeared. He could almost picture the Northern Lords on their backs, watching over the world far beneath them. Then the loremaster came to the tragic and terrible betrayal where all the world—including many weak and covetous Lords of the Manticorian Prides—conspired in their jealousy to bring low the might of Drakosia and take on its glory for their own. In sorrow at the betrayal, Drakis removed himself from the circles of the world. Then came the mournful song of the dragons as they in turn were brought to a terrible awareness of their own guilt and began the ages-old lament even as the great cities of Drakosia vanished into the mists, never to be found again among mortal lands. The song, the loremaster told them, was still sung today by the dragons of the north country beyond the raging waters of the oceans, calling to the night stars in the hope that Drakis would hear their sorrow, accept their regret, and return once more in might and power to establish justice for all the races of Dunaea who longed once more to be free. This was the great hope of the loremaster for the Khadush Pride; for though they, too, were cursed as all the manticores for the betrayal, they had been among the prides that had broken with the Lords of the Manticorian Clans and would not allow themselves to become toothless puppets of the Rhonas oppression.

By the crackling bonfire around which he and his brother had gathered with the rest of the Khadush Pride, Belag heard the loremaster speak of their glorious destiny: to resist the Rhonas, to free the enslaved prides, and to look for the day when Drakis—the mystical human of divine power from the north—would again take form among mortal men and, having been a slave himself, would lift the curse that held the manticorian nation in chains and awaken the power of the Khadush once more to hunt their true enemies.

Watching the embers from the fire rise up among the stars, Belag saw the firelight shining in Karag's eyes. His elder brother believed the words of the loremaster with all his heart. In time, Karag had even studied under the lore-master with the thought in mind of becoming his apprentice and one day perhaps even becoming the loremaster to the Khadush Pride. But in the end, Karag discovered that it was not his calling, that recitation of the lore was not enough for him; he had come to believe with unquestioning fervor that Drakis not only would come but that he *had* come and that the greatest thing he could do would be to leave the pride and journey into the world to find the prophesied liberator and serve him in his coming battle against the Rhonas oppressors. It would require hardship and, in the end, great sacrifice, but the glories of the songs to be sung and the stories to be told of those who served Drakis in his return would last down through the ages.

To Belag, who lived on every word of his elder brother, the dreams and the glories that awaited them in such service were intoxicating, and any sacrifice seemed but a small matter by comparison. His brother believed and so Belag, too, believed. For him, in those early years, it was just that simple.

So when Karag left the pride to search for the promised emancipator of the manticores, Belag went with him without a second thought. They journeyed northward because the legends said that Drakis would one day come from the north. Their track also took them somewhat westward around the northern foothills of the Aerian Mountains as Karag wished at all costs to avoid the bizarre and devious chimera of Ephindria. As they traveled, Belag learned all that his brother knew about Drakis Aerweaver and the Dragons of Armethia, committing each detail to memory. Belag could still remember the smile his brother gave him with each correct recitation or whenever Belag answered his questions correctly.

Then came the day they were ensnared by the Rhonas slave hunters on the verge of the Vestasian Savanna—and with their first enforced Devotions all the memories of their great quest and hopes for their future vanished under an avalanche of lies and false memories.

And so they lived for nearly four years as slaves of the

Rhonas, asleep to their true natures and fighting battles for the elves in which they had only artificial loyalty and illusionary allegiance to their master's Houses. Belag, in hindsight, now considered that time as a trial of his faith and part of the sacrifice by which the gods test their heroes. By then both he and his brother knew a human slave named Drakis, but their memories were so buried beneath the miasma of House Devotional spells that they did not even recognize the object of their quest when they saw it.

Then Karag died in their final battle—died saving this Drakis. Belag believed that somehow Karag must have known, even through the damning House Devotions, that protecting this human was his greatest moment and the culmination of his faith. His brother, Belag now knew without doubt, was a martyr whose death atoned for the curse on the manticores of their pride's clan.

Then came the Awakening. Drakis utterly destroyed the Aether Well of House Timuran and freed Belag's mind from the interwoven chains of lies, deceptions, and falsehoods that his life had become. In that moment he remembered it all—how the elven hunters had taken both him and his brother and every painful, humiliating day since. Most of all he remembered the legends of Drakis and attached them at once to the Impress Warrior that he knew so well. Especially since his brother had died defending him in the battle of the Ninth Throne.

It was a sign . . . it *had* to be a sign. It *had* to be significant. His brother *had* to die for a greater cause and his death *had* to be on behalf of his lifelong dream so that his spirit could rest among the honored dead.

In that moment, standing amid the chaos as House Timuran tore itself apart—in that moment, Belag knew the reality of it with his entire soul. His fragile sanity hung suspended by that single, inviolable truth: This human Drakis was the embodiment of his brother's every hope, and his life gave meaning to his brother's death.

Belag withdrew his face from its close proximity to the carving on the wall and shook his head, repeating his words. "They have it wrong."

"They see it differently," a small voice said casually next to him.

The large lion-man jumped slightly at the sound. Belag had not believed it possible for a human to be able to approach so near a manticore without been heard. "No, they are wrong, Lyric."

"Not so much wrong as you are both right in a different way," the Lyric replied, her own gaze fixed on the carvings adorning the wall. Her hair had grown into a wild nimbus of near-white radiating from her head. Its soft strands seemed to float in the air around the crown of her head. "They do not know what you know, Belag—how could they see through your eyes?"

Belag spoke quietly down toward the much shorter human woman. "And whom have I the pleasure of addressing today?"

The Lyric looked up at him, her large eyes shining up from her narrow face. "Of course, you are a manticore and from a far and strange land. I wonder not that you have never encountered my kind before. Fear not, good creature, I am a beneficent spirit and mean you no ill."

"A spirit?" Belag furrowed his furry brow.

"Aye," the Lyric responded with a sad smile. "I am the ghost of Musaran the Wanderer. I am most often invisible, but I show myself to those whose stories I wish to take with me . . . and to those whom my stories may help. Every creature of the world has a story, and I am fated to know them all."

Belag let out a relieved breath. The Lyric changed her persona unpredictably, and more often than not lately she had taken to adopting strange and sometimes dangerous characteristics. Yesterday had been a challenge. She had proclaimed herself Clarinda, the throat-cutting harlot of Chargoth Bay and had everyone more than a little wary of her. A ghost of some wandering story-gatherer sounded like a good deal safer personality for all concerned. "Then you know the legends of Drakis Aerweaver."

"I do—and a good many more," the Lyric said with a sad darkness in her voice. "There is one story that interests me most right now, one with which you can help me. I have the beginning and the middle right, but I do not yet have the ending."

"You need my help with a story?" Belag chuckled.

"It is a story that will interest you, I think," the Lyric replied, arching her eyebrows.

"Thank you, spirit," Belag replied, turning back to the carvings on the wall. "I have no need of stories."

"But this one involves you," the Lyric replied. "It is the story of RuuKag, the manticore who lost his tale."

"Lost his tail?" Belag snorted. "He should look behind him!"

"Not his 'tail,' Belag, his *tale*," the Lyric said with surprising impatience. "His story, his personal legend. Every creature is the hero of his own story but RuuKag lost his. Now I fear he has gone to find it."

Belag hesitated. "Find it?"

"Yes," the Lyric replied, shaking her head. "He left yesterday late in the evening. I followed him—invisible as I was—for a long as I could. He crossed over the Cragsway Pass toward the . . . where are you going? The story isn't finished yet!"

Belag was already throwing open the doors of the Elders' Lodge, his pace picking up quickly toward the bay.

"Aye, that's a fine ship, lass," Jugar said through his wide-toothed grin. "I've never seen the like!"

"Then you've never encountered the corsairs of Thetis," Urulani replied, swinging around a backstay to land on the planked deck beneath her feet. "She's just three hands under thirty cubits in length from stem to stern, and we can pull her at a respectable speed with a crew of twenty—given a good sea. She's the smallest of our corsairs, but I rather like her."

"It is a wonder!" The dwarf said, shaking his head as he gazed at the ship where it was moored to the dock. The *Cydron*, as Urulani called it, was a beautiful craft, its hull tapered fore and aft with such elegant lines that it looked as though it could fly across the waves with barely a feather's touch. She was not a terribly large ship—completely unlike the large and rather ponderous galleons that the Rhonas employed against their rebellious cousins on the southern borders of the Empire—but was built for grace and speed. Three slightly angled masts gave a powerful rake to her lines. Her main deck was a single level though a raised walkway just above the level of the oarsmen's heads connected a small enclosed forecastle and a more elevated afterdeck that held the long, ornately carved arm of the rudder. He was a dwarf and his expertise was largely relegated to the realm of stone, but he certainly could appreciate the art involved in such a fine piece of woodcraft. His eyes twinkled as he took in the lines of the ship. "How fast will it sail?"

"She'll cross the Bay in less than three days," Urulani said. "We've raided coastal towns in Nordesia when necessary and been back in less than a week's time."

"A wonder . . . a marvel of our age," Jugar nodded with appreciation. "Perhaps I will have the privilege of sailing aboard her one day. You know, Drakis is such a strange human, even seen through the eyes of his own kind, I might venture to say, that I wouldn't wonder if he would request passage to the north . . ."

Urulani was no longer paying attention to the dwarf. "It looks as though someone else of your group has taken an interest in boats."

Jugar turned and was astonished—if not a little frightened—to see Belag bounding toward them, crouched over and rushing toward them on all fours. The great manticore slid to a halt on the planks of the dock, rising back on his hind legs as he spoke.

"Urulani . . . Jugar . . . have either of you seen RuuKag today?"

Jugar looked up. "No, but I would not consider that an unusual occurrence. He is, as you well know, a most reclusive individual prone to rather moody withdrawals from our company . . ."

"Urulani," the manticore said, turning hastily to the dark-skinned woman. "Have you seen RuuKag . . . the other being like me?"

Urulani smiled slightly through her puzzlement. "I do *know* what a manticore is, friend Belag . . . but I have not seen RuuKag since last night when . . ."

Urulani stopped speaking.

"What is it?" Belag asked.

"I was discussing Drakis with some of the Elders last night," Urulani replied, her smile having fallen. "We were considering additional sentries to be posted in the Sentinel Peaks and along the Cragsway Pass. The discussion turned to whether we should have our warriors travel in pairs to watch each other."

"Watch each other?" Jugar said, raising his own thick eyebrows. "Why should you be concerned about your own warriors?"

"Because," Urulani said, stepping up from the deck onto the dock, "the stories of Drakis being spread by the Hak'kaarin and the Dje'kaarin both also now speak of incredible rewards being offered for the location of your friend and any of the rest of you. We were talking of this when your friend suddenly appeared. We changed the subject of our speech, but now I wonder if perhaps he didn't overhear us."

"The traitor!" Jugar's word's exploded from his mouth. "He's finally done it! We've got to stop him! He'll be the ruin of us all!"

"What do you mean, dwarf," Belag snarled.

"It's him!" Jugar said, grabbing his pack and shoving at Belag to get him moving as well. "He'll bring the Iblisi down on all of us if we don't reach him first . . . without a doubt!"

CHAPTER 41

The Crossroads

THE MANTICORE STOOD silhouetted against the bright backdrop of the stars in a cloudless night. He was hunched over, his massive head turning furtively from side to side. The tall grasses of the savanna stretched to the south, west, and east under the starlight. To the north, the dark towers of the Sentinel Peaks stood as a great, jagged wall blotting out the stars. But here, almost exactly beneath his padded feet, two widely trampled roads came to an intersection. One curved down from the mud gnome's city to the northwest and plunged deep into the Vestasian Savanna to the southeast. The other carved a wide path from the Tempest Bay colonies of the Dje'Kaarin gnomes to the east and wound its way to other more southern mud gnome cities to the southwest. Both roads were formed by the passage of gnomes who were in too great a hurry to stop at this singular place and who, in the depths of the night, had left the manticore entirely alone.

The creature continue to shift nervously under the stars, first on one foot and then the other, turning from time to time to look behind him. All the while he held a small stone gingerly between the thick fingers of his right paw, tapping it nervously onto similar stones he held cupped in his right paw.

The manticore stopped for a moment, holding perfectly still in the night, his head straining upward. He shivered abruptly though the night was far from cold, the hairs on his growing mane shaking momentarily. Then he resumed striking the small stones together once more.

"So it is you," a voice said from the darkness.

The manticore wheeled around, dropping to a crouch, his legs contracted and prepared to spring.

"Peace, friend," the voice said, seeming to come from every direction at once around the startled manticore.

The manticore relaxed slightly, his eyes straining at the darkness. He spoke quietly into the night. "I am a servant of the Empire!"

"And you have done well," came the voice in reply from a shadow that appeared out of nowhere before the eyes of the manticore.

"Have we met, Master?"

"Not before tonight," the shadow responded. Its shape was more defined now against the stars: lithe and tall after the form of the elves. Its head was cloaked in a great hood, and in its right hand it held a long ornate staff. "Although I have followed you for some time. By what name are you known?"

"RuuKag, Master," the manticore answered, bowing down before the robed elf. "I was a servant in the House of Timuran and the Beacon of that House."

"You have done well, RuuKag," the shadow answered. "Are the others near?"

"No, my Master."

The elven silhouette stopped. "Then why have you called me, Beacon of Timuran?"

"The stones, my Master," RuuKag replied with evident pain in his voice. "The dwarf has discovered them. He stole most of them from me as I slept and doubtless plans to use them to confuse you, my Master. He will send them away with someone else and instruct them to mislead you—to take you farther from me. I would be lost to you, my Master. I would be . . . lost . . ."

The manticore fell to the ground, burying his head under his forepaws.

"Peace, friend," the hooded elf said once more, his staff lowering slightly until the glowing blue gem fixed in its head shone down on the manticore.

The groveling creature relaxed slightly and looked up. "Please, Master! Please take me back! I want to forget. I want to go back and forget everything I ever was or did. I had no part in this rebellion, I swear it! Please . . . I don't want to remember any more!"

"In time," the elf replied calmly. "When you have finished your task."

"My task?" RuuKag asked as he pushed himself up. Even kneeling his head was still nearly level with the elf's chest. "But, Master, I have done all that was expected! I have led you to me. You have found me!"

"You are not the one I seek," the elf said softly. "Until I have taken him, you will not have peace."

RuuKag stood suddenly.

The elf's staff shifted menacingly.

"But . . . Master!" RuuKag grumbled. "I've done all you asked of me! I stayed with the rebels, dropped the beacon stones as I promised . . ."

"And where are they now?" the elf demanded. "I could have taken you any time I wished . . . but just getting recaptured wasn't your task, was it? You were supposed to lead me to the *rest* of the bolters . . . not just you! The entire point of *having* beacons planted among the slaves is so that you will lead us to all the *other* escaped slaves, not just yourself."

"Please, Master," the manticore said, wringing his large, fur-covered hands. "I just want to go home."

"Home?" the elf spat. "You *have* no home, RuuKag . . . it's burned to the ground, its walls caving in on itself as a ruin because your companions wrecked it all. If you're going to have any home at all, it will only be after you finish your task by leading me to the bolters with whom you've been traveling."

"I don't know where they are!"

"What?"

"They ... they moved on," RuuKag said. "That Drakis human said something about going east—maybe finding a ship or something. They've probably left by now ..."

"Then find them!" the elf insisted. "By the gods, you're a manticore!"

"But, Master," RuuKag asked with uncertainty in his voice. "I know you are powerful, but they have magic of their own ... powerful and deadly. How many of your brothers are with you?"

"It's just me," the elf replied. "And it will go a lot better for all of us if it *remains* just me."

"I don't understand," RuuKag said, shaking his head.

"Listen to me, manticore!" the elf was losing patience. "There are three—maybe four full Quorums of Iblisi on the plains who are trying to keep up with *me*. *They* are hunting *me* in order that they may be led to *you*. When they *find* us—*should* they find us—then I can promise you as certainly as the sun will arise in the morning, things will go much worse for all of us—you included—if you do *not* get me to this Drakis friend of yours *first*."

"I don't ... please, Master, I've got to think ..."

"Think!"

The manticore flinched at the elf's shouted word.

"You don't have to *think* about anything! Thinking is what made you a coward!"

RuuKag whined, his ears flattening back against his wide head.

"I may not have Timuran's Impress Scrolls, but I *did* read the Devotion Ledger—especially of certain bolters," the elf said, stepping closer. "RuuKag, once of the Shakash Pride was supposed to be a warrior—supposed to rush into battle—but he *thought* too much, *felt* too much. So he came home ... just walked back to his pridelands because the thought of battle and death and pain frightened him. The frightened manticore! A freak and an embarrassment to his father and mother and brothers and everything his Shakash Pride had stood for and taught since the rise of

Chaenandria. You were useless, so they banished you to the Vestasian Savanna."

RuuKag shrank back.

The elf pressed his face so near the manticore that his scent was overwhelming. "How was that for you, RuuKag? Too afraid to fight and your own family not understanding why? They still loved you, still cared for you, but in one way or another they all turned their backs on you and banished you from the pride. You might still be among them, but you could never again be *one of them.* So you banished yourself, making the long way to the cursed lands of the Vestasian Savanna, nursing the wounds in your heart. How was that for you, RuuKag of Shakash ... oh, pardon me, RuuKag of no pride at all ... to come again just weeks ago back to the old lands of your punishment? Did even the mud gnomes remember the story of the manticore with no pride?"

"No," whispered RuuKag. "Not even that."

"No, you were forgotten—not even important enough for the mud gnomes to remember your story," the elf sneered. "No wonder you prefer to forget."

RuuKag closed his eyes. Great tears fell down his fur-covered cheeks, glinting in the moonlight.

"Now, I'm the one who knows your story, RuuKag," the elf continued. "You could try to take me, I suppose, try to summon that famously vicious warrior heart, and we could do battle right here. Or you could do as you were *told* to do: lead me to Drakis and his companions, serve the Imperial Will and, as your reward, I will see to it that you never remember again who you were and the shame you brought on your family and pride."

RuuKag's breath was ragged. He held very still.

"Take me to Drakis," the elf whispered. "And RuuKag can be completely forgotten. No one will remember that name ... not even you."

RuuKag opened his eyes and stared into the blackness that was encompassed by the elf's hood.

"I will, Master," the manticore said.

The elf smiled, his sharp teeth shining in the starlight.

"But I will need a new set of beacon stones," RuuKag continued. "They're going to use the old ones to take you in the wrong direction."

"Here," the elf said, reaching into the folds of his cloak and pulling out a small, plain pouch. "These are my own—made by my hand. They will answer to my staff only."

"Thank you, Master," the manticore said. He took a few steps up the northwestern road and then stopped. "Master, is it true that you do not wish to harm this Drakis-human?"

The elf chuckled. "RuuKag, I may be the *only* one I know who does *not* want him dead."

"But," RuuKag persisted, "why do you wish him alive?"

"I have my own reasons," the elf replied.

"Surely such things are beyond my understanding," RuuKag said, his eyes gazing once more upward toward the stars, "but it is a wonder that an elf should cross all of Chaenandria, concern himself with the obscure backgrounds of a handful of freed slaves, and cross the length and breadth of the Vestasian Plain just to meet this Drakis."

The elf paused. "You're thinking again, RuuKag."

"Sorry, Master," the manticore said, lowering his head.

"Just don't let it happen again."

"Yes, Master."

The manticore turned once more to face the elf. "They will have questions, Master—about my absence, especially since they discovered the stones. What do I tell them?"

"Tell them . . ." The elf thought for a moment before he continued with a bright lilt in his voice. "Tell them that you were their traitor."

"They would kill me," RuuKag said. "You cannot be serious!"

"On the contrary, I am most serious," the elf continued. "They wouldn't believe you if you lie. Tell them that you have been dropping these stones so that they could be tracked and followed and that the Iblisi are searching for them. Then tell them that after getting to know them you have changed your mind and want to help them instead."

"They will believe this?"

"Absolutely," the elf said, folding his arms across his

chest, his staff casually crooked in his arms. "Any lie is far more easily swallowed when it is mixed with a liberal amount of the truth. Besides, from what I know of this Drakis, he would be more willing to forgive a penitent traitor than a professed friend. Most humans are."

RuuKag nodded. "Then I shall do your bidding . . . but, Master, by what name shall I speak of you?"

"Soen," the elf replied. "Just Soen."

CHAPTER 42

Heart of the Manticore

BELAG WAS STRAINING at his own patience. Urulani knew the Cragsway Pass, and the dwarf simply could not be stopped from coming. Even the Lyric—who still insisted that as Musaran the Wanderer her spirit could easily keep up with them all—was moving with them through the night. Fortunately, Belag mused, Drakis and Mala were nowhere to be found or they, too, might have insisted on coming. As it was, the group was moving far more slowly than Belag liked. He would have preferred them to have just stayed behind and let him deal with RuuKag himself—a stealthy hunt and a quick kill would have been more to his liking. But he did need Urulani to help him track down the traitorous manticore, and there seemed no stopping the dwarf or the Lyric. At least Jugar had managed to close his mouth and keep silent as they passed to the south.

It was well into twilight when they descended the southern slopes of the Sentinel Peaks. RuuKag's tracks had been easy to follow through the pass; he had made no effort in his haste to disguise them. Darkness fell fully upon them as the foothills gave way to the savanna beyond. The tracking became more difficult through the tall grasses, but Urulani had more success here. Soon it was evident that the trail had straightened.

Urulani lifted her arm and pointed southward. Belag stopped and stood silently in the night for a time, finally lifting the dwarf up so that he could see above the tall grass.

The trail led straight toward the mud city of the Hak'kaarin—the same city they had left just days before.

Even from three leagues distant, they could see that something terrible had happened there.

The mud city was burning. Tongues of flame flared above it from the opening in its enormous roof. Smaller fires burned outside the great dome. Black, greasy smoke was billowing from the opening, marring the night sky with a great absence of stars overhead.

Belag put the dwarf down, and they began a more wary approach to the city.

It was well after midnight when the four of them arrived at the clearing surrounding the city. Gaping pits had opened up all around the base of the dome—part of the defensive system that Belag had observed surrounded each of the mud mound cities of the Hak'kaarin. Many of them appeared to have been activated. Other places in the ground and across the dome were marred with long, charred furrows.

"Look," Urulani said in hushed tones as she pointed along the base of the dome. "Most of the gates are shut, but those two are broken inward—as is that third farther down."

Belag nodded and then raised his head, his ears swiveled forward as he listened intently. Only the crackling and rush of the fires came to his ears. No cries ... No battle ... just the sound of burning.

"He came here," the Lyric said with sadness filling her voice.

Belag turned to her. "Lyric, I don't think . . ."

"RuuKag came here because he was in pain," the Lyric said, her eyes fixed on the nearest shattered gate. "He was

in pain because he knew that he was once again part of a
great story. He had listened to you, Belag, and heard more
than you knew. For all his anger came from his pain, and
his pain was that he had too great a heart. He believed you,
Belag. In the end, he believed in Drakis, too."

Belag, Urulani, and the dwarf stared at the Lyric. Her
eyes gazed far away, as though she were seeing a scene that
was beyond the vision of mere mortals. She began walking toward the shattered gate as she spoke. "But his own
story was sad and tragic. He had bragged about going to
war when he was a cub, but in his heart he had doubts. He
feared pain and death, and so in the end he was branded
a coward by his own pride and exiled. He was forgotten—
even among the Hak'kaarin who once had sheltered him."

Urulani whispered. "How can she know these things?"

"That girl knows more than she's letting on," Jugar said,
his eyes narrowing as he considered her.

Belag shook his head. "Come . . . look there in the
ground. Those are RuuKag's tracks. The Lyric's walking
in them."

They came to the shattered gate. The long tunnel beyond curved gradually upward toward the center of the
enormous mud dome as in every other city they had visited, but here they stopped in horror.

The floor was carpeted with the dead.

"What a struggle they must have put up," Jugar breathed.

Urulani pressed her lips together, unable to speak.

Belag turned to the Lyric. "What happened here?"

"He came," the Lyric continued, her eyes staring past
the end of the rising tunnel toward where the glow of
fire could be seen. "He had accepted your faith in Drakis,
Belag, and the old fear returned to him . . . but this time
that he *would be* remembered as the manticore who failed
the human of the prophecy. The battle was already raging
when he arrived. He had come for solace from these gentle
creatures of the Hak'kaarin, the only family he felt left to
him. He saw the battle, heard the desperate cries of the
mud gnomes . . ."

The Lyric turned and pointed at the ground. "Here he

ran, charging past the bodies of the gnomes who had fallen. He picked up a weapon—taken from this gnome's cold hands—and with a great warrior cry leaped forward."

The Lyric stepped carefully among the fallen dead, their blood staining her sandals and the hem of her skirt as she walked down the tunnel. Belag and the others, entranced by her words, followed down the hall with gingerly steps.

The Lyric stopped where the tunnel rose sharply upward toward the center of the dome. A great, jet-black stain swept from one side of the tunnel to the opposite wall where some of the mud had melted into dark glass. "Here he saw the first of them—a robed elven hunter whose magic was killing the Hak'kaarin in terrible numbers. Seeing the gnomes being murdered thus, at last RuuKag found his warrior's heart—or perhaps he found a cause for which he could fight."

At the apex of the stain lay a robed figure missing its head.

"Here, for the first time," the Lyric said, "RuuKag found the courage to kill."

The Lyric, her hem now dragging a terrible bloody stain across the floor behind her, stepped up the ramp and into the great open space beneath the center of the dome.

The fires were burning out in the upper levels but still gave all too bright illumination on the grizzly scene. Two sections of habitat walls had collapsed and buried part of the central floor of the common area. The bodies of the dead gnome defenders were a terrible blanket across the floor.

"Where are the children?" Urulani asked.

"What? What children?" Belag growled.

"That's my point," Urulani said, her eyes shifting across the mass of the dead. "These are all warrior gnomes. Some men and some women but none of them old—none of them infirm—and there are no children here among the dead."

"She's right," Jugar said in astonishment. "In such a calamity one might expect an even greater number of noncombatants to fall prey to the terrible confusion of war.

"And there's not enough of the dead," Belag nodded. "This was terrible, indeed, but even so there are nowhere near enough dead to account for the entire city."

"He saved them," the Lyric said simply.

"Who saved them," Belag asked.

The Lyric pointed again, this time to the far side of the commons.

Belag's eyes opened wide.

RuuKag—or what was left of him—lay dead against the wall. His eyes were dull and blood stained the corners of his open jaws and his bared teeth. The hair was burned entirely off his left side where the raw red of his muscle was exposed. His right arm hung at an impossible angle, flopping limply over one of the three shafts that pierced his chest.

Next to him was a crumpled form in robes, an elf whose throat had been torn out.

"Elves!" Belag snarled.

"Back again, eh?" The dwarf gritted his teeth.

"Look! There are more of them," Urulani said, again pointing to various places around the hall. "Four ... six ... wait, there's one up there, too. Seven of them!"

Belag nodded as he stepped quickly through the carnage to reach RuuKag's side. He stood over the fallen manticore for a few moments and then reached down and closed his eyes.

"Well fought, brother," he murmured into RuuKag's ear. "You've proved your heart this day. Your story will be told ... and I will tell it."

Jugar considered RuuKag for a moment then took in the rest of the dead. "He bought them time ... time to escape."

"Yes," Belag said, straightening up. "The rest of the Hak'kaarin are fleeing to the other cities. Within days the story of what happened here will be told from one end of the savanna to the other."

"I don't understand," Urulani said, shaking her head. "Slave hunters have no reason to attack the mud cities. The Hak'kaarin have no possessions worth the attention of any elves and they make terrible slaves."

"These aren't slavers," Belag said, turning suddenly. "This is a full Quorum of the Iblisi—the Inquisitors of the Imperium. They have no interest in gnomes."

"What do they want then?" Urulani asked. "Why attack this city?"

"Because they thought *we* were here," Belag replied. "Because they thought *he* was here."

"Drakis?" Urulani sputtered, "All these gnomes destroyed and your friend slaughtered . . . just because these elven magicians think your friend is part of this moldy prophecy?"

"Come!" the manticore said as he began moving back toward the tunnel as quickly as the gore-coated floor would allow. "We have to get back . . . we have very little time left."

"Time?" Urulani said with astonishment. "Time for *what*?"

"Lyric . . . uh, Musaran," Belag called. "You must come and tell this story to Drakis."

"As a spirit I am above such things," the Lyric replied.

"Yes, but Drakis is fond of communing with spirits," Belag continued. "Come quickly. Jugar, Urulani. We must get back at once!"

"Get back?" Urulani was losing her patience. "What about any survivors? What if there are more of those 'Ubisee' things around?"

"I tell you that there *will* be a lot more of those 'Ubisee things' around soon enough!" Belag said, stopping at the top of the ramp and turning to face the warrior-woman. "This was a single Quorum, but as soon as the *other* Quorums get word of what happened here, they're going to *know* it was one of us who did this . . . and it won't take them long to figure out that the only way we might have gone is through the Cragsway Pass."

"And to Nothree," Jugar said as he nodded.

"They've found us," Belag said. "And our backs are to the sea."

CHAPTER 43

Relentless

"WHERE HAS EVERYONE GONE?" Mala asked casually. "Do I care where everyone has gone?" Drakis answered back, soft warmth in his voice.

They walked as one along the sloping sands of the bay's shore, their bare feet digging into the residual warmth of the sand as the cool offshore breeze flowed past them. The sun was setting on a perfect day in the first place of peace that Drakis had ever known. The totality of its experience was almost painful to the human warrior who had never known tranquillity—never even had the ability to imagine it. Yet here they were, Mala's arm wrapped around his waist and his around her shoulders, walking beside the gently lapping waves of Nothree Bay and looking in awe at the encircling mountain peaks, fading to purple under a vibrant orange sky at sunset.

"But I haven't seen anyone all day," Mala said.

"What do you mean 'haven't seen anyone?'" Drakis spoke through a crooked smile. "Look ... over there behind that corsair galley. There's a whole group of 'someones' working on those nets. And just up there ... entirely too many 'someones' who are trying to keep those children out from under foot while they cook dinner. The whole village is absolutely lousy with 'someones.'"

Mala slugged him in the chest with the boots in her hand just hard enough so that he would not let go of her. "You're terrible! That's not what I meant and you know it. Where's the dwarf or the Lyric ... or either of the manticores from our old House for that matter?"

"You forgot the chimerian."

"Well, I'd just as soon *forget* the chimerian altogether."

"Can't argue with you there."

"But seriously, Drakis." Mala stopped walking, pulling him around to face her just before they came to the beached prow of one of the Sondau ships. "Where are they? Don't you think it odd that they follow you all this way and then run off without a word to you? They've been gone more than a full day now. It's like they all vanished at once."

"Mala, stop worrying," Drakis said, turning toward her and taking her by her shoulders. She looked so beautiful to him in the soft light of the closing day that he nearly forgot what he was about to say. "I spoke with Elder Shasa this morning. He said that most of them went off to try to find RuuKag ... who apparently had gotten it into his mind to return to the Hak'kaarin on his own. No one knows where Ethis went, and to be honest, I'd be just as glad if he remained lost."

"But, Drakis ..."

"Mala, listen to me ... there's something I want to talk to you about." Drakis took her hand and led her higher up the beach just short of the seawall. He gestured for her to sit and then sat next to her as they both looked out over the waters of the bay. The evening was deepening but through the narrow channel that entered the bay between the towering rocks could still be seen the fading remnant of the sunset illuminating the northern horizon.

"What is it, Drakis?" Mala asked quietly.

Drakis sat still for some time before he spoke. "Have you ever enjoyed quiet like this?"

"Quiet?" Mala laughed. "I hear those pots in the kitchen behind us ... I hear the laugher of those men mending the net ... those children squealing up the beach—and the birds around here can be downright obnoxious."

Drakis smiled. "That's not what I mean. I mean the luxury of *being* quiet . . . of just holding still and looking out over the water with someone next to you to share that stillness. To not have to say a word and know that no one needs you to speak because the quiet around you speaks for you."

Mala leaned toward him, resting her head against his shoulder. "I've never known that quiet before here . . . it's painful."

"Yes, that's right," Drakis nodded. "Painful because we never knew it existed and now the thought of losing it is unbearable. Mala, I'm tired of running toward a horizon that is always getting farther away . . . tired of pretending to pursue some destiny that isn't even mine."

"What are you saying?" Mala asked.

"I'm saying that this . . . right here . . . is everything that I want or could ever want out of my life." Drakis reached down and pulled up a handful of the white sand from between his feet. It glittered slightly in the fading rays of the day. "This place . . . this peace. I don't want or need any great destiny that may not be mine to begin with. All I want is this quiet . . . right here . . . with you."

"But, the song in your head . . . the music that calls you . . ."

"It's still there," Drakis replied, looking through the narrow passage to the north. The light on the horizon was rapidly fading. "If anything it is stronger than ever, but, Mala, that doesn't mean I have to follow it. Let it just be a song in my head . . . from what Elder Shasa tells me there are plenty of other humans who have heard the song, too, and *they* didn't have to go out and become this great prophecy fulfillment either."

"What are you saying?"

"I'm saying I don't want to run anymore." Drakis turned to Mala. "I'm saying I want to stay . . . right here with you as my mate or wife or whatever the Sondau call it, bury my sword, have a family of our own, and live a quiet life."

"I . . . I don't . . ." Mala stammered. "Is it possible, Drakis? I mean, we've run for so long, and we barely know ourselves who we are . . ."

"We can be whoever we choose," Drakis persisted. "If anything, I've learned that over the last months. It doesn't matter who we were, Mala; we can *become* who we want to be. We can forget about our past; what we cannot forget, we can forgive and start anew."

"Can we, Drakis?" Mala said, looking up into his face. "I don't know . . . if people can change. Maybe we're so broken that we *can't* change."

Drakis smiled down at her. "How will we ever know if we don't try?"

"It would be wonderful to try," she replied softly.

An unwelcome shout behind Drakis shattered the moment. "Drakis!"

"It would be him," Mala said distastefully.

Drakis pushed himself up from the sand and turned toward the voice. "Yes, Ethis, it is me. Now that you have completely ruined my evening, I'm sure you've thought of some way to ruin my night as well. What is it?"

The chimerian paused, glanced at Mala rising to stand next to Drakis, and then took in a deep breath.

"Yes," Drakis urged, "You've got my attention. What is it?"

"I . . . I thought we might discuss our next move."

"*Our* next move?" Drakis responded. "Just what *move* would that be?"

"Why . . . northward, as you said," Ethis spoke, choosing words as a warrior might choose his weapons in battle. "The Sondau have these corsairs that are legendary in the open sea. You might prevail upon them to take us farther on—perhaps across the Bay of Thetis into Nordesia or even . . ."

"No," Drakis said flatly.

"They might take us along the coast to the west, or we could travel by land to Point Kontantine but we would still need the corsair ships to . . ."

"No, Ethis," Drakis repeated more firmly. "I'm not going anywhere."

"But . . . your destiny . . ."

"*My* destiny? You've been repeating that lie so long

that you've started believing it yourself." Drakis shook his head. "It's not me! Even if it *were* me, I wouldn't want it! It was all just a story the dwarf told, Ethis, so that gullible folks along the way would feed us and give us a bed! It got us here and that's enough . . . I'm not going anywhere!"

"So that's it, then," Ethis spat, his blank expression vanishing for the first time that Drakis had ever known him into what passed for a scowl. "You just give up, tell the rest of the world to jump into the Chaos while you play in the sand?"

"Yes!" Drakis shot back. "It's my life . . . for the first time it *is* mine . . . not yours . . . not the dwarf fool's . . . certainly not the Empire's . . . and I'm not giving it up to anyone else, either!"

Ethis shook his head. "You selfish, blind, narrow-minded idiot! It's gone way beyond time for you to hide! You think the Iblisi will just *give up* . . . that they'll wake up one day and say, 'This is too hard, let's just let this one go?' They *never* give up, Drakis, and they *never, ever* forget. They will hunt you down and murder you, you and anyone who has been with you. The very first they'll take will be those closest to you. The safest thing you can do is get off this continent—across the sea—somewhere they can't reach."

"Oh, please," Drakis sneered. "You're scaring the women."

Ethis growled under his breath in frustration. "You have no idea who these Iblisi are . . . or who *I* am for that matter!"

"Oh, I think I have a pretty good idea about *you*," Drakis snarled. "I've seen what you're capable of . . . just how honest you can be!"

"I'm trying to *help* you, human!"

Drakis looked behind the chimerian. There came a rising tide of shouts from the village. Suddenly one appeared, then three, and then entire families were running frantically about. Soon a number of them ran toward the various ships beached along the crescent of sandy shore that marked the edge of the harbor.

Drakis eyed the chimerian. "What did you do, Ethis?"

Belag and the Lyric appeared behind the dwarf, all of them running directly toward Drakis and Mala.

"Well," Mala sighed to herself. "It looks like everyone found *us*."

Urulani came with them but ran past Drakis without as much as a nod, shouting toward the beached ship beyond. "Kanshu! Get up!"

A head poked up over the gunwales, staring blearily back.

"Raise me a crew of twenty!" she shouted, plunging into the water without slowing, then pulling herself up a rope that Kanshu hastily tossed over the side. "We've got to get the ship provisioned and ready for sail at once. And I want warriors and sea-crafters only—and pray we don't need them!"

"Aye, Captain," Kanshu replied at once, himself jumping over the side and pushing shoreward through the shallows. "How long a voyage, Captain?"

"I don't know ... bring as much as is at hand," Urulani shouted as she at once set about readying the ship. "I've told the Elders to abandon the village. We'll hold the beach until everyone is safely away on the other ships."

"Are we being raided, Captain?" Kanshu asked as he surged out of the water and onto the shore.

"Yes! I don't know when but soon," Urulani called out. "We have to get everyone out ... they can't kill us if we aren't here."

"Now what?" Drakis groaned.

"Drakis!" the dwarf shouted, his short legs churning up the sand atop the seawall. "Ah, good it is to see you, my friend, and most blessed by the gods indeed that you are well! We've not a moment to waste ... gather all that is needful, and let us away while we can!"

Drakis closed his eyes and turned his face up toward the dark sky. "You, too? I finally find a place where I am content to stop and now all of you want to leave?"

"I am sorry, Drakis," Belag said. "But we must."

"We don't *have* to do anything," Drakis protest.

The manticore drew himself up before the human warrior and looked down at him with kind eyes. "Sometimes, friend, we must do a thing or we stop being ourselves."

"What does that mean?" Drakis asked.

"It means that we have just returned from the mud city south of the Sentinel Peaks," Belag said. "We tracked RuuKag there. There is much to that tale that we will tell when there is more time, but for now all that needs to be said is that RuuKag is dead . . . and so, too, is the city of the Hak'kaarin."

Ethis caught his breath sharply. "Dead? *All* dead?"

Belag looked curiously at the chimerian. "Yes . . . though we know that most of the mud gnomes escaped thanks, I believe, to RuuKag. He found his heart at last."

"But," Mala struggled to find her words. "Who would do such a thing? I mean . . . the mud gnomes weren't a threat to anyone and had nothing anyone would want."

"They had Drakis," Belag said, his gaze fixed on the human warrior.

"No," Drakis said, closing his eyes as he shook his head.

"There were seven robed elves among the dead," Belag continued. "Nearly a full unit of what the Iblisi call a Quorum. It took only seven of them to destroy perhaps a thousand of the gnomes, but RuuKag managed to help stop them at last—stop them to protect you, Drakis."

"No, please," Drakis moaned. "Not for me."

Beyond, among the huts of the village, the shadows were moving swiftly. Men emerged from the edge of the jungle forest, all rushing with sacks and chests shouldered as they charged down toward the ship behind Drakis. Elsewhere along the shoreline, the other ships were being readied in haste to depart.

"They tracked us to that city," Belag said. "They tracked *you*. Perhaps the death of their Quorum was enough to give them pause but if there is more than one Quorum pursuing us . . ."

"They'll know where we went," Ethis finished. "They'll come directly here."

They won't stop, Drakis thought. *They'll never stop.*

Mala started to ask, "How much time do you think . . . ?"

An explosion rocked the ground. An enormous ball of flame shot into the sky south of the village. The heat of it burst against their faces as they watched it roll upward into the night.

"How much time?" Ethis drew his sword. "I would say . . . not enough."

Chapter 44

Fury

"NAME OF THE ANCIENTS!" Urulani swore from the deck of the ship as she watched the fireball climb high into the night. "Those are the inner defenses. They slipped past the outer two!"

"How close are they?" Drakis called up to Urulani.

"One hundred yards from the edge of the village," she replied. "They are very close, prophet-man!"

Belag turned at once to Drakis. "They know we have ships, and their objective is to destroy every breathing thing here. Their first move will be to cut off our escape."

"That means they'll try to take the beach," Drakis nodded as he drew his own sword, "probably from the sides—or at least they'll try to destroy the ships."

"If they manage either one, we're finished," Ethis agreed. "We've got to protect the flanks of the beach until the ships are away."

Drakis turned to the manticore. "Belag, you and Ethis take the east end of the beach. Gather as many of the Sondau raiders as you can. There's a jumble of boulders about a hundred yards down there just above the seawall ... do you see it?"

"Yes, Drakis," the manticore nodded.

Two more explosions erupted over the treetops, followed shortly by a third. The beach was getting crowded with people from the village, many of them readying the boats and others tossing supplies and children in as well. The Sondau raiders were just as readily tossing the children back out, shouting for others to wait until the ships were ready to sail. The cries and confusion were both rising precipitously around them.

Drakis kept talking to the manticore. "Take anyone you can gather there. You'll have a good view of the eastern side, and the position is defensible. Fall back below the seawall if you have to and make your way back here, got that?"

Belag nodded.

"Ethis!"

"Yes, Drakis?"

"It looks like you'll get your wish after all," Drakis said. "Don't let them through. If they close off this beach it's all over."

The chimerian nodded; then, drawing his two long scimitars from their scabbards at his back, he followed quickly on the heels of the manticore.

Drakis turned to Mala. "You get the Lyric aboard this ship. Help Urulani get it ready to sail . . . do anything she says . . . and wait for me here."

"Drakis, don't go," she said, her voice in near panic. "I've seen you go off to battle so many times but . . ."

"I'll be back," Drakis repeated. "I've got to come back . . . you're here."

Mala nodded then looked away, unable to watch him go.

Drakis turned, slapping Jugar on the back. "Let's go, dwarf! Have you ever actually been in a battle or do you just talk about them?"

"Oh, I've been in a few," Jugar chuckled. "Mind you I prefer just talking about them, but I believe I'll manage."

With that, the dwarf drew his broad-bladed ax in front of him and charged west down the beach, dodging between the humans rushing toward the edge of the water.

Drakis shouted and followed after him.

Soen stepped through the fold just as an explosion to his left rocked the ground. He lost his footing and fell to his knees.

He cursed again, his eyes wide with anger and frustration. Everything had gone wrong. He had come to the northern reaches of the Empire with a simple plan and, he had hoped, the blessing of Keeper Ch'drei to recapture this Drakis quietly so that they might use him for their own purposes. But Ch'drei was always a devious woman and never made an honest wager when she could concoct a dishonest one. Soen had not been more than a few days out on his journey when he knew that he was being followed and tracked through the folds. It didn't take him long to determine that he as the hunter had become the hunted—the bait for a rather bloodier and more bludgeonlike approach to solving the problem. The subtlety that Ch'drei mastered in her politics had apparently failed her in execution of policy, and she preferred the finality of death to more delicate influences. Still, Soen had hoped to complete his mission as he had originally intended—confront this Drakis human and determine if, indeed, he was the prophesied doom of the Imperium.

Information like that brought opportunities that he could scarcely calculate—and capabilities that even the bloodthirsty Ch'drei could not deny.

But all of that was crumbling around him. Even as he was making contact at last with the Beacon among these bolters, the Inquisitor who had been tracking him had grown impatient and clumsy. A Quorum had attacked and laid waste to an entire mud city of the Hak'kaarin—managing somehow also to get themselves destroyed in their zeal—and leaving behind such undeniable wanton carnage that even Soen was appalled. Worse, the stories of the slaughter were now spreading like a grass fire across the savanna by the surviving mud gnomes. The two stories were already merging—of Drakis and of the Iblisi Quorums out to destroy him at any cost. Soon, if it had not happened already, these stories would reach the Dje'Kaarin townships around Yurani Keep. Within a week, every ministry and Order of the Empire would know that there was a "Drakis" loose in the northlands who was being hunted by the Iblisi. Their very hunt would give the rumors credit—and what was once a containable flicker of an idea would become a raging bonfire of debate in the courts of the Emperor himself.

He had managed to find their fold Standards and followed them here to this human village on the shores of the Bay of Thetis, where once again this blundering Inquisitor was trying to capture a butterfly with a two-handed club. The outer homes of the village were already blazing, the walls of several of them blown flat. The smell of burning flesh filled the air. He could see robed figures hovering at the edge of the town, the spells from their Matei staffs creating a wide clearing all around the village where no one could cross unnoticed. The path was closing toward the beach as he watched.

He had to put a stop to this.

"There!"

"I see them, Drakis," the dwarf responded.

They had gathered a dozen men of the Sondau with them toward the western edge of the village. All of them were arrayed along a jagged, low ridge a few yards from the beach.

"They're moving to the right."

"Aye. Now, lad, there's a few things you need to know about this particular enemy that in your experience you may not have considered before tonight."

"What?"

"These are, if I may be so bold as to inform you, Quorums of the Iblisi Order—Keepers and Guardians of the Truth. They're rather powerful, experienced users of the elven Aether magics and are superbly trained warriors. For someone like yourself, skilled warrior as you are, to attempt to best one of these in single combat would be an act of supreme foolishness and what I believe is commonly referred to as a 'sucker bet.'"

"You're telling me this now?" Drakis answered in a hoarse whisper. "What are you suggesting ... that we just surrender and get it over with?"

"I never counsel surrender, my friend, unless there is profit in it," the dwarf chuckled back. "I only tell you this so that you will have no romantic notions about this combat. The Hak'kaarin were fine warriors despite their size: organized and efficient. There were only seven of these Iblisi, and the mud gnomes died by the thousands. In the end the gnomes won because their numbers—and the key help of RuuKag—overwhelmed the Iblisi."

"So you want us to charge them in force?" Drakis asked, his voice skeptical. "I don't think we've got quite the numbers that the mud gnomes had ..."

"Nonsense!" The dwarf winked. "This calls for subtlety and a large dose of legerdemain. I want you to keep an open mind. If nothing else, remember this: There are only seven in a Quorum. They are each powerful beyond belief, but with each one you kill they are diminished just as greatly. In such a contest there are no rules but one: He who lives, wins. You cannot take any of them in open combat. No one can. You have to be where he does not suspect you, attack from where he cannot see you, and kill him before he knows he's dead."

"Clever trick," Drakis agreed, "but they're almost to the beach. Their fires are burning a path before them, and anyone who tries to cross it is being burned to cinders before they reach the other side. We have no time for an elaborate defense."

"Not elaborate," the dwarf grinned. "Just subtle. I've been saving this one up."

The dwarf reached inside his waistcoat.

In his hands he held the dwarven Heart of Aer.

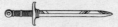

The rocks shattered before Belag's face, collapsing in front of him into a blue haze. The manticore instinctively fell back away from the powerful eye of the Iblisi staff that was searching him out among the rocks, and he tumbled down the seawall.

"Ouch! Get off!"

Belag rolled over, pushing up off the sand while throwing himself against the seawall. "Ethis! We need to get closer to them!"

"Closer?" the chimerian shouted over the roar of the fires burning from the shore to the heart of the village. The Iblisi were incinerating them from thirty yards away.

"We can't hurt them if we're not close enough for our weapons."

"What about the Sondau?" the chimerian asked over the din. "Don't they have archers?"

"Great ones, but their volleys aren't hitting their marks," the manticore answered, his face peering over the sands toward the advancing enemy. "Something is deflecting them."

"I can only imagine what *that* might be," Ethis groused.

"If we can get around their flank," Belag said, licking his incisors. "Then we'd be close enough to taste their blood."

"Around their flank?" Ethis drew himself up next to Belag. "Do you *see* a flank?"

"At the water's edge," Belag pointed. "We just need to draw them closer to the village . . ."

Two small hands clapped them both on the back at the same time.

"Fellow warriors, take heart! The Wind-princess of Nordens has come to your aid!"

With that, the Lyric leaped blithely over the seawall and began running with all her might toward the burning village.

"NO!" Belag roared.

Drakis floated upside down in the night. He had to close his eyes from time to time to avoid being dizzy, but he clutched his sword in his right hand so hard he thought the grip might snap.

The fires spread by the Iblisi drifted below him. The heat from them was making him sweat, and this worried him as much as anything because he somehow knew that a single drop falling from his brow could easily call death upon him.

He twisted slightly as he opened his eyes. The dwarf was back behind the ridge of stone beyond the lane of fire. *Trust the little fool not to mention that he had some skill in magic. Just when was he going to tell the rest of us,* Drakis thought, *at my funeral or after?*

Beneath him he could see his target: a robed Iblisi just below him, his staff gushing fire across the landscape only three feet below him. Drakis opened his left hand, readying it for the plunge, his right hand coiled with the sword, ready to strike.

The dwarf had said they never look up.

He hoped this worked.

Suddenly, Drakis fell from the sky.

In a swift motion, Drakis grabbed the sharp chin of the elf beneath him and, using the Iblisi's shoulders as leverage, swung his knees down his victim's back. The tip of his sword connected at the base of the throat just above the collarbone and slid with satisfactory force into the rib cage and tore through the creature's heart.

In the next moment, Drakis lay on the ground surrounded by the dense ground cover of the jungle with the dead elf lying on top of him.

That's one, Drakis thought. *But it's not enough. They're moving too fast.*

In the next moment, he was yanked skyward by the dwarf's magic once again.

"Wait! Look!" Ethis shouted.

The Lyric ran across the line of Iblisi, diving at the last moment behind a tree. The trunk exploded into a thousand splitters, toppling the tree—but she was no longer there.

The Iblisi saw her at once, their Matei staffs shifting to

strike her with their full force. Blue and red rods of light arced toward her, waves of flame and sound engulfed her . . .

. . . But never *reached* her.

"She *is* the Wind-princess!" Belag said with shock.

"Wind-princess or not," Ethis said with a smile as he pointed, "look what she's doing!"

The Iblisi continued to train their power against her as she darted about the village ruins, drawing them inward and away from the beach.

"There's your flank, Belag," Ethis said. "But I've got something I have to tell you before you go . . . something you have to do that can mean all the difference in the world to us all."

The manticore looked quizzically at the chimerian.

"You must do this for Drakis," he said, reaching into his pocket.

Drakis once again floated over the landscape. They were moving too fast, and this was taking far too long. Good plan or not, the end result would be the same.

Another of the Iblisi was below him now. He needed the dwarf to move him just a little more to the left.

The fires below were unbearable. The heat was making it hard for him to concentrate, and his eyes stung.

He opened his left hand again and drew back his sword.

The dwarf was moving him slowly, carefully . . .

A gust of wind drifted over the fires, carrying with it a wave of smoke just as Drakis drew in his breath.

He coughed.

The Iblisi looked up just as Drakis fell. He jumped sideways but not far enough. Drakis caught him on the way down, dragging him along, but the sword did not enter properly and plunged into the elf's body at an angle.

The elf screamed.

Drakis tore the blade from the body of the elf just as Jugar's magic dragged him into the air.

Two of the Iblisi leaped into the air to follow.

CHAPTER 45

Fall of the Inquisitor

DRAKIS FLIPPED OVER IN MIDAIR, turning toward the rustling sound behind him. Two of the Iblisi were rising into the sky in his wake, their dark reddish robes rustling as they rushed toward him. He gripped his sword and was suddenly aware of how useless it was; there was no place in the sky where he could plant his feet and get any leverage with which to strike a blow.

The dark spirits of death flew closer to him by the moment as he watched in helpless horror.

In that instant the two figures vanished in a roaring vortex of whirling sand. Drakis felt the magical power that supported him in his flight falter for a few, staggering moments and then vanish altogether as the cyclone tossed and tumbled the robed figures in its grasp. Drakis fell, his free hand clawing at the air. He glimpsed the beach rushing up toward him just before he closed his eyes . . .

Something shoved him sideways, and in the next moment he was rolling across the sand.

ChuKang was yelling at him. "Standing still on the field of battle is an invitation for death to find you."

Drakis pushed his feet under him, dragging his sword from the sand and taking a defensive stance though what he saw astonished him. The Sondau raiders were crouched down, prepared to meet the enemy, but it was Jugar who was commanding the cyclone.

The vortex was spinning along the shore, dancing before the short, upstretched arms of the dwarf. Jugar's face was nearly beet-red with the effort as he stood with his feet pressed hard against the sand and the Heart of Aer in his left hand shining with a purplish light that made Drakis uneasy just to look at it. Jugar glanced at Drakis, saw that he was once more on his feet, and flicked the wrist of his extended right hand.

One of the Iblisi shot from the vortex, spinning with frightening speed directly toward Drakis. The human warrior's trained muscles reacted before the thought entered his mind; he raised the blade over his head and stepped into the onrushing target. The whirling target did most of the work against the keen edge of the blade, nearly dividing the elf in two across the abdomen. As the target fell squealing to the ground, Drakis quickly reversed the blade in his hands and plunged it down directly into the creature's heart.

"Three," he counted. As he turned to stand, more movement caught his eye. "Jugar! More! On the ground!"

The dwarf shifted at once. The vortex collapsed, tossing the suddenly freed Iblisi into the jungle trees. Drakis heard with satisfaction the elf slamming into a tree trunk with the sound of a smashing melon. Instantly, this was followed by an enormous wave drawn up from the bay. Its sea-foam face rose higher and higher, shimmering in the light of the burning village as it arched over and crashed down upon the advancing reddish robes. The waters flowed on into the village and over the fires, snuffing out a wide swath of the flames and filling the air with dense smoke.

Through the smoke leaped four more of the robed horrors—one of them soaring directly toward the dwarf, its Matei staff pointed at his heart.

The dwarf turned toward his attacker, but the Sondau chose that instant to rise up. Three of them intercepted the Iblisi charging Jugar, physically knocking the magic-wielding elf down as he approached the ground. The Iblisi obliged them, countering with his staff in a blur of moves, killing the three of them where they stood around him nearly at once. More of the Sondau had joined in the fray but they, too, were faring no better.

Drakis ran to the dwarf. "Jugar!"

"I'm nearly done, boy," the dwarf said as he tried desperately to catch his breath.

"Get up! We've got to keep moving!"

"We can't hold them," the dwarf grimaced. "Back, Drakis! We've got to get back to the boats!"

Drakis dragged the dwarf to his feet. The Sondau line of battle was literally evaporating into a bloody mist before the power of the Iblisi magic.

They turned toward the boats that were still hovering near the shore, still struggling to load people aboard.

They ran, knowing that the Iblisi would be right on their heels. They had tried to purchase enough time for the ships to get away, and they knew they had failed.

Soen strode through the village, a circle of frost crackling around him wherever he stepped. His footfalls froze the fires beneath them, snuffing them out in a swath behind him.

As he walked he became two ... walking side by side with a duplicate of himself.

Then he became four, then eight, sixteen, thirty-two.

Each laid frost in his wake, turning the fires of the village cold, their light extinguished with each step.

They broke ranks, dozens of Soens moving through the burning paths of the village, drawing cold darkness behind them.

Occasionally one of their number would happen upon an Assesia and beckon him to follow. Twice different Soens of their number came upon Codexia, all of whom were astonished to see him but followed as well. Slowly, the members of the Quorums were being drawn into the center of what remained of the village.

It was only a matter of minutes before one of them encountered the Inquisitor who was leading the raid.

"Drakis? What is it?"

The warrior stood looking down the beach and then along the line of the still burning homes nearer the water's edge. "They've stopped! They're moving back into the village."

"We've beaten them?" the dwarf said doubtfully.

"No, they *never* give up," Drakis said as he considered. "But ChuKang used to say if the gods are offering you gift in the middle of a battle, you take it! Everyone! Fall back to the boats! It's time to leave!"

"Who here has countermanded my orders!" screamed the Inquisitor as he strode into the small village square, still burning brightly in places around what had once been a green but was now trampled and utterly spoiled. Around the square, ten red-robed Iblisi stood silently watching and listening. "The rebel Drakis is known to be harbored here. This village and everyone in it is an offense to the Imperial Will, and by decree its utter destruction is ordained! Who ordered this withdrawal? Who ordered you here?"

"I did," a voice answered from atop the stairs that once led to the now burned-out lodge.

The Inquisitor looked up and then, through a tight smile, drew out the name as he spoke as though tasting blood in each syllable.

"Soen."

"Yes," Soen replied as he carefully descended the steps, his hood drawn back, his black eyes shining in the light of the fires. "I thought perhaps you and I should talk this out before you carelessly murder anyone else on your little crusade, Jukung. It *is* Jukung, isn't it?"

"It is," Jukung replied, pulling back his own hood. The

burn-scarred tissue drew his lips back hideously from his teeth, and one of his eyes had gone a flat gray. "Sorry, I've no more time for you."

"That always was your problem," Soen continued, pushing past the robed Iblisi around the square. "Always in such a hurry, always wanting to smash things and get it over with so you could move one more step higher in the eyes of the Keeper."

"And your problem," Jukung sneered, "was always one of insufferable arrogance. Some of us, however, prefer action over talk."

Jukung raised his hand. The robed elves around the square lowered their Matei staves, leveling them directly at Soen.

"Wait! There's something you need . . ."

"Good-bye, Soen. I'll convey your regrets to Keeper Ch'drei."

"But you don't know . . ."

Jukung dropped his hand.

Instantly, the Matei staves of all ten of the surrounding Iblisi flashed rods of incredible blue, pulsing as they converged directly on the Inquisitor. Soen raised his own staff but too late; he was engulfed by the power of the magic. His flesh turned to ash on his bones, his black eyes ran momentarily as a black liquid down his crumbling cheeks. What once had been Soen, Inquisitor of the Keeper and Envoy to the Imperial Courts, collapsed into an unrecognizable pile of ash and bone smoldering in the center of Nothree's village square.

Jukung grinned as he swaggered back to the center of the square. "How sad that you had to come to such an end, Soen. But take comfort that I have taken your place . . . and that it was I who taught you the last lesson of all."

He reached down to pick up the skull of his vanquished rival . . .

. . . and his hand passed through it.

"What . . ."

Jukung's own skull was suddenly pulled backward, pain overwhelming him as a blade slid across his exposed neck, cutting deeply across his windpipe and vocal cords. He gasped reflexively for breath, but his lungs were filling quickly with his own blood.

A voice spoke into his ear.

"*This* is *your* final lesson," Soen said as he kicked away the Inquisitor's Matei stick while still holding him from behind. "Sometimes the old ways are the best ways. Just be grateful that I am in a hurry, Jukung. You'll die quickly. I had wanted to let you bleed to death slowly, but I just haven't got the time for such amusements."

Gasping, Jukung glanced at the surrounding Iblisi.

All of them were pushing back their hoods.

Each of them was the image of Soen.

"They're all away!" Urulani shouted. "Now it's our turn! Are we ready, Master Ganja?"

"Aye, Captain!" the tall Sondau warrior called back from the prow. "Anchors are all in!"

"Six men over the bow," Urulani called. "Everyone else aft! All ready, Master Ganja—NOW!"

"Aye! Put your shoulders into it, men of Sondau!" Ganja shouted.

Three men on each side of the bow pushed back and up, raising the prow from the sand.

"Push for your lives, men of Sondau!" Ganja shouted.

The bow shifted and the ship rolled slightly.

"Sooner would be better, Master Ganja," Urulani called.

"Aye, Captain! Push! Push!"

With agonizing slowness, the shore reluctantly relinquished its grip on the hull. In moments she was drifting slowly away from shore.

"Board those men at once, Master Ganja!" Urulani called out then stepped quickly to the tiller. "Everyone to your duty! Quickly!"

The six Sondau who were standing waist deep in the water by the drifting bow were quickly hauled aboard.

"Oarsmen!" Urulani called. "Out with the sweeps!"

The Sondau men pushed the oars out the ports on both sides of the ship.

"WAIT!" came the shout from the beach.

Drakis, standing with Mala and Jugar on the afterdeck, looked up sharply at the sound. "Belag? It is! Urulani, wait! There's someone on the beach!"

"Oars down!" the captain cried.

The manticore was running down the beach, holding something in his hands.

The Lyric!

"Please," Drakis said to Urulani, "we can't leave them here."

"The Iblisi could return at any moment, Drakis, I can't . . ."

"They are *my people*," Drakis said.

Urulani peered into him as though she were trying to look into his soul. He matched her stare for stare until she turned away. "Oarsmen . . . HOLD! Master Ganja, get those two aboard at once!"

Speed won over grace. Both the Lyric and the now soaked manticore were hauled over the side as though they were the catch of the day and dropped unceremoniously onto the foredeck.

"Now if there is nothing else?" Urulani snapped at Drakis.

"Let's leave," he said.

"Aft . . . PULL!" the dark woman shouted and the Sondau raiders responded at once. The *Cydon* surged backward so quickly that Drakis nearly lost his footing on the deck. The ship glided backward into the deeper waters of the bay.

"Port Aft—Starboard Fore . . . PULL!" Urulani called from the tiller, and the oarsmen responded, turning the great ship around its center.

"PULL!" the captain called again, and the prow of the ship had nearly swung to point at the harbor passage.

"All together, Fore . . . PULL!" Urulani called, and this time the Sondau men responded with their full strength, all pulling back on their oars at once. The ship fairly leaped forward now, her sleek prow cutting smoothly through the night waters of the bay.

Drakis and Mala leaned against the aft gunwales near where Urulani stood at the tiller. His arm was around her as they watched the village—and so much more—burn.

Neither of them spoke. Mala shuddered under Drakis' protecting arm but could not bring herself to look away. A single tear carved a furrow down Drakis' soot-darkened cheek.

"There's someone else on the beach," Jugar said quietly to Drakis as he pointed. "And not a passenger, I'll wager."

Drakis looked up and saw a single robed figure silhouetted against the fires run down to the edge of the beach and stop. He could not be certain, but there was something familiar in his stance, as though they had met somewhere before, but it was far too dark and too far for him to be certain.

One thing Drakis *was* certain about was that the figure was one of the Iblisi . . . and that they, too, were hunting him because of this nonsense about a legend. They had murdered a city of the Hak'kaarin and, had they been able, would have murdered all the Sondau as well. They had taken from him the one place he had ever hoped for happiness.

"Shorten the sweeps!" Urulani shouted from the helm. The twenty Sondau men at the oars complied at once, pulling the oars halfway inboard on both sides. The *Cydron* slid out between the harbor pillars, the last of the Sondau ships to leave. Within moments, the twisting passage obscured their view of the beach and snuffed out Drakis' hope once more.

"We've the wide Thetis Sea before us," Urulani said to Drakis. "The ships of Nothree will go west along the Forgotten Coast and gather at an anchorage about ten leagues to the west of here. But I'll tell you, Master Legend-man, I've got a provisioned ship and a good crew, little stomach for you and what you brought down on my people, and the deep desire to hurt something. What do you suppose I should do?"

Drakis looked up at her. "I know exactly what you should do. How far will this ship travel?"

"As far as I take her," Urulani replied.

"Beyond Nordesia? Beyond the Straits of Erebus?"

Jugar looked up in surprise.

"Why?" Urulani asked.

"Because beyond the Straits is the land of this prophecy," Drakis replied.

"So now you *are* this legendary hero?" Urulani scoffed.

"Please!" he sneered. "Of course not—not that anyone will believe me. We're going to go there—beyond the northern ocean into the lands of these myths. We're going to see this place for ourselves, and I'm going to prove once and for all that I am *not* this legend that everyone wants to believe that I am."

"What are you saying, boy," Jugar asked.

"You'd like to prove that I'm a fraud," Drakis continued talking to Urulani. "And I *want* you to prove it . . . because until you do, people are going to keep dying for a dream that doesn't exist."

Urulani thought for a moment.

"Well?" Drakis asked.

Urulani smiled. "Prove you a fraud? That would be worth the trip."

"For both of us," Drakis replied.

"Then we go north."

Book 4:

THE SIRENS

CHAPTER 46

Do Dwarves Float?

URULANI SET two of the *Cydron's* three sails after clearing the passage and set her course north from Sanctuary Bay toward Pilot Island, a nasty piece of rock that jutted up from the Thetis Sea. The island offered nothing beyond a place for the merfolk of the deep ocean to occasionally sun themselves and a point of navigation for the Sondau corsairs. By the light of the stars, Urulani caught sight of its southern shore sometime after the midpoint of the night, took her bearings, and after putting the ship on a more western course turned the tiller over to Ganja. Then she found a spot on the deck on which to sleep.

Watch by watch, the *Cydron* held its course across the Thetis Sea. The winds were not entirely in their favor, coming at them from three points off the port bow, so their progress was slower than the captain might have liked. It took another full day and night before the dark profile of Point Kontantine came into view off their port bow as the morning rays were spreading across the sea.

Beyond the point was the open Charos Ocean, a vastness that had yet to be tamed. Urulani chose not to make landfall at the Point—she would only say that they would not be welcomed there and that some things in the world were best left undisturbed—then turned their tack more north by northwest, laying on more sail. Now the quartering wind was to their advantage; the *Cydron* heeled over slightly and cut through the waves with vigorous speed. The sunlight was just failing by the time the ship eased toward the gentle slope of Cape Caldron and made anchor in a small protected harbor.

It had been a journey of just over one hundred and eighty leagues... and to Urulani it seemed that the dwarf had talked the entire way.

"Where's the manticore?" Drakis asked as he pulled himself up on the deck. "I thought he was down below."

"Aye, my boy, and I can certainly understand why you would have thought to look there first," the dwarf said, beaming his wide-toothed smile. He sat on the afterdeck, its planks sloping forward gently toward the galley benches just forward, a piece of driftwood in his hands. A small pile of shavings was growing next to his crossed legs as he carved the wood with a thick-bladed knife. "Indeed, our friend Belag does not seem to have taken to this travel by sea as so many of the rest of us have. Captain Urulani has expressed her concern for him on a number of occasions, and I have personally assured her that manticores are perfectly capable of sea travel. There are many stories—both ancient and in times nearer our own—in which seagoing manticores have figured prominently and acted most bravely. This does not seem to apply to friend Belag, however, who was most anxious to get off of 'this barge' as he put it and feel the ground under his feet for a while."

Drakis was only half listening to what the dwarf was saying. He stood with a wide stance on the deck and looked about. "So where is Mala?"

"There you have the collision of both stories, for she went ashore as well," Jugar continued. "I believe the captain called it 'provisioning,' and she seemed most anxious to do so regarding water stores. Apparently the next leg of our trip is a rather lengthy one, more than a week at sea or longer still even should the winds prove themselves favorable."

"Belag won't much care for that," Drakis laughed. "So why didn't you and the Lyric go ashore as well?"

"So I did earlier, but in truth I found it rather dull," the dwarf shrugged, shaving another curling piece from the driftwood. "I attempted to enliven the conversation with the captain by regaling her with stories of famous shipwrecks—trying in the interest of better relations to build some sort of rapport with her—but she did not seem to appreciate the subject matter as much as I had hoped."

"Is he still *talking*?" Urulani was pulling herself up over the side of the ship. The water shone on her dark skin, pooling at her feet on the deck. Drakis found himself staring at her muscular figure as she pushed the water out of her hair. "By the Ancients, how do you ever get him to stop?"

"I don't . . . but I'm open to suggestions."

"Well . . . do dwarves float?"

"We could find out," Drakis agreed.

"Now, both of you just stop that kind of talk right now!" Jugar said, his face becoming red at once as he pointed the tip of his broad knife at them in turns. "That is a poor jest at my expense . . . especially as I'm an important and critical member of this expedition whose knowledge will be invaluable in the days ahead! Threatening me with a watery grave . . ."

"It would appear," Drakis commented to Urulani, "that dwarves are not entirely fond of bathing."

"Which is easily discerned if one remains upwind of a dwarf," Urulani added.

"Why, I'll have you both know that dwarves consider their hygiene to be of the highest personal priority in all levels of their society!" the dwarf sputtered.

"I never doubted it," Drakis said bowing slightly.

"You'll be granting me a far greater measure of respect once we reach the Desolation of the North!" Jugar said, wagging his wide fingers at the two humans. "There, at the end of the River of Tears, in the far reaches of the Sand

Sea we'll find the God's Wall . . . from which mountain peaks the dragons issue their mournful call! And who will interpret the ancient words for you then, eh? The power of the ancient magic of the Aesthesian dragon warriors rivaled that of Rhonas itself, and who will protect you from the ravages of its pent-up forces if it isn't this humble fool of a dwarf, eh?"

"Humble fool of a dwarf?" Drakis said looking down his nose with suspicion. "I've been meaning to ask you about that ever since Nothree. This 'humble fool of a dwarf' was spinning some rather impressive magics of his own that night."

"Oh, well, not really as impressive as it seemed at the time," Jugar said at once, his countenance shifting with remarkable swiftness from belligerent to shy. "It really was mostly the Heart of Aer that was impressive. I just used it to conjure a little trick or two."

" 'A *little* trick or two?' " Drakis said, his words slower and with more consideration. "You bested not one but four or possibly five Iblisi with those 'little tricks.' "

"It is most kind of you to say so, but, in all fairness it was only with your most able and impressive aid that such a feat was accomplished," the dwarf said smiling once more.

Drakis was not convinced. "You're a wizard, Jugar. When were you going to tell us . . . ?"

"It was a terrible battle, indeed, my boy, but at least we are rid of that chimerian Ethis," Jugar continued as though he had not heard the man. "I dare say that each of us sleeps better at night knowing that he has gone on his way. I do not say that I wish the fellow harm—never let it be said that Jugar would be so cruel—but there was something about him that I did not trust. True, it is most likely that he is a fallen comrade lying scorched and broken among the ruins of Nothree, but, tragic as such an end may be, it has brought us to this fine ship and furthered us on our very honorable journey in search of your destiny."

Urulani just shook her head. "Unbelievable! How does he do that?"

"Listen to me, dwarf," Drakis said, squatting down on the deck before Jugar, but the dwarf continued to look down at the wood he was working in his hands. "You've been making me out to be this legendary hero to everyone we've met since the fall of House Timuran. It kept Belag sane when he might have fallen into madness ... and I'm glad for that. It even managed somehow to bluff us through the Faery Kingdom although I find it hard to believe that Queen Murialis didn't see through the lie from the first. It got us fed on the Vestasian Savanna ... and it seemed like just a convenient little lie then."

The dwarf continued to look at his hands as they worked the wood.

"But now people are *dying*," Drakis continued. "The city of the Hak'kaarin is filled with the dead—and RuuKag with them—because of that lie. All of Nothree was burned to the ground and who knows how many of the family and friends of this crew may be dead for all we know—certainly all of them now homeless—because of that lie."

"It's not a lie," Jugar huffed.

"I am *not* the man," Drakis said each word with emphasis.

"*You could be!*" Jugar shouted.

Drakis stood up.

"How do you know?" The dwarf continued as he, too, stood, turning his face up so that their eyes could meet. "You've lived your entire life so far as you recall under the thumb of your pathetic elven masters—*masters*, they call themselves! They stomp about the world taking what they want, bleeding the world pale just to satisfy their whims while the *rest* of us die for them. They *destroyed* your people, Drakis ... they hated humanity so much that they killed as many as they could and enslaved those that remained *not* because you were such prized slaves or warriors but because they wanted every day ... *every* day, Drakis ... to see the evidence in the flesh of their superiority over conquered humankind. When the dwarves wouldn't bow to them, they destroyed them, too—oh, yes, they took them apart throne by throne until only the Ninth Throne stood, and even then they would not bow to the Imperial Whim. They paid for it with their last blood!"

"But *you*!" the dwarf said, taking a step toward Drakis, "You can change all that. One man alone is worthless ... but a *legend*? A legend can forge a new destiny, Drakis. A legend can change the world! You—me—we're nothing— lumps of flesh who just wander the world for a few years before we return to the ground that spawned us. But a *legend* lives forever, boy! A legend has a destiny beyond the life of anyone!"

"I've seen the fruits of this *legend* you're so pleased about," Drakis said in a voice that barely carried across the deck. "So far it has motivated hundreds—maybe upward of a thousand—very inspired deaths."

"You're missing the grander picture, my boy," the dwarf replied not unkindly.

"Nonsense," Urulani interjected. "I'd say he's got a rather clear understanding of the situation."

"This from a corsair! A woman whose people subsist on the scraps they can steal from their neighbors while they hide in coves along a coast that no one wants!" Jugar suddenly changed his gruff tone after the look on the captain's face conveyed her sudden desire to test her dwarf-floating hypothesis. "My apologies, good Captain, it was an ill-advised phrase that I used in the heat of the argument. I should have suggested—and, indeed, *do* suggest—that the perspective of the Sondau Clan should be broadened beyond their pressing and immediate concerns. Rhonas is at war with the entire world and has brought it to heel."

The dwarf turned back to Drakis. "The *one* thing that survived the fall of humanity was this legend—this tale of the great dragon warrior who turned his back on the world and would return again to save it in its hour of most desperate need. The hope of this redemption—this story of justice to come—has found its way in one form or other into every nation and race from the Charos beaches of Mestophia to the breaking waves of Chaenandria's Lyrac shores. They all look to the north—and wait for the legend to fulfill his destiny and bring peace to their lives.

The sands have fallen again and again through the glass of time, our need has grown more desperate with each passing year, and still he has not come."

"But *now* you're here, Drakis," the dwarf poked the human with the tip of his knife. "Mortals do *not* get to choose their fates . . . their fates choose them. You're going to be the Drakis . . . *that's* your fate."

Drakis gazed down at the dwarf and shook his head. "When we get to these God's Wall Peaks you keep talking about, then we'll find out whether I choose my fate or it chooses me. There is only one way to be absolutely sure."

"Indeed?" the dwarf asked.

"Yes . . . the same way one can be absolutely sure as to whether a dwarf floats or not."

Chapter 47

One Among Us

M ALA WATCHED Cape Caldron fall astern as the *Cy-dron* sailed northwest from the anchorage, her eyes never leaving the coast until it vanished at last below the horizon under a brightening morning sky.

As the sun crossed the tops of the masts, shore again was sighted to the east, this time the Westwall Cliffs rising through the haze on the eastern horizon. This, Urulani informed Drakis, was the farthest western end of Nordesia. Their conversation was somewhat disjointed, however, as Jugar was constantly interrupting with some prattle about the giants that lived in the Westwall Cliffs and who occasionally waded out into the ocean to capture and play with boats that passed too close to the shore. Urulani scoffed at the "child's tale" as she stood at the tiller, but Drakis quietly noted to himself that she nevertheless kept the ship far from those shores.

It was perhaps two hours later that Urulani pushed the tiller over slightly and the ship's bow responded, changing their course perpendicular to the falling sun. They were heading truly north now. The Straits of Erebus lay far to the east—that body of water that separated the Lyranian and Drakosian continents. Their course, however, would take them directly north across the eastern expanse of the

Charos Ocean as that was the course the song in Drakis'
head seemed to dictate to him.

There was nothing now between them and the sirens
that called to Drakis but the open sea.

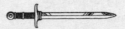

Drakis stood on the afterdeck of the *Cydron*, his hand on
the tiller as he watched the bow and, more importantly, the
stars beyond.

From where he stood he could see the length of
the middeck below him. The oars—sweeps, he corrected
himself—were pulled in and stored beneath the galley
benches. The night had been a clear one and remarkably
warm with the trade wind blowing from the southeast off
of Nordesia. Urulani had instructed the crew to strike the
canvas that they had spread days earlier like a tent over
the middeck. There was a lower deck to the *Cydron* where
the crew could bunk among the stores—and where poor
Belag had elected to spend most of the voyage, miserable
in his seasickness—but tonight most of the crew elected to
sleep on the deck beneath the gentle breeze and the great
dome of the star-filled night sky. He could see them as
shadowy figures on either side of the elevated decking that
ran the length of the ship between the port and starboard
ranks of galley benches and around the masts, ending at
the forecastle deck at the bow.

Come to the shores of the sorrowful . . .
Come to the Northerly Lands . . .
Come on the ocean . . .
Come with devotion . . .

Drakis was fancying himself something of a corsair.
There was something about the water, its freedom, and the
motion of the ship beneath his feet that called to him like
the song that still ran through his head. The seas were relatively calm this night and the breezes generally favorable
as they made their way northward. Urulani had instructed
him on how to man the tiller and steer a course directly
north by keeping the bow directed toward a particular

place about which all the heavens overhead revolved. She kept a critical eye on him for some time and then, at last satisfied that he would not be a danger to the ship or her crew, she sat with her back against the aft bulwark, folded her arms, and drifted off to sleep.

One is the Guardian of our hope . . .
One is the poison we drink . . .
Pity the last one . . .
Keep the course true on . . .

Since leaving the Westwall Cliffs five days before, everyone aboard had settled into a comfortable routine and, being in such confined quarters, got to know to each other quickly. Ganja, the ship's master, was next in command on board, a tall and powerfully built man of Sondau who kept his tightly curled hair cut close to his scalp. Drakis knew that the man was deeply distrustful of both him and his companions, but he also sensed that he was unswervingly devoted to his captain. He often would take a watch at the tiller—as did Kendai and Dakran, the two sailing loremasters aboard. Then there were the eight men on each side who manned the oars whenever Uru- lani found the wind not to her perfect liking and tended to other duties aboard when the sails were full. Yithri, Kwarae, Gantau, Djono the Giant, Zinbar, Lukrasae, whom all the rest kidded about his diminutive height and whom Jugar had taken to defending—Drakis was coming to know them all as they worked shoulder to shoulder on the ship.

He looked down at Mala, who lay on a bedroll he had prepared for her, curled tightly under a blanket, her back turned against the breeze. Her hair had completely cov- ered the tattoo atop her head that had branded her—and branded Drakis and so many of his companions—as slaves to the House of Timuran. Now her auburn hair fluttered slightly in the night breeze, and he realized how beautiful it had become to him—more beautiful with each passing wave of the ocean below.

Nightmares and dreams are for dark of night . . .
Sometimes we sleep while awake . . .

Tears for our sorrow . . .
Weep for the morrow . . .

Perhaps, he reflected, that was what he liked about the corsair ship—that here on the open waters he was far from the cares of the Rhonas or the fear of being brought into bondage. He had tasted the free air of the sea and felt the ship beneath his feet go wherever his mind willed his hands to take her. This was what a man was meant to be . . . to master his fate, to be his own . . .

Drakis froze.

A tall, robed figure stood silhouetted at the bow. Its face was in darkness, but its form was all too familiar to him.

And the magical Matei staff, its headpiece glowing a painful blue, was unmistakable.

"ALARM!" Drakis screamed, letting go of the tiller at once and charging down the central decking as he reached for his sword. *"ALARM! ALARM! ALARM!"*

He could hear the crew around him struggling up from the depths of their sleep. The deck beneath his feet rocked with the motion of the Sondau warriors clambering to get their feet under them. Their shouts grew, and the sound of their weapons being gathered filled the air.

"Hold, Drakis of Timuran!" the figure shouted at him, as the glowing head of the staff shifted.

Drakis realized there were two figures on the forecastle.

The Lyric! The lithe woman stood quivering in front of the Iblisi, her back turned toward him and his left hand on her throat. The blue glow of the Matei staff cast shadows across her frightened face.

Drakis came to a stuttering halt, his feet sliding awkwardly across the planking. The Sondau warriors hesitated as well, looking aft toward their captain. Drakis glanced back as well and saw Urulani, now standing silently on the afterdeck with Mala at her side.

"Well you should pause to consider, corsair," the Iblisi called down the length of the ship. "One poor decision on my part could tear this ship from stem to stern—and I know that it is too far from land to swim, even for the much-storied Sondau."

Jugar struggled up from belowdecks, his ax in hand. "Where's the fight?"

"That's what we're about to find out," Drakis said quietly.

Urulani stood so still that Drakis could not tell if she were breathing. "What do you want?"

"What I have always wanted," the Iblisi snapped, his voice cracking. "What I have crossed continents and oceans to achieve. What has caused death and destruction everywhere in its wake. I want to speak with the slave Drakis!"

Urulani raised her hand. The Sondau drew back slightly. "You've come a long way to speak with a slave, friend. Who are you?"

Mala quickly made her way down the central deck to where Drakis stood. He tried to reassure her with a thin smile as she came to his side.

"Come far? I have come too far," the Iblisi stated in contemptuous tones. "And my name is Soen . . . just Soen."

"What do you want . . . Soen?"

"You, Drakis," Soen replied from the folds of his hood. "You and your bolters have eluded me far better than any have before, I will grant you that, but I have found you at last."

"Found us? You didn't find us at all!" Jugar shouted. "You were led to us, you lying bastard elf! You would never have discovered us without traitorous assistance."

"There is no shame in accepting help . . . especially if the help is so very willing." The Iblisi said casually as he released the Lyric, letting her fall with a heavy sound to the deck at his feet. "I'll admit that I was nearly lost when you left Nothree without me . . . until I discovered this."

Soen reached his right arm inside his cloak and pulled out what appeared to be a small ball of mud about the size of a pea. "It is a beacon stone, a magical object that calls me to it, dropped by one of your closest companions along the way so that I would not be left behind on your journey. This particular one was the most useful to me . . . because to my surprise I found it at Cape Caldron. That's what led me to you here ... and the end of your run, bolters. It's time to come home."

Drakis gripped his sword and glanced around him. Miles from shore and only the boat beneath their feet.

"Peace, friend," Soen said in even tones.

"Peace is not what I have in mind," Drakis said, his breath coming quicker.

"Peace, friend," Soen repeated.

"What?" Drakis did not understand what the elf meant.

Next to him, Mala took her arms from around his waist, and started walking toward the Iblisi.

"Mala! No, stand back!" Drakis cried.

"Please?" Mala said in a quivering voice. "Please, take me? Please take me home?"

The Lyric looked up in astonishment at Mala from where she lay on the forecastle.

"Mala!" Drakis called, tears blurring his vision. "No! Come here!"

"Please take me home?" Mala's voice grew stronger with every step, her hands reaching out toward Soen. "I've done everything you asked. I've gone with them and followed them and been with them ... I've eaten with them, slept with them, smiled at them ... I've done all that the demons have spoken from the dark dreams. I looked for you, *longed* for you to come."

"NO!" Drakis screamed as he rushed forward, grabbing Mala by the arm. "You can't! Everything we have together! Everything that we were ..."

"Pretend!" Mala shrieked, tearing her arm away from him. "You said it was pretend ... and the demons said it, too! They said you lied and made me remember, and as long as I remember, they'll tear at me in the night. But I won't let them!"

She turned and ran forward, throwing herself at the elven Inquisitor's feet. "*You* won't let them! You'll take me back home and free me from the demons just like before! You'll send them back to the forgotten places! I did everything they said I should do, and now you've come for me! You've come to take me back!"

Soen gazed down at her with his black, lifeless eyes.

"You promised!" Mala screamed. "I gave them to you! I dropped the stones just as the demons said I should! I slowed them down! I was clever!"

Soen looked up at Drakis. The human had fallen to his knees on the deck, quaking in his agony.

Mala turned, too. "You promised to keep me away from him most of all! The demons are nothing next to his pain! He loved me! He hurt me! I want him! I hate him!" Her voice dropped to a whimper. "Please take me home! I cannot live with what he feels. I cannot live with what *I* feel. I want to never know that pain again. I want to forget."

She began to sob. "Please take me home . . ."

"Mala," Soen said in a soft, warm voice. "You have, indeed, done everything that you were meant to do. I am sorry . . . but the demons must stay with you."

Mala looked up into the Inquisitor's face, her shoulders shaking as she spoke. "But . . . Master . . . you've come for me! You . . . you've come to take me home!"

"No, Mala," Soen replied, "I cannot do that."

"Why?"

"Because, I am not the Inquisitor whom you serve," the elf replied. "I am not Soen."

The robes began to shift as the Matei staff fell heavily to the deck. The black elven eyes contorted, and the flesh around them shifted. The robes collapsed into smoother forms. Two arms became four as the expressionless and all too familiar face looked up.

"I am sorry, Drakis," Ethis said from the forecastle, where Mala lay quivering at his feet. "There was no other way."

CHAPTER 48

Chimera

"ETHIS!" Jugar sputtered. "You! I have seen a number of feats of legerdemain in my time, but how is it that you have thus magically appeared on this ship?"

"In a moment, friend Jugar," Ethis said looking toward the afterdeck. "Captain Urulani, may I suggest that a few of your crew take charge of this human woman. I believe she is now beyond doing us any further harm, but her actions, I believe, warrant some prudent caution."

Urulani broke from her astonishment and nodded. "I agree. Zinbar and Gantau . . . go forward and take charge of her. Bind the woman hand and foot, but I don't think a gag is necessary. Make her comfortable, but I want her secure."

"Aye, Captain!" they responded and moved forward, Zinbar picking up a coil of rope stowed next to the main mast.

Urulani raised an eyebrow as she spoke to the chimerian, "Anything else?"

Ethis bowed slightly, "It's your ship, Captain."

"And I'd like to see that it *remains* my ship," the captain replied. "Is there anything *else* you would like to tell me?"

"Only that my name is Ethis, that I am—as you plainly see—a chimerian shapeshifter, and that I serve you aboard this ship."

"That's all?"

"Oh, and that you'll find that there is no longer a sea-sick manticore in your hold."

"Which is because?" Urulani urged.

"Because ... because *I* was that seasick manticore."

"Ah-*ha*!" the dwarf crowed. "That's how you got aboard!"

"And how I've been aboard since we made our hasty retreat from Nothree," Ethis replied taking a step down the deck then turning back to the dwarf. "Oh, here is something I need to return to you."

The chimerian reached into folds in his flesh that had been smoothed over moments before and pulled out a shining, black-faceted stone.

The dwarf's eyes went wide as his hands instinctively patted down his waistcoat and discovered it empty. "The Heart of Aer! How did you ... ?"

"I am a creature of many talents," the chimerian replied. "Besides, I could hardly have a real wizard conjuring up spells against a fake one, could I?"

The dwarf frowned, holding out his open palm.

Ethis shrugged and set the stone carefully in Jugar's hand.

"I am just a poor fool of a dwarf, but it occurs to me that the shapeshifting talents of the common chimerian do not include the ability to mimic clothing and even hair down to a degree of complexity that would pass even a cursory examination." Jugar's eyes narrowed, but there remained a brightness to them as he spoke. "Such capabilities are rare, indeed, and often put to rather specialized use in behalf of the chimerian state interests. Such dangerous creatures have been rumored to be abroad in the land. You wouldn't happen to be one of them, would you now, Ethis?"

"And are you, friend Jugar, no more than a common dwarven fool?" The chimerian's face remained as blank and inscrutable as ever, but he leaned forward as he continued. "Just as a pure matter of speculation, it would be an interesting contest, though from what I have heard of such beings, it would be better *not* to know them. You, of all creatures, should recognize the advantage of anonymity. However, should any such creatures be made known to me ... I should be glad to direct you to them."

The dwarf, for once, held his silence.

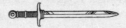

Drakis was vaguely aware of Ethis as the chimerian turned and stepped carefully over to where he remained kneeling. His head hung down, his chin nearly resting on his chest. His mouth hung slackly open and his eyes were closed. Drakis was still aware that he held his sword loosely in his hand, his shoulders rising and falling with his quick breaths. But the rest of the world seemed so far away ... and the sounds so muffled.

Ethis knelt down in front of the human. "Drakis."

He continued to breathe raggedly, the sound of his breath roaring in his ears. Ethis was saying something to him.

"Drakis, I'm sorry," Ethis continued. "It was the only way I could have convinced you."

The human opened his eyes slowly, his head still hung down to his chest.

"You would not have believed me," Ethis continued. "You haven't really trusted me since that day we awoke in House Timuran. Your suspicions were only strengthened in the Faery Kingdom. You thought I had betrayed you there, but in truth it was the only way to save you ... to save us all. The Iblisi were closing in on us. Murialis was our only chance, but I had to prove to her that all of us were who we claimed to be. She trusted me to find that out."

"You did," Drakis said, his voice rough from deep in his throat. His words sounded disconnected, as though he were talking through a dream.

"Yes," Ethis continued. Drakis could feel himself being drawn out through the chimerian's words, being coaxed to come back to the realm of consciousness and pain. "We had met many years before when ... well, it doesn't matter when ... and I knew that she could help you."

Drakis' eyes shifted upward and peered at Ethis from under his brows. "So . . . you were only *helping* me."

"Yes, Drakis," Ethis urged. "I had suspected Mala ever since my interrogations in the Faery Kingdom, but it was not until the dwarf discovered the beacon stones on the savanna that I knew with certainty. The Iblisi were closing in on us. I had to act . . ."

"For my own *good*," Drakis found the words distasteful as he spoke them.

"For your own good," Ethis nodded. "I waited for an opportunity. Then, when we reached Nothree, that day she was bathing at the pool . . ."

Drakis shuddered violently, closing his eyes again, but Ethis' words kept coming at him.

". . . I took some of her beacon stones from the hem of her gown. I went back through the pass to a crossroads on the fringes of the savanna and used the stones to call him. I suspected the Inquisitor did not actually know which of us was helping him. I changed form and appeared to him as RuuKag. He never suspected me. I told him the stones had been compromised by the dwarf, and he gave me an entirely new set of stones. Now that same Inquisitor Soen is chasing the *wrong* stones instead of us."

"Who's dropping these wrong stones then . . . and drawing what will soon be a very angry Iblisi after them?"

'Belag," Ethis said. "I told him to lead him east, back toward the Dje'kaarin."

"And he did this for my own *good*," Drakis said through clenched teeth.

"Yes," Ethis nodded. "Everything we've done has been for your own good . . ."

Drakis' grip on his sword tightened as he sprang toward Ethis with a terrible yell that started from the darkness of his soul and rushed from his mouth with animal ferocity. He pressed his left forearm against the chimerian's throat, his weight and momentum pushing Ethis back against the main mast. His body pinned the lighter chimerian, the edge of the blade suddenly biting at Ethis' throat.

Drakis' crazed face was within inches of the chimerian's

own face. "For my own *good*? Everyone seems to be working for my own *good!* House Timuran fell for my own *good,* and it brought me memories that are *still* too painful for me to even think about—it stole my life from me! *You* took us into the Faery Kingdom for my own *good* and because Murialis would either be entertained by us or kill us, you cheated me out of my deepest thoughts, hopes, and fears. RuuKag . . . RuuKag *died* for my own good and the gods only know how many others! And now you . . . you show me *this*! You take away from me the one thing I ever wanted . . . the one really honest, good thing I ever asked for myself . . . you tear out my soul, and you have the gall to tell me it's for my *own good?"*

"Drakis, my boy," Jugar said in a careful voice. "It's truly a calamitous situation—deplorable and tragic—but a little calm reflection and distance might . . ."

"And you!" Drakis wheeled on the dwarf. "You started this all! You and your talk of legends and humanity's lost greatness. You packaged it and sold it to everyone we've met along the way, but it was all a lie!"

"You don't know that, lad," Jugar said, holding his hands up. "Those stories that I told are true . . ."

"It's *NOT ME!*" Drakis wailed at the dwarf. He turned back to Ethis, his sword cutting across the chimerian's skin just below his jaw. "What did you do to her? How did you make her *lie* like that?"

"It's not him, lad," the dwarf said.

"You then?" Drakis said, his wild eyes fixed on the dwarf as he turned.

"No, my boy," Jugar said with as much calm as he could muster in the face of the crazed Drakis. "The elves . . . *they* did this to her."

Drakis stood on the deck glaring at the dwarf. He was vaguely aware of the rest of the crew watching him, of the damning concern in their eyes, and of their pity. He hated them for that, too.

"She's . . . she's what they call a *Seinar*—a beacon," Jugar continued, his eyes fixed on Drakis as he spoke. "It's an old-fashioned custom that was the tradition in elven households for nearly a century—may Nexog damn them forever for it. The Rhonas elves would take one of their household slaves and 'train' them to be a *Seinar*. But this wasn't 'training' as you know it, my boy. They would take them when they were youths 'just in their beards' as we say among the dwarves—both male and female—and afflict them with such terrible horrors—tortures, lad, of mind and body—until they had burned these trained scars into their minds, seared them so deeply that they would never be free of the orders they were given. Then they deviously buried the memory of this training under the Devotion spell so that the slaves themselves would not be aware of it. They were trained to betray their own kind—to run away with any slaves who might somehow break the bonds of their Devotions—just as we did, lad—and lead the Iblisi to them."

"They did that," Drakis said, his eyes shifting to where Mala lay bound on the forecastle. "What did they do to her?"

"It wasn't magic," Jugar said quietly. "It was not some spell that could be released and make her right. It was her mind they broke—as they did with every other *Seinar*. Then, in a cruel blessing, they gave them their Devotions in the households and allowed them to forget all the carefully, torturously impressed commands that they had burned into their minds . . . leaving them buried there against the unlikely day when the Devotions would fail . . . and their precious slaves would escape."

Drakis dropped his sword, barely aware of it clattering on the deck at his feet. "Then she didn't choose this . . . they made her do it . . . they . . . they *broke* her?"

"Aye," Jugar nodded. "Intentionally, but, aye, they broke her. It is a difficult and costly proposition. Most of the lesser Houses of the Empire no longer go to the expense of what has become such a luxury. But Timuran was just proud enough and just vain enough to want to own a traitor to her own kind."

Drakis walked slowly up to the forecastle. The two Sondau warriors stood on either side of Mala, who looked pathetically small where she lay on the deck between them. Drakis reached down slowly, pushing back the hair that had fallen over her face.

She looked up at him with the eyes that he had long remembered with such depth of feeling though now they were unfocused and seemed to dart about, unable to fix on any one thing.

"Take me home," she said to no one in particular. "Please take me home . . ."

Drakis stood up and drew in a long, shuddering breath.

"If you like," Ethis said quietly behind him, "I can take care of this for you."

Drakis turned. "What did you say?"

"This needs to be taken care of," Ethis said with a little more emphasis. "She's a *Seinar*, Drakis. She'll do whatever she can to lead the Iblisi to us."

"She's Mala," Drakis said, shaking his head.

"No, she's not," Jugar said. "She has betrayed us and, beyond doubt, she will betray us again."

"No," Drakis insisted, "She doesn't want to be this."

"It isn't a question of what she wants," Ethis said with conviction. "She has no control over this any more than you can control whether you breathe or not! She is broken—deep within—and she *cannot* be fixed."

"NO!" Drakis shouted. "She was fine before we began this insane quest and she'll be fine again! If I find a way to put her back under House Devotions, she'll be . . ."

"What? *Your* slave?" Ethis countered. "Is that what you're hoping for?"

Drakis wheeled on Ethis, slamming his right fist into his face. He felt the bones of the chimerian's face flex as was the inherent trait of his kind and his fist give into the soft flesh of the face, but the blow did force Ethis back a few paces and gave Drakis back his focus from the satisfying blow.

"We sail north!" Drakis made the statement as though he dared anyone to contradict him. "We find the Siren

Coast and this ... River of Tears or whatever it is ... and see what there is to this damn legend. Until then Mala is *mine* and under my protection."

"It's my ship," Urulani said. "If she stays, then she stays under guard."

"You, too, I see," Drakis replied. "Then take me north, O Great Captain! We have a legend to bury."

CHAPTER 49

Voice of Dragons

DRAKIS STOOD at the tiller that night. He shifted the course of the *Cydron* five points to starboard and held it there for nearly three days. All Urulani's arguments were brushed aside by him as he held that course ... because, he said, the song was calling to him, and this was the course where he heard it the loudest.

By the dawn of the second day the distant shoreline could just be made out on the northern horizon. It took until just before noon for the coast features, such as they were, to become defined: short, gnarled trees and scrub brush painting a dark line above a bright sand shore. Here and there a tumble of rocks could be seen, but for the most part it was the most unremarkable coast Urulani or any of her crew had ever seen.

Drakis leaned hard on the tiller, his red, sleepless eyes struggling to peer over the bow. Despite the lack of landmarks, however, he steered the ship with remarkable precision up one of a dozen channels that flowed over a wide sandy delta. The *Cydron* was made for shallow-draft river raiding and passed smoothly over the delta waters and into the main channel of what Jugar at once proclaimed to be the River of Tears. Only then did Drakis relinquish the tiller to Urulani ... and he collapsed on the deck just as Urulani called for the sweeps to be set and the oarsmen to start pulling.

Drakis did not awaken again for another day and a half.

"How is your head?" Urulani asked.

"Much worse," Drakis replied as he stretched. "Where are we?"

"I can report that we are definitely somewhere," she replied, "And we are making good time."

"Wonderful news," Drakis responded, looking around them. The river had cut a meandering course, which Urulani was trying to make her ship follow. "I see that the riverbanks are sand. What's beyond?"

"More sand," Urulani replied with a twinkle in her dark eyes.

"Then I think you are wrong," Drakis said, drawing in a deep breath. "We've gone right past somewhere and have definitely reached nowhere."

The shores of the Sand Sea drifted past them for a time, the silence broken only by the rhythmic stroke of the oars to the drum below.

"How is your Mala?" Urulani asked.

"She is . . . she is doing better," Drakis replied. "She has calmed down and is speaking again . . . but she is still undoubtedly broken."

"Then why keep her with us?" Urulani said to him with surprising softness in her voice. "I do not ask you this to be cruel, Drakis, but what kind of a life can you have together without trust? She is clearly a danger to you and perhaps to us all. What kind of a life can she have beyond the forgetful lie that the elves offer to all their slaves?"

"You make sense, Urulani," Drakis responded. "In fact, all of you make sense . . . even Ethis is starting to make sense to me. I cannot explain it, but I feel responsible for her."

"You did not break her, Drakis," the captain said. "It is not your fault that she is how she is."

"Yes, I know," he said gazing out over the bow. "But I made promises to her when she was whole—when I thought she was mine—and now that she is no longer whole, I feel that those promises should still mean something. Maybe it wasn't real for her, but it was for me—or at least as real as I believe anything to be any more."

"So, are you this Drakis they all want you to be?" Urulani asked through a smile.

"You really want to know?"

"Yes."

"Then I'll really tell you . . . I don't know."

"That's no answer," Urulani scoffed.

"That's all the answer I've got," Drakis said, reaching up for one of the back stays and leaning against it. "There's only one thing that I'm certain of and that is that I need to know—one way or the other—if this is my destiny. So much has happened, so many people have sacrificed so much—even their lives from time to time—that I have to wonder if all of this has some meaning . . . some purpose. Belag once told me that he *had* to believe in me or his brother's death would have had no meaning. All I'm left with now is that thought and this terrible song in my . . . wait! Look ahead, just around this bend!"

The bow was swinging around another turn in the river.

Urulani's face shifted into a crooked smile.

"Is that a *road?*" she asked.

"Ethis! Jugar!" Drakis shouted. "Break out the packs and make sure they're stocked! We're going on a little trip."

"Master Ganja, you are in charge," Urulani said, checking her pack and closing it. "I've got six of the crew with me . . . the rest are to stay here."

There was a groan among those left behind. They would have liked the opportunity to see this new land.

"Drakis, are you ready?" she asked as she shouldered her pack.

"We're *all* ready," he replied.

Urulani turned to acknowledge him when she was caught up short. "You're not serious!"

The captain had expected Ethis and Jugar to be joining the expedition but there, too, was a brightly beaming Lyric and, most surprising of all, Mala holding her pack and looked down at the deck, seemingly avoiding anyone's eyes.

"There is no way they are coming with us!" she said.

"There is no way they cannot," Drakis replied.

"I'm not dragging those women across the Sand Sea!"

"*You're* not dragging anyone," Drakis said. "Both the Lyric and Mala need to be watched . . . and not out of my sight."

"You don't trust my crew?"

"Not with Mala," he replied.

"Fine!" Urulani shouted. "But if she so much as spits in my direction, I'm going to kill her myself, and I promise you I will *not* be asking your permission ahead of time, you understand?"

"I understand," Drakis answered.

Urulani turned on Mala, jabbing her finger at her collarbone. "And do *you* understand, princess?"

"Yes," Mala answered, not looking up.

"Well, what a happy crew," Urulani said though there was nothing happy in her tone at all.

Urulani had beached the *Cydron* on the riverbank, so they jumped from the bow of the boat onto the sands of the shore. Their feet sank down into the warm sands, causing them to struggle slightly until they managed to clamber up onto the remains of the roadway. There was some concern about the dwarf, who panicked for a time in the sands trying to get his footing, but in the end they managed to pull him onto the path as well.

The road of tightly fitted stones was broken in many places and completely obscured by drifting sand in so many more that Jugar feared they would lose it altogether, but in time they followed it up, at last cresting the sand dune at the edge of the river's channel.

They were greeted with the sight of a chain of towering mountains that seemed to stretch from horizon to horizon. Purple-blue in the distance and appearing to waver in the heat of day, their peaks were sharp, jagged pinnacles whose crests were still draped in the white of perpetual snow. They looked as though they had been pushed up angrily from below, rising abruptly from the sands at their base in sheer granite crags and towers—the savage teeth of the world.

"The God's Wall!" Jugar cried and began dancing a strange, dwarven step on the ancient stones.

"How did we miss *that?*" Ethis blurted out.

"We've been in the river channel," Urulani shrugged. "The dunes must have hidden them from us."

"That doesn't prove anything, dwarf," Drakis said, his eyes narrowing to try to examine the mountains better. He raised his arm and pointed. "What are those?"

"What?" Urulani asked.

"There at the base ... those tall shapes at the base of the range. They're too evenly spaced to be natural, and they seem to run down the length of the range."

"They are my brothers," the Lyric said with pride. "We are home!"

"The Sirens!" Jugar crowed. "Those are dragons, my boy! The dragons of the prophecy calling to you!"

"Is it ... is it *possible*?" Drakis whispered.

"We came to find out," Ethis said. "It must be four ... maybe five leagues to the base. We could make it before dark, but we'd have to make camp and return in the morning."

"You want to make camp ... with dragons?" Urulani asked.

"Do dwarves float?" Drakis asked as he started down the road, which ran straight toward the base of the mountains.

Drakis stared up at the dragon.

The dragon's dead, stone eyes stared back at him.

Drakis stood on a wide, black marble platform. The surface had been pitted and scarred by the blowing sands over time, scuffed to a dull finish. Fixed to it, the great carving of a dragon rose above him, its neck craning downward until its chin also rested on the pedestal. Enormous wings, also of stone, rose high above them nearly one hundred feet into the sky, brightly cast in the red light of the sunset. The front and back claws clutched enormous crystals in their talons that were embedded into the marble base. The crystals looked dark and common, but the dragon carving was intricate and detailed with pictograms of people now long dead and fallen to dust pursuing great deeds that were now otherwise forgotten.

Drakis considered the statue in silence.

"I ... I'm sorry, my boy," Jugar said next to him. "More sorry than I can say."

Drakis started to speak, considered for a moment, and then continued. "It's hollow. Can you see it? The head cavity all the way up the neck and into the body is entirely hollow."

"Yes, lad," Jugar said sadly.

Behind him, the rest of their party stood in the sand or sat on the edge of the pedestal. The Song of the Dragon rose and fell around them, a mournful, hollow sound. As far as they could see down both directions of the range, duplicates of this same statue stood on their own pedestals. Each of them in turn was making the same music across the Sand Sea to the south.

"The wind," Drakis continued dispassionately, pointing toward the head. "It blows here constantly through that hole in the dragon's mouth. I saw a musician once who played an instrument by blowing into it. It looked about the same size as that hole. You know, there must be some mechanism in the head that varies the pitch so that the song can be played over, and over, and over, and over ..."

"Come, lad," Jugar said, pulling at Drakis' arm. "A little supper, perhaps, and a story or two ..."

"There it is, dwarf!" Drakis shouted. "There's the great destiny of humanity! There are *no* dragons to save us, just these lovely, marble dreams we created for ourselves. All myths and stories and lies we tell ourselves to comfort us and make us think there is some *meaning* to what we do. Well, here they are, dwarf! Here are the dragons that I'm supposed to raise from the storybook past and make war with on the elves! Here's the source of the song that calls me back to a dead land filled with dead dragons! Here are your Sentinels—the sirens of the desolation—watching over us with stone eyes and weak songs!"

"Please, my boy," Jugar tugged at the human's belt. "Enough of this."

"Enough?" Drakis' laugh had a hysterical edge. "This weak, windy song? Let's make a decent noise of it! Let's call the whole world up here to see just how hollow this legend of yours is!"

Drakis turned back to the dragon's head, drew in a deep breath and blew as hard as he could through the hole.

A thunderous blast of sound shook the ground, raising a pall of dust two feet high. Drakis staggered back from the statue, his hands clasped to his ears.

Mala stood up, her jaw dropping in wonder.

The crystals under the statue's talons flared suddenly to life, brilliant light radiating outward, then curving back in on itself, forming a ball on the platform directly beneath the statue.

Ethis turned, his eye widening.

All down the range the other statues were answering in kind. Ethis watched as the bases of each, as far as he could see, were being illuminated by crystals as well.

Jugar's cheers were entirely engulfed in the sound.

The progression of the song began, note after over-whelming note—*Nine notes . . . Seven notes . . .*shaping the globe beneath the dragon statue until it flashed once and stabilized.

The Lyric smiled.

Five notes . . . Five notes . . .

Drakis staggered back off the platform just as the song concluded, its final chords echoing off the sunset-glowing mountain peaks to the north.

He took his hands from his ears.

The song had stopped . . . it was gone from his mind.

"It's a fold!" Ethis shouted.

The sphere of light beneath the dragon had become a portal. It was ancient—certainly older than any known in Rhonas. Beyond it was a land of dense green forests and bright towers in the distance.

Mala screamed.

Drakis looked up.

The peaks of the God's Wall range suddenly began to move.

Drakis' legs lost their strength.

As far as he could see, from every crag and mountaintop, dragons had awakened . . . and were filling the skies.

They answered the call.

They were coming for him.

Chapter 50

Celebrations

THE OLD ELVEN WOMAN had all the credentials of a Court Adjudicator of the Ministry of Occupation—a wizened post well suited to her age. If anyone looked more closely as she traveled the Northmarch Folds, they might discover that she bore the name of Liu Tsi-Feing, Third Court Adjudicator of the Arikasi Tjen-soi Prefecture and a Sight-maiden of the Paktan Order. Liu would tell you that she was a devout follower of Kiris, the elven Goddess of Light and Dark and that her mission on behalf of her master Arikasi dealt with trade disputes in the northern territories.

All of it was perfectly correct.

None of it was true.

The elven woman stepped uncertainly from the fold portal, gripping her walking stick tightly. The fold itself was guarded on both sides by rather impressive Warriors of the Nekara Order with a single Occuran Foldmaster sitting with his feet over the edge of the platform.

Young, the old woman thought, *on his first posting for the Order and wondering if there was any part of the Empire more distant from all he wanted than this one.*

The woman struggled forward, her staff dragging against the stone of the platform. The day was pleasantly cool. She could smell the breeze coming off the bay beyond the mud and stone walls of the town below. There was music rolling over the walls, and she could hear happy shouts and laughter punctuating the music drifting up the slope.

The Occuran Foldmaster did not bother to stand. He only turned to see who had come through and, seeing no one of importance, turned back to his idle consideration of his own importance.

The old woman would not be put off, however.

"Young Foldmaster," she said in a quavering voice. "What town is this?"

"Yurani Keep," the youth replied, though the effort seemed to pain him. "That stack of mud buildings is the capital city of this region."

"They seem to be celebrating," the woman noted. "Do you know the cause? Is it a holiday?"

"I do *not* know the cause . . . nor do I care." The youth stretched at the aching in his limbs. "They have given us three days of rest and peace from their constant trafficking of their wares through this fold, and that is as good a cause as any to celebrate so far as I am concerned."

The old woman smiled and nodded as she hobbled down off the platform and wound her way toward the city gates. The Foldmaster was typical of elven youth: spoiled, proud, lazy, whining, and lost in his self-importance.

She silently put him on her list.

In time she arrived at the gates through the city walls, finding them both open and unattended. The narrow, winding avenues with their cobblestone streets were filled with short, rust-brown gnome men, women, and children laughing and chattering at one another. Wherever there were small bands of drummers, lute players, trumpeters or other musicians playing together, they were surrounded by other gnomes who were invariably dancing and cavorting through the streets.

She came at last to the large, paved plaza of the city and climbed with stiff and pained strides the wide stairs up to the Great House Hall of the Caliphate of the Dje'kaarin. Several gnome guards stood before the great doorway that led into the hall. The Captain of the Guard stepped out from their number and held his hand up.

"Stop!"

"Yes?" the woman asked weakly.

"You wish to see the Caliph?"

"That is why I have come."

The captain's hand flipped palm up. "Ten Imperial decella for ten minutes. Hard coin only—no paper!"

"Could the Captain of the Guard manage to give me a private audience . . . undisturbed . . . for, say, twenty decella?"

The captain considered for a moment, then nodded. "He's all yours . . . for twenty."

The woman sighed, then produced the coins for the captain. He stepped aside and motioned the rest of the guards to do likewise. She passed through the large doors and turned her stooped form back to close the doors behind her.

As the doors rang shut, the old elf woman turned, gripping her staff firmly with both her hands. She took in the disgusting room with practiced eyes. Bent over and with shuffling steps, she moved slowly toward the throne of the Caliph.

Ch'drei was in no hurry; she knew how to play a part well.

Few alive remembered that the Keeper had been a great Inquisitor in her day. Down the years of her rise to the highest position in her Order, she had increasingly affected the roll of a withered elven matron. While it was true that her skills had diminished over time, it was not nearly to the extent that even her closest associates in the Order thought. She held them against those times when it was necessary that she travel alone.

This had become one of those times.

It had all gone wrong. She first knew it when reports came back of entire gnome cities being massacred by Iblisi Quorums in the Vestasian wasteland. Jukung had been her choice to quietly contain the problem; he became her mistake, and she could see that now. She thought his pas-

sion would give him strength to do the job; instead it consumed him to the point where he forgot what the mission
was about. The surviving members of Jukung's Quorums
whom she questioned confirmed her worst fears. He had
substituted his own orders for hers. Now Jukung was dead,
and all the Empire, it seemed, was talking about how the
Iblisi had been hunting a human named Drakis . . . and suc-
ceeded only in killing everyone they met *except* him.

This disaster was bad enough—but not enough to bring
her out of her lair. Ch'drei had come north for her own reasons: One of the Assesia she interviewed had given her a
message from the one person she had no wish to hear from.

Soen.

He seemed to have vanished almost the moment after
he had killed Jukung in some obscure human coastal village. The Codexia could not say where he had gone. They
had followed rumors of an elven Iblisi tracking a manticore eastward along the Thetis Coast; there were other
reports of him among the mud gnome cities, or passing
east into Ephindria, or bartering for a ship in Menninos.
None of it could be confirmed. All that remained was the
message given her by the Codexia.

*"Tell the Keeper I leave my answer with the Caliph of
Yurani."*

She stopped and looked up at the foot of the throne.

At the sight, Ch'drei straightened at once, tossing back
the hood from her head.

The Keeper of the Iblisi stood staring at the form of
Argos Helm, the former Caliph of the Dje'kaarin and now
a rapidly rotting corpse impaled on the top of his own
throne.

"You always were a clever boy," Ch'drei breathed
through clenched teeth.

No wonder the town was celebrating. Argos Helm was
a despot of the worst kind, but he had been a despot the
elves could easily control. Now it would be only a matter of time—days perhaps—before the warlords of the
Dje'kaarin threw the region into an uproar over which
of them would be dominant. The guards outside were un-

doubtedly making their coin letting the jubilant citizens in for a peak at this freak show that ...

A mark on the frame of the throne caught her eye. It would have been invisible to anyone else, but those trained in her Order had it so ingrained into them that it would call their attention even without an active search.

Ch'drei moved quickly around the throne. The blood of Argos Helm had dried down the back of the throne, but she paid no attention to it or the rotting corpse. She pried at the back board. It came away in one piece exposing a hollow space.

Within lay a vellum scroll tied with a brightly colored ribbon.

Ch'drei snatched it from its place, pulled the ribbon free, and unrolled the vellum. The writing on it was in an ancient script known now only among the Iblisi and used generally for messages intended for their ranks alone. She recognized the concise and careful hand that wrote it at once.

> *My Respected Ch'drei;*
>
> *I always repay the kindnesses shown me. As you can see, I have done so with the Caliph—and all he ever did for me was to lie.*
> *How ever shall I ever repay you?*
>
> *Soen Tjen-rei*

Ch'drei looked up at the broken form of the gnome Caliph. The sounds of laughter and music, muffled and distant, filtered into the hall.

"So it's begun, Soen, you fool" she murmured to the empty hall. "And you do not know how terribly it will end for us all."

THE END OF BOOK ONE

Dragon Raid

THE THROATS OF A THOUSAND DRAGONS answered the call.

Drakis took several steps back from the towering statue, awestruck by the shapes rising from the craggy peaks beyond. He glanced back at the statue, the craning neck with the ridge of scales curving down to the horn-spiked head with bladelike long teeth onto the ancient marble base, the enormous stone wings rising straight up over a hundred feet, and the gigantic claws gripping the glowing crystal globes. His gaze jumped back to the mountaintops and the shadows pulling their way closer to him through the evening sky. Dragons . . . real dragons! Even from this distance of several leagues he could make out some details of the enormous monsters, their great wings sweeping forward and scooping the air down and back with every stroke. The sound of their shrieking calls rolled down the mountainside and shook the wide pedestal on which he stood, carrying away with it every other sensation. It encompassed him, shot through him and drowned out everything else. Somewhere nearby the muffled voice of Urulani shouted through the noise, calling her men to gather closer around the statue and ready their weapons. What were their names, he vaguely thought. The dwarf, he knew, was also shouting nearby but his voice sounded more distant than the dragon calls and his movements were somehow slow. Ethis was pulling at the dwarf, dragging him back on to the pedestal and closer to the fold—the magical portal sphere of radiant blue light that had opened at the base of the statue. Beyond the portal fold and through its shining blue haze he could see a land of dense foliage and distant towers but it seemed so very far away. Mala lay sobbing hysterically at his feet. . . .

Mala, his Mala . . . the Mala that had betrayed them all because he had heard the song of these dragons and brought them here.

Drakis grabbed her arm, dragging her to her feet. The muffled, confused sounds filling his ears suddenly cleared and he was at once keenly aware of his surroundings. He had been a warrior not so many months ago in a different lifetime; his training acted for him. He reached for his sword, pulling it from its scabbard and finding comfort in the sound of the steel blade as it cleared the leather.

"Urulani! Get everyone back to the ship!" Drakis shouted.

"We can't outrun that!" Kendai yelled.

"It's coming here," Drakis snapped. "It's coming for me. I'll stay here—cut back and forth through the fold—and keep them at bay until you can get to the ship and think of some way to get me out of this."

"I'm staying," Ethis said.

"We'll take them together," growled the dwarf.

Urulani opened her mouth but Drakis spoke first.

"You have to get the rest out of here," Drakis said in the firm voice of command that he had heard so often before from his commanders and which he, in turn, learned to use on those under his leadership. It was a voice that carried its own authority. "You're the captain. You're the only one who can. Take Mala and the Lyric with your crew and get help!"

Urulani gritted her teeth and then turned to her men. "Yithri, you and Kwarae bring the Lyric! I've got the Princess. We're going back to the *Cydron!* NOW!"

Kendai, Djono, Gantau, and Lukrasae did require another word. All three bolted from the platform, following their footprints back across the sands.

"So, are you glad you came along, Princess?" Urulani said, grabbing the arm of the auburn-haired woman, pulling her away from Drakis. The harder she pulled, however, the more firmly Mala gripped Drakis as though he were her only island in a sea of fear. Urulani, after considerable effort, managed to pull her free. "Let's go!"

"NO!" Mala screamed, her hands shaking as her head and eyes began darting about. "The monsters are out there! They've come from my dreams! They've come for my soul!"

"We don't have time for this!" Drakis barked, his eyes fixed on the dark shapes wheeling around them in the sky.

"You heard the man, Princess. . . ."

Mala shoved Urulani backward with a mindless, animal roar.

The captain quickly recovered her footing.

"Fair warning," Urulani said as she pulled back her arm and thrust a quick fist across Mala's cheek.

Mala, however, did not drop. She staggered backward several steps before her eyes went wide—and Mala erupted into a fury. She clawed suddenly at Urulani's face with a ferocity and speed that shocked Drakis.

Just as suddenly, the Lyric yanked her arms free of Kwarae and Yithri, and leaped on Urulani's back.

"By the gods!" Drakis shouted, reaching over to try and pull the Lyric off the captain. "Get them out of here!"

"Gantau!" Bloody red streaks opened up along Urulani's midnight skin. "Get back here! Lend a hand!"

Gantau slid to a stop in the sand, turned, and rushed back to the platform. By the look on his face, Drakis knew the man was afraid but obeyed.

Drakis managed to pull the Lyric off of Urulani's back. He shoved Mala behind him but she was still sobbing, as afraid of the portal as of the approaching dragons. She pushed back against him from behind. Drakis struggled to keep his footing on the marble under him.

"Good luck, Princess!" Urulani said. "Men of Sondau! Let's get out of here!"

"It's too late, they're already here," Drakis bellowed. "Ethis! You and Jugar watch the sides and each other's backs! Urulani, get what's left of your men to form up with our backs to the fold. The plan's still good ... we'll drop back through the fold if we need to and hold on the other side until your men bring help."

"What kind of help do you think they can bring against that?" Urulani asked, pointing to the sky.

Three of the great shadows in the deepening evening sky were ahead of the rest, their shrieking cries seeming to cut directly through Drakis' ears.

"When do we fire?" Kwarae said, but there was a strange quiver in his voice.

The song returned to Drakis' head like a thundering chorus of a thousand voices.

Back to the homeland of fallen dreams ...
Is this the prophet returned?
Wandering so long ...
Wandering so strong ...

"Wait, I ... what?" Drakis stammered.

"Do we fire?" Kwarae repeated.

"No! We wait!" Urulani replied.

"What?" Yithri yelped.

"That's no welcoming party, lass!" Jugar growled.

"So you want to fire arrows into *that*," Urulani pointed as the first of the dragons banked above the sands, its enormous leathery wings held tight against the air through which it rushed. Sweat was breaking out on her brow. "Do you see the scales? Do you really think we can do any damage to that at this range? We have to wait until it is closer!"

"I think it's already too close," Ethis shouted, "We've got to retreat through the portal!"

"NO!" Jugar yelled over the tumult of voices around him. "We don't know where the fold leads! It could be a thousand leagues from ..."

"What does it matter where it leads?" Ethis shouted back. "How can it possibly be worse than this?"

Drakis barely heard the words around him. The song filled his mind and thoughts.

Come to the claw and the forehand . . .
Come to the land of the dead.
Come quiet stealing . . .
Come to the healing . . .
Mala screamed.

The dragon had turned above the sands, pulling at the air so hard that the dunes beneath it exploded upward in billowing, sunset clouds. In an instant, the enormous gaping jaws were closing on the platform, its mammoth, razor-sharp fangs nearly as tall as Drakis as the mouth gaped open. The fifty-foot wings of the beast struck down and forward, slowing the monster in mid-flight just short of the platform, the sudden hurricane gust knocking Drakis back two steps. The dragon's great, left fore claws extended down toward Drakis.

It was the eyes, Drakis realized in the last moment, which caught his attention. Slit pupils and a terrible yellow color but focused, determined, alert . . .

Intelligent.

Drakis reached forward with his left hand, transfixed by the eye of the dragon.

The sound of crashing metal brought him out of his stupor. Urulani, Gantau, and Yithri had all charged forward; their swords and weapons flashing against the open claws, slashing at the leathery flesh of its palm, which soon welled up with blood.

The dragon's cry was deafening, causing everyone on the marble platform to involuntarily raise their hands to their ears. The dragon pulled back its arm, landing with a resounding boom on its hind legs as it clawed at the air in pain and outrage. Its tail whipped frantically about, crashing through one of the statue's claws. Rubble from the broken leg of the statue flew across the platform, slamming into Gantau's chest and smashing him against stone at the back of the platform's statue.

Two more dragons landed with such force around the statue that the platform shook Drakis and all of his companions completely off their feet. Gantau lay unmoving in a growing pool of blood.

"Do you think we could leave *now?*" Ethis shouted.

"Out!" Drakis screamed as he grabbed Mala's arm once more. "Everybody out through the fold!"

Drakis got his feet under him just as the dragon's head once more thrust down in his direction. He pushed Mala through the glowing sphere and prepared to jump after her . . .

Something connected at his back, rushing him toward the sphere. His hands were pushed backward with the sudden rush and he could feel the smooth, hard and wet surface behind him.

The dragon's fang.

The dragon had lunged at him but misjudged his prey. The massive head was pushing him through the portal, rushing through it with him. Drakis saw the glow of the fold rush past him and the broken stones of a ruined plaza suddenly surrounded him, as he looked at the astonished faces of his companions.

Just as suddenly, the rushing stopped and he flew forward, rolling across the broken stones of the ruined plaza that cut at his arms and legs. The last impact with the ground pushed the air from his lungs and he struggled to stand up.

The sight before him was not to be believed. The ancient plaza was illuminated both by the twilight sky above and by the quavering glow of the fold portal. The ruins of the plaza itself had been nearly completely reclaimed by the dense, impossibly lush growth all around it, shadows illuminated by the fold as the day was ending. The only remaining feature that might have had any recognizable function from a more civilized time was a short altar near the glowing portal, a pair of crumbling low walls along the edges, and several broken columns.

But there was no time to consider this vision. Out of the soft radiance of the portal sphere extended the head and neck of the dragon. The horns of the beast were thrashing back and forth, its jaws snapping at Urulani as she tried desperately to avoid its deadly maw, horns and the raw power of its blows while striking out against it at the same time. Jugar was urging the Lyric into the jungle despite her protests. Ethis had also drawn both of his weapons and was attempting to distract the creature. This resulted in one of the horns connecting with his chest and flinging him with such force into a tree that he seemed to nearly be wrapped backward around its trunk.

"By the gods," Drakis muttered as he painfully sucked in the air and adjusted the grip on his sword. "How are we supposed to deal with that?"

Drakis charged the front of the head, then dodged to the side, trying to strike, but the dragon reacted swiftly, knocking Yithri into his path. The two men tumbled into each other, ending up on their backs, scrambling to get up again. Drakis had barely found his footing when he was forced to leap suddenly to his right to avoid one of the many spiked scales protruding from the monstrous snout. There was a strong, sulfur smell in the air that struck Drakis as out of place but he had no time to think about it.

"Yithri! Kwarae!" Urulani shouted. "Stay over on the right!"

"My right or the dragon's right?" Yithri yelled back.

"You're right, you stupid . . . watch out!"

The dragon was fast, faster than Drakis would have thought possible in a monster its size. Yithri had just leaped toward the beast, his ax raised over his head when the maw of the creature snapped in his direction.

Yithri's scream was quickly choked off as the massive, razor sharp fangs and teeth plunged through his body. The dragon's head jerked back in distaste, rising up high above the plaza as it pulled in a great breath through its nostrils.

"Take cover!" Jugar yelled just before diving behind the remains of a pillar at the edge of the plaza.

Drakis caught a glimpse of Mala standing shaking in front of a low wall. He sprang forward, catching her shoulders and pushing in backward over the broken stones.

Drakis felt the blistering heat against his back, saw the flash in his peripheral vision. He could not help himself. He had to look.

The dragon was spewing fire from its upturned maw, a churning conflagration that exploded throughout the large plaza with roiling flames. The center was a brilliant blue color, a place hotter than Drakis had ever known. The strange trees, brush, and foliage encroaching on the far side of the plaza erupted into flame, adding to the conflagration.

What remained of Yithri lay across the plaza, the stench of its burning flesh filling the air.

Proud are the dragons that hear the call . . .
Come at the sound of the song.
Why come attacking
in discourse lacking?

Drakis stood up.

Mala quivered where she sat, her knees drawn up to her chest and her back against the wall. "Drakis," she whimpered. "Stay with . . ."

Drakis stepped over the wall, his sword swinging loose at his side as he walked directly toward the creature.

The eyes of the dragon fixed on him, its spike-crowned head turning toward his approach. Drakis was barely aware of Ethis, the four-armed chimerian, running across the plaza toward him with the dwarf Jugar at his heals.

The song in Drakis' head was overwhelming.

Come is the brother of ancient day . . .
Come to the land he once lost.
Why come in anger?
Who was the traitor?

The dragon's flame choked off and its eyes focused on Drakis. The head flashed downward.

The fold vanished.

The neck and head of the dragon crashed down onto the shattering stones of the ancient plaza, blood rushing from the cleanly severed neck.

Drakis stood still, blinking at the unexpected change in their situation. The thunderous song in his head had vanished, leaving him disoriented by the sudden silence in his mind. He glanced uncertainly at his blade.

"Help!"

Drakis looked around.

"Help me out!"

It was the dragon . . . the dragon was speaking a good deal like Jugar.

Drakis walked toward the dragon's head. The eye that had so enthralled him had gone dull now that the creature's life had fled.

"Jugar?" Drakis asked.

"Get this beastie off of me!" the dwarf yelled.

The lower jaws of the dragon lay across the legs of the dwarf, pinning him against the fitted stones of the plaza with the rest of his body unfortunately now situated in what had once been the mouth of the mammoth creature.

Drakis examined him for a few moments. "This is awkward."

"Awkward?" Jugar yelled, his face purple with rage. "I think the damned monster has broken my leg!"

Drakis looked around, still feeling in something of a daze. Urulani was picking herself up off the stones. Kendai was helping Lukrasae to his uncertain feet. "Djono! Kwarae! Give me a hand here . . . we've got to free the dwarf."

Ethis came to stand next to Drakis.

"You all right?" Drakis asked in flat tones.

"Yes, I'll be fine," the chimerian replied. "Although I'm not certain for how long. We had better find some shelter—defensible shelter—and soon. We've already run out of daylight and I suspect this will not be friendly territory in the night."

"That should keep anything too curious at bay for a while," Drakis nodded over toward the still raging fire in the forest at the northern end of the plaza.

"And the smoke will attract them in the morning," Ethis replied.

"I don't suppose you know the way back to the ship?" Drakis asked though he already suspected the answer.

Ethis actually chuckled as he looked around. "No. The dwarf was right about one thing: that portal could have taken us a thousand leagues in any direction. Jugar might have better luck with knowing where we are by morning—dwarves seem to have an innate talent for that sort of thing—but if you're asking my opinion, I believe we're lost in a land of legend . . . and a dangerous one at that."